Also by Jean_Rezab

Crocus Hill Inn Mysteries
The Last Owners
The Last Scam
The Last Cake

Richmond Sibling Series
Chokecherry Valley Comfort
Chokecherry Valley Joy
Chokecherry Valley Love
Chokecherry Valley Faith
Chokecherry Valley Collection

Standalones
In This Place Together (Biblical)
The Prediction (Mystery)

CHOKECHERRY VALLEY COLLECTION
BOOKS 1-4

JEAN REZAB

CHOKECHERRY VALLEY COMFORT
Book 1

ACKNOWLEDGMENTS

Special thanks to the excellent editor, Krista Venero at Mountains Wanted Publishing & Indie Author Services for great suggestions. She helped create a better book than I could have envisioned on my own. Any editing errors found upon publication are due to the author's urge to rewrite after the editing process was finished.

Thank you to the book cover artist at Sunset Rose Books for an amazing cover.

Considerable thanks to my family who have encouraged me in my writing journey.

Thank you to Sally, Ruth, and Amy, great friends who also are great at running book ideas and cover designs past. I couldn't have finished this book without your help.

Special thanks to Connie Victoria Volk for helping by editing and making suggestions for a stronger book. She writes her own books. www.connievolk.com

Thank you to the Wordsmiths writing group for their helpful suggestions in making this a better story.

NOTE: This book was written before the pandemic, so protocols in some medical facilities may be different from this novel.

CHAPTER 1

Dr. Paul Richmond looked around the exam room from the hard plastic patient chair. He resolved to be on time for his own patients in the future.

Would Riley find an aneurysm? A clot? Some other reason for his hallucinations? She'd been the best in their graduating class and became a respected neurologist, while he opted for family practice.

The door opened, and he let out a deep breath.

Riley walked in and held out her hand. "Hi, Paul."

He grasped her hand. "Hi, Riley. Thanks for fitting me into your busy schedule."

She set his MRI films on the desk in front of her and sat down. Her shiny black hair bobbed just below her chin as she gazed at him. "No problem. You're always at the top of my list. How else would I have gotten through med school?"

His strained laugh echoed in the small room. "You helped me too. You'd have managed, driven as you are."

"That's me. But let's talk about you. I looked at the films before I came in, and everything looks fine."

"Nothing?" There must be a reason he kept seeing and talking to Amy even though she died two months ago.

"I'm sorry, Paul. I know you think there is a medical reason you keep seeing your daughter, but I can't find one. We've done all the tests I can think of that would cause hallucinations." Her soft voice held only sympathy.

"Maybe I've got some psychiatric problem? Is that what you're telling me?" His loud voice cracked. "I know you're doing what you can. I don't believe I'm imagining her because of some need I have to see her again. I miss her a lot." He lowered his head and stared at his hands clenched in his lap.

Riley wheeled her stool away from the desk and faced Paul directly, a few feet away from him on his own patient chair.

"Have you thought there might be a third option? Something other than a neurological or mental problem?"

At her words, he raised his head. He didn't try to hide the tears pooling in his brown eyes. "Such as?"

"That she's really there?"

"What?" Paul was confused. "But you know she died in that car accident, Riley."

Riley's face showed a compassionate understanding. "I know. But I meant, what if she came back from Heaven?"

His confusion remained—a maelstrom of confusion—and he didn't know what to think. His daughter was real? From Heaven? "What?"

"From Heaven. She's been sent back to Earth to comfort you." Riley waited while he absorbed the idea.

It took a few minutes of silence while he tried to wrap his mind around what she'd said. He'd always pictured Amy in Heaven with Samantha. They'd been in the same vehicle crash. They both died at the scene, and he couldn't say goodbye to either of them. It seemed more likely he imagined seeing Amy than she was real and came back to comfort him. He missed Samantha as much as Amy. "Then why don't I see Samantha? Why is it just Amy?"

"I don't know." Riley shook her head. "It's only a thought, Paul. I know it might be hard to believe, but I've seen some interesting things in my life. I don't think you're hallucinating. You don't hear or see anyone else. Amy only comes to you when you're having a hard time and need some moral support. That's what you said, anyway?" Her brows lifted in question.

"Right. Whenever I want to have another drink, she appears. But how would she even know? Even if she's from Heaven, she can't read my thoughts." He didn't even want to know half of his own thoughts since his daughter and wife had been killed.

"Have you thought about taking a vacation? You haven't taken a vacation in a long time."

Not since the Grand Canyon. But Riley didn't need to say it out loud. The Grand Canyon trip turned out to be one of those magical vacations, exactly as the brochures pictured. One of those times that would be forever etched in his mind and heart no matter how much time passed or how many other things happened to him. Just him and Samantha and Amy.

Any issues that came up on the trip, they laughed away. They relaxed for the first time since Amy was born and felt like a settled couple for the first time in their marriage. Paul's position at the clinic and Samantha's interior design firm were successful. Three weeks later, they were gone, and he was on his own.

"Paul, what are you thinking?"

"I don't know what to think. Maybe I do need a psychiatric consult," Paul said.

"Maybe. I can refer you to Dr. Ted Whitaker. He's seen some interesting things in his life. It's rumored he has visions himself."

"What?" Paul felt his head about to explode. When he entered the exam room, he'd never have guessed Riley would suggest a psychic psychiatrist. Or that Paul really saw his daughter. "Do you believe in Heaven?"

"Of course. I grew up believing, and nothing I've seen has changed my mind. I'm betting Samantha and Amy are in Heaven. But that doesn't preclude Amy from coming to see you now and then," Riley said.

"And you believe I could be seeing my daughter for real, and not in my imagination?" He and Riley hadn't discussed religion much in the time they were in med school. Every class they attended was scientifically based.

"Definitely. Look, Paul, I know this is hard to believe, and I'm not sure I should have even suggested it to you. See Dr. Whitaker. He's a great psychiatrist. He won't bring this up with you like I did. He'll listen, and he'll tell you if he thinks you've got a medical problem, or if he thinks you're imagining your little girl into existence to comfort you, like an imaginary friend. Or if he thinks you have schizophrenia or any one of several conditions. You know them yourself. You've studied some of them and looked up the rest since this started happening. That's all he'll do. Unless you bring up the question yourself, he won't bring up visions.

"He's a private man, and it's not his way to push his opinions of visions onto others. Not many people even know about his visions. It's a well-kept secret for obvious reasons, so please keep the information to yourself. If you don't want to see him, then try Dr. Isabel Dacey. She's traditional but not narrow-minded. She'll consider all the angles and give you her honest opinion."

Paul agreed to start out with Dr. Dacey. Riley said she'd send his test results to her; and if he changed his mind and wanted to see Dr. Whitaker, to let her know.

He stumbled out of the room and made it to his black Ford Escape. He sat in the driver's seat, numb. No obvious reason. None. No reason why he saw Amy, except she might be real and from Heaven.

"God, help me," he prayed, banging his head on the steering wheel until he realized someone tapped his arm.

"Daddy."

He turned his head to the right, and there she sat in the passenger seat beside him. She had on a pair of purple leggings, a lilac-colored short-sleeved dress, and white sneakers with butterflies on them. Her blonde hair was one long braid down her back. He thought she might be cold, as it was fifty degrees outside. Spring in Bismarck, North Dakota, remained chilly with occasional warm days.

"Aren't you cold?"

"No. It feels the same to me all the time. No matter where I am," Amy said.

"Where do you go when you leave me?"

"All around."

"All around where?" Paul asked.

"Here and there." She shrugged.

"At the hospital?" He looked around outside his vehicle at the other cars in the parking lot, realizing someone might be watching his weird display. From the head banging to the talking to himself. No one was around. Just him and the big parking lot, with the cars and the trees with bare branches. Chilly, fresh, and wonderful when Amy visited with him.

"Yes. I see the new babies here in the hospital. And Hannah," Amy said.

"Who is Hannah?"

"I don't know for sure. She comes to see the babies sometimes and talks to Sheldon."

"You see Sheldon?" He knew Sheldon Carlisle was the director of the NICU. Amy visited the very sick baby nursery. Why?

"Yes, I see him."

"Do they see you?" Paul asked.

She laughed. "No, silly. Only you can see me."

"Why? Why am I the only one who can see you?" He felt like the seven-year-old, not Amy. He had so many questions, and so few answers.

"Because God sent me here to help you." She put her hand on his forearm again.

He felt comforted but afraid. Glad she was here. Yet afraid of when she would disappear again. "Did you see God?"

"Of course. He's in Heaven."

"Were you in Heaven?" Paul asked.

"Of course," Amy said, as if his question didn't need an answer.

Of course. Paul did believe in Heaven. He believed Samantha was there too, along with Amy. But Amy was here now. Alone. Confusing.

"Do you leave Heaven to come here?" Paul asked.

"It's not really leaving. Heaven is kind of here. Kind of there. It's hard to explain. I blink, and I'm back in Heaven with the other kids." Amy shrugged.

"So, how do you get here?"

She scrunched up her nose and pursed her lips. "I don't know. I end up here with you sometimes."

He could see it wasn't going to be easy talking with her if he kept asking her how Heaven worked. "Are you a ghost?"

"Of course not, Daddy. I'm your little girl."

"Of course you are." He wanted to reach out and hug her, but he didn't know if that was allowed.

CHAPTER 2

The sun shimmered across the brook as it gurgled through the middle of the emerald fields stretching out across the land. Orange and yellow daisies covered the fields on either side of the brook.

Amy, seven, and Joshua, eight, had their bare feet planted in the muddy bank beside the brook. There were no parents in the vicinity. It didn't matter. They were in Heaven, where nothing bad happened.

Amy giggled at the frog croaking in the brook. "He's funny."

Joshua laughed with her. "Watch his throat."

Each time the frog croaked or swallowed, causing his throat to bulge, the children started giggling all over again. Soon they were watching other frogs leaping along the bank.

"Let's see which one is the fastest." Amy pointed to a little frog. "I bet he's the fastest."

Joshua picked out a fat bullfrog. "I bet he can beat your frog."

"No way. He's too fat. Watch."

They leaned forward in unison, but both of their picks decided to sit in the mud and croak. "Ribbit. Ribbit."

Amy waved her hand at the little one she'd picked to win. It took one tiny jump and stopped.

Joshua took his turn, and his plump green frog took a giant leap. "Wow!"

Amy laughed. "You win."

The children watched the multi-hued fish that were all colors of the rainbow swim in the crystal-clear water of the brook.

CHAPTER 3
HEAVEN

I haven't seen my daughter, Amy, and I've been in Heaven for three months. Time doesn't mean much here, since it's forever, but somehow I know how much time has passed on Earth.

I thought I'd see Amy by now because, when I was on Earth, we were taught we'd see our loved ones when we got to Heaven. My Amy is the most loved of my loved ones.

Strangely, I don't feel sad over her not being here. For some reason, I know she's in a good place, and I'll see her eventually. I may not be sad, but I am impatient. When?

My first day as a Gifter was a surprise. My name is Samantha Richmond. I don't know what I expected to do in Heaven once I arrived, but it wasn't giving gifts to people on Earth. Of course, I'm not the only Gifter. Many of us do this, and Gerard leads us.

Yesterday, Gerard shared one horror story. Well, he didn't tell me what happened. He said I needed to watch the dates and times on the gifts and not be late. He said I didn't want to end up like Kate. I agree. Although I have no idea what he is talking about or who Kate is. Anyway, this is Heaven. I doubt anything bad happened to her. She probably got moved to a different section.

My fellow Gifter is Lily Price. She's three years older than me. She gifts houses but started in the hand tools section, so she knows what she's doing. She's been in Heaven for seven years. She died before Amy was born. I think she has seen Amy, but she's never said anything to me.

I haven't had a chance to ask her about Kate, as we're kept busy. Of course, in Heaven, keeping busy isn't a hardship. There's no pain in my mind or body. I feel free. And best of all, I'm young. Does that mean I'm vain? I don't think so. There's so much love; even if I looked old, no one would care. Nor would I. Especially since there is no black feeling in my mind, and the sun shines in a glorious blue sky. The trees are emerald; the birds sing.

Yes, I can hear and see all that. Although the rooms where I work are filled with gifts, many round, square and odd-sized objects aren't solid but luminous, variegated lights in strange shapes. Like fireworks shot into the sky and, in a bright moment, stop in place and levitate. I don't try to figure it out. I just enjoy it.

All the lighted, luminous objects are labeled with gold tags with dates and times. You would think we're inside a big warehouse, but we're outside. The luminous objects float in orderly rows and go on forever. When we give out the current gifts, more move in to take their place. They're all suspended in space. Sometimes I look at the beauty of the colors and lose myself in the moment. Then there's a little nudge somehow or other, and I know it's time to give out another gift.

I even get to see the receivers of these gifts. It's beautiful—because I'm in the child gifting section, babies to seven-year-olds. God's children.

CHAPTER 4

Hannah listened to the ideas being thrown out to fund new equipment for the Neonatal Intensive Care Unit. The meeting for fundraising had been going on for almost an hour. As the director of the foundation, she would end the meeting soon.

Featuring a family helped by the NICU topped the list, but they were having a hard time deciding which family. "Maybe we should include two families."

"Good idea." The agreement came from the other three in the room: Sheldon Carlisle, Judy Henke, and Diane Carter.

"What else do we need to decide?" Hannah looked at her watch. Almost four. She had a few more things to finish in her office, and she could leave for the day.

"Nothing today. If we know which families we want, I can contact them and discuss whether they're interested in helping promote by sharing their story at the fundraiser." Sheldon got up from the table. As the director of the NICU, he worked hard to keep the department staffed with warm, caring people who could handle the stress of dealing with sick babies day after day.

Hannah left work and headed for the gym. She'd skipped working out the past few days, and the stress of the job was starting to get to her. Between work and her arthritis, she was achy and in need of exercise. She'd been diagnosed with arthritis at twenty-five and didn't understand why her joints always hurt. Most of the time, it was under control, but stress made it worse.

She met her friend Thea at the gym. They spent a half hour on the treadmill and twenty minutes lifting weights. Neither talked much until they were on their way out.

"Monroe's working late at the clinic. Want to get something to eat?" Thea asked as they exited the gym.

"Sure. I don't have much at home and need to get groceries. What do you have in mind?" She followed Thea to the parked cars.

"The Golden Dragon?" Thea asked.

"Sure. I've been hungry for Chinese food for a while. I'll meet you there."

On the drive to the restaurant, she thought through the cases for the foundation. Would Dr. Paul Richmond be at the benefit? She heard he'd had a rough time of it since his wife and little girl died, but he was Casey Anderson's doctor. Casey was one of the kids being recognized at the benefit, and usually their primary doctor would come to promote the foundation.

Hannah hadn't told anyone she wanted to meet Paul, but she did. She found him attractive and interesting. She'd heard about his past. Everyone in the hospital knew. Of course, gossipers twisted the truth. Unless someone talked about their own experience, there was no way to know the truth from the lies. She'd like to hear his story firsthand.

She parked in the lot beside the restaurant, and Thea stood waiting at the door, bundled up in a coat with her arms tightly hugging herself. The sun sank behind the horizon, and the wind picked up speed. Without the direct sun, the cold gusts penetrated her skin.

Once they were seated, the waiter took their order and left.

"What's up?" Thea asked.

"Nothing new. We met about the NICU benefit today."

"Was Sheldon there?"

Sheldon was a close friend of Thea's husband, Monroe. Thea volunteered at the local food pantry, and Sheldon invited Thea to help there.

Hannah smiled. "Yes. He and two of the NICU nurses. The whole plan is working out. The only problem is going to be getting Dr. Richmond involved. I don't know how things stand since his wife and daughter died."

"You've never met him, have you?" Thea asked. She and Hannah met at a local charity and remained friends. Thea also worked at the hospital as a child psychologist and had patients in common with Paul.

"No. He's never been involved in the foundation since they hired me. I'm sure he must have referred some of his patients to you for psych evaluations though."

"Yes. A few. He's easy to work with." Thea's eyes lit up. "You're interested in him."

Hannah could feel the heat rising on her cheeks. "Well…"

"He'll come to the fundraiser if that's your question. Invite him to a meeting about the NICU. Ask him in front of Sheldon. He won't say no then."

"Would he say no otherwise?" Hannah asked.

"I doubt it, but I'm sure you've heard his wife and daughter died a few months ago in an accident. He hasn't taken any time off from work, but who knows what he's feeling these days about being in the public eye."

"That's for sure," Hannah said. "You have a good idea, though. I'll invite him to the meeting, or Sheldon can."

"Chicken."

"You're right. Sheldon will get a positive response. Paul doesn't know me." Hannah concentrated on her egg roll.

Thea laughed. "You're right. And then you'll get to meet him."

CHAPTER 5

Classes were done for the day at St. Gertrude's Elementary School. With the children dismissed for the day, Beth Garvey enjoyed the peace in her third-grade classroom as she sat at her desk grading math papers.

She'd been teaching at the school for four years. Her husband Jeremy taught English but didn't find helping kids fulfilling like she did. His goal to be a published writer had been put on hold while he worked at a job with regular pay.

Her dream to be principal at St. Gertrude's Elementary School could still happen. She knew her younger age could be a detriment, and she might be seen as inexperienced, but she also knew she had a good shot at the job. She'd earned her master's degree and PhD in a short amount of time.

Jeremy's sudden wish to have another child could put a snag in the whole plan. He wanted her to put her dream on hold until she had the baby. He also wanted to stay home and watch the baby, which was fine with her.

Except, where would the money come from to pay all the bills, especially the school loans and the medical bills for having the baby? If she got the job as a principal, they could probably financially afford to do it. And if Jeremy sold some of his writing, that would help too.

Jeremy's lack of ambition added to the other problem with the whole plan. Sure, he wanted to write. But he hadn't written in a long time. Not since Brad died. So, what were the odds that even if he stayed home with the baby, he would actually write? And was the baby a replacement for Brad? Jeremy must know somewhere below the surface that one child couldn't be replaced with another. They would still miss Brad.

Her cell rang. She knew it would be Jeremy asking if she was ready to go home.

She realized she'd been contemplating the future too long and hadn't finished grading the papers. She packed them up in her satchel to take them home. It would only take her a half hour anyway, and Jeremy could cook while she graded papers. Of course, he might have his own papers to grade.

She answered the phone. "Hello."

"You ready?" He sounded stressed.

"Sure. Meet you outside?"

"Yeah." He hung up.

She looked at the phone before putting it in her purse. What was up with him this afternoon? Could be a student, a parent, something else. No way of telling. Jeremy was usually an easy-going guy.

When she got outside the building, he had the truck parked in the circular drive of the school, a little past the doors. The cool air revived her as she walked to the truck. She opened the truck door, got in, and buckled the safety belt. "Hi. Tough day?"

"So-so." He started the truck and drove around the circle to the exit.

She waited two more blocks. "What happened?"

"Steven didn't show up again today. We notified the police."

"And?" This was pulling teeth in a big way. Steven chronically skipped school. Why did it bother Jeremy so much today?

"He wasn't home. His grandmother hasn't seen him for two days."

"Today's Monday. He's been gone since Saturday night?"

"Yeah."

"And she didn't think to call the police sooner?" Beth asked.

Jeremy shrugged as they waited at a red light. "You know how she is."

"She thought he'd be home and didn't want to cause problems for Steven."

"True. But she loves him and feared what might have happened to him the whole time he was gone. The police are following some leads. I don't know what we'll find out. On the plus side, this is a small town. News travels fast. If something bad happened, we'd already know."

"He'll show up like he always does. Do you want to do fast food tonight?" She cared about Steven, but she didn't know what else to say.

"What if he drags Tyler into drinking? Maybe he already has." Jeremy tapped his fingers on the steering wheel as he drove.

"Tyler is fine. He wants to go to med school. He's not going to mess that up by following in Steven's footsteps."

"Ever since Brad died, he's been different."

Beth took a deep breath, waiting for the pain to pass. She missed their youngest son so much, and Jeremy rarely spoke about him. He'd taken her by surprise when he mentioned him now. "He feels guilty."

Jeremy shrugged. "It's not his fault."

"But that's not how he sees it. He says he should have been driving because Brad just got his license, and the streets were icy."

Jeremy didn't disagree out loud, and Beth didn't ask him what he thought. She wasn't sure she wanted to know yet.

CHAPTER 6

When Dr. Isabel Dacey came to the waiting room to get him, she was nothing like what Paul expected. When Riley told him Dr. Dacey was traditional, he'd expected a woman in her fifties or sixties. Dr. Dacey looked about twenty-five, but Paul knew that wasn't possible. She had to be at least in her forties considering her medical degrees and experience.

She led him back to her office, and he took a seat across from her. She leaned against her chair and studied him. "What brings you here today, Dr. Richmond?"

"You can call me Paul. Didn't Dr. Adira send you the information and the MRI results?"

"Yes, but I'd like to hear it from you."

He swallowed and took a deep breath. It had been one thing to open up to Riley, whom he'd known for years, but he didn't know Dr. Dacey. He put that against the fact he felt like he was going insane, and he needed to know. "I keep seeing my little girl, Amy. She's dead."

"I see." Her expression remained calm. She read his chart, and Riley told her the other information. She knew the score. Riley kept the visions out of her reports as he requested. Dr. Dacey wouldn't do the same. Anonymity was over as far as records went.

"Dr. Riley sent you the lab and test results. She told me nothing showed up in a physical sense to explain it, and she suggested I see you," Paul said.

"You're concerned about hallucinations, and rightly so. There can be a lot of explanations and treatment options."

"I'm not interested in taking drugs." Paul thought about the testing he agreed to when the clinic let him come back to work after his alcoholic rehabilitation program had been completed. They weren't going to go easy on him a second time. Medications would be the last resort.

"Let's see what happens." Her face remained neutral. "Tell me more about Amy."

"Amy's an amazing girl. She could read by the time she entered first grade. Longer stories like *Goodnight Moon*. She loved any kind of stories and said she was going to be a doctor like me when she grew up." He stopped talking, willing the tears away. He took a deep breath.

"She went to work with my wife Samantha until she was old enough for kindergarten. Samantha was an interior designer. When work made that impossible, she left Amy with my mother-in-law. Samantha's parents live on a farm about an hour away, and they loved having Amy visit."

Dr. Dacey didn't take notes while listening as Paul continued, "Amy spent her evenings with me when I was home." He thought about the times he missed telling her good night when he worked late or drank too much and got home after Amy was already sleeping.

"What were you thinking about then?"

"Amy going to bed before I got home from work."

"And how did you feel about that?"

"Guilty. I felt guilty. Like I should have been there for her all the time. Especially now when it's too late to change."

"Was it possible to be home sooner?"

"Part of the time, yes. Part of the time, no. But maybe they wouldn't have died if I had been home more often."

Dr. Dacey nodded. "What happened in the accident?"

Paul shifted on his soft padded chair. "I try not to think about it."

"But you asked the police what happened, right?"

"Yes. They told me it was a drunk driver." He closed his eyes.

"There's something you don't want to tell me about the drunk driver, isn't there?" Dr. Dacey leaned forward, encouraging him to continue.

He couldn't. "No. I didn't know him."

"I heard you didn't want them to prosecute him."

He shook off the shock. "How did you know?"

"I read the coverage. The reporters were intrigued by that bit of news."

"And lots of Mothers Against Drunk Drivers were mad at me."

"Right. But you had your reasons."

So, she already knew about his drinking problems. How? For some reason, the reporters missed that piece of information when they reported on the accident that killed his wife, daughter, and a young man. He didn't know how his privacy held during that time.

"I had my reasons." He wasn't going to tell her about the other people he'd met while he went through treatment. Not today anyway. It had nothing to do with seeing Amy.

"Tell me when you started seeing Amy after her death."

Paul thought back. "About a month ago, she first appeared. She'd suddenly appear out of nowhere. She didn't talk to me. After a few weeks, she'd start saying my name, and we'd talk a little bit, and then she'd disappear. Lately, she seems to have more control over how much time she spends with me and seems to be able to go places as she pleases, and it doesn't surprise her when she finds herself with me. She'll say she has leave, and then she's gone."

Dr. Dacey didn't show any skepticism. "You're thinking like she's learning how to navigate?"

"Yes."

"But you're also afraid you're going crazy, imagining Amy visiting you, and she's not really there."

"Yes. That sums it up."

"Do you see Samantha? Or anyone else you know who has passed away?"

"No. Just Amy." He waited for her response, clinging to the hope she had some reasonable answer.

"Have you dated anyone since Samantha's death?"

Why did she want to know? He hadn't, but he didn't see any reason why they needed to get into it this session. "What does that have to do with anything?"

"Do you have any close friends you confide in? I'm trying to see what kind of support system you have."

That made sense. "I talk to my father-in-law."

"In any depth?"

"Occasionally." Frank was a rock despite his daughter and granddaughter having died. He and his wife, Nina, lost as much as he had. "He understands."

"But nobody can totally understand what you've gone through, Paul."

"Agreed. Thank you for putting it that way because that's the way I feel. How can anyone know what it's like to lose their daughter and wife at the same time, except for someone else it's happened to?"

"Are you thinking of anyone in particular?"

"No, I don't know anyone else it's happened to."

"Do you have any siblings?"

Her question caught him off guard. She was thorough, that was for sure. "A brother and a sister."

"Do you talk to them?"

"We're not close." Thinking about his brother Alex irritated him. Alex wouldn't let him visit him in jail. And it was his fault his sister Ashley wouldn't talk to him. Not after the way he'd treated her when he was drunk. When he had his life together, he needed to make amends with her.

"What do you and Amy talk about?"

Glad she'd changed the subject, he said, "Not much. She tells me she loves me. She talks about seeing other kids where she's at. She mentions playing with them."

"Does she seem happy or bothered in some way?"

"Happy. She always seems happy, which makes me glad. She's concerned more about me and my feelings. It's disconcerting."

"In what way?"

"She's my little girl. She's dressed in the purple leggings and shoes with butterflies she always wore, but sometimes she acts older than me. Like she knows things, things I don't know yet."

"Which is probably true, if she's visiting you from Heaven, don't you think?"

Paul had one of those surreal moments. Those moments when he looked at himself from outside, seeing himself sitting here with a psychiatrist, talking about Amy as if she really visited him and was alive in a different way. His mind froze there.

"Paul?"

He realized Dr. Dacey was watching him. "Just feels weird talking about her. Like I'm going to go home and see her."

"But you probably will, isn't that right?"

He thought about that.

"How often does she visit you?"

He noticed she didn't say "appear to you."

"This week, every day," Paul said.

"And before that?"

"A few times a week."

"So, there must be some reason why she's suddenly visiting you more often," Dr. Dacey said.

"It's like she's trying to comfort me."

"Do you need more comforting lately?"

"I've been thinking more about drinking lately. She always comes to me when I'm ready to take a drink." He thought about going to a bar the day he left Riley's office. He'd decided since there was nothing physically wrong with him, he should go and get hammered. But then Amy appeared. And he hadn't wanted to disappoint her.

"Let's talk about your drinking. Are you going to AA, or do you have some other plan to make sure you don't start again?"

He lowered his head. "No."

"Let's plan now. Do you have a sponsor?"

"I haven't connected with him for a few years," Paul said.

"Now seems to be a good time." She started tapping on her keyboard. Soon a paper spit out of the printer beside her desk. She handed it to him. "Here's a list of AA meetings. Choose one."

"Now?" He was a little put out by her attitude. Hadn't he come here to talk about Amy?

"Now. The sooner the better."

He looked at the list. Maybe this one at 7:00 a.m. "Tomorrow morning at Christ the King Church." He almost asked, "Are you happy?" but refrained.

"Great. And your sponsor?"

She was hard-headed, which he guessed he needed right now. "I'll try him tonight."

"And if he's not available?"

"I'll get a new sponsor tomorrow." Paul didn't want to, but he figured if he wanted her help, he'd have to walk through these steps.

"Just because you do this doesn't mean you won't see Amy again. I don't think she's coming to see you only to help with your drinking."

His relief at that statement made him light-headed. Convinced the only reason Amy came back to him was to keep him sober, he was afraid if he got help, she wouldn't return. He hadn't admitted that to himself until this moment. Hadn't realized it on a conscious level. "You don't think, when I get help, she'll disappear again?"

"I don't."

"What's causing me to see her?"

"I don't know, Paul. I think we're going to need to give this some time and talk about it. You filled out the questionnaires I gave you, and everything seems completely normal. I don't see any signs of schizophrenia or any other disease process like that, or biological mental issues. Dr. Adira covered the complete range of neurological tests, and everything seems to be in order. Your tests show you're suffering from depression, which is normal under the circumstances."

"I told you. I don't want medication."

"I don't think that's necessary at this time, but I'd like you to come for two appointments a week for a few weeks, to be sure. I'd like you to go to regular AA meetings. Every day if you must."

"Sure." He would. He didn't need to fall back into the well again from drinking.

"Keep the list with the meetings, and plan ahead."

"I know what it can do to a person's life." Samantha taught him that years ago.

"How long has it been since you drank?"

"Almost two years," Paul said.

"Let's make it two." She stood up. "Do you want to come again in a few days?"

"Sure." Why not? What other choice did he have besides Dr. Ted Whitaker, and he wasn't ready to go there yet. "I'll set up an appointment on my way out."

She shook his hand and ushered him through the door.

He couldn't figure out if he'd been helped by the visit or not. She'd focused more on drinking than Amy. But he brought up the drinking himself, and if he were the doctor, he would have followed up on that too. If he started drinking again, no one would be able to help him until he stopped. Better not to start.

CHAPTER 7

Beth took the leftover chicken from the table, covered it with plastic wrap and put it in the fridge. She looked at the papers sitting on the couch, then plopped down beside them and grabbed the remote. Clicking through channels, she finally settled on a mystery and picked up the batch of papers and her marking pen.

Halfway through the show, she heard the shower as Jeremy cleaned up from his exercise. He'd spent a half-hour on the treadmill before they'd eaten, and he'd been in a better mood throughout dinner. She could tell he was worried about Steven though.

Jeremy appeared in the doorway ten minutes later. "I'm going out." He put on his sneakers.

"Just a minute." With ten minutes left in her show, they hadn't identified the murderer yet.

He stood there waiting, juggling his keys from one hand to the other.

She'd have to watch the ending later. She clicked on the recorder to record the ending and leaned forward on the couch. "Where are you going?"

"To find Steven."

"You don't know where to look. He could be anywhere. Bismarck has lots of places for him to hide. He could be with friends."

"I know most of them. I've looked for him before."

"I know." She held back her fear. Steven went to some shady places. There were news stories of knifings every day. "He'll be fine."

"What if he's not?"

"What are you going to do? He's not going to listen to you."

"Maybe he will."

"Stay here."

"Maybe Tyler's with him. I have to go." He stood there a little longer, and when she couldn't respond with a negative, he walked out the door.

She plopped back onto the couch with a grunt. What had gotten into him lately? He was obsessed with Steven and ignored Tyler's pain.

Jeremy seemed convinced he could make Steven turn over a new leaf. As if it would turn back the clock and save Brad, but it was too late. And when Steven didn't give up the rough life, what would Jeremy do?

As she distractedly watched the end of the mystery, Tyler returned. After grabbing an apple from the fridge, he went to his room without a word. She continued to worry about what was happening with Jeremy. Where was he?

Two hours, a pint of ice cream and half a bag of chips later, Jeremy finally returned home. Beth looked at him, relieved to see him in one piece, even if the scowl on his face didn't bode well.

He shook his head. "No luck."

"I'm sorry, Jeremy."

"I know you care, but sometimes you don't show it," Jeremy grumbled.

She dug her fingers into the couch. "What does that mean?"

"I mean you don't care about what I care about." He nudged one shoe off with the toes of his other foot. He did the same with his other shoe. He set his keys on the end table and sat on the recliner.

"What are you talking about? Of course I care. I care about Steven." She did care about Steven. She just cared about Jeremy more and didn't want Jeremy to get hurt. Physically or emotionally.

He leaned forward, his hands clasped, hanging between his spread legs. "You didn't come with me."

Her mouth formed a circle. "You wanted me to come with you? You never said."

"I never used to have to tell you. You'd come."

She shook her head.

"We'd do everything together."

She couldn't comprehend what she heard. "Jeremy, we didn't do everything together. You went hunting. I didn't go with you. You took off for weekend camping trips with your buddies. I didn't go with you."

"That's not what I'm talking about."

"Then what do you mean?"

"You'd be there for me."

"I'm here for you." She hadn't left him. She hadn't even suggested leaving him. Sure, they were going through a rocky patch over the baby thing.

"It's about the baby, isn't it?" she asked.

He hung his head. "I want a baby with you. Is that too much to ask?" He looked at her again.

She turned her face away from him. She couldn't think with his brown eyes pleading with her. If she said yes, she'd have to give up her plan. The principal's job was going to open soon. She knew it. She couldn't fight morning sickness and gain thirty or forty pounds and learn a new job. She looked back at him. "I want one too."

"When?" Hope flickered in his eyes.

"As soon as I get the job." She took a deep breath. There, she'd decided.

"What job? Have you applied for something?"

"The principal job I want. No, it's not open yet," Beth said.

His eyes dulled. "So, it's not even posted yet."

"No. But it will be soon."

"How can you know?" Jeremy asked.

"I just know."

"And you said, 'As soon as I get the job.' What if you don't?"

That stung. "I have as good of a chance as anyone else."

"What if you don't get the job, Beth? What then?" Jeremy's question hung in the air.

Why was he pushing her? "I don't know. I'll try for another one."

"How long?"

"How long what?"

"How long do I have to wait?" He didn't stay for her answer.

She heard him stomping around in the bedroom, getting ready for bed. When she got in bed beside him an hour later, she could hear his steady breathing. She didn't fall asleep for hours.

CHAPTER 8

The morning sky turned light yellow as Paul drove to work. The lights of a few morning commuters shone as cars came toward him on the street, passing and leaving the semi-dark morning quiet again. He liked this time of day before he got busy with patients and coworkers.

His thoughts centered on Hannah. Ever since Amy mentioned her, he knew he had to find out more about her. Sheldon Carlisle agreed to see him at the end of the day, and Paul planned to stop by the NICU on his way to his office. If Amy saw Hannah in the NICU, then Sheldon would know who she was. Only visitors and staff were allowed into the NICU to prevent anyone from stealing a baby, so Hannah had to be staff. Amy would have told Paul if Hannah had been there to visit a baby.

While St. Gertrude's Medical Center wasn't a small hospital, it was a small community, and he was aware of a lot of the staff. Especially the nurses. He would see them sometimes when he stopped by to see his patients. Even though there were now hospitalist doctors who specialized in inpatient care, Paul would sometimes see his own patients in addition to the hospitalists.

Paul entered the staff lounge to get some coffee, pleased to see a fresh pot ready to fill his mug. Someone arrived before him. Staff agreed the first person to arrive made the coffee and hot water for tea.

His nurse, Danielle, entered his office behind him and started running through the phone messages from patients, noting his instructions as they went. Finished with that, he looked through his scheduled patients for the day. Most were familiar to him, and he looked up a few of their charts to view labs and other results.

He wanted to ask Danielle about Hannah but decided against it. He trusted Danielle to keep quiet, but he didn't want them to be overheard. Time got away from him, and he didn't get to the NICU that morning. He would wait until the afternoon meeting with Sheldon to find out what he wanted to know.

He was distracted throughout the day, waiting for the meeting. It was the first step in finding out why Amy would be able to see Hannah, Sheldon, and the babies in NICU. He didn't like not understanding what was going on with him or with them. He was acting as if Amy was real. Like she wasn't a hallucination of his grieving mind. He decided that was the only way to get through each day.

Sometime he would know what was going on. For now, he would go to AA like Dr. Dacey suggested. He'd treat Amy as if she were alive when he got to see her, and he would see what was going on with the NICU involving Amy. Especially Hannah.

Sheldon's office was on the NICU floor, and Paul arrived before him for the meeting. As Sheldon kept his office door locked for security reasons and didn't have a secretary, he waited in the hallway.

Paul heard steps behind him and turned to see Sheldon striding toward him, his bald head gleaming under the fluorescent lights. He stood somewhere around six feet tall, about the same as Paul.

"Thanks for waiting." Sheldon held out his hand, and they shook. He pulled out his key and unlocked the door.

The light automatically came on as they entered, and Sheldon gestured to the chairs in front of his desk. "Have a seat. I'll be with you shortly."

He dropped his briefcase on the desk and opened his top drawer, pulling out a folder before he sat. "I'm glad you called to meet with me. As I said on the phone, I have a favor to ask of you about our next fundraiser."

"I'm not sure how I can help. I've never had anything to do with fundraising before now. What were you thinking?" Paul was getting a little nervous about the idea. He'd kept out of the spotlight since Samantha's death by going to work and then going home for the night. He'd occasionally stop at the gym, but that was about it for a social life. He wanted to be home and remember Amy and Samantha. And drink. Although he'd resisted the urge and followed Dr. Dacey's directive to get a new sponsor and attend meetings for alcoholics.

"We're having a benefit dinner that features two patients who were helped by the NICU. One of the patients is now a patient of yours, a one-year-old named Casey Anderson."

"Definitely one of my patients. She's doing well, thanks to the NICU's early intervention here when she was born."

"And she continues to do well because of you. We'd like you to be at the benefit if possible." Sheldon's expression was sympathetic. "I know you're trying to keep a low profile, but this would help the hospital out if you could attend."

Paul hesitated. The NICU was important, but he kept to himself and preferred to stay out of the spotlight. "Who's spearheading the effort for the benefit?"

"That would be Hannah Johnson. She's our director of the foundation here at St. Gertrude's Medical Center."

Paul kept his lips from turning up into a smile. Meeting and spending time with Hannah was practically being gifted to him, but Sheldon certainly wouldn't understand at all if Paul smiled at Hannah's name. Paul hadn't even met her yet, and he didn't need Sheldon's curiosity. "I don't think I've ever met her."

"She's a terrific addition to the foundation. I believe she'd been with us about a year now at the hospital. She's an upbeat person, and though this is the first time I'm working with her directly for the NICU's benefit, we've talked about other fundraising efforts she's done for the hospital. I think you'll like her and find her easy-going."

"I'd like to meet her soon, then. I'll be happy to help with the fundraiser. Although not as excited to attend the actual benefit, I'll be there. I believe in the NICU, and that's what matters right now. I can get through one evening facing the public." He smiled wryly.

Sheldon nodded. "We'll keep it as painless as possible. You can count on Hannah to make you feel comfortable. She's great at events like these."

"I'd like to meet her when it's convenient for her." Paul couldn't believe his luck.

"We're meeting tomorrow about the benefit. Would you be able to come to the meeting? It'll be at seven in the evening because of the people who need to attend. They can't all leave work during the day."

"I'd like that. I'll be there."

They shook hands again, and Paul left, elated at the conclusion of the meeting and excited to meet Hannah.

CHAPTER 9

Hannah spent the day wondering about Dr. Paul Richmond. She'd seen him around the hospital occasionally and wasn't sure why she was interested in meeting him. Would he be willing to help with the fundraising benefit? His part in the proceedings would be limited to a few comments during the meal and visiting with possible donors during the pre-dinner drinks. He would be free to leave after the meal.

If she hadn't wanted the Andersons to take part in the benefit, he wouldn't have needed to be involved. He already told Sheldon he would do it, so why was she worried he'd change his mind? His family's death a few months ago would no doubt keep him from being in a party mood. Hannah sat in the conference room a few minutes early for the 7:00 p.m. meeting, trying not to worry.

Sheldon, Judy, and Diane all came in together, laughing at something one of them said. As they stood by the table, Dr. Paul Richmond entered the room. The others on the committee knew him from working in the NICU.

"Hello," Dr. Richmond said to them.

"Hello," they chorused as Hannah stood up to meet him.

"Hannah, this is Dr. Paul Richmond," Sheldon said.

Dr. Richmond held out his hand, and Hannah shook it. He had a firm grip that sent warm tingles through her hand. She smiled and cleared her throat, so her voice wouldn't squeak like a teenager's. "Hello, I'm Hannah Johnson. Thank you for coming this evening."

"As I mentioned, Hannah's our foundation director," Sheldon explained. "Judy and Diane are part of this committee since they work in the NICU. Now that you've met Hannah, let's get comfortable at the table and start the meeting."

They all sat down, and Sheldon continued, "I talked to Paul, and he's agreed to be at the benefit and speak briefly to the crowd."

Hannah nodded, relieved he hadn't changed his mind. She'd been worrying for nothing. "Let's hope there's a crowd."

"I have no doubt with your management, there will be," Dr. Richmond told her.

She smiled at him, pleased by his compliment. "Thank you for the vote of confidence. I hear you're a popular doctor among your patients, so you're probably right. They'll come to hear you speak. Did Sheldon tell you we're celebrating two families during the charity event?"

Dr. Richmond nodded as a brief flash of sadness appeared in his eyes and then disappeared. "Yes. I understand the other family's doctor will speak first, and then it's my turn. Is there something specific you want me to talk about? Of course, I'll promote the NICU and explain a bit about how it helped Casey. I'm assuming Sheldon will be doing a longer speech about the NICU."

"That's right," Hannah said. "You could give a few examples of how Casey benefited from the NICU, and how that gave her a better start in life. Maybe add how it even gave her a chance to live. That would be great."

She felt nervous around Dr. Richmond. He was attractive and had a kind manner. Perfect for a child's bedside. She'd glimpsed the sorrow in his eyes a time or two, though his manner was quite pleasant. He smiled easily and often. She wanted to get to know him better, but he had suffered a double loss and might not be interested in socializing yet.

Sheldon slid a few sheets of paper across the conference room table toward Dr. Richmond. "Here are some notes I thought might be helpful. Hannah put them together for you. They will give you some idea of what other people have said at fundraising benefits to inspire people to donate. You can pick and choose or use them as a starting point."

Dr. Richmond glanced down at the papers and then at Hannah. "Thank you. These notes will help. I'm not much of a public speaker."

"I'm sure you'll do fine," Hannah said.

He turned to Diane and Judy. "You two are quieter than usual. When I see you at the NICU, you've usually got something to say."

Diane glanced at Judy. "You all seem to have it covered. If there's anything we can do, ask. That's why we're here."

"You helped a lot with the planning we've already done. The night of the benefit, you'll be there to keep things running smoothly, along with Hannah," Sheldon said.

He looked at Paul. "Hannah can give you her contact information if you have questions later."

Hannah dug a business card out of her day planner. "Here's my card. Feel free to call any time, even if it's after hours. I realize, as a doctor, you don't exactly have time during the day."

"Thank you." He took the card from her. "I'll call if I have questions."

She hoped he'd have a question or two, so she'd have a chance to talk with him again. She chided herself. She was not a teenager with her first crush.

CHAPTER 10

Tyler wasn't sure what to do next. Every time he came out of the school after practice, he found Dr. Richmond glaring at him from his vehicle in the parking lot. Tyler hadn't told his parents, and he didn't want to let them know. Dr. Richmond was hurting. He understood because he hurt too.

He missed Brad every day. He wanted to find someone to glare at also, but unlike Dr. Richmond, he blamed himself. He felt he should have prevented his younger brother from getting behind the wheel. If he had been the one driving, maybe Brad and Dr. Richmond's family would be alive.

He knew intellectually the accident wasn't his fault, but he felt guilty anyway. He started going to a counselor, though he hadn't told his parents that either. They were hard to talk to since Brad's death. It was like they were too busy with their own grief to see he had his own to deal with. And he had been the one in the car with Brad. He had some lingering pains the doctors thought would disappear in a few more months. He had been lucky to escape with his life. He'd been the only one of the four in the accident to live. Some luck.

Sometimes he wished he had died with his brother. He told the therapist that, and the therapist was okay with Tyler's feelings. He couldn't get that understanding at home. His parents couldn't seem to put aside their own problems long enough to help him with his. He missed his mother's empathy.

His parents' fights were starting to get to him. He wanted them to get along again and life to go back to the way it was before the accident.

"What are you doing?" Steven sat across from him at the library.

"Waiting for time to pass. I don't want to go home yet."

"Why don't you want to go home?" Steven pushed his hair out of his eyes. "If I had parents like yours waiting for me,

I'd be home more."

"Not anymore." He knew Steven had only his grandmother at home, and she was strict. Steven rebelled all the time. Tyler also knew his dad spent a lot of time looking for Steven to make sure he was okay. "I know you think Dad's some kind of hero."

"At least he seems to care about me. Most of the teachers think I'm a loser." He slumped further into his chair.

"That's not true. They think you don't care. They know how smart you are. I wish I were half as smart. I have to study twice as hard as you. I don't think my dream of being a doctor is going to happen." He threw a resentful glance at Steven. "You could probably ace the entrance exams for med school. I'm going to be studying all hours to get in. Plus, I need a referral from a physician."

"Why don't you get Dr. Richmond to send a letter? He owes you for everything." Steven stared at him.

"He doesn't owe me. The accident was my fault. I shouldn't have let Brad drive."

"That's not true." He sat up straight, emphasizing his point.

Tyler slid from his chair and grabbed his laptop. "I don't want to talk about it. Do you want to get something to eat?"

"Sure. Where do you want to go?"

"Arby's okay with you?"

"Sure."

Tyler wanted to talk to Steven about him disappearing in the evenings. He didn't want his dad to have to go searching for him in some of the places where Steven went. Maybe Tyler could get him to at least text to let him know where he was. That way Tyler could keep better track of him for his dad. Maybe that would make him feel better.

CHAPTER 11

Despite his busy schedule at the clinic, the afternoon dragged on for Paul as he waited for Hannah. They were going to go out for coffee for the first time, and happiness zinged through him. When he left the building, Tyler Garvey waited for him in the parking lot. He stood beside a small car, one of the few among a lot of SUVs and pickups.

Tyler looked like he was trying to decide whether to approach Paul or not, but finally moved toward him at a slow pace. "Hi," he said.

"What do you want?" Paul's pulse raced. The white-hot rage running through his veins made his vision hazy.

The hesitancy on Tyler's face intensified. "Just to talk for a minute."

"We have nothing to talk about, do we?" His fists clenched. He wanted to punch this kid, even though he knew his response was out of all proportion to the situation. Tyler posed no threat. He took a deep breath.

"I wanted to say I'm sorry for your loss." As he spoke, Tyler's hesitancy vanished. "I know how hard it is to lose someone you love. I wanted you to know I want to be a doctor too. My friend Steven said I should ask you for a referral."

The white haze intensified. "You want to get a referral from me? After your brother drove the car that killed my wife and little girl? You want me to do that?" Paul's voice rose to a roar.

"I thought..." Tyler stopped and took a step back as Paul stepped forward.

"You thought what?" Paul continued to yell and raised his fist. "I would help you after everything that happened? If it weren't for your brother—" He felt a tug on his shirt, and he looked down. Amy stood there. She stared at him mutely.

When he stopped yelling, he caught a glimpse of Tyler's confused expression. Then Hannah stood beside him too. No one else looked in Amy's direction, so he assumed no one could see her. When he looked down again, Amy had disappeared.

"What's wrong?" Hannah asked. She smiled uncertainly at Tyler.

"This is Tyler Garvey. He was the passenger in the other car." He spoke calmly, and the release of adrenaline left him shaky. He wiped his hand across his forehead.

Hannah didn't ask which car.

"I'm leaving." Tyler backed away, warily watching Paul. Then he slid into his car and zoomed out of the parking lot.

"What was that all about?" Hannah asked.

"He wanted a referral to medical school and thought I would give him one." Irritation rushed through him again, but he held himself under control. "I don't know why he thought I'd give him one."

"Maybe he thought you owed it to him after everything that happened."

He didn't understand the expression on Hannah's face. He was tired of people alluding to something he couldn't grasp. It seemed to be a common occurrence lately. "Do you still want to go for coffee?"

"Yes," Hannah said. "I'll need to drive separately because I'm meeting Thea at the gym afterwards."

"Okay."

They each headed to their own vehicles. Paul covertly glanced around for Amy, but she was gone for now. He didn't like that she saw him when he lost control of his anger. Even if she lived in Heaven, he didn't think she needed to be aware of the painful realities of life on Earth. However, she'd probably seen more than him since she was in Heaven. She seemed to be able to come down to Earth a lot, and if she visited the NICU, she'd probably seen some of those parents in distress over their sick children.

Why did Tyler think he would give him a reference for medical school? Paul didn't understand what was going on with the kid. This wasn't the first time he'd seen him in the parking lot, but it was the first time Tyler approached him to talk.

He got into the pickup and left to meet Hannah.

CHAPTER 12

Paul pulled up to Myrtle's Coffee Shop and smiled. He'd been looking forward to seeing Hannah all day. For the first time in a long time, he was interested in something other than seeing Amy. He'd barely gotten through the days at work, only to get home and find himself with too much free time.

His AA sponsor told him to find something to do in the evenings, so he started researching the life of Moses. Although his interest mostly kept him occupied, his focus wasn't the best, and he found his mind drifting. While at work, engaged with the patients, his focus returned, which was good. He needed something to fill his hours, and his patients deserved his full attention.

Hannah drove into the parking lot in her black Honda CR-V, and he got out of his vehicle to meet her. She opened the driver's door with a smile. "This is nice. I like it here."

Myrtle's Coffee Shop had been there fifty-some years and probably changed owners from the original Myrtle. The place was far enough away from the hospital, and Paul hoped they wouldn't run into any hospital staff. He wanted to have a nice cup of coffee and a quiet talk with Hannah. He found her personality soothing, and she seemed to smile a lot—something he needed right now. He probably wasn't the best company for her, and that bothered him.

They entered the coffee shop together and went to the counter to order. They stood there in comfortable silence until their drinks were ready. While she picked up some napkins from the dispenser beside the counter, he carried the drinks over to a booth.

"Is this okay?" The booth had a view out the side window of the café. They could see people walking along the sidewalk outside.

"It's fine," she said and slid into the booth. "I haven't been here for a while."

"Me either. I haven't been getting out much." He shouldn't have added that last sentence. He sounded desperate. Setting her tea on the table in front of her, he slid into the seat across from her and took a sip of his drink.

She didn't seem concerned at the allusion to his wife and daughter. "It's good to go out occasionally. Even if it's coffee and tea with a friend."

He wanted to change the subject fast. He refused to talk about Samantha or Amy today with Hannah, although he suspected a time would come when he would. In the short time he'd known her, he found her to be a good listener, and he reminded himself not to take advantage of her kindness. "Tell me something about Hannah Johnson, other than where she works."

"I like to paint with acrylics for fun," she said. "I'm especially bad at animals, so my friends like to guess what I've painted whenever there's an animal in the picture."

He laughed, surprised at himself for enjoying a simple story. "You must be good at painting something. What's the best painting you've done?"

"I once painted a terrific-looking fence. One of those fences out in the country that's wooden and old and falling down. The only problem was the fence was twice the size of the barn." She laughed. "My dimensions weren't all great, but the fence would have looked good if I'd left the barn out of the picture."

"I'd like to see that picture." He'd also like to spend more time with her. "My in-laws live on a farm, so I'm used to those old fences."

"Sometime when you come by my house, I can show you some of my atrocities. Don't be concerned about hurting my feelings. I know they're bad, but I love to paint. It relaxes me, and when I'm doing it, my concentration keeps me from thinking of other things." She took a sip of her tea.

He wondered what thoughts she needed to avoid. It sounded like maybe she needed a distraction from something too. Just like he did when he studied the time of Moses. He hoped it was simple stress relief for her, and she didn't need the diversion for something major. Relaxation was a necessary part of everyone's life.

The rest of their time at Myrtle's Coffee Shop passed quickly, and they parted, agreeing to meet again the following week at the same place. The NICU benefit was two months away. It would be an excuse to stay in contact with her through the spring months.

Tyler didn't intend to approach Dr. Richmond again. Something was going on with him he didn't understand. When the doctor blamed Brad, there was something strange about it. Almost like he didn't know what happened at the accident scene.

Tyler found that hard to believe. He, himself, asked the paramedics to tell him everything that was going on at the time. While the events were hazy, he knew what caused the accident. Dr. Richmond must have asked for details too, but he must have blocked out some important ones.

Maybe Hannah knew what was going on with the doctor. She might also help Tyler find someone else who could give him a reference for medical school. He would say some prayers for Dr. Richmond when he stopped by the church later.

He hadn't told his parents or Steven he'd started going to sit in the church during the day when he didn't have class. It calmed him, and for some reason, he felt close to Brad there. It was almost as if Brad sat beside him and gave him advice, even though he didn't see or hear him. The peaceful atmosphere soothed him, something he couldn't find anywhere else.

His parents fought constantly, and school had turned into a drag. Steven kept disappearing, and he worried what trouble Steven would get into while he rebelled. He wanted his brother back. He squinted against the sudden tears. He didn't want to cry.

When he got home, his mom sat at the kitchen table grading papers. He went to the fridge to find a snack. "Hi."

His mother looked up and pushed her papers aside. She smiled at him. "Hello. There are some cookies in the cookie jar."

She was in a cheerful mood. Good. He opened the lid of the cookie jar. "Yay! Chocolate chip." He took the container over and set it on the table. "Are you almost done grading?"

"Just about. Don't eat too many of those. I'm going to make something special for dinner, so save some room."

"Wow. What's going on? Cookies and a special dinner?"

"I have some news." She had a big smile on her face.

"What is it?" he asked and munched on his cookie. He felt much better seeing his mother happy again for the first time in a long time. Maybe they'd be okay with Brad gone after all. That brought a lump to his throat, and he pushed back the tears again. They were close to the surface today.

His mom shook her head, though she kept smiling. "Sorry. You're going to have to wait until dinner when your father is home to hear the news at the same time."

"So, Dad's going to be here?"

A slight frown marred his mother's face. "He said he would be."

"Then I'll text Steven and ask him to be on his best behavior. I don't want to miss this." He jumped up from the table and gave his mom a quick squeeze around her shoulders. "Thanks for the cookies." He whistled on his way to his room.

Later, the three of them gathered around the table. His mom made lasagna, garlic toast, and mentioned apple pie for dessert.

Tyler found himself smiling as his parents laughed and joked with each other. He didn't have anything to say himself, but he watched them with contentment.

They were nearing the end of the meal. His mom stood at the counter and cut the pie into large pieces. There was even a choice of whipped cream and ice cream. He preferred ice cream but knew his dad preferred whipped cream. His mother had gone all out.

"Are you going to tell us what we're celebrating?" Tyler asked when he got up to help his mother dish up the pie.

"I applied for a different job today." His mom licked a bit of whipped cream off her finger.

His father's head jerked up, and he stared at her. "The job?"

"The job. The principal gave his notice, and I applied."

A big smile crossed his dad's face. "Does this mean what I think it means?"

His mom carried a piece of pie to his dad and kissed the top of his head. "We'll talk later."

Tyler sensed there was more to this celebration than his mother applying for the principal's job, but he didn't want to know what was going on between his parents. He wanted them to be happy.

Steven texted he'd kept his word and stayed home with his grandmother for the evening. He said he'd played some cards with her, and Tyler thanked him. He thought Steven should spend more time with his grandmother anyway, so he didn't feel a bit guilty about asking Steven for the favor.

They finished their pie with his parents happily talking together, and Tyler enjoyed every bite of his pie and ice cream.

His dad volunteered to do the dishes, and Tyler helped. They loaded plates into the dishwasher.

"I saw Dr. Richmond today at the hospital." He dropped some forks into the silverware holder in the dishwasher.

His dad stopped whistling and stared at him. "Why did you do that? You should stay away from him."

"He's not dangerous." Tyler paused. Well, Dr. Richmond's face turned red before that woman interrupted the conversation. "He's a doctor. He wouldn't do anything to me."

"You don't know that. He lost his wife and daughter in the accident, and he blames you and Brad."

Tyler started in on the dishes again. "I know that. But I thought if I explained what happened, it would help him."

"We're not the ones who can help him, Son." His dad gave him a sympathetic look.

Tyler felt tears coming again, this time for real. His dad hadn't called him "Son" since Brad died. He mumbled, "Thanks," and hurried out of the room before his father saw his tears.

CHAPTER 14

After they finished the dishes, Tyler said he needed to get some studying done and went to his bedroom. Beth settled on the couch in the family room and picked up a magazine to read, but Jeremy sat down on the couch beside her and put his arm around her.

"We've had a nice evening, but I feel there's something I need to say to you. I hope this doesn't make you mad," he said.

She gripped the magazine and clenched her teeth. Their evening had been nice. The nicest time since Brad's death. She felt a little guilty about that, but they had to continue living, and never having fun wouldn't bring Brad back. She braced to hear what Jeremy would say.

"I feel like I've put you in an awkward position about having another baby."

She opened her mouth to protest and then shut it. He had put her in the position of either saying yes or no to him when he had already made up his mind. She hadn't considered having another baby so long after Tyler and Brad.

Tyler would graduate in the spring, and Brad was sixteen when he died. She bit her lip. She would have had two more years with Brad, but with Tyler leaving for college in the fall, they'd have an empty nest next year.

She hadn't totally objected to Jeremy's suggestion for that reason. Was she ready to be without a child in the house? Was that a good reason to have another baby? No, it wasn't. She had been thinking so hard, she missed what Jeremy said. "I'm sorry. What did you say?"

Jeremy shifted so he faced her and took the magazine from her hand. It was crumpled from her grip. He set it on the coffee table. "I ambushed you with my request for a baby. And that's what it was. A request. I should have asked what you

thought of the idea instead of making it sound like we had to
have a baby, or our marriage was over. It's just, I miss Brad."

"I miss him too."

They both had tears in their eyes. Jeremy patted her
hand. "I think we both try too hard to avoid talking about him. I
notice Tyler never brings up his name in front of us. We need to
set an example for him, let him know it's okay to talk about
Brad. He's still part of our family."

Beth started crying. "I miss him so much. I thought if we
didn't talk about him, I would get over the grief sooner, but
that's not happening."

Jeremy held her in a tight hug, and she felt comforted.
Her tears stopped, but she knew they'd come again.

"It hasn't been long, honey," Jeremy said. "I hate to say
this, but the grief is never going away, and we need to accept
that. I've been trying hard to protect Steven, which distracted me
from losing Brad. Yes, I care about Steven. He's Tyler's best
friend, and I feel responsible for him since we've known him so
many years. And, yes, for Olympia's sake and for his, I'm
concerned about him and so I'm looking out for him. I've gotten
obsessive about their situation, so I don't have to look at what's
happening at home. I'd like to pay more attention to what you're
feeling. I'm sorry I've been distant."

"What about having another baby?" Beth asked.

"I'm still interested." Jeremy smiled down at her. "But
let's not talk about it for a while. Let's try and learn to live with
things the way they are now. Maybe you'll get the principal's
job, and then we can discuss it. That will give me time to do
some planning of my own. If I'm going to be home writing, I'll
need something to occupy me if there is no baby. We both need
to think about what we want and then discuss it. What do you
think?"

Beth was relieved Jeremy was talking sensibly again. It
wasn't that she didn't want to have a baby. She didn't know
what she wanted anymore, and that was the crux of the matter.
Jeremy was right. "Yes. We both need to think about our needs
and then talk about it."

They hugged and held each other.

CHAPTER 15

Hannah's week crawled by as she waited for the next time she and Paul would meet at Myrtle's. Her distraction amused her friends, but she decided to keep her visits with Paul a secret for now. She didn't want them to get the idea she was going to have a romantic relationship with Paul. His loss was fresh, and she didn't know what his relationship had been like with his wife.

She knew she had to proceed slowly, for her sake. She was attracted to him and already halfway to seeing a future for them, and he still mourned his wife and daughter. It was too soon for him, and she could get hurt if she fell for him too fast. She would have to hold on to her patience, though she was usually an impulsive person.

She smiled. Yes, God knew she needed some patience. He certainly put her in the right position to try and develop it now.

Hannah had already ordered her tea and sat down before Paul arrived. She decided not to wait for him in a cold vehicle in the parking lot. There wasn't any sense in running her engine to keep warm. Besides, Paul might be busy at the hospital and not arrive at the agreed upon time.

Paul arrived on time, smiling at her when he came into the cafe. He stopped first at the counter to order, then came and stood by the table while he waited for his coffee to be ready. "How are you today?"

"Cold, but the tea is helping," she said.

"We're supposed to get some snow tonight. I'll be right back." He went back over to the counter where his coffee was ready.

She watched him until she noticed he was watching her in the mirror above the counter. It had been a long time since she blushed, but she couldn't stop the flush spreading across her face.

He smiled at her when he came back to the table. "I guess we had the same thought."

"What do you mean?"

"Try and figure out the other person when they aren't watching." He swirled his coffee with the stirrer.

She took a sip of tea to buy some time. She decided to be honest with him. "We don't know each other, and I'd like to change that."

"Me too."

She held up her hand to stop him. "But it's only April, and your wife and daughter… It hasn't been long." How crass could she get? She stopped before some other tactless remark escaped her mouth.

His smile disappeared, but he didn't look mad. He looked thoughtful. "You're right, but I feel like I've known you much longer than a few weeks."

"I feel like that too, but I don't want you to get the wrong idea, Paul. We need to take things slowly."

"I'd like that too. Let's say we're good friends." He held his hand out to her, palm flat.

She set her hand in his and felt his warmth. "Friends." She quickly squeezed his hand and dropped hers before he had a chance to respond. "Now we've got that out of the way."

Their laughs were awkward, but soon they were discussing Hannah's latest painted animal, and she relaxed. They had needed to get that conversation out of the way, and she hadn't been looking forward to it.

There was a pause after Hannah's story, and she asked Paul, "How do you spend your time when you're not working?"

"My AA sponsor suggested I find a hobby, so I'm studying the time period when Moses lived."

"Oh, that sounds interesting. I don't know much about that time. Just what I've read in the Bible."

"You read the Bible?" Paul asked.

It mattered to her that he wanted to know. He seemed to be a Christian, which was good. But she should probably ask for sure since non-Christians might study the time of Moses too. "I hope it doesn't bother you I'm a Bible-reading Christian."

He grinned. "Not if it doesn't bother you that I'm a Moses-studying Christian. I realized I knew the stories in the New Testament better than the Old Testament, so I started with Moses." He shrugged. "I don't know why. It seemed a good place to begin. Noah and the ark's two-by-two felt a little daunting."

"It sounds interesting. When we have more time, let's discuss it."

"That sounds good." He looked at his watch. "I have to go. I'm meeting a friend for racquetball. My time with you and Myrtle," he looked around, "always seems to go by fast."

She laughed. "I don't think Myrtle's alive. I've only seen people around twenty running this place, though they do it well."

He got up. "Yes, they do." He reached out to help her to her feet. "Do you want to meet again next week?"

"I'd love to. Bring an interesting tidbit about Moses for me."

"Only if you bring a picture of your worst animal painting."

"Deal," she said, pulling her zipper up all the way.

She parted ways with him and thought about him on her drive home. He mentioned AA in a casual way. Did that mean he no longer drank or used drugs? She didn't want to ask, but next time he brought it up, she would. After all, she'd only seen him a few times, and they had a lot of things to learn about each other. She didn't know if this relationship would go anywhere; but he made her laugh, and she liked him.

CHAPTER 16
HEAVEN

Samantha couldn't believe she got to go along on another Gifter journey. She'd been to one birth, but this birth was going to be at the hospital where her husband worked: St. Gertrude's Medical Center. She was excited to see if she would see anyone she knew.

She still hadn't seen Amy, and she was beginning to wonder what circumstances God would use to bring them together again. The thing about Heaven was there were no worries. She wasn't worried about Amy. She knew God was taking care of her, and someday, when He wanted them to be together again, they would be.

CHAPTER 17

Paul wondered why his boss called him into the office. They talked on a frequent basis, as they saw each other often, but this sounded official. He could tell from Joel's tone on the phone the news would shake up his world. The fact the administrative assistant hadn't made the appointment hinted at some unwelcome information.

He approached the CEO's office and took a deep breath before letting it out. Whatever came, he could handle it. Maybe it pertained to the upcoming NICU benefit. That thought calmed him down. Of course it was about that. There was no need to believe something terrible was about to happen.

He entered the office and smiled at the assistant, Marci, as she looked up from her computer. "Good morning."

"Good morning." She smiled back at him. "Mr. Killian will be with you shortly. Would you like some coffee or something else to drink while you wait?"

"I'll get a water." He motioned to the small refrigerator that held a coffee maker on top, along with some bottled water and other supplies to handle liquids. He took a bottle of water and sat down on one of the upholstered leather chairs. He twisted the cap off and took a long swig. He was nervous. Even if this was about the benefit, he was unsure of himself. He seemed unable to handle anything out of the ordinary right now.

The five minutes of waiting felt longer before Joel came out of his office to get him. They exchanged greetings and headed into Joel's plush office, which held a couch, a glass coffee table, two upholstered chairs, a conference table with chairs and Joel's large desk.

Joel led him over to the couch and chairs, which gave Paul the impression this would be an informal meeting. Joel's gray hair gave the appearance of an older man, but Paul happened to know he was in his late thirties, which was only slightly older than Paul. His hair was a genetic aberration as far as Paul knew.

Joel's face was serious today. There wouldn't be any jokes between the two of them, which left Paul feeling even more uncomfortable as they settled into the two chairs.

Joel looked across the coffee table at Paul. "You weren't gone long for bereavement leave. How are you settling back into work?"

"It's going okay. The flu season is dragging on this year, as you already know from the inpatients at the hospital. I'm always kept busy with lots of patients, which is a good thing right now. I don't like to go home to an empty house." He winced. That came out a little self-pitying, but he couldn't take the words back now. Besides, Joel already knew.

"I think we're reaching the end of flu season, so things should become a little more routine now."

"We're all hoping, anyway," Paul agreed.

"Which is why I feel we need to talk about you taking some time off, Paul." Joel ran his hand through his short gray cut.

Paul's stomach clenched. This was it. He'd known this wasn't a routine catch-up with the CEO. Joel didn't have time for that. "I took time off for the funeral, and I'd rather be working."

"I understand, but there are other reasons why it would be a good thing for you to take time off right now. I don't believe you're thinking clearly enough to be working."

Paul frowned. "I'm not sure what you're saying, Joel. Has some patient complained? Are we going to be named in a lawsuit? Or am I going to be named, and the hospital isn't?"

Joel leaned forward, put his elbows on his knees, and clasped his hands together. "That's not what I'm talking about. As far as I know, all your patients are satisfied with the care they've received from you. This is about you, Paul, and no one else."

"I told you. I'm fine working."

"How about Tyler Garvey? What's going on with him?"

Paul's confusion increased. "Why are you bringing him up right now? What does he have to do with this meeting and the hospital?"

"Nothing with the hospital, but I did hear you were outside in the parking lot a few times yelling at each other."

Paul stood up and started pacing. "He won't admit his brother caused the accident and killed my wife and daughter. I don't know why he thinks I'll sign a referral for him for med school."

Joel straightened in his chair. "His parents have stopped here at my office and complained about your behavior toward their son. We can't have this happening at the hospital."

"Did you tell them their son shouldn't be accosting me in the parking lot, and that would end the situation?"

"I would have, but that's not true, is it? I heard you were also standing outside their house late one night yelling at him."

Paul lowered his head. "That wasn't what I intended. I ended up there, and before I knew it, I was standing outside on the sidewalk yelling." He could admit it since Joel already knew.

"That's what I meant. They've threatened to get a restraining order against you. I don't know why they came to me instead of telling you directly, but perhaps they're trying to be sympathetic. You need some time off, and if you don't take it willingly, I'm going to force the issue. The Garveys will not follow through on the restraining order if you take time off to get your act together."

Paul didn't like the grim look on Joel's face or the ultimatum. This wasn't his friend. This was his boss and the CEO of a major hospital talking to him. "What do you mean, force the issue?"

Joel stood up, as if he knew Paul wasn't going to take this lightly. "I want you to take a two-month leave of absence. If you don't sign the paperwork, I'll suspend you for two months. That will satisfy the Garveys and give you time to deal with some things. Take your pick between the leave or the suspension."

Paul only needed a minute. No matter what, he was going to be on leave. He should take the leave himself and not have a suspension on his record. "Have Marci send the paperwork to my office for a leave of absence."

"You're not quite understanding me. It's effective now. Marci has the paperwork, and then you'll be leaving the hospital. If you need some personal possessions from your desk, you can get them after the paperwork is signed."

"But all of my patients are booked for the day."

"They've been reassigned. I've told the staff you're not feeling well, so they aren't expecting you back today."

Paul had no intention of going back to his desk if the staff thought he was sick. He didn't have any possessions there he needed in the next few months anyway. If he ever came back. He'd call his nurse to put his possessions in a box and get the box from her in a month or two when he felt like it.

He stalked out of Joel's office to Marci's desk. He felt Joel watching him from his office door. "I understand there's something I need to sign."

"Here it is, Dr. Richmond." She handed him papers with a few sticky arrows on the page. "If you could sign where the arrows point. It's a leave of absence form that says you'll be gone until June seventeenth for personal reasons. The bottom page is a copy for you to take."

He signed his name and took his copy. "Thank you," he said to Marci. Ignoring Joel, he left the office and, stunned, strode to his vehicle.

He was on leave for two months with nothing to do. He couldn't wrap his mind around what just happened. He thought of Hannah. What was he going to tell her? Did this mean he couldn't attend the benefit?

At some point, he'd have to get over his anger enough to check with Joel. As mad as he was at him right now, he didn't want to lose his job over this. It was the Garveys' fault. Complaining to his boss. Who did that?

CHAPTER 18

Beth had dressed in her usual school-teaching attire for her third-grade class. She was unprepared when the superintendent of schools called and asked her to come in for an interview at 2:00 p.m. The superintendent arranged coverage for her classroom, but that didn't give her any time to run home and change clothes.

She looked down at her cheap polyester flowered shirt, black slacks, and black sneakers. Her pants had started getting tight around the waist. It was all those cookies she bought for Tyler. Like that would help his grief. At least the clothes all matched today. She'd been rather sloppy with her appearance since Brad's death.

She didn't have much time to gear herself up for the interview. Lunch time was busy with taking care of some of the children's last-minute problems before they left the classroom for lunch. She grabbed her sandwich from the teachers' lounge fridge but ate at her desk. She wasn't in the mood for socializing today. She needed the time alone, even if it was only fifteen minutes.

By the time the children settled back at their desks, and they'd completed math class, the substitute teacher arrived in the classroom. When Beth knew a substitute teacher would be coming in for the afternoon, she left the spelling words and the reading portion of the day for them. There was no sense in giving them a harder class to teach when they had no chance to prepare.

"Good afternoon, Mrs. Garvey." Superintendent Richards got up from her desk and greeted her with a handshake. "Thank you for coming on such short notice. I didn't realize I'd be at the school until today. When I knew I was coming, I hoped you wouldn't mind seeing me at the last minute."

After seeing the gray suit, crisp white shirt, and black heels Superintendent Richards wore, Beth felt even more discouraged. How could she possibly get a job as principal?

"This is fine." Beth wanted to object to this late appointment, but, of course, it was out of her hands. The interview would happen, and it would be what it would be.

"I see you've been teaching the third-grade class here for about seven years." She read Beth's resume and then looked at her. "Do you like that age group?"

"I do." Beth smiled at the thought of her third-graders. "They're old enough to be almost self-sufficient, but not quite old enough to have the system figured out. For the most part, that is."

"Yes," agreed Superintendent Richards. "There are always a few who have it figured out from the day they're born."

"Not always their fault either," Beth said.

"No. It's not." She leaned back in the chair, her hands resting lightly on the armrests. "Can you tell me why you'd like to change from the teaching job to the administrative work of being a principal?"

Beth sat up straighter. This could be the most important answer she gave. "I've gone to school, and I'd like to put into practice some of the things I've learned. I feel my years of being a teacher would be helpful, as I can bring that experience to the principal's job."

"And what specifically about the principal's job do you think you would like to work at?"

Beth thought carefully. How could she word it without criticizing the out-going principal? "Sometimes I think each student's discipline could be more tailored to their situation. All our students have their own backgrounds to be considered."

"That would take a lot of coordination and knowledge. We don't always know what the situation is at home."

"I think we'd need an overall policy that covers everyone because we couldn't look like we're singling out anyone for special favors. Within that framework, though, I think we could have a little more leeway."

"I see."

The rest of the interview was standard background questions, and Beth was happy when the forty-five minutes were up, and she could escape home. She took a drive around town to unwind, wondering if she wanted the principal's job or not.

When she reached home, Tyler was there alone at the kitchen table eating cookies again. She rarely got to see him when she didn't have a lot of homework to grade or classes to plan, or when Tyler was without Steven.

"Hi." She sat down across from him, waiting to see if he'd want to talk, or if he'd go to his room.

"Hi." He stayed and took another cookie. "What's got you all bothered?"

She laughed. "I must look awful for you to notice."

"You don't look awful, but you look upset."

She shook her head. "I'm not upset. I interviewed today for the principal's position."

He set the half-eaten cookie on the table. "Why didn't you tell Dad and me? We could have said some prayers or talked about it with you. Or something…" He trailed off at the end.

She patted his hand. "Eat the rest of your cookie. I didn't know until I got to school today. The superintendent happened to be at our school, and she asked if I'd do the interview today. She scheduled the appointment at the last minute. I didn't know, or I would have dressed up." She looked down at her clothes and grimaced.

Tyler ate the rest of his cookie. "You look fine, Mom. You always do."

She felt like laughing for the first time that day. "Thanks, dear."

"So, how did the interview go?"

"I think it went okay. I did okay with the answers to her questions. It depends on what she's looking for in a principal."

"You'll get it, Mom." Tyler stood up and hugged her. "You're what that school needs."

She felt tears come to her eyes. "Thank you. How are you doing?"

"I'm fine now that Dad talked to Dr. Richmond's boss. I'm worried about him, though."

"Why are you worried about Dad?"

"I meant Dr. Richmond. I don't think he's quite right about some things. He seems a little mixed up about the accident."

"I'm sure it's a lot for him to take in. It has been for us." She tried to hide her bitterness. Tyler didn't need to deal with her feelings in addition to his. "He'll be fine. It's nice of you to think of him though."

"Thanks. I'm going to my room until dinner," Tyler said.

"Okay. Spaghetti and meatballs."

"Yum." He high-fived her before he left the room.

CHAPTER 19

Paul had no idea what he would do with his time. His heart raced, and his palms got sweaty. Two months off was not a good idea, but he admitted he brought it on himself by yelling at the Garvey boy. He was mad at Tyler for living while his own daughter hadn't survived. He was ashamed, too, that he didn't allow Tyler to grieve his own brother. That must have been hard for him because the two boys seemed close in age. He needed to talk to Dr. Dacey about getting over his anger at Tyler because it was eating him alive.

He needed to find an AA meeting to attend because, right now, he wanted to go to the liquor store and then go home to drown his sorrows. He felt too angry to even think clearly about not drinking.

After the AA meeting, where he'd gotten the idea to talk to his father-in-law, he headed out to the farm. The farm was about forty-five minutes west of Bismarck. As it was close to noon, he fully expected Frank to be in the house instead of working outside on the farm.

As he turned into the driveway, he was met by a barking Rex. Paul hurried to get out of the pickup to pet him. He scratched Rex's back. When he finished and looked up, Frank stood on the top step of the three steps leading up to the front door.

"I see you've dug up some of the yard since I've been here," Paul said.

"A few places where Nina wants to put in some flower beds," Frank agreed. "A few weeks ago, when it was nice out, and the snow melted, we did it. I know we'll probably get a few more snowfalls before we can plant, but it's nice to have it ready. It's been a dry spring, so we'll be out in the field in a few weeks unless the rain comes heavy."

Paul nodded. "Mind if I come in for a bit?" He had no idea what his father-in-law's reaction to his request was going to be. There had been some issues when both he and Samantha drank, and he didn't know how the man felt now his daughter was gone. They talked a few times since the funeral, and he'd been treated civilly by both of Samantha's parents.

"Come on in." Frank held the door wide for him.

Paul patted Rex, and then entered the house.

"Outside," Frank said sternly to Rex. "You know that."

The dog sat down on the front step and eyed them as Frank followed Paul into the house.

"Is Nina around?"

"In the kitchen. We'll go in there and have some lunch. Unless you've already eaten?" Frank looked at him in inquiry.

Paul shook his head. "Haven't had time yet." He wasn't surprised Frank hadn't asked him what he was doing there in the middle of the day. He was a quiet man and let people volunteer information if they wanted, or he left the subject alone. If he did speak up, it was time to pay attention. He'd only ever spoken to Paul about Samantha one time to give advice. Otherwise, he'd left them alone to run their own lives.

"Look who I've brought with me for lunch," Frank said to Nina, who stood by the fridge.

She looked over and smiled at Paul. "Welcome. We haven't seen you for a while."

Paul's face reddened. "Hi. It's been busy at work. Flu season, you know."

Nina nodded. "Are you okay with tuna salad sandwiches and baked potatoes?"

"Sounds good to me." Paul was suddenly hungry, and he ate almost anything put before him. "But you won't have enough baked potatoes to go around."

She laughed. Her laugh, a musical melodical sound, reminded him of a Samantha. "I don't put them in the oven. That's why we have a microwave. Frank makes the baked potatoes these days."

Paul looked at Frank, and he nodded. "I'm getting good at it. Nina's been helping me outside, so it's only fair I do part of the cooking." He hugged her around the shoulders and was tall enough to rest his cheek against the top of her head for a moment.

"I'll set the table then," said Paul, wanting to help and grateful they were greeting him normally. They accepted him as part of the family even though Samantha was gone. He should have visited them sooner, but he hadn't been out to the farm since the funeral. He'd been mired in his own misery and ignored everyone else. He'd come here for his own reasons and to get help, but he'd help them while he helped himself. He hoped they'd see it that way.

He didn't realize he'd been standing by the kitchen table holding a plate and not moving until Nina nudged him with her elbow. "Hey, wake up." She laughed again.

He smiled at her. "Sorry. Just carried away with my thoughts."

Paul set the plate down and looked at them where they stood by the fridge watching him. "First, I'm sorry. I should have come by to check on you both. I haven't got any excuse."

Nina rushed over to him and hugged him briefly around the waist, and then took his face in her hands. She stood on tiptoe to do it. "We're okay. We were worried about you, but we didn't want to interfere where we weren't welcome. Are you okay?" She looked deep into his eyes, and he wanted to turn away, but he didn't.

"I don't know," he said.

She patted his cheek and turned back to the fridge. "I'm glad you came. We'll take care of each other."

After that, the three of them bustled around the small kitchen getting lunch on the table. Paul asked Nina what she planned on planting, and the talk centered on her plans until they sat at the table.

Frank said the before-meal prayer, and they helped themselves to food. "You didn't come out here just to eat with us, did you?" he asked.

"No," Paul said. "I want to work out here with you for the spring. Help you get the crop planted and whatever else you need during the next few months. I'm free now, and I'm guessing you could use the help?" He turned the last part of his sentence into a question. Did Frank and Nina want him hanging around? They'd been cordial to him today and seemed to enjoy his company, but would they want him around daily?

Frank looked him over for a few moments. "You'd probably have to stay out here at the farm. Would you be willing to do that?"

Paul paused. He hadn't thought about that, but the idea had merit. He wouldn't be at home with all the reminders of Amy and Samantha. Amy seemed able to be with him wherever he was. He didn't believe his moving would stop her from showing up to visit him. "That would be great. That is, if you want me around?"

Nina and Frank didn't even look at each other or hesitate. "We'd like you here," they both said at the same time, then looked at each other and laughed.

Paul gave a relieved sigh. "Thank you. I'm on leave from the hospital until June seventeenth, so until then, I'm all yours. Or until you get sick of me being around."

"Or you might be sick of us before we're sick of you," Nina said.

Paul sat there and smiled happily for the first time since his wife and daughter's death.

Paul's first week at the farm was uneventful. He helped Frank fix machinery for the spring planting. He bottle-fed a few calves that lost their mom or wouldn't latch on to the mother. He did whatever Frank requested.

Being outside in the warmer April air, away from all his other responsibilities, released some internal turmoil. The weather cooperated and stayed in the lower sixties.

When he was busy taking care of the calves or feeding hay to the cows, he let his mind wander. His thoughts mostly centered on Hannah, his Moses research, and occasionally Amy.

The peace and stillness of the country relaxed him. He had been afraid his lack of working at the clinic would leave him bored, or worse yet, consumed with thoughts of Amy and Samantha. He hadn't seen Amy since his move to the country, but he wasn't concerned. She always showed up sooner or later in her own time. He had gotten used to that. He couldn't will her to come. She just came.

He didn't understand why it happened and avoided thinking about when it would stop for good. He hoped if he wasn't going to see her again in this life, he'd at least get to say goodbye to her before she disappeared back to Heaven.

He wondered where his relationship with Hannah was headed. And he wondered what her reaction to his forced time off would be. Would she decide he wasn't worth getting to know better? Would it put her off? He had no idea. He hoped they'd at least get to continue their weekly get-togethers. He'd even thought of asking her if he could take her to church. He'd go to hers, as he hadn't been to his since Samantha and Amy's funeral. He didn't think he could take the sympathy. He wanted to go to church, be anonymous and pray.

He took a moment to thank God for the times he'd gotten to see Amy, for Hannah, for his in-laws' acceptance. Even for Joel, who forced him to take the time off from work.

He was blessed. Yes, the country air was good for him. He put the pitchfork back in the barn and patted the dog, Rex, on his head. "Good boy."

He smiled at the dog, who followed him as he left the barn. When he looked up, he saw Hannah standing by her vehicle. His smile widened. "Hello."

"Hi," she said. "I wasn't sure if it was okay to visit out here, but Frank and Nina seemed okay with me coming to see you."

"Frank and Nina?" he asked as he walked over to her.

She blushed. "They said to call them that. They're nice."

"Yes, they are. They didn't ask you any awkward questions, did they?" He wasn't sure what his in-laws would think if he was interested in another woman so soon after Samantha's death. They weren't meddlers though.

He got the feeling they were aware of the tough time he and Samantha were having in their marriage at the time of her death, but he doubted Samantha told them anything. She had been annoyed at her parents for years over their views on her drinking. She stayed away from them except on some holidays, but she let Nina or Frank pick up Amy on a frequent basis, so Amy could spend time with her grandparents.

"No."

He was brought back to the present by Hannah's answer.

"They pretty much stay out of people's business unless you ask them for advice. They're thoughtful if you want to know something," Paul said.

"They seem nice." She nodded. "I could tell they were curious, but they didn't ask me anything, just told me where to find you."

"How did you know to come here in the first place?" he asked.

"The hospital grapevine is robust. No one was surprised Dr. Richmond needed to take a vacation. Except me." She looked him directly in the eye. "What's up?"

"I was told to take time off, or I would be suspended for two months. I told the CEO I'd take the two months off. Here I am." Paul didn't mind that she knew the truth. He was going to be honest with her. If that became a problem, then their relationship wasn't going to work.

They walked along the path between the barn and the house, and he veered over to take another path leading to one of the fields he would soon be plowing.

"Why was the CEO going to suspend you?" Hannah shaded her eyes against the afternoon sun.

"Let's face this way." He pointed to the north, so the sun warmed their backs and stayed out of their eyes. He looked into the distance at the fields and valley. The spring green went on and on. The view soothed him. Nature always calmed his soul.

She turned as he suggested, waiting for him to tell her what happened.

"You remember about a month ago when I yelled at that kid, Tyler? The one who'd been in the accident?"

She nodded. "You were angry."

"I was, but not much anymore. Being here at the farm, being outside, doing things has settled me. I'm calmer. I think I'm finally getting things settled in my mind."

She touched him lightly on the arm and then dropped her hand to her side. "It's going to take time."

"I know." He hesitated before continuing, "I went to Tyler's house and yelled at him from outside that I was going to prosecute their family for what they did to Samantha and Amy."

Hannah gasped. "You what?"

He hung his head in shame. "I was wrong, but I was beside myself with grief."

"That's not a good excuse, Paul."

The criticism stung, but she was right. "I know. Like I said. I kind of went crazy with grief. I'm better. Anyway, Tyler's father went to the CEO of the hospital and told him to either force me to take time off and deal with my grief, or they would get a restraining order against me. Which wouldn't look good for me or the hospital."

"No, it wouldn't."

"So, that's what Joel did. He told me to either take two months off, or he would suspend me for two months. I chose to take the two months off. When I tried to think of what to do during that time, I thought of my father-in-law out here running the farm by himself with Nina. It seemed like a perfect solution as long as they were willing to have me out here with them. I didn't know if I'd be a reminder of what they lost, but they aren't looking at it that way. They welcomed me, and my father-in-law put me to work."

"It seems to agree with you," Hannah said gently. "I'm glad they were okay with you being out here with them. You're probably a comfort to them. Do they have any other children?"

"Only Abby...Abigail. She's Samantha's twin sister. She lives in Houston and doesn't come back to North Dakota very often. I'll be honest. She doesn't like me, and she blames me for a lot of things that went on with Samantha and me."

"You can tell me if you want someone to discuss it all with."

Paul wasn't sure he wanted to open up about the past situation with Samantha and his drinking problem. It didn't speak well of either him or Samantha. But if Hannah was going to be in his life for longer than a short time, and he hoped she would be, he was going to have to tell her the story.

"You're hesitating," she said.

He couldn't read the emotions on her face. "I plan to tell you, but not today. It will take too long."

"I have the time," she said.

"I have to get back to help Frank. That's not a way of putting off telling you, although I'm not enthusiastic about you knowing some of the harsher truths about myself." He smiled ruefully. "It's not a pretty picture."

"I can guess some of it if you're in AA."

"That's right. Drinking played a big part, but it really is a long story, and I do have to get to work." He turned back the way they came, and they started walking back to the farmhouse where she'd parked her vehicle.

"Do you want me to come out here instead of meeting at Myrtle's? Or do you want a chance to come into town?"

"I'm fine talking out here, but it's up to you. It's a long way for you to drive."

She shrugged. "It's peaceful. I like it here. I'll come out unless it's too snowy or icy."

"Good. That means you plan on coming back."

They reached her Honda, and they stood there awkwardly for a moment before she opened the driver's side door. "I'll see you in a week. I'll text before I come to make sure you're available."

"That sounds good." Paul placed his hand on hers where it rested on the door handle. "Thank you, Hannah. You've been a good friend. Next time I'll listen to what's going on with you. I'm sorry. I've been self-involved."

"That's okay. You'll get to listen your fair share." She tapped his hand playfully, then moved to get into the vehicle.

"Next week," she said through the open window, and then drove away.

CHAPTER 21

Tyler was home alone when he heard Dr. Richmond had left town for a few months. Steven heard the information and called to tell him. Tyler wanted to talk to Dr. Richmond and tell him everything was okay, but Dr. Richmond hadn't been willing to listen. Instead, he ranted and became verbally abusive. Tyler was embarrassed his father told the CEO they'd take out a restraining order against Dr. Richmond. His father had been livid when he found out what happened between Tyler and Dr. Richmond.

His dad told Tyler he didn't have to put up with that abuse. When Tyler said he wanted to get into medical school, and this might cause a problem, his dad told him, no matter what, they'd find a way to get him into medical school, and he shouldn't put up with abuse to accomplish his goals. He didn't know how his dad could come through on the promise of medical school, but the situation was what it was. He had only a few months of high school to finish, and it was probably too late to get into pre-med for next year anyway.

He had a wild thought to talk with Hannah. Ever since he'd seen her with Dr. Richmond in the parking lot, he'd thought about getting her perspective. His mom and dad probably wouldn't like that idea. The idea kept popping into his mind, and he knew some day he was going to talk to Hannah.

Steven knocked on the door and walked in. Tyler was used to him doing that. When Steven called, he said he would be over to see Tyler soon, so he'd known Steven was coming.

Steven plopped into the chair in the corner of Tyler's room. Tyler lay on the bed sideways, feet hanging over the edge. It stretched his back out, which he needed after spending all that time in the library today. "Thanks for the info on Dr. Richmond. I'm glad he's gone for a while. I was tired of being glared and yelled at every time I turned around."

"I knew you'd want to know. Poor guy. He doesn't know which way he's going these days," Steven said.

That was the thing about Steven. He had such empathy for people in pain. Too bad he hadn't found what he was looking for yet. Steven needed a goal in life besides taking care of his grandmother. He was at loose ends, which wasn't good. "What do you want, Steven?"

"Now? Something to eat."

"That wasn't what I meant, but I think Mom left some cookies in the cookie jar the other day. I tried to finish them all, but I couldn't." He laughed while he struggled into an upright position. "Let's go see what's in the kitchen."

They raided the fridge and set some bananas and grapes on the kitchen table, along with the cookie jar from the counter.

"Looks good," Tyler commented. He grabbed a banana and started peeling it. After he swallowed a mouthful, he looked at Steven. "What do you want to do when you graduate? Are you going to get a job or what?"

"I suppose. It's probably my only option." He finished a homemade chocolate chip cookie in two bites. "It's not like my grandmother has a lot of money. I know my mother sure doesn't."

Tyler knew Steven's mother used any extra money for either drinks or drugs. Steven's grandmother wouldn't let her stay at the house when she was using, so Steven and his grandmother fended for themselves because she was seldom around.

Tyler slumped in his chair. "Medical school seems like it might not happen, so maybe we can get an apartment together, if we can find work."

Steven shook his head. "No way. I'd like to find an apartment with you, but that's not going to happen. Somehow, some way, your dad's going to find a way for you to get into school, and even if you start out with a different major, I guarantee you're going to end up in medical school."

"You sound sure. I wish I was as sure of it." Tyler stuffed the rest of the banana into his mouth.

"Hey. You've got your dad. He's looking out for you."

"Maybe." Tyler couldn't think of anything else to say. His dad didn't always get what he wanted. He'd learned that with Brad's death. His dad would have stopped that from happening if he could.

CHAPTER 22

Hannah enjoyed the drive on I-94 and then the five miles off the highway on gravel roads to see Paul. She loved getting out of the city. If her job didn't demand she be near a bigger city, she would love to move to a more rural area. Unfortunately, there weren't many fundraising jobs in small towns or the country, so she'd stick with Bismarck.

Paul greeted her eagerly and gave her a swift hug when he saw her. He mowed the lawn earlier. She could smell the freshly cut grass and knew it was Paul and not Frank. Nina had taken a moment at an earlier visit to let Hannah know she appreciated Paul doing some of the more manual tasks, so Frank could take it easier. Nina confided Frank had taken Samantha and Amy's death hard, and she worried about Frank's health.

Hannah smiled and squeezed the woman's hand. She couldn't do much more than listen to comfort either Frank or Nina. She didn't know them, and even if she had, there wasn't anything you could say to someone who lost their daughter and granddaughter suddenly in an accident.

She decided to come out earlier next time she saw Paul and visit Nina for a while first. She could at least keep the woman company and talk with her.

Paul came out of the garage pushing two bicycles. "Hey there. I thought we'd take a bike ride if you're interested. I found these in the garage and think they're in pretty good shape."

Hannah looked them over. They looked like someone had taken a rag over them and shined them up. "Did you clean them up?"

"I did. What do you think?" he asked eagerly.

"Other than a little dust you missed, they look fine," she teased him.

He looked at them and took another swipe at a spot of dust. "How's that?"

She smiled back at his engaging grin. His brown eyes showed the first real spark of life she'd seen in a long time. "My jeans can handle a little dirt. Let's go."

She took the short one from him and got up on the seat. It was a little high for her, and she wobbled. Once they got going, it wouldn't be too bad. Paul could easily help her off and on the bike if it became necessary. The bikes must have been made for taller people.

She thought of Nina and Frank. They had twin daughters, Samantha and Abigail. These were boys' bikes. She wondered who rode them but didn't ask. Maybe there had been another tragedy in their lives. She didn't want to bring up any of that today. Paul needed some relaxation time, and they were going to talk about happy things. Take a bike ride on a sunny day and unwind.

They started down a path through fields of freshly plowed earth. The path must have been used for getting to and from the fields because patches of new greenery from spring shoots of grass or crops studded the center of the lane. She wasn't sure which.

The sky was a bright, brilliant blue, and the sun blazed down on them. She stopped once to tie her jacket around her waist as she got too warm. The beginning of the ride passed in companionable silence as they enjoyed the beautiful day.

They reached the end of path between two fields when Paul said, "Let's stop here for a while."

She readily agreed and hopped nimbly off the bike. She was getting used to its height. There was no kickstand, so she laid it gently on its side and stood there stretching, letting the breeze cool her down. "It's beautiful out here."

She was looking at the chokecherry bushes lined up along the path. Five bushes growing in the middle of nowhere. Their white blossoms were beautiful.

"I know. That's why I like it so much. I find it peaceful and refreshing." He rummaged around in a sack she noticed he brought with him. He pulled out two bottles of water and some granola bars. "Want a snack?"

She realized the ride made her thirsty and hungry. She took one of the water bottles and a peanut butter granola bar. "Thanks. That was a good idea to bring something."

"I've ridden out here a few times before."

She noticed the bike tire tracks along with the weeds sprouting up on the track. She imagined Paul getting away as often as he could to be by himself. Maybe it wasn't quite as healthy as it seemed, but he looked a lot better. She wouldn't say anything for now. Time would tell if he needed more interaction with humans, but nature and God were doing a good thing for the present.

"I see my daughter out here sometimes," Paul suddenly said.

Hannah wasn't sure she'd heard him right. Maybe the solitude wasn't good for him. "You see Amy?"

"Yes." Paul dug the toe of his work boot into the dirt on the track. "I thought you might understand. I don't see her all the time."

Hannah didn't know how to respond. "What happens when you see her?"

"We talk for a little bit, and has to go back to Heaven."

Hannah tried to remain non-judgmental of his mental state. "Do you think she's real?"

"I know she's real. She talks about Heaven and Earth, and she said she's seen you."

That freaked Hannah out. "What do you mean she's seen me?"

Paul was watching her reaction. "I probably shouldn't have said anything. You think I'm insane. I've seen a psychiatrist and a neurologist if that makes you feel better. They both know and don't think I'm a danger to myself or anyone else, so here I am uncommitted in the hospital."

"I don't think you're crazy," Hannah said. "You took me by surprise. Yes, it does make me feel odd to think your daughter has seen me and mentioned me to you."

"She said she was in the NICU one time and saw all the sick babies. She met Sheldon when she was alive. She mentioned him and said you were with Sheldon. That's all."

"That makes me feel a little better." She frowned in concern. "Why does the psychiatrist think you're seeing Amy?"

"She doesn't know. She hasn't given me a diagnosis. Of course, depression would be the main reason."

Hannah looked down at the dirt Paul piled in a small circle with his boot. He opened up to her, and she could tell that made him nervous. He had taken a giant leap in trusting her.

"If they don't seem concerned, I'm not either," she said emphatically. "I'm glad Amy is helping you. Do you ever see Samantha?"

"No. Just Amy. She comes when I feel like drinking or I'm really sad. It's strange to have her know about my drinking. When she was alive, Samantha and I kept that part of our lives to ourselves. We never discussed it in front of Amy."

"But if you and Samantha were both drinking, Amy saw. She was old enough to know what was going on, even if she didn't fully understand it." Hannah spoke without thinking.

Paul shook his head. "I don't think so."

"But you believe she understands the past when you talk to her now."

"She seems almost grown up when I see her, although she still appears as a little girl in her favorite outfit. She's an old soul."

Hannah nodded. "It's okay, Paul. I understand. You can talk about this with me again if you want. As you can see, I'm not treating you like we need to get back to the house as fast as we can."

He smiled at that, and she caught the look of relief on his face.

"I wanted to tell you. I like you, Hannah. I hope we can be friends, but I've got a lot going on right now, so can we take this friendship thing slowly?"

"Of course. I'd like to remain friends." She held out her hand to him. "Shake?"

He took it in his, but instead of shaking her hand, he squeezed firmly. "Thank you," he said as he let go of her hand.

"Any time."

CHAPTER 23

Paul and Frank worked on the seeder that broke down when they planted the wheat crop. They carried on mostly in silence with a few desultory comments.

"Thanks for letting me get away to see Hannah when she comes," Paul said. He held a flashlight pointed at the place where Frank worked. Frank's eyesight wasn't as good as it used to be, and in the shadow of the machinery, the area he worked on was dim.

"I figure she's good for you." Frank adjusted Paul's hand holding the flashlight to get a better view.

Paul grinned. "I think she's good for me too."

"She makes you happier, and she isn't as dramatic as Samantha."

Paul was surprised Frank brought up Samantha. Did Frank want to talk about her? What was he supposed to say? Samantha had been a drama queen. Always hyperactive and giddy about something. "Was Samantha hyper when she was younger?"

Frank looked up from the machinery. "Definitely. She showed off from the day she was born." He cleared his throat. "We encouraged her. Always wanted to see what she was up to. Abby was quieter. They were sure different, even though they were identical twins. Abby would hardly say a word if we had company, and Samantha always put on plays and acted in them in front of the three of us or whoever visited." He put his head down again and started screwing in a piece they took off to get to the problem.

"I think Amy took after Samantha that way. She was always a talkative little thing. I miss them."

Frank lifted his head again. "Me too. So does Nina. We talked about Hannah. We're glad you've found someone nice and good who can help you. Friends are good."

Once more, Frank surprised Paul. He wasn't a garrulous man, and feelings weren't brought up.

"Thank you. I appreciate your approval. I like her." He smiled again. When he thought of Hannah, he couldn't help smiling.

"We wanted you to know, we don't blame you about Samantha."

Paul was unsure where the conversation was headed. "About what?"

"About her drinking. We knew you'd quit. We hoped Samantha would too, but she didn't. Guess there's no use thinking about it anymore. She tried a time or two."

Paul remembered when Samantha was pregnant, she quit drinking. He hoped it would be the end of it, but it wasn't. She started up again when Amy was young. She said she couldn't deal with the stress of a toddler and a job. Paul said she could quit work, which she did, but it didn't stop the drinking. "Yes, she tried. She said once she wanted to make you proud of her again, like when she was a little girl."

Frank shook his head. "We always loved her. We only said something about the drinking once, and she wouldn't listen. We didn't feel like it would do any good, so we let it be."

"I tried too, but we fought over it. It didn't make a difference. I look back and wonder what I should have said or done. I don't know."

Frank shrugged. "She was a grown woman making her own choices."

Frank changed the subject. "Nina and I like Hannah. We think she's good for you, so don't you start thinking you're not good enough for her. You are."

Paul's face turned red. "Thank you for saying that."

Frank smiled at the look on Paul's face. "You're welcome. Enough reminiscing. Let's get some work done today."

CHAPTER 24

Jeremy was worried about Steven. He hadn't shown up to class for the day, and even though Steven liked to wander at night, his class attendance was pretty good for the most part. He didn't miss too many days. Although he left earlier than he should. His last period of the day was study hall, and he was known to skip that time. It wasn't considered mandatory for a senior to attend, but it was encouraged. However, Steven missed the whole day.

Jeremy texted Beth he intended to look for Steven after school. Beth texted back she'd get a ride home from someone else, so he didn't have to drop her at home. She texted a heart emoji, so she seemed okay with him looking. Ever since they discussed her applying for the principal's job, she'd been upbeat and happy.

Their marriage suffered from the accident with Brad and Tyler. Brad's death caused a distance to form between them, and they were both trying to navigate their own grief. He was ashamed he hadn't tried to help Beth deal with hers. He'd been too wrapped up in his own grief, Tyler's troubles with Dr. Richmond, and Steven's problems. He lost sight of the fact Beth lost her son too.

When he returned from finding Steven today, he'd talk to her and see what he could do to help. He knew healing would take time, and there would always be a wound that didn't go away. He missed Brad. Missed telling him stupid dad jokes and playing basketball with him on their home court in the driveway. Brad wanted to be a professional basketball player. Although they both knew that was a dream. Not that Jeremy ever said that to him, but Brad knew he wasn't good enough to play pro ball.

It felt good to think about him, and it was the first time since Brad died he didn't feel a searing anger along with the sadness. Their family, what was left of it, needed to pull together and help each other. He'd talk to Beth about an evening family mealtime, instead of the random pattern they'd fallen into in the past month or so.

He pulled into the driveway of Steven's house to talk to his grandmother, Olympia. He always smiled at her name. It reminded him of the Olympic games and great athletes. And Olympia could have been a great athlete when it came to determination. She had it all there in her winning attitude.

She opened the door even before he'd shut off the vehicle's engine and stood there waiting for him on the front step. He got out of the vehicle and stopped at the bottom of the two steps leading up to her front door. This almost put them at eye level.

"Do you know where he is?" Olympia asked. She wasn't wringing her hands but stood there ramrod straight, as if ready to give Steven a good tongue lashing as soon as she saw him.

Jeremey admired her. If Brad or Tyler were missing, he'd be worried sick. Not that he underestimated Olympia's feelings. She was worried. She chose not to show it to many people, but he'd seen it a time or two.

"When did you see him last?" Jeremy asked.

"We ate together at six last evening. He said he was going to see some friends and left. That's the last I've heard from him."

"Did he say any names?"

"No. Just friends."

"Okay. I'll go look." He left her standing there on the front step. He knew she wouldn't go with him. He'd asked before this time. He also knew she was frustrated because she didn't know how to drive, so she had no way of looking for him herself, unless she went with him.

He got in his vehicle and didn't waste any more time. He went to a bar he knew where they didn't care what age their patrons were. The place kept getting shut down and then reopened as soon as the fine was paid and the waiting time lifted. The patrons helped hide the younger group in two of the back rooms. Jeremy didn't like the place and hated going into the building, but he had to look there. He might as well get it over with.

He drove by the building first, looking at the vehicles in the parking lot. He didn't see Steven's scratched and dented blue pickup. Plenty of other vehicles were in the lot, so the bar wasn't shut down.

Jeremy debated going into the place but decided to text Tyler first. He pulled into a parking spot along the curb and pulled out his phone. He texted his son, "Have you seen or heard from Steven today?"

Jeremy realized he should have texted before he even went to see Olympia. If Tyler had seen him, this trip around town would have been a waste of time.

A ding sounded, and he looked at his phone. "No. He wasn't in school."

"Thanks. I'm out looking," Jeremy texted back.

"Want help?" Tyler texted.

"Not yet. I'll let you know. Thanks." He put his phone back into his pocket and considered Steven's acquaintances.

He spent the next hour driving around to the various acquaintances of Steven's he knew and didn't find him.

He finally stopped by to talk to Olympia again. The dark blue pickup was in the driveway, and Jeremy felt a rush of anger. How dare this young man worry his grandmother? He could have driven away, but instead he got out of his vehicle and knocked on the front door.

Steven opened the door, and Jeremy didn't even let him say hello.

"How dare you worry your grandmother this way?" Jeremy asked. "You've been gone all night, and she's been worried sick."

He noticed the black eye Steven failed to hide. "What happened?" he asked in a quieter voice.

Steven opened the door further. "You can come in and hear the story. I just got home and was going to tell Grandma."

Jeremy followed him into the tiny kitchen. It had cracked linoleum on the floor, a small table that fit only two people, and a few cabinets with a marbled countertop. Everything was in its place and immaculately clean. Olympia sat in one of the chairs by the table, and Jeremy gestured to Steven to take the other one. "You look like you could use the chair. I can stand."

Steven sat and looked between the two of them. "I should have called you, but I was ashamed. I thought it would be better to see you in person. I went to the bar you told me not to go to, and there was a fight."

Jeremy opened his mouth to say something. He wasn't sure what, but Steven held up his hand and said, "I shouldn't have been there in the first place. I didn't start the fight or contribute to it. I was trying to get out of there when this guy swung his arm, and his fist connected with my face. I fell. People were fighting, and I heard the police coming. I managed to get up and get out of there. I drove out of the parking lot, and then I didn't know where to go." All defiance left him at those words.

Jeremy knew how hard it was for Steven to say he didn't think he had any friends.

"So, you decided to worry me instead of coming home and worrying me?" Olympia asked quietly. They were the first words she'd spoken since Jeremy arrived.

"I thought my face would look better today. Besides, I was drunk. I didn't want you to see me like that."

Olympia gently took his face between her wrinkled hands. "You're drinking too much. I know you want to be out of school. I know you don't like it here."

He took her small hands in his large ones. "If you mean I don't like it here, meaning your house, you're wrong. I love you, and I love this house. I don't fit in anywhere else, like school and with other people." He looked at Jeremy. "Except you and Tyler, of course. I feel like I'm always letting you down, Grandma."

"You're not letting me down, Steven. You're letting yourself down. A few ground rules are going to start today. You're going to abide by them, or we will have a talk you won't care to hear at all."

Jeremy caught the quirk of Steven's lip and thought it might be a hint of laughter. Not a disrespectful laugh though. More like real amusement.

"Okay," Steven said.

"I saw that smile," Olympia said, smiling too. "I'm glad you're back in one piece. Now, the ground rules. No skipping school. No drinking. No drugs. Come home right after school unless you're with Tyler. We're going to see the guidance counselor this week to find out what you will be doing when you graduate. You're smart, and you shouldn't waste that."

"But, Grandma," Steven objected, "we don't have the money for me to go to school."

She looked at Steven. "You want to go to college? You keep skipping school or at least some classes."

"Study hall is boring, and so are half the classes I'm taking."

"That's because they're too easy for you," Jeremy agreed.

"Exactly. So, what do you want to go to school for?" Olympia asked.

"Environmental engineering. I thought I'd get a job and work when I wasn't in class. I'd go here to the local community college to start out with."

"You want to go to college?" Olympia asked. "You're not saying that to make me happy, are you?"

"No. I really want to go if I can get into the classes I want."

Jeremy smiled. "You have to take some basic classes unless you go to a trade school. Trade school gets you into the meat of the classes sooner."

"Is there a trade school for what you want to do?" Olympia asked.

"No," Steven said.

"Then you'll go to the community college to start out, and you will go to every class unless you're sick," she said. "I'll pay for classes, and you can stay here until you graduate. If you want, that is."

Steven got up and hugged his grandmother. "I can't believe you're offering to pay for college and letting me stay here. I've given you so much trouble."

"Yes, you have." Olympia hugged him back. "I believe in you, and I love you. You need to find your way. Make some better friends and don't keep making the same mistakes. Stop drinking and go to class." She held up her hand to stop him. "You're going to say you're bored. That's life. Find something creative to do while you're sitting there bored in study hall. Maybe you can see if you can sign up for a college class early and do it online. You can work on it in the boring study hall."

Steven's face broke into a grin. "That's a great idea, Grandma. You're the best." He hugged her again, and then a frown crossed his face.

He sat back down in his chair and slumped. "But where is the money coming from? This is going to cost money. I need to work."

"Yes, you do," agreed his grandmother. "You're going to get a job this summer, and then you're only going to work a few hours during your freshman year. I want you to get good grades. I have some money set aside for your school. Don't worry about it."

"You saved money for my school?"

Jeremy caught the shame in Steven's expression, but he was happy for him. Olympia seemed to have saved up money somehow for Steven to get a good start in life. Jeremy had been ready to add some money from somewhere. He knew Beth wouldn't be too happy with him for offering, since he wanted to have another baby and stay home and write.

He would have continued working as a teacher if Steven needed the money for school. Jeremy believed in him. Steven didn't need him anymore because he realized his own grandmother believed in him too and would help him establish himself in life. Jeremy loved to see the happy ending—if Steven would behave, study, and stop drinking. Jeremy prayed that was the case.

CHAPTER 25

Hannah watched Paul as he plowed the field, getting it ready for the spring crop. The time outside and away from the hospital seemed to be doing him a lot of good. His mood swings were fewer and his temper slower to ignite. It helped that he didn't run into Tyler at the farm.

She hadn't told Paul about meeting with Tyler to help him prepare for medical school. She expected when Paul remembered the truth about the accident, he would be willing to help Tyler get into medical school.

She planned to tell him the truth today. If he chose not to believe her, she didn't know what would happen. He would probably break up with her. She trembled at the thought, but she believed it was the right time to tell him. She questioned when, or if, he had ever acknowledged the truth.

He moved closer as he plowed the dirt and stubble in the field on the side where she parked her SUV. She watched idly as she stood outside in the wind, the dust blowing her way. Deciding it was only going to get dirtier the closer he came, she got back into her vehicle and waited for him to stop. He drove the tractor past her about fifty feet and then parked and got out.

She loved the smile on his face as he greeted her and gave her a quick kiss on the cheek, carefully leaning forward and not touching her to keep her from his dust-covered clothes.

"What are you doing out here in the dirt?" he asked.

"I came to see you. I wanted to tell you something, and this seemed the place to do it."

Her serious tone must have registered because the smile on his face disappeared, and wariness crept into his eyes. "That sounds ominous."

She should get it over with. "I went to the hospital and talked to Sheldon. He heard a rumor you might be returning to your practice soon."

Paul shook his head and waved in the direction of the tractor and plow. "I'm not ready. Going around the field in circles helps me think. It's peaceful, and my father-in-law has gotten used to my crooked driving. He'll have fun at harvest time." He smiled again. "I need the serenity of this time alone."

"Have you seen Amy lately?" She knew sharing Amy's visits was a big step for him, and she was glad he was willing to tell her.

"No. She hasn't come to any of the fields I've worked for my father-in-law, but I'm fine with that. I'm okay with her not appearing, and I feel her near anyway."

"Did she tell you why she gets to see you?" Hannah wondered if Paul would tell her if he knew, or if he would keep it a secret from her.

"I think she and God don't want me to drink again, and that's the way to stop me. I don't feel like drinking out here." He threw his hands wide to encompass the outdoors. "I feel free and unpressured here. I'm thinking of not going back to my physician practice."

Hannah's mouth dropped open. "Not go back to medicine? Isn't that who you are, Paul? Healing and helping people?"

"Maybe not much anymore. I'm not sure what's going to happen. I'm taking it one day at a time."

Hannah hesitated. Maybe today wasn't the day to tell Paul the truth. He looked calm, but it unsettled her to hear him talk about not going back to his previous job. His mood appeared upbeat, but this was unexpected.

Paul must have sensed something because he crossed his arms over his chest. "What did you come to tell me, Hannah? Are you breaking up with me?"

"What? No!" She put her hand on his sleeve and then hugged him, despite his dirty clothes. He felt rigid under her touch, though he did uncross his arms and hug her back. "That's not why I'm here at all."

"Let's go sit in the SUV and out of this wind," he suggested.

She nodded, happy for a few more minutes to gather her thoughts. Should she tell him? Should she wait for him to remember on his own?

She settled into the driver's seat while he sat in the passenger seat. She gripped the steering wheel, and then let go and gripped her hands in her lap. "When was the last time you looked at an article about your wife's accident?"

He turned slightly in his seat, so he faced her sideways. "What has that got to do with anything?"

"Go along with me for a minute."

He wore a puzzled frown. "I've never read any articles. The press wanted to interview me, and I only answered a few questions, but refused a full interview. I don't want to go online and see anything about it. People told me what they said in the news."

She turned toward him and grasped his hand. He curled his fingers around hers. "There's a reason for that, Paul. I know you've been seeing a therapist, but it doesn't seem to be getting you any closer to the truth. Are you ready to know what happened that day yet? Or do you want to continue living with your presumptions of what happened during the accident?"

"What are you talking about? That kid Brad ran a red light and hit Samantha's vehicle." His grip strengthened, and she winced. He noticed and let go of her hand.

She set it back in her lap and shook her head. "That's not what happened, Paul. Brad did not run a red light. His vehicle did not slip on the ice that evening either."

"What are you talking about?" He gripped his own hands in his lap.

"That's not what happened. Do you want to know, or not?" she asked.

"Why are you asking me this when I'm finally happy?" he shouted and yanked the door open.

"You didn't answer my question. Do you want to know?"

"No." He stumbled out of the SUV and slammed the door.

She watched him stalk back to the tractor. She didn't know how they were going to continue their relationship if he kept lying to himself. She shouldn't care. He did it to protect himself, not for any malicious reason, but she didn't want to keep tiptoeing around the subject for the rest of their lives—if they had a life together in the future.

CHAPTER 26

Paul jerked the tractor into motion and set off around the field again. His emotions skittered from being mad at Hannah to confusion. She made it sound like he missed something about the accident. Something he wouldn't admit. He didn't know what she meant. What was she suggesting by saying Brad didn't run a red light?

Joel acted the same way when he strongly suggested Paul take time off from the job to figure things out. There was a moment in their conversation when Paul felt like Joel held something back. He thought Paul should know something.

He felt lost and alone. He wasn't sure Hannah would continue to put up with him. How much baggage did she want to deal with?

Amy popped in and sat next to him in the tractor. "Hi."

"Hi, sweetheart." He gave her a hug. "It's great to see you."

"You must have needed me because here I am."

He kept his one arm around her shoulders and steered with the other. He did need help. Amy comforted him, but did he want to ask her for the truth? Who should he ask if not Hannah? He'd made her angry, but she wouldn't hold on to her anger.

He could ask that Tyler kid. Tyler wanted to talk to him, and he shut him out. Amy seemed too young to clear up his confusion, but she appeared now. Did God have a reason?

"I always love to see you, but I didn't feel like drinking this time. It's the first time you've shown up when I needed you for some other reason." He regretted that slip. His daughter didn't need to know he wanted to drink to drown out his sorrow. Maybe she didn't show up just because of his drinking. Maybe God had another reason he let her come to Earth.

"Mom drank the day of the accident." She patted his shoulder.

"I know. It bothered me she drove you anywhere when she drank. I told her not to do that, but I was at work and couldn't always stop her. We weren't the best parents for you, but we loved you then, and I love you now."

"I haven't seen Mom in Heaven," she confided but didn't seem concerned.

"I'm sure you will see her. God has His own timing, and we're in more of a hurry than He is sometimes." Like now. He wanted the grief to pass.

"I play with my friend Joshua. We have a lot of fun. It's beautiful, Daddy. I wish you could come with me, and I could show you."

He smiled at her gently. "Someday. We can't hurry God's plan. At least I get to see you now and then. I'm lucky we get to talk."

"I'll always be here when you need me."

Paul wasn't sure God would allow that, but for now, he got to see her. "Thank you, honey."

He decided not to ask her anything more about the accident. It was time to talk to Tyler or Hannah and find out what happened. He obviously missed something, and it was time he faced it. Maybe Amy hadn't been sent for him to talk to, but she did give him courage to face whatever he needed to face. He smiled again at the thought of his little girl being his strength, but it was true. God came through for him in a way he never expected.

CHAPTER 27

Paul crossed his arms over his chest and stared at Dr. Dacey. "I'm not sure why I'm coming to see you, except Joel insisted I continue my appointments with you while I'm on leave."

Paul waited for Dr. Dacey to respond. She took her time today, as if she wanted him to fill in the gaps of their conversation.

"I think he's concerned you will hide away on the farm, start drinking again, and never return to your medical practice," Dr. Dacey finally said.

He dropped his arms and leaned forward. "First, it's my in-laws' farm, and I would never do that to them."

"I think he's underestimating you too, but he only knows what he sees. He's going by your actions in the past, not the present. Have you been going to AA like we talked about?"

"Yes, I go weekly since I'm out at the farm. If I feel the need, I go to extra meetings." Paul was tired of the talk about his drinking. He handled the cravings okay. "I fought with Hannah, and I didn't even think about drinking afterwards. I was too worried about her."

"That's a good sign. Why were you worried about her?"

Paul hesitated. Yes, these sessions were confidential, but what would Dr. Dacey think about him not remembering aspects of the accident everyone kept alluding to? But then again, he saw his dead daughter, and she knew, so she could probably handle his lack of memory. "Something's wrong with my memory. I don't seem to be aware of all the details people think I should know, even though they say all the information was in the news accounts."

Dr. Dacey nodded like she knew what he meant, but she couldn't. He thought of it as her psychiatrist pose. "What details do they think you should know? Is it something they've talked to you about, and you don't remember?"

"No. I remember conversations and things with my patients, but it seems to be about the accident. I've listened to what the police said, and I've avoided the news. I don't see how I could be wrong about what happened."

"So, tell me what happened in the accident."

"Now?"

"Sure. I know what happened. You can tell me what you know, and we'll see what details are missing." She leaned back in her chair, prepared to listen.

His gut started churning, and his palms got sweaty. Why was he afraid suddenly? "I'm not sure this is going to help."

"Let's try," she encouraged softly.

He took a deep breath and let it out. "Samantha and Amy were out running errands. The roads were slippery that day, but Samantha wanted to get some things done. They drove through an intersection, and another car didn't stop at the red light and hit them. The car was driven by a sixteen-year-old boy, and his older brother was in the car too. He survived." His gut clenched again.

"The fact that boy survived makes you angry."

He didn't detect any judgment in her voice. "Yes. Amy should be alive."

"Is that why you keep seeing Amy? She's alive?"

Paul shook his head. "She's gone." He couldn't use the word "dead." "I don't know why I see her. And, yes, I am angry Tyler is alive. Intellectually, that isn't fair. His brother drove and died from the accident. Tyler has his own grief."

"Do you think maybe he feels the same way you do? Angry his brother died?"

Paul sat there for a minute, breathing deeply, trying to get his feelings under control. "He misses his brother. How could he not? But when I see him, I get angry his brother caused the accident, I see a red haze in front of my eyes and want to hit Tyler. It's wrong, but that's how I feel."

"Tyler must know his brother caused the accident, but his brother is dead, and he can't get him back. What else do you think he's feeling?"

"Guilt. I feel guilty."

She let that statement hang there in the room for a few minutes. When he didn't say anything more, she finally asked, "Why do you feel guilty?"

"Because I should have stopped Samantha from driving while she'd been drinking. But I don't know how I could have done that. Unless I took Amy and moved out of the house. But Samantha still would have wanted to spend time with Amy, and I wouldn't have stopped her. I loved them, and I couldn't take Amy away from Samantha. I feel I should have been strong enough to do that, and they would both be alive today. I'm starting to talk in circles."

"You can't know that they'd be alive if you'd done any of what you've told me. Accidents happen. You said Brad caused the accident."

"I didn't say the boy's name," Paul said.

"I've also read the reports," Dr. Dacey said.

For some reason, Paul's stomach started churning again, and he dropped his gaze. "Accidents happen," he managed to say.

"What do you think everyone knows about the accident that you don't?" she asked.

His mind went blank. His patients told him that, and he never understood. They must have some thought in their mind, but he couldn't think of anything, except his mind was blank. That was his thought. "My mind is blank."

She nodded again. "Do you want to ask one of those people what they are talking about next time?"

"I've thought about it."

"And who would you ask?"

"I think Hannah would tell me. We argued last time we talked, but she understands."

"Do you want to ask her about this?"

"She's the only one I feel comfortable talking to besides you. I don't feel judged by her. We've only known each other a short time, but I think we have a future together. I've talked to her about seeing Amy too."

"Did she understand?"

"Yes. Hannah believes in Heaven, like I do, and I think that's where Amy is most of the time. Or all the time. If she can be in two places at once. Heaven and Earth."

"I think you're doing well, Paul. Your losses have been a heavy burden. Continue talking to Hannah if you feel comfortable with her. I think it would help you to have a friend you can share your feelings with. Do what you feel is right, and when you're ready. It might be a while before you talk to her since you've just had an argument. Or maybe you or she is ready to apologize. If an apology is necessary."

"I should apologize to her. She was being kind, and I treated her like a jerk."

"We all have moments we want to take back in life. The only way to do that is to apologize and move on, if she's willing. Only you and she will know."

He left her office with his gut churning, though it calmed down somewhat. She hadn't told him anything new, but he felt like she had done what she could. There was something about the accident, but Dr. Dacey wanted him to find out for himself when he was ready. The fact he didn't push her to reveal the information today suggested he wasn't ready. And maybe he wanted to hear it from someone like Hannah. A friend.

CHAPTER 28

Hannah spent the day after her fight with Paul wondering what to do about him. He didn't seem to have the whole story about the car accident, or he couldn't process it. Despite their argument, they were friends. Although sometimes she thought of Paul as more than a friend. She could almost see a future with him, but it was much too soon to start thinking that way. He lost his wife and daughter, and it would take a lot of time for him to recover, if he ever did.

Soon he would admit what happened in the accident. She had to be patient with him. He had closed his mind for so long. She wondered if seeing Amy was part of the problem. He needed to see Amy in the beginning to keep from drinking and to get through his guilt about the accident. Was he afraid that if he admitted the truth, he wouldn't see Amy again?

Hannah knew she had to leave it all up to God. He obviously let Paul see Amy for a reason, and it wasn't up to Hannah to question how long that would go on. If it helped Paul get through this time of mourning, she was thankful God let him see Amy.

Hannah needed to concentrate on her own problems for a while. Her younger sister needed some of her help too. Christina's arthritis was flaring, and she had difficulty watching her two kids while in pain. Hannah needed to go over to Christina's house and make her some meals and help with the laundry.

She also needed to finalize the banquet preparations for the benefit and see if Paul was going to attend. Sheldon and Joel okayed it, but she hadn't told Paul they would still like him to be there. It would give her a reason to go see Paul in a few days when he cooled off. She wouldn't bring up his wife's accident. Paul obviously wasn't ready to talk about it yet.

CHAPTER 29
HEAVEN TO EARTH

Samantha smiled happily at the activity in the birthing center at St. Gertrude's Medical Center. This would be her first birth as a Gifter, and she anticipated the excitement of a new life. She'd watch how Lily handled the birth of the baby for the couple.

Lily, another Gifter whom Samantha met on her first day in Heaven, mentored her. They worked together in the home goods section for a while, and then Samantha got to join the Baby Gifters. The home goods section had been all about people gifting home repair or improvement items.

As one of the training grounds for the Gifters, all new Gifters had to take their turn there. It was as much fun as anything else in Heaven. It wasn't hard. They got to spend time with people on Earth, even though the people on Earth had no idea they were even there.

Gifting was an art form, and Samantha loved watching the faces of people get what they wanted when it came time for the gift to be given. She saw men and women getting hammers, screwdrivers, shelving, and flooring. The excitement on their faces was as much fun as watching them get some more exotic item. People exhibited such thankfulness.

Samantha could tell the birth was near when the doctor came into the room. She stood back in a corner of the room where she could see the action but be out of the way. It didn't matter because no one could see her, but she had a full view of the room this way. Lily stood by the mother, gently holding the mother's free hand. The father of the newborn-to-be held the mother's other hand. The mother couldn't feel Lily's hand touching hers, but Lily exuded kindness and comfort Samantha felt all the way on the other side of the room.

As Samantha watched Lily, she decided it was all about comforting the people in the room. Lily patted the father's back when the baby was born. She gently touched the arm of all the medical personnel at one time or another, as if she was spreading God's grace and goodness over everything and everyone.

The baby cried angrily at the new world he'd entered, and then settled quietly into his mother's arms with the father sitting on the bed, holding them both. Tears started in Samantha's eyes at the sight. She didn't think she could get any happier. The moment reminded her of the night she had Amy. For a moment, she missed Amy, and then the feeling was gone. She looked up and saw Lily watching her with a tender smile.

Oh. So, this birth had also been about Samantha remembering her time with Amy before everything went wrong in her family. She smiled back at Lily, at peace again.

CHAPTER 30

Paul took a few days to get over his anger at Hannah as he continued circling fields in the tractor, planting the crop. He realized the anger was directed more at himself than her, and he wondered how to make it up to her. He wasn't an easy man to be around these days. He knew that. He mostly kept to himself to avoid other scenes like the one with Hannah. He felt more adjusted each day, but it was difficult.

Amy didn't come to see him as often, but she always came when he needed her. He wondered about that and why God chose to send his daughter to take care of him. He was grateful for every moment he got to see her. He had a feeling his time with her was going to end soon. He wondered if this time he'd get to say goodbye to her.

He needed to call Hannah to apologize and see if she'd come to visit him. Maybe he should go to the city and meet her at Myrtle's Coffee Shop. He had gotten used to her coming out to see him, which he liked.

He didn't miss city life at all. He knew his time at the farm would come to an end too. For now, he knew Frank needed him, and he needed Frank and Nina. They were treating him as if he were their son, and he appreciated it. God was being good to him, and he needed to start counting his blessings.

He walked around by the seeder, stretching his legs from being seated. He was nearly done with this field, and then it would be time to move over to another. He'd call Nina in a few minutes, and she'd either bring him lunch or take him to the farmhouse to eat.

He went with whatever Nina cooked and preferred that she decide if it was a sit-down meal or something he could eat in the field. He thought it also depended on what she had going on. Nina was busy in the community helping a lot of the older people and was often away from the farm. He was happy for her. She needed things to keep her occupied.

He knew Frank and Nina wished Abby lived closer, but she settled in Houston and didn't get to North Dakota to visit often. She didn't have any children, and both she and her husband worked. Nina and Frank flew down in the winter to visit sometimes.

Paul's thoughts skewed back to Hannah and the apology she deserved. He only put it off because he didn't know how she would react. Would she say she was done with their relationship? He should call her. It was almost noon. She'd probably be on her lunch break at work and could take his call. If not, he would have to wait until the evening to reach out to her.

He dialed. No sense in procrastinating any longer. It rang a long time, and he was preparing a message in his head to leave on her voicemail when she answered, "Hi, Paul."

He couldn't tell anything from the tone of her voice. "Hi. I wanted to call and apologize."

"Apology accepted."

She hadn't even hesitated, and he was suddenly tongue-tied. What to say next? "You were trying to help. I guess I'm grieving, and I don't feel like I can handle some things yet." He heard a door close on her end of the phone.

"I understand, Paul, but I don't like to be yelled at by anyone."

"I'm sorry about that. Please forgive me." He planned to keep his temper in check from now on.

"You're forgiven. I do understand."

She sounded like she meant it. He wished he had asked to see her at Myrtle's Coffee Shop so he could see her face. He should have done that, instead of apologizing over the phone. But he hadn't wanted to wait.

"Thank you. I'm finishing up a field here, and Nina will be here soon. I'm sure you need to get back to work."

"I do."

"Can we get together again soon?" he asked.

"Sure. Do you play cards?"

"Some. Depends on the game."

"How about pinochle?" she asked.

"Yes. Nina and Frank even belong to a card group that gets together monthly to play."

"Perfect. How about if I come on Friday evening, and the four of us play together? Do you think Nina and Frank would be interested?"

"I'm pretty sure they would. They like you."

She laughed. "That's good because I like them. I'll be there on Friday. I'll let you ask them if they want to play with us."

"Sounds good." He smiled and relaxed again. Hannah was good for him.

"See you then." She hung up.

He put the phone back in his pocket and jumped up onto the tractor seat, reinvigorated.

***

Friday evening, Paul opened the door to Hannah. She arrived as he was setting the table. After he took her coat and laid it on the couch, they joined Frank and Nina in the kitchen.

Nina dished up the food, and Frank finished the table setup. "We're having mashed potatoes, pork chops, green beans, and apple pie for dessert," Nina announced to Hannah.

Hannah smiled at her. "That sounds lovely. I'm always in such a hurry, I usually don't cook much. Sandwiches are my main meal source."

Nina shook her head as she continued dumping the beans from the saucepan into the serving bowl. "That's not good for you."

Hannah laughed and gave Nina a one-armed hug. "You're right. I'll have to come out and have you feed me more often."

Paul saw Nina's quick glance at him, probably to see if he was paying attention to her next words: "You come every day if you want," Nina said to Hannah.

102

They all sat down at the table, and Frank said the before-meal prayer. Soon they passed around the food, laughing and talking.

Paul wasn't sure how Hannah would treat him, even though she accepted his apology quickly and gracefully. She was cheerful and her usual self. Paul heaved an inner sigh of relief. Samantha would say she forgave him, but then he suffered through her silence and cold shoulder for days after any disagreement. He was happy to see Hannah didn't share that personality trait.

He didn't like comparing Hannah to Samantha. They were two different people. Hannah never cared about the limelight while Samantha craved attention. Hannah didn't shun attention, but she didn't seek it either.

"You okay over there?" Hannah asked, drawing him out of his thoughts.

"I'm fine. Just waiting for dessert." He winked at Nina.

She smiled back at him. "You know where the plates, the pie, and the ice cream are. You can serve."

He stood up, bowed, and went to get everything together.

Hannah sat back and watched him, then looked at Nina. "Think I should help him?"

"No. He needs to get up and move around. He hasn't done anything today except sit on that tractor."

Paul laughed and looked at Frank. "They don't understand how hard the work is."

"That's right. They think it's like sitting in a chair in the living room watching television. They don't realize the bumps and jarring a body takes when sitting on a tractor seat all day long."

"I stand corrected," Nina said. "However, I do thank you, Paul. If you weren't here, it would be my seat sitting there getting a workout every day."

Paul set down the knife he used to cut the pie and walked over to give Nina a hug. "You're welcome. I'm thinking of doing this every year. I like the peacefulness and solitude."

No one said anything for a minute. Then Nina spoke up. "I think you'd get tired of it, but we're happy to have you as long as you'd like to be here."

Paul went back to cutting the pie and serving it, wondering about the silence that greeted his statement. They seemed okay with him being here, but maybe they thought once his leave from work was over, they wouldn't see him again. He had been an absentee son-in-law, so he didn't blame them for thinking that. He would have to be sure to continue visiting them, even when he went back to work.

The rest of the meal passed in laughter, and they sat down to play pinochle when the dishes were done. They all pitched in to clean the table and sink, and it hadn't taken long. Paul felt like part of a family again.

He realized he hadn't felt that way since he and Samantha took their last vacation to the Grand Canyon. After that, their lives revolved around his work and Samantha's tantrums. She drank heavily before her death, and they constantly fought.

He was happy when they started playing cards, and his mind was occupied with thoughts other than Samantha. Laughter rang around the table throughout their game. Frank even shared multiple jokes, and Hannah laughed with him when he stumbled through the punchline.

Paul was happy to sit back and enjoy the evening and tried not to think of going to his room after Hannah left. She'd be back. He knew that, but he didn't want tonight to end. He began to realize how important Hannah was to him and how he could picture a future with her. He knew it hadn't been long since Samantha died, but his marriage had been floundering for a long time. He refused to believe it at the time until it was too late to do anything.

CHAPTER 31

Frank and Nina went to bed around 11:00 p.m., and Hannah and Paul sat in the living room. Paul found the space comforting. Nina had quilted for years, and a soft cotton quilt lay on the couch where he sat. Hannah settled into the rocker recliner across from him and slowly rocked.

"This is peaceful," she said.

"You don't have to stay. It's getting late to drive back to the city."

"That's okay. I used to drive a lot at night when I drove back and forth to do fundraising in other cities. There were several conferences I attended in North Dakota. We don't do them as often anymore since online meetings are possible."

"Do you like your job at the hospital?" Paul realized they hadn't talked much about Hannah's work or the benefit she was preparing for right now.

"I do. I get to meet a lot of people, and I'm always seeing the best in people. You'd be surprised at who donates to the causes. There are people who have so little themselves, but they find some money to give for others. It's enlightening and inspiring. There are many good people in the world."

"It's sad the bad happenings always make the news," Paul said.

"Yes, but we can only work on our little corner of the world."

He laughed. "Sounds like that's part of your work speech."

Her face flushed, but she smiled. "You're right."

"You're preaching to the choir. I agree with you. We haven't talked about the benefit since I've come to the farm. Does Sheldon still want me there? I'd like to be there. Is that okay?" He did want to be on hand to help Hannah and to promote her fundraiser.

She rocked a little faster. "Sheldon and I talked about it. We both agreed we want you to be there. We even talked to Joel, and he agreed too. No one wants you to quit your job, Paul. We all think you're a good doctor."

"Then why am I here on the farm bottle-feeding calves and planting wheat?" He heard the bitterness in his voice, and it surprised him. He thought he had come to terms with the leave of absence. He even knew he needed the time to deal with his emotions.

Hannah stopped rocking and got up. She sat by him on the couch and took his hand. "I thought you were okay with this leave from the hospital. What's wrong?"

"I don't know. I'm as surprised as you appear to be that I'm still angry. I feel like Joel forced me, and I don't like to be forced to do anything." He knew he sounded like a two-year-old having a tantrum but couldn't stop the words.

Hannah squeezed his hand. "Joel asked me how you were doing when we talked about the benefit. He's genuinely worried about you. He wasn't just making small talk."

Paul took a deep breath and let it out. "I guess I'm going to have to pray for some peace about the how of being here. Joel forcing the leave from work. I do feel okay about working on the farm. It's been good for me."

"I've noticed. You seem a lot calmer. You'll come through this okay, Paul. It's going to take a long time to get through the grief of losing Samantha and Amy. You can do it though. I know the loss will never go away completely, but you can deal with it."

"I feel like I've dealt with Samantha being gone. Our marriage wasn't over, but we had a lot of problems. We continually fought over her drinking, and I thought of taking Amy away from her." He hadn't intended to share that information with Hannah tonight. He had been ashamed of the idea of separating Amy from Samantha but began to think it was the right thing to do for Amy.

"She must have been drinking a lot." Hannah squeezed his hand again.

It felt nice to be sitting close to Hannah and sharing his feelings. He was usually close-mouthed about what went on with his emotions and his personal life. He hadn't felt like he could say anything to Frank and Nina, though he suspected they guessed. He prayed a lot, but he hadn't noticed anything change.

He realized Hannah was waiting for him to say something. "I tried to get her help, but she wasn't at an emotional place to make the change. I thought if I threatened to take Amy away, it might change her mind. I was too late to do anything. The accident happened, and they're both gone. I saw Amy the day you and I argued." He waited for her to withdraw, but she sat there beside him holding his hand. He relaxed further.

"She knows when you need comforting," Hannah said.

"We talked about her mother's drinking. It was surreal. She seems grown up, although she still looks like she's seven."

"I find the idea of Heaven interesting. You get the rare opportunity to talk to someone who is there already. I'm jealous." She punched his shoulder lightly with her free hand.

Paul smiled at her. "She doesn't tell me anything about Heaven. In fact, when we're together, it's all about me. I've tried to ask her what Heaven looks like, but she describes it so fleetingly, I can't get an idea. I guess I'll have to wait until I'm there myself."

"At least you get to see her. That's something."

Paul pondered that for a moment. "I don't think I'll get to see her much longer. I feel like soon she'll be gone, and that's it. I wonder if I'll get to say goodbye this time."

Hannah's eyes were filled with tears when she looked at him.

"Hey. I didn't mean to make you cry. Let me get you a tissue."

"It's okay." She wiped her hand across her eyes. "The thought is sad for you, and it's sad for me too. I like that you get to talk to her."

"I wish you could see her." He hugged her close, and she rested her head on his shoulder.

"I don't think that's in God's plan."

"Probably not. I'm grateful for what I have."

"And I'm happy for you, even though I don't get to see her. God is good to send her to you."

"Yes. He is."

They sat quietly with Paul's hand over her shoulders, enjoying the quiet evening.

"Are you coming to the benefit?" she asked him.

"I'll be there. It's for the good of the NICU, and I'm happy to do it."

"Good. I suppose I should be going back. It is late."

He walked her to the door, wanting to give her a goodnight kiss but knowing it was too soon. "Be careful driving, and text me when you're home."

"I will." She squeezed his arm and left.

CHAPTER 32

Beth spent the time since her weekend getaway trying to come up with a way to tell Jeremy everything she wanted to change. They had been mostly distant since Brad's death, although a few times they experienced the closeness they'd had before losing him. She wanted to get back to sharing their lives again.

Sometimes she didn't know how she kept moving from day to day with the knowledge of Brad being gone. She kept picturing him in Heaven, doing the things he loved to do, and that helped her get through some of the times when she missed him. She also spent a lot of time crying the first few months, but she did it in secret, away from Jeremy. She hadn't wanted to add to his misery. The shattered look in his eyes nearly undid her— she knew she needed to hang on for him and Tyler and herself. They all needed to stand together as a family.

The weekend away had been good for her. She felt more herself than she'd felt since Brad's death, and she wanted to continue feeling this way. The news she had to share with Jeremy and Tyler would change their lives again, and she didn't know if they were ready. Ready or not, life was going to change.

They had dinner together that evening, and she told them they were having a family meeting after the dishes were done. It was Tyler's turn for dishes. She wanted her boys to grow up helping in the kitchen and always enforced the rule of taking turns cooking and doing dishes.

While Tyler did the dishes, Jeremy joined Beth in their bedroom. She told him she wanted to talk to him for a few minutes before they all met in the living room for the family meeting.

"What did you want to say?" Jeremy looked braced for bad news. His hands twisted together, and he stood by the bedroom door looking like he would run out of the room at the first sign of trouble.

Beth took his hand and led him over to the bed. "Sit down."

He did, and she sat beside him, keeping hold of his hand. "We are going to have another baby."

He looked at her as if she'd spoken in another language. "What?"

"We're going to have another baby," she said gently. "I'm pregnant."

"What?" He looked bewildered, and she gave him time to process what she'd said. Finally, it seemed to register in his mind because a big smile crept across his face. "We're…you're already pregnant?"

"I am. When I went away that weekend, I started thinking about how much I ate and why. I thought it was because of grief, but then I realized I was really hungry. I wasn't just stuffing my face. I thought about the queasiness I felt, but it wasn't too bad. I took a home pregnancy test, and it was positive."

"So, this has nothing to do with the job or anything. You're pregnant?" He sounded like he finally got the picture.

"Right. It wasn't planned or anything. It happened."

"I'm done with the dishes," Tyler yelled from the kitchen.

"Give us five more minutes, and we'll meet in the living room," Beth yelled back.

"We're having another baby," Jeremy said with wonder, no longer questioning the good news. He hugged Beth. "This is great."

Then he frowned. "Is it? Are you happy about it, or just saying it? I know you want that principal's job."

She gave him a soft smile. "It is great, isn't it? We didn't even have to decide. It happened. I'm glad, and I could get the principal's job. And I'm happy you're happy. We talked about waiting, but I guess God and this little guy or girl had other plans."

"I guess they did." He kissed her on the lips. "Let's go tell Tyler he's getting a sibling."

Beth held him down when he was ready to jump up. "Let's go easy with the revelation. I'm not sure what Tyler's going to think. He may not be as excited as us. I've had some time to think about it since I left for that weekend, and you've been thinking about having another baby for a while. I'm concerned about what Tyler's going to say and feel."

Jeremy nodded thoughtfully. "You're right. We need to be careful of his feelings."

They made their way to the living room, where Tyler lay stretched out across the couch. He sat up and braced his hands on his knees. "You two look happy."

A relieved smile crossed Tyler's face when they appeared, and Beth realized he had been afraid of what they would tell him. He kept that fear to himself throughout the meal, and she was sorry she hadn't told him it was good news they were sharing. She looked at Jeremy's smiling face. "Do you want to tell him, or should I?"

"You go ahead," Jeremy said. "I think you have a few things you want to say, so you run this family celebration."

Beth sat down beside Tyler, and Jeremy sat in the armchair across from them. "I'm pregnant, Tyler. I'm going to have a baby."

Tyler looked at her, and his expression reminded her of Jeremy's in the bedroom. Stunned. "But…"

"I just found out," said Beth, giving him time to absorb the news. "When I went away for the weekend, I was emotional. I guess part of that was the hormones wreaking havoc." She laughed. "But you're a teenage boy and don't want to hear about women's hormones."

Jeremy leaned forward. "He's eighteen. It won't be too long, and he might have to start dealing with women's hormones."

Tyler's face flushed. "Dad," he protested. Then he looked at Beth. "That's great, Mom. I'm happy you're going to have another kid."

"Are you really? Because things have been difficult lately, and this is a big thing."

Tyler interrupted, "No. It's great. It's great. I mean that. I'll be gone next year at college, and it will give you something to do." He grinned and looked so much like Jeremy in that moment.

She laughed. "It's not like I don't have anything to do. I do have a house to run and a job I go to every day."

"That's true. But now you'll have someone else to take care of. I know you like that."

What an astute observation from an eighteen-year-old, Beth thought. "I raised you right." She hugged him, relieved he didn't seem upset about a new baby. She deliberately didn't say anything about being a big brother, as it would only start the conversation about Brad making him a big brother, and she wanted to avoid that for the evening.

"I know we don't get to choose, but I'm hoping for a little girl." Tyler's face turned red. "But, whatever."

Jeremy looked at Beth to save Tyler from his embarrassment. "I think you have a few more things you haven't told me that you want to say to both of us."

She got up and hugged him too, and then sat on the couch by Tyler again. "You both know I had that interview for the principal's job. I don't know if I got it or not. They haven't called. But I've decided I don't want to take the job. I like teaching third graders. I'm not ready for a principal's job."

"But you really wanted that job, Mom."

She looked at Tyler. "And I do, someday. But not now. It's not time."

"Does it have anything to do with the baby?" Jeremy asked. "Because we can work it out, even if I do continue to work full-time."

"I appreciate the support. But, no, I want to stay as a third-grade teacher. I'm happy doing it. I don't know if I'd be happy as a principal. Like I said, not right now."

"Okay then," Tyler said. "We're going to have a baby. I should make a cake this weekend, and we should celebrate." His eyes sparkled, and Beth took in a relieved breath. Her men were okay with a baby in the house. One more change to adapt to, and they were dealing with it well.

"Sounds like a good idea," Beth said.

"I'm going to do some homework." Tyler left the room, humming under his breath.

Jeremy joined Beth on the couch. "He took that well."

"I think so too. I was nervous about how both of you would handle the news."

"We're a family." Jeremy hugged her.

He let her go, and she moved away enough to be able to look at him. "We have some things to discuss."

"What could that be?" He looked puzzled.

"You. This affects your job too."

"I can't be a writer," he said.

Beth stood up and put her hands on her hips. "You can be a writer. We need to make some plans about how you can do that. A baby isn't going to change that, nor is the fact I'm not going to change jobs for a while."

"We need the money," Jeremy said glumly.

"We don't need much money to live on. We saved for Tyler's and Brad's college. We can use Brad's money for the new baby." She stumbled through that and felt a few tears fall. Jeremy noticed and pulled her close again. "I think we've found out how quick life can change. If you want to write, you should write. But could you work half-days?"

He gave her a tight hug. "I'll work full days if you want me to."

"No." She leaned away from him. "It's your dream to write. It's time to go after your dream. Time's wasting."

He hugged her close as Tyler came back into the living room. "Oh, hey, sorry!"

"Don't worry, honey," Beth said. "Your father and I are done talking. Do you have a minute?" She saw the worried look cross his face. How long until he regained his balance and didn't expect the worst?

"I have a minute."

"Your dad's going to find a part-time job teaching and stay home with the baby part of the time and write."

A grin split Tyler's face. "Hey, that's great, Dad. You've always wanted to be a writer."

Jeremy's smile matched Tyler's. "It is great."

CHAPTER 33

Paul got in from the field, ate with Frank and Nina, and then excused himself for the evening. He thought they deserved some time alone, and he was ready to read a book in bed. He had ordered a few mysteries online and looked forward to a relaxing night of reading.

He turned on the lamp beside the bed and settled back with his phone and his book. First, he wanted to check out the articles online about the benefit Hannah was putting on for the NICU. Now that he was going to attend, he needed to read the information about the fundraiser. He realized he should have looked at the articles before, but he talked to Hannah and thought she'd given him enough inside information about the occasion.

When he searched the internet, he noticed the headline first: *Bereaved Doctor to Speak at Benefit.* He struggled not to swear. He kicked that habit years ago. Young patients and a child of his own cured him of the habit.

Why did the headline have to announce his personal business? This was a benefit for sick children. They could have avoided bringing up his loss.

He scrolled through the story. Nothing new. Hannah told him all the information the article listed. It only briefly mentioned his wife and daughter had been recently killed in a car accident. Thank goodness they didn't spend much time on his life story when the NICU was the beneficiary of the banquet and needed the exposure. He was lucky Joel and Sheldon okayed him attending. They must have known he would be newsworthy for months after the accident.

He skimmed through some other articles on the benefit, and then, for some reason, started scrolling through the articles about Amy and Samantha's accident. He had avoided reading any articles for this long, but tonight he felt up to it. He felt he could handle it, and he needed to see what people said because he wouldn't be shielded tomorrow at the banquet. Someone was sure to pass on condolences, and he needed to be prepared.

Suddenly, a headline screamed out at him, and he gripped the phone. He stared at the screen: *Doctor's wife drives drunk, kills teen.*

He sat stunned by what he read. And then, in a frenzy, he searched and scrolled through all the articles on his phone. The meaning of the past four months came to him. His own wife killed their daughter because she drove drunk. How could he not have known? How could he have blocked that out?

All the hints from people now made sense. He thought of his conversation with Hannah when they argued. She tried to tell him Tyler and Brad weren't at fault. Samantha was. But she had been kind and let it go. Hannah let him wait until he was ready for the truth.

Tears blinded his vision, and he threw his phone across the room. He heard it crack as it hit the wall.

Frank came pounding up the stairs to the bedroom and knocked. "Are you okay?"

Paul struggled for breath. "I'm fine. Sorry. Just dropped something." His voice showed his tears, and it took forever before he heard Frank reply.

"Okay. Let me know if you need something."

"Thank you," Paul said.

As he stared off into space, he heard Frank's footsteps slowly return down the stairs. What an idiot he'd been. Did this have something to do with Amy visiting him? Samantha had driven drunk. He knew that. But he hadn't known she ran the red light.

He thought of the times he'd yelled and glared at Tyler. The poor kid. He just wanted to talk to Paul. Tyler seemed reluctant to leave him alone, like he was afraid *for* Paul and not afraid *of* Paul. Now Paul knew why.

They were all concerned about him because, when he talked about the accident, he blamed Brad, not Samantha. It made sense why Joel insisted he take time from work. He was surprised they were going to let him speak at the banquet.

Did Hannah check on him weekly to make sure he was okay, not because she wanted to spend time with him? He almost slapped his cheek with his hand. Of course not. That wasn't Hannah. She spent time with him and Frank and Nina because she wanted to. He was ashamed of his suspicions.

How could he ever speak with his coworkers again? How could he face Hannah and go to the banquet? How could he undo the damage he'd done to the Garveys when he accused their son? He needed to make it all right somehow.

But he needed a drink first. He needed something to get through this terrible morass of feeling swirling in his gut. It was the same feeling he'd had when Dr. Dacey would speak about the accident and make him recite his knowledge. She was waiting for him to admit the truth. They all were.

Suddenly, he was angry. He stumbled from the bed and grabbed his phone off the floor. The case was cracked, but not the phone itself. He stuffed it in his pants pocket and grabbed his wallet and his keys. He was going to the liquor store, and then back to his house in town to get drunk. He deserved it after everything that happened.

He said a quick goodbye to Frank. He lied and told him he was going to his own house to sleep for the night.

Frank stared him in the eye and didn't offer any objection. "I'd say you've had an unwelcome realization. Just remember, son, Nina and I love you. You don't need to do this. I'm here if you want to talk."

"Thank you." He walked out the door, having one second thought, and then back on the path to a drink.

He stopped at the liquor store and took the bottle home. Was he daring God to have Amy show up? He wasn't sure, but so far, she hadn't appeared.

The lifeless house was depressing without anyone around, and he stared at the furnishings in the living room as if he'd never seen them before that night. He set the bottle on the glass coffee table.

The furniture didn't offer up the soul comfort like Nina and Frank's cloth plaid couch did. The leather seats were fashionable and comfortable, but not comforting. He grabbed the bottle of booze and sat on the couch to flick on the television to find something, anything to keep him company. He finally settled on a house fixer-upper show and opened the bottle. He had the bottle halfway to his mouth, and then set it down on the coffee table again. He didn't want to do this. He stared at the open container for a while.

He'd come far. He thought of Hannah. She'd probably be disappointed if he drank, but she'd understand. And Amy. Amy watched him sober up and watched her mother drink. She'd been with her mother when she crashed into another car and killed them both and another person's son. He couldn't take a drink.

"I'm glad, Daddy."

Amy spoke to him from across the coffee table where she sat on the matching leather armchair. "You didn't drink. All by yourself, you stopped."

He dredged up a smile for her. "All by myself."

"You're afraid I'm going away, aren't you?"

"Yes, I'm afraid of being all alone."

She smiled at him as if he'd said something funny. "You're never alone, Daddy. There are angels in this room now. You always have angels. And God and Jesus are here. I can feel them even when I don't see them. Can't you feel their warmth?"

After his astonishment listening to her, he sat there quietly and waited to feel something. At first, he didn't notice anything, and then he felt lighter, like all the tension in his stomach from the past four months disappeared.

Amy bounced up and down on the armchair. "You feel something. I can tell. You're almost smiling."

"I'm feeling," he said to her. "Are there really angels and God and Jesus here?"

"Really. They want you to be okay. Are you okay, Daddy?"

He smiled at her. "I'm okay." And he meant it. He felt okay. "It's weird thinking I'm never alone though."

"But comforting."

She'd used the words he thought of for Nina and Frank. Love equated to comfort now. An all-encompassing love.

"I have to go." She ran around the table to give him a hug. "Hannah's coming. She'll be here soon."

"How do you know that?" he asked. But the room was empty. She was gone.

He looked at the booze, took it into the kitchen, poured it down the drain, and threw away the bottle. He had angels and a beautiful daughter. He didn't need it.

He heard the doorbell. He looked at the clock in the kitchen. 1:00 a.m. Who would be stopping now? Hannah. That was what Amy said.

He hoped it wasn't Frank. He was sorry he'd worried him. He should call the farm and reassure him everything was okay, even if it was the middle of the night. He thought all this as he went to the door. It was Hannah, like Amy told him.

"Hi," she said uncertainly. "Frank asked me to check on you."

"Just Frank?" He thought of Amy's comment Hannah would be here shortly.

"Yes. Who else would call me?" She looked puzzled as she stood there in the doorway.

"I'm sorry. Come in and sit down. We need to talk, and I know it's late, so let's make it short. Then you can get back home. I'm sure you need some sleep."

"I do need some sleep. The benefit is tomorrow night. But I care too much about you and what's going on. I needed to make sure you were okay after Frank called me."

"What did he say?" Paul asked, remembering Frank's offer of a listening ear.

Hannah followed him into the living room and sat down in the same chair Amy had just vacated. "He said he thought maybe you remembered the truth, and it might steer you in the wrong direction."

"Meaning, I know Samantha caused the accident, and I might drink to suppress the knowledge to deal with it?"

"Yes. I'm glad you know, Paul. You can deal with it now. It's hard to deal with things you avoid."

"I've found out," Paul said.

"It got you through these months. Don't give yourself a bad time over it."

"That's not what's bothering me. It's that Tyler kid. I need to make it up to him. What I can, anyway. I can't give him his brother back, but maybe there's something else I can do for him. He tried to tell me his brother didn't cause the accident, and I kept screaming at him because I thought his brother was responsible."

"You were trying to deal with a lot. You have to give yourself a break, Paul. You can do something about it, and it will all work out."

"I didn't drink, by the way. I bought some, and I put the bottle down before drinking. Even before Amy came, I didn't take a drink."

"Amy was here?" She looked around.

"She's gone. She came and talked to me and told me there are angels everywhere and not to feel alone because I'm never alone. I'm a little freaked out about there always being someone with me."

Hannah laughed. "Eyes everywhere. You'll be okay, Paul."

He frowned. "She talked to me like it might be the last time I see her. I don't know if she'll ever be back on Earth. I wanted to say goodbye this time, but she disappeared suddenly again."

"Maybe you can say a temporary goodbye in your heart, knowing you'll see her again in Heaven. That doesn't mean you can't talk to her all the time. Maybe she can hear you even if you can't see her, and she can't be here with you. Sometimes, I feel like my mother hears me when I'm speaking to her. It's a closeness I feel."

"Maybe." He felt doubtful. Everything he thought for months had turned on its head, and he wasn't sure of anything anymore. "I need to text Frank, and then get some sleep. I'll make sure you get home okay, and then I'll come back here to sleep the rest of the night."

"You don't have to get me home. I can make it by myself," Hannah said.

"Yes, I do. I'll follow you, and when I'm sure you're in your house, I'll come back here. I don't want to bother Frank and Nina tonight. It was nice of Frank to contact you to check on me."

"He cares for you like you're his son. See, you're not alone. You have Frank and Nina. And me," she added.

"Thank you." He gave her a brief hug. "Let's get some sleep. You've got a big day tomorrow."

"It's a good thing I wasn't going to the office until 10:00 a.m. anyway because of the banquet."

CHAPTER 34

Paul was nervous about the benefit. He hadn't seen anyone from the hospital since he left about two months ago. Sheldon and Joel each called him a few times to see how he was doing. Dr. Monroe Carter, who saw Paul's patients, called and conferred over some of their patients and kept in touch. Paul knew Monroe was married to Hannah's friend Thea, so he thought the four of them might get together someday.

Frank and Nina greeted him with a big breakfast when he got to the farm that morning. It counteracted his strange feelings about sleeping at his own house, where he'd felt more like a stranger than he did at the farm.

Unfortunately, he needed to stop at his house again to get ready for the benefit. The banquet required dress clothes, and he didn't have any of his suits with him at the farm. When he walked into his house, he was immediately hit by a sense of depression.

He felt the walls closing in and took a deep breath to dispel the feeling. He could do this. He needed to get ready and go to the banquet. He could pack any other items he wanted before he left for the benefit, and then he wouldn't have to come back to live here. He'd rent a place to stay until the house sold, and then he would see what he wanted to do.

He realized he wasn't going to live in this house again. Since it was a Friday evening, there was nothing he could do about listing the house. As soon as he found a realtor, the house was going on the market.

He would keep some mementos of Samantha and Amy. He'd keep his personal items and donate the rest of the things in the house. Maybe even have someone else come in and clean it out. He'd have to think about it this weekend. Right now, he had to get through the evening.

He was glad he had Hannah to speak to at the benefit. Monroe would help him through the evening as well. He had to remember he had friends there. And, according to Amy, angels and God were always with him.

No one knew anything about what happened, except for the accident. They weren't aware of anything else that had gone on with him. No one would question him for leaving work and taking a few months off.

He arrived at the banquet with his hands gripped together and his mouth dry. He greeted a few people at the door, and then Hannah joined him.

"Are you okay?" she asked quietly. "You look a little peaked in spite of all that time you've been spending in the sun."

"Too much sunscreen," he joked.

She smiled. "You'll be okay. Look who I have with me." She motioned to Monroe, who quickly joined them. "He thought you might want some company tonight, so he's joining you at the table."

Hannah left them together, and Paul watched her walk away, feeling marooned on a desert isle.

Monroe laughed. "I can tell what you're thinking. She'll be back. She likes you."

"I like her too. She's been good to me."

"I know. I've gotten updates from her," Monroe said.

Paul turned to look at Monroe. He didn't like the thought of others talking about him.

"Don't worry. We didn't get into details. I asked if you were doing okay and told her to let me know if you needed anything."

Paul breathed a sigh of relief and laughed shortly. "I guess I'm a little touchy. I feel like everyone's watching me to see if I'm going to be okay or fall apart."

"Only those who care about you matter. The rest of them are gossipers. Best to ignore them and stick with those of us who care," Monroe advised him.

"Thanks, Monroe. And thanks for taking care of my patients. I miss them."

Monroe smiled. "So, you're not going to give up medicine and become a farmer?"

Paul smiled too and finally relaxed. "I thought about it for about a week, but it isn't me. It's great to get away from all the gossip and to get myself back together, but I couldn't do it as a way of life. I'll be taking regular vacations from now on though. Frank and Nina could use the help, and I like to spend time on the farm. I hope to be back at the clinic in a couple of weeks. I'll work out the time frame with you and Joel. We can meet next week and go over the details."

"Come in your jeans."

"Oh, I intend to. This suit isn't exactly what I'm used to wearing." He gestured at the navy-blue suit, light blue shirt, and patterned, matching tie.

"Me either," Monroe agreed. "Last time I wore a suit was at my wedding."

Hannah interrupted them and showed Paul where he would sit at the table with the other speakers.

Paul pulled her aside for a minute. "Is it okay what I've got planned?"

"Yes, Joel has agreed it's fine."

"Good. I talked to Dr. Fishbine, and he is going to start a scholarship too. He's naming his after his patient, like I'm naming mine after my patient."

"That's great."

Paul left it up to Joel to contact everyone and get the proper paperwork to have a medical scholarship set up. He thought of putting it in Amy's name, but then he decided it would be better to keep his family out of it, except to be the sponsor for the scholarship. He would contribute the money, and they'd name the scholarship The Casey NICU Scholarship in his patient's honor. He would give out the scholarship once a year to a medical student.

He made it through the cocktail hour with no problems. He wasn't even thinking about drinking. He thought about the speech he would give for Casey and the other speech he prepared for the scholarship fund. Hannah was unable to stay by his side, as she organized the fundraiser. He kept getting glimpses of her moving around the crowd in her emerald-green dress.

She looked beautiful tonight. She always looked pretty, but tonight there was something different about her. He didn't know if it was his own new awareness of everything. He felt more alive than he'd felt in years.

"She's beautiful," Monroe said.

He looked behind him where Monroe stood. "Yes, she is." The admiration in his friend's eyes triggered a moment of jealousy.

"Don't worry," Monroe said. "I only have eyes for Thea."

"How are things going with her?" Paul realized he'd been out of touch with everything going on while he retreated to his own private sanctuary.

"We're doing great."

"Wonderful. I've been thinking, since Hannah and Thea are friends, we should all get together sometime," Paul said.

"Sounds like a good plan. I look forward to it, and I'm sure Thea will agree."

"That's great."

"Would you think about getting married again?" Monroe asked.

"I hadn't thought about it until lately." He grinned at Monroe. "Let's say there's a lady in an emerald-colored dress who's giving me second thoughts tonight." He frowned. "However, I think it might be a while until we're both totally ready. Because of the way Samantha died, Hannah may be hesitant. There will probably be news articles if we do get married. She might not like the publicity."

"I wouldn't worry about that." Monroe clapped him on the shoulder. "Hannah can handle a lot."

Paul thought about the past few months with Hannah by his side. She saw the worst of him on a few occasions, and she stuck by him and kept visiting him at the farm. She was behind his return to the hospital via this benefit. He knew once Joel saw him giving his speeches and how he conducted himself tonight, he would be invited to come back to work at the hospital when he was ready.

Joel had been waiting for him to come out of his denial and admit Samantha's role in her and Amy's death. His eyes were open. It hurt to think about it, but he felt clear-headed and ready to get back to his job at the hospital as soon as he finished helping Frank. He sometimes got the feeling Frank thought up work for him and didn't need his help since the crops had been in the field for a while.

They were seated, and the evening progressed as each speaker got up to make their speech during the meal. Paul couldn't eat. He toyed with his water glass and waited his turn. He spoke first after Joel introduced them all, and he gave his speech about the NICU being a great place to give high-risk babies a great start in life. He indicated his patient Casey and how well she was doing. Her parents spoke briefly and thanked him. Then Dr. Fishbine discussed his patient and gave his endorsement of the NICU. The speeches continued, and when dessert came, Paul knew the time had come to give the most important speech of his life.

When Joel got up to re-introduce him, he took a deep breath and looked at Hannah. She nodded and smiled at him from her place at the next table. He got up and thanked Joel.

"I've got a lot to be thankful for," Paul began his speech. "You all know I've recently lost my wife and little girl in an accident, but I wasn't the only one who lost someone that day." He indicated the Garvey family, who had been seated on the opposite side of the table from him, and as far away as they could get from his own place.

Paul asked Hannah to do that, so they would feel as comfortable as possible. He passed the message on through her to the Garveys he was sorry, that he understood now and would make it up to them. She said they understood Paul's grief and were happy he was done glaring at Tyler.

They looked bewildered as they sat there at the head table.

"They don't know why I asked them to come today, but it's a special occasion for us here celebrating the NICU. I would like to give a chance to young men and women who want to become doctors. I understand Tyler Garvey would like to go to medical school. I'm happy to tell him and his family, Tyler will be the first recipient of the Casey NICU Scholarship, which we will be giving out yearly. As this is the first time we are giving out the award, we'd like to give it to Tyler for his continued dedication to his schoolwork and his humanitarian efforts in the past year."

There was loud clapping after this part of his speech.

"As Tyler and his family were not given the reason for their invitation to tonight's celebration, we will not be hearing a speech from them."

Tyler interrupted him by standing by his chair, his face flushed. He looked down at his parents and then up at the podium where Paul stood. "I'd like to thank Dr. Richmond for this opportunity. It's a surprise to me and my parents, but thank you, Dr. Richmond. You're a special doctor." He nodded at the other diners and sat down.

"Thank you, Tyler. I know you'll be a credit to our profession." He handed the microphone over to Dr. Fishbine to announce his own scholarship and recipient and sat back down in his place at the table. He'd have to talk to the Garveys after the speeches were over, but at least they'd have a little time to get their thoughts together before he apologized more fully.

After dinner, as the guests were beginning to depart, Paul found the Garveys huddled in a corner. They didn't know any of the guests, and he felt bad for them.

He looked first at Tyler. "I'm sorry. You tried to tell me the accident was Samantha's fault when I blamed Brad. I can never take back the pain I caused you or your family, but I'm sorry. The scholarship was not to absolve my conscience. I'll probably always feel guilty. The accident was Samantha's fault. The scholarship is because you deserve it. You kept your grades up despite your own grief. Hannah tells me you were concerned about me, and for that, I thank you. I didn't deserve your compassion after the way I treated you. You'll make a great doctor."

"Thank you, Dr. Richmond. I won't let you down," Tyler said.

"I have no doubt you'll do great." He looked at Beth and Jeremy. "You have a fine son. I want to thank you also. Because of you, I got the help I needed with those two months' leave from the hospital. It helped me to get away and see what's important. I can see where Tyler gets his humanity from."

They both spoke at once, "You're welcome."

Jeremy continued, "Thank you for what you're doing for Tyler. We didn't get a chance to say this before, but it's not necessary for you to make this up to him. We only want him to have the scholarship if he deserves it, not to pay us back in any way for anything. That's not what we're about. What happened was between God and your wife and our children." He took a gulp of air. "We both lost our loved ones that day."

"We did." Paul hugged them both, though he generally wasn't a hugger. "I'll leave you now, so you can go home and relax. I'm sure you're ready to get out of this place."

"It's not our thing," Beth agreed with a big smile. "Thank you again."

CHAPTER 35

Paul spent Saturday doing some shopping and whistling throughout the day. He'd been up early to help Frank on the farm, did his shopping and then returned to the farm to help. Paul saw the end of his usefulness to Frank. The bottle-fed calves had been sold, and the other cows and calves were kept in a pasture and didn't need to be fed any longer. Frank would have a neighbor and Paul help move them to a larger grassy area. After that, Paul wouldn't be needed.

He had a short talk with Joel, who was amenable to him returning to his practice within a few weeks. Paul would take the time to get his house cleaned out and put on the market once he finished helping Frank.

He was no longer depressed when he was in the house. He felt, with his new knowledge of the accident and Hannah and Nina and Frank's help, he was going to be okay. He missed Samantha and Amy, but he was more settled in the fact they were gone.

He called Hannah and invited her to lunch and a bike ride at the farm after church the next day. She said she would come, and he looked forward to the look on her face when she found out he was coming back to work. They'd be able to see each other occasionally at the hospital, and he hoped to see her frequently when they weren't working.

Nina brought his lunch to the field, and he stopped the tractor near where she parked the pickup.

"Thank you," he said to her when she handed him the food.

When she didn't leave immediately, he asked, "Is there something you want to talk about, Nina?"

"You've been busy and whistling today. You don't usually whistle all day long."

He couldn't help the big smile that split across his face. "I'm happy for the first time in a long time."

"I can see that. Hannah's worth it. I'm glad you found someone who makes you happy. Do you make her happy too?"

Paul frowned. His self-assurance in Hannah's feeling took a nosedive. "I hope so. I assume so since she's kept coming out here to see me. She didn't have to do that."

"No, she didn't. She's a nice lady." Nina started back to the driver's side door.

Paul followed her. "Nina," he said gently. "Are you okay? Samantha hasn't been gone long. Do you think I'm rushing things?"

She paused with her hand on the door handle and kept her back to him. "I'm fine."

Her voice was muffled, and he could tell she was trying not to cry. Paul set his lunch on the ground, not caring what happened to it. He put his hand on Nina's shoulder. When she didn't shake it off, he squeezed gently and held his hand there. He appreciated it when someone cared enough to hug or touch him.

"I'm going to tell you something," Paul said. "Something I've kept mostly to myself since it happened. I don't know if you or Frank will understand, but you can decide if you want to tell him."

She sniffed and turned around to look at him. Her eyes were red, and she fished a tissue out of her pocket and blew her nose. He patiently waited, and when she stuffed her tissue in her pocket, she seemed ready to hear him. "Go ahead."

"I miss them both. I miss them a lot. Samantha and I were going through a rocky time in our marriage. I wasn't a good husband for the first few years with her, and I know you and Frank weren't happy with her choice in me. You were right. I drank, and she drank. It was a bad combination."

"But then you stopped," Nina interrupted. "We loved you from the beginning, Paul. We didn't like what you and Samantha did. Especially when Amy came along."

Paul felt the hot wave of shame roll through him. "I can never take those years back and change them, but they changed me. I'm trying to be better."

"But it's been hard. Right? You want to drink again."

"I wanted to drink again. Every day since they've died, I've wanted to take a drink, and I came close a time or two." He took a deep breath. What was Nina going to think? "And then I saw Amy."

Nina stared at him while he prepared for her judgment. But she stood waiting for him to continue.

"Every time I came close to having a drink, Amy would show up, and we'd talk. She'd stay with me until I was okay, and then she'd disappear."

Nina's shoulders slumped. "Are you sure that's normal? To see someone who's not here?"

"No, it's not normal. God gave me a great gift. Amy would mention things she'd seen, and she'd talk about Heaven. It made me want to join them. Not that I'd do anything to hasten my end, but it seems, well, heavenly." He grinned. "Nina, don't worry about me. Please. I've been to a neurologist, a psychiatrist, and AA meetings. I've talked to my AA sponsor. They all say it's not unusual for victims of grief. They think I'm imagining her, but she says things I couldn't imagine. I believe God sent her from Heaven to help keep me sober and to get me through the first period of mourning.

"You think I'm crazy," he said to her. "I didn't want to tell you or Frank because I didn't know what you'd think, and I needed you. I needed you as much as I needed Amy, and I can never repay you for taking me into your home these past few months. I thought if I told you about Amy, it would help you feel better, the way it helped me. But maybe I should have kept my experience to myself. I hope this hasn't made things worse for you."

Nina hugged him, and he felt her slight frame shaking. "No, it helps."

She stood back from him again and studied his face. "You've helped Frank and me by being around. We couldn't have gotten through these months without you. And I don't mean the farm work. We would have managed that. Having you around the place made it feel less lonely." She sighed.

She said, "I wish I could see them one more time. I said some bad things to Samantha. I hoped she'd quit drinking. I told her to think of Amy, but the pull of drinking was too strong. I wonder if there was something I could have done or said to get through to her."

He shook his head. "Nothing another person says can stop the drinking. It must come from within. I've found that out. It's a lesson I've come to know. I don't know if I'll see Amy again. I think that part is over."

"Because of Hannah. She's good for you. Treat her well." There was a small smile on Nina's face.

"She's special. I've invited her over tomorrow for lunch and a bike ride after church. I hope that's okay," Paul said.

"It's fine. I better go make one of those peach pies she likes so much." She opened the driver's side door and then stood there.

He couldn't see her face.

"If you see Amy again, will you tell her I love her?" Nina asked softly.

"I will."

"And once you go back to work at the hospital, come visit us whenever you can." She turned around and hugged him quickly, then got back in the pickup without waiting for a response.

Paul had tears in his eyes, waving to Nina as she drove out of the field. He wondered if she'd tell Frank about him seeing Amy. Probably. He was okay with it. Maybe it would help them not feel quite as lonely. He certainly planned to visit them more often, hopefully with Hannah.

CHAPTER 36

Hannah agreed to go to church with them all on Sunday, and Paul waited for her on the front porch. The early June sun shone in the bright blue sky. A perfect day for a bike ride. It was supposed to get to seventy degrees, a nice temperature for riding bikes. He straightened up as he saw dust in the distance, and her vehicle turned into the driveway.

She waved and then got out. "It's a gorgeous day, isn't it?"

"Perfect. Not a cloud in the sky. Nina's made a peach pie for you."

She reached the porch steps and climbed them in a pretty white dress with navy flowers. She wore a pair of white slipper shoes on her feet.

He wanted to reach out and kiss her, but he didn't. Frank and Nina were probably watching them through the living room window. He opened the front door into the house. "Let's tell them we're ready for church."

He barely heard the priest speaking as the mass proceeded. He was too busy planning what he would say to Hannah on their bike ride together. She nudged him a time or two when he was slow to stand or kneel. One time, he thought he caught a stifled laugh from her, like she knew he wasn't with it today. He turned and smiled at her, and her answering smile lit his heart and soul. As Nina said, he better not let her get away.

Lunch passed with a lot of laughter. Frank and Nina told stories of past years when they were kids themselves, and Hannah showed every interest in what they said. She exchanged smiles with Paul on several occasions.

Finally, it was time for dishes, and Paul got up to help.

"No," Nina said. "You two go change clothes for your bike ride, and I'll do the dishes. Frank can go take a nap."

133

"That doesn't seem fair," Hannah protested. "You did a lot of work already. The least we could do is help you clean up."

"That's okay." Nina winked at Paul. "I think it's time you two got out and got some fresh air. These early summer days aren't always sunny and warm. Go enjoy yourselves. We'll see you when you get back. Hannah, you can change in the bathroom or our room."

"Thank you."

Paul kissed Nina on the top of her head. "Yes. Thank you."

He raced up the stairs to change and heard Hannah come up the stairs a short time later to change into bike-riding attire. He pulled on his jeans and navy t-shirt and hurried back down to wait for her.

Frank stopped him before he stepped out the front door. "She'll say yes, son." He laughed and left Paul standing there speechless.

So, Frank knew what he'd planned. He was a wily man, that Frank.

Paul got the bikes out of the garage and had them ready to go when Hannah came outside in her jeans and white t-shirt. She looked stunning to him, like she always did.

They started out happily in the same direction they always took to the path between fields. It wasn't hot yet, but in a few hours the lack of clouds would make it warmer. They were going out at the best time of the day.

They stopped for a breather in their usual place by the row of chokecherry bushes that were in full bloom. Paul got out some water from the backpack he'd slung over the bike's handlebars.

"Thanks." Hannah took a swig of water. "I'm full from Nina's lunch. I'm not in the mood to go far today. I guess that means we should bike longer since I ate so much."

"I don't think we need to worry about that today. Let's enjoy the moment." He took a swig of his own water, and then rooted through the backpack.

"What are you looking for? It can't be food," Hannah joked.

"It's not food. It's this." Paul held up a little square box.

Hannah's mouth dropped open. "Is that…"

"A ring." He opened the box to show her the gold band with a brilliant square-cut diamond in the center. "Hannah," he went down on one knee, "will you marry me?"

She stood there staring at him and shaking her head. He heard the water bottle she held drop to the ground.

"Hannah? Are you okay?" He snapped the box closed and stood. He took a step toward her. Her mouth was wide open in astonishment, and she hadn't answered. Was she mad at him? He couldn't tell what she thought. He took another step toward her, and she finally moved.

She flung herself into his arms, taking him by surprise, so he almost fell. "Yes. The answer is yes. I didn't expect this."

He started smiling and breathed again. "I had more to say, like I love you."

She squeezed him tighter. "I love you too."

"I had more to say, but I guess this is all that matters."

"Yes. This is all that matters." She smiled at him.

They finally kissed. When they stopped, and Paul looked around at the sunny fields, he caught a glimpse of Amy disappearing. She was gone. He'd tell Hannah later.

CHAPTER 37

Samantha knew the birth she attended today was special. She wasn't sure why until she heard the name: Beth Garvey. The mother of Brad. She was sorry for her responsibility in the accident that killed him.

At the last moment during the accident, she tried to swerve, but it made no difference. Too late, she understood her drinking was responsible for a lot of hurt, and she was sorry. The words kept ringing in her head while she lived for a few more moments. She looked over at Amy and saw it was too late for her, and she was sorry about that too.

But sorry didn't bring back the dead. God did. She'd been blessed that He had the grace to forgive her. She hoped Paul forgave her. She knew the pain he would be feeling with her and Amy gone. But she couldn't go back.

Beth was doing fine with her pregnancy, and the birth process started. Jeremy held her hand and encouraged her. Tyler was in the waiting room, and that was where she went. She felt called to be with him while he waited for the arrival of his new sibling. When she got to the waiting room, only two people were sitting there.

She stood there stunned and watched Amy talk to Tyler.

Amy looked up when Samantha made a slight noise entering the room. She jumped up and rushed to her side and hugged her. "Isn't this exciting? Tyler's getting a new sibling. It's a girl."

"Can he hear you?" Samantha asked.

"Sometimes. Not right now. He doesn't know it's a girl yet."

"Can he see you?"

"Yes. Just for now. As soon as the baby is born, he won't be able to see me any longer. He doesn't know who I am either."

"Can he see me?"

"No."

"Won't he be wondering why you're hugging the air?"

"He's not paying any attention." She dropped her arms. "Now he is, and I have to talk to him. I'll see you after the baby is born." With that, she went and sat by Tyler again.

Samantha felt the warm rush of love that told her God was near, and she thanked Him for letting her see Amy again. From what Amy said, she'd be seeing her again soon.

She needed to get back to the birthing room and her Gifter responsibilities.

~~~
~~~

CHOKECHERRY VALLEY JOY
Book 2

ACKNOWLEDGMENTS

Special thanks to the excellent editor, Denise Roeper of Eloquent Edits, LLC, (www.eloquentedits.com), for her great suggestions. They helped create a better book than I could have envisioned on my own.

Thank you to the book cover artist at Sunset Rose Books for an amazing cover.

Considerable thanks to my family who have encouraged me in my writing journey.

Thank you to Sally, Ruth, and Amy, terrific friends who are also great at running book ideas and cover designs past. I couldn't have finished this book without your help.

Special thanks to Gayle Larson Schuck for helping by editing and making suggestions for a stronger book. She writes her own books. www.gaylelarsonschuck.com

CHAPTER 1

Abby glanced at Mark as she packed her suitcase that sat on their bed. He lounged in the armchair on the other side of the bedroom, his dark hair tousled from running his hand through it constantly as he worked. Half the time he watched her, and half the time he looked down at the laptop he held.

"Are you sure you don't want to come with me? You can work remotely." Abby added another pair of jeans to her suitcase. She'd debated how many shorts and jeans to pack based on the forecast being in the seventies and low eighties—and on the insect population on her parents' farm in North Dakota.

"I'll fly out to Chokecherry Valley like we planned for a few days next week. I'm deep into this project and need to be free from distractions. We have to get it done this week."

She walked over to him and planted a kiss on his cheek. "I'll miss you. North Dakota is a long way from Texas."

He laughed. "The time will pass quickly. It will give you a chance to spend time with your parents before I get there."

"I know. You're always so loud while you're working on that computer." She looked around the room to see if she'd missed anything.

"Do you think you'll see Paul while you're there?" Mark closed the laptop and studied her expression.

"Maybe. He stayed at Mom and Dad's house for a few months, so I imagine they get along pretty well at this point." She wasn't sure how she would feel about seeing him again. She'd been so mad at him at Samantha and Amy's funeral.

She didn't know if she still blamed Paul, or if she was over her anger at him. Time would tell. She closed the top of the suitcase and zipped it shut. "Let's have breakfast, and then you can drive me to the airport."

She stepped over to the mirror and took one more look at her smooth, brown, shoulder-length hair. She'd applied a quick swipe of eyeliner and mascara. Good enough for the plane ride. Picking up her purse and carry-on bag, she left the bedroom.

Mark went over and lifted her packed suitcase from the bed. He followed her out of the room and down the stairs. "You didn't have to make breakfast today."

She laughed as he set the suitcase down by the front door and followed her into the kitchen. "I didn't make anything. Either you make something, or your choices are fruit, yogurt, or cereal."

"I think there might be a boiled egg or two," he said, rummaging around in the fridge.

"I'm having yogurt and a banana."

He passed her a yogurt. "What if you do run into Paul?"

She finished taking the lid off the yogurt container, and then looked up. "I don't know. Why are you so concerned?"

"I just don't want you to get upset."

"You mean like when I screamed at him at the cemetery, when they buried my twin sister and my little niece?" She heard the bitterness in her own voice and realized she had a long way to go to forgive Paul, even though he hadn't caused the car accident. She had wanted someone to blame, and Paul was the scapegoat. He wasn't even in the vehicle when the accident happened.

"Like that," Mark said pointedly. "You'll be okay. Just call me any time. You know I'm able to be interrupted most of the time. I only have to be at the office a few hours today and tomorrow."

"Thank you. You may regret that offer."

Mark got up from the table and gave her a hug. "You'll be okay. Call me if you need to. I'll be joining you in North Dakota soon. I love you."

"I love you too," she said. Maybe she should have told him about quitting her job yesterday, and all the things she had been thinking about recently, but she didn't want to deal with his reaction before she visited her parents in North Dakota. She needed the time to get her feelings sorted out. She was relieved about the job but felt guilty she hadn't told him how bad the situation had gotten at work.

Anxiety pressed against her chest as she thought about the future. She and Mark had drifted apart. She wasn't afraid they'd separate, but she did need them to connect again. At this point, she was too confused to even talk about her feelings. A week on the farm would relax her and take her out of her current thoughts enough to get some perspective.

They'd have plenty of time to discuss everything when Mark joined her in Chokecherry Valley. She knew procrastination wouldn't be a good thing. Mark would just have more reason to be upset with her.

CHAPTER 2

Abby got off the plane in Bismarck, North Dakota, not knowing who to expect to meet her. She wasn't sure if both her parents would be picking her up at the airport, or if it would just be one of them. Summer at the farm was a busy time. The forty-five-minute drive out to her parents' farm by Chokecherry Valley would add more time to the trip.

She looked forward to seeing them and spending some time relaxing out in the country. Houston had become so busy, and the job at the hospital where she worked had been extra demanding lately.

She sat down in the waiting area of the airport and checked her phone. Then she caught a glimpse of her dad's graying head. His tall stature was easy to see, although the airport traffic had thinned of people fairly quickly once they reached the waiting area. Then she saw her mother walking beside her father and rushed over to hug them.

"It's so good to see you." Abby felt a guilty twinge that she'd only been back once to see them since her sister and niece's funeral in January.

"Hi, Love," her mother said, hugging her back.

She got the same treatment from her father, and then they went to get her luggage.

"You both look great," she said.

They were looking much better than when she'd seen them in March three months earlier. Her father stood upright instead of emphasizing the slouch he'd developed since the funeral, and he had a summer tan that made his complexion look even darker than usual. Her petite mother smiled and looked more rested.

Abby had hated to leave them last time she visited, but she had to get back to her nursing job in Houston. At least she had these two weeks with them now.

"We caught a break this spring when Paul stayed with us and helped out with the calves and the spring planting." Her mother smiled at her. "He helped a lot."

"Now, Nina," her father said. "Paul grew up on a farm before he became a doctor, so of course he knew what to do. And he has helped me some over the years."

Not often, Abby wanted to say, but she held her tongue. She wasn't going to disrupt her parents' peace over her own anger at Paul. "Is he back working at the hospital now?"

"Yes," her mother said. "He's working full time and seems to be doing okay. He's met a nice young woman. Her name is Hannah."

"Isn't it a little soon for him to be dating?" She regretted the snippy tone, but it was too late to take it back. Abby felt irritation on her sister's behalf. Did Paul feel he could replace Sam so easily?

"They're taking it really slow."

"Too slow if you ask me," her father said.

"Frank!" Her mother playfully tapped him on the arm. "Not everyone proposes on the first date, like you did."

"When you know, you know." He hugged her.

Abby was pleased to see that they were doing so well, and some of the guilt of her neglect eased a little. She still needed to get back to see them more often though.

They left the airport and reached the pickup. Abby lifted her suitcase and carry-on into the back area of the extended cab and slid onto the seat.

"You could have sat in the front seat and talked to your dad while he drove." Her mother got into the passenger seat in the front.

"That's okay. I can be a back-seat driver from here and talk to you both."

Their drive to the farm was mostly on the highway and then about five miles on country roads. They didn't pass through the town of Chokecherry Valley, but the farm was only about three miles from the town. There was a grocery store, bar, community hall, St. Anne's Church, and a small café. For anything more, they would have to travel to one of the bigger towns in the surrounding area, or travel to Bismarck.

Abby figured Chokecherry Valley would have anything she needed at the little grocery store. Her parents tended to keep all the basics well stocked at their house.

When they got to the farm, her father carried her suitcase up to her room. Her parents had remodeled her room and Samantha's when they had both gotten married within a year of each other. Her room didn't feel the same as when she grew up, which was a little sad, but it helped that Samantha's room had also changed.

She and her parents didn't need constant reminders that Samantha was gone, even though the thought wasn't far from Abby's head for long, and she doubted it wasn't far from her parents' thoughts either. It was hard to think she wouldn't see her sister on this trip.

She sent a quick text to Mark that she had arrived, and everything had gone okay. She'd call him that evening before she went to sleep.

CHAPTER 3

I'm a Gifter. God has me gifting children to parents on Earth. I love doing that. I even get to go to Earth once in a while to help with a birth. My name is Samantha. My daughter is in heaven too, and she was at the hospital talking to another child at the last birth I attended. Ever since then, I see her often in heaven.

I got to attend little Chloe's birth. Her mother, Madison, lives in Chokecherry Valley, and Madison's mother knows my mother. I wonder if I'll be in Chokecherry Valley again? I never know why God sends me where he sends me. It's just that suddenly I'm attending a birth and giving out comforting vibes to the mother.

CHAPTER 4

Abby spent the rest of the afternoon unpacking and just talking with her parents. They had arrived at the farm from the airport about 4:00 p.m., and there wasn't much time to do anything else. She helped her mom prepare the evening meal of meatloaf, potatoes, green beans, and blueberry pie.

After they'd eaten, she helped her dad with the outside chores, and then they talked for a while before bed. Abby didn't tell them the real reason she'd taken two weeks to come visit in addition to seeing them. She was tired of working in Houston and thought a career change would help, but she needed the time away from Mark to get some perspective.

She was even thinking of moving out of Houston, and that would be a big change for Mark. She was ready for the change, but would he be interested in moving? She didn't know, and she needed to figure out a way to talk to him about it. Their marriage had developed a divide due to their constant work schedules, which she didn't like.

Her dad sent her off to bed at 10:00 p.m., saying she made him tired just watching her yawn. She laughed and said goodnight to her parents. Once she settled into the queen-sized bed in her old room, she lay there for hours, unable to sleep, but too uninterested to get up and retrieve one of the books from her suitcase to read. She'd called Mark, and they each ran through their uneventful day before hanging up.

Now, as she lay awake, she kept going through make-believe conversations with Mark about quitting her job. Since they were simply hypothetical conversations in her own head, she had no idea if they'd bear any resemblance to what the actual conversation would be once she started talking to Mark.

***

After only a few hours of sleep, she woke early and heard her parents already moving around getting ready for the day. Days on the farm started early. She showered, dressed, and joined her mom in the kitchen. Her dad had already gone out to start the farmwork for the day.

"What's your plan for today?" her mom asked.

"I'm going to help you with whatever you need." Abby took a grapefruit from the counter and poured herself a cup of coffee.

"I have to be in Chokecherry at ten to meet with the Community Helpers group. There are five of us meeting this morning, and we're going to be working on a drive for donations for a family who lost their home in a fire. I think we have a few other things on the agenda, but Melissa keeps track of that. She's our secretary."

"That sounds like a good idea. I'll go with you." Abby finished her grapefruit and sipped her coffee.

"Are you sure? This is your vacation, Love. Do you really want to come to this meeting?" Her mom finished wiping the counter and folded the dishcloth in half before putting it across the double sink.

"I'm sure." Abby shrugged. She sure didn't want to sit around the house wondering any longer about mythical conversations with Mark, or what she wanted to do with the rest of her life. Talking about someone else's problems would be good for her and take her mind off her own troubles.

A half hour later they were driving into town, which was only a few miles away from the farm. Abby was enjoying the peaceful nature of the drive. She had her window open enough to breathe in the fresh air, and the warm summer air streaming in the window blew her hair in her face. She smiled as she moved a piece of hair away from her eyes. Tall green grass and weeds filled the ditches, and she knew her dad would be out haying the ditches and grass fields that belonged to him.

"Does Dad have someone to help him with the haying now that Paul is back working at the hospital?" she asked.

"There's a neighbor whose son helps us. The kid's name is Jason. Actually, he's in his thirties, so maybe only a kid to me." Her mom glanced over at her and then back at the road. "I'm not sure if you remember Jason Allmen. His parents are Patricia and Gary."

"I remember them all. Jason was just a few years younger when Sam and I graduated from high school."

"Well, he's grown up now, but he's still cute. We're trying to find a nice girl for him."

"Mom, I know you and his mom, Patricia, are friends, so I don't envy Jason. When you get together with her, you two are always a force to fear. I imagine Jason will find himself married in the not-too-distant future."

"That's not all bad, is it? You and Mark are happy, aren't you? I was afraid that since you came without him that there was something going on."

Abby went from smiling to frowning in an instant. "Mom, I'm sorry you're worried. There's nothing wrong with Mark and me. We're just fine. We're here," she said.

Her mom pulled up in front of St. Anne's Church where the Community Helpers group was meeting. She stopped the car and shut it off. "Are you sure everything's okay with Mark? I don't want to get into your business, but I can listen."

"Really Mom, there's nothing wrong. I just needed to get away to think about work and some other stuff, but our marriage is okay. We can talk later. It looks like there are a few of the ladies standing outside waiting for us." She pointed at the church entrance.

"You're right. Now's not the time."

Abby reached out and put her hand on her mother's arm. "Thank you. And don't worry. I'm fine."

Her mom patted her hand. "Good. I'm here for you."

As they got out of the vehicle, Abby knew her mother would still be worrying about her. They would need to talk today, or her mother would imagine all sorts of things that weren't true.

Her mother introduced her to the Community Helpers group. Abby had met most of them before but was glad for the refresher in names. She'd been living with Mark in Houston for ten years and hadn't seen the women for a long time.

Christina had brought along her four-year-old granddaughter. Abby instantly fell in love with the cute, little, brown-haired child. Brooke was shy and peeked from behind Christina's leg once in a while as they all walked into the church. They settled into one of the classrooms in chairs at a round table set up for the occasion.

Melissa had already set a pitcher of water and paper cups in the center of the table along with plenty of pens and paper for any notes. Melissa smiled at Abby and pointed to the supplies. "Help yourself if you need anything. We keep this group low tech, but we do send out emails to update everyone as to what's going on with whatever project we happen to be working on."

"Thank you," Abby said. "You can add my email address to the group for this project. I'll be in town for a few weeks, and I'd love to help you out. I understand a family lost their home and belongings in a fire, and that's what you're working on right now. I'll do what I can."

Melissa's face lit up. "Thank you for being so helpful. I should have known that a daughter of Nina's would jump right in."

Melissa looked at the others seated around the table. "Since Abby has started us on the subject, let's say a quick prayer and begin."

The others agreed and then bowed their heads as Melissa said a prayer of gratitude and asked for the Lord's help in their endeavor.

When they finished praying, Christina handed Brooke a pen and some paper. "Would you like to draw a picture while we're talking?"

Brooke nodded happily and sat quietly drawing throughout the meeting.

"Our group agreed to find kitchen needs and clothing for the family. We've had enough donations from the local community to buy plates, bowls, cups, and glasses. We've also got enough money to buy each family member three sets of clothes and shoes. Who wants to take them shopping?" Nina asked.

Ellen raised her hand. "I'll take them shopping for clothes. They'll all fit in my SUV. We'll go to Bismarck. It's got enough variety for the whole family." She turned to Abby. "It's a family of four. There's a couple and their two kids. One is an eight-year-old girl, and one is a six-year-old boy. The couple is Renee and Thomas Meyer, and the kids are Zachary and Esme."

She turned to the rest of the group. "Once they've all got clothes, I'll take Renee shopping for the dishes."

Christina nodded. "I'll work on flyers for all of the surrounding communities to post in grocery stores, community halls, and churches. We'll ask for donations of items and money. She looked at Peggy. "Do you want to help me pass out the flyers to all the local communities."

Peggy nodded. She was a woman in her forties and appeared to be the shyest of the group. She listened but didn't speak much. Between Nina, Melissa, Christina, Ellen, and Peggy, they had covered a lot of ground in the hour they gathered. When the meeting broke up, Nina and Abby had agreed to try to find a new home for the family to rent until they could either rebuild or decide what to do for a permanent home. Right now, the family was spending time at Renee's parents' house, but the home was too small to be a long-term solution.

On the ride back to her mother's house, the conversation remained focused on the Meyer family and their need for accommodations.

"I really can't think of anyone who has room for the family. I don't know of any places that are available to rent that are habitable." Her mother frowned. "I wish we had agreed to help Peggy with the flyers. Christina is much more aware of housing in the area. She sells her arts and crafts at flea markets and other events, so she knows more about what's available."

"Maybe we could have Christina help us. I'd love to watch Brooke. She's a sweet little girl. I'd be happy to do that, if it helps, so you and Christina can work on finding a home for the family."

"That's a good idea. I know Christina doesn't like to leave Brooke with a babysitter very often, but she'll know she can trust you."

"We've got two weeks while I'm here, so that should give you and Christina time to help the Meyer family find a place to live and make it habitable."

Nina smiled. "You'd think so, wouldn't you? I hope we can, but I don't know what community they're going to end up living in, and it would be nice if it's somewhere near to Chokecherry Valley since that's where their farmhouse was that burned down."

"We could spend tomorrow driving around if you want," Abby suggested. "I'd like to see what's been going on in the area where I grew up. I haven't really driven around for years. Mark and I just don't usually have the time when we visit from Houston. It'll give you and me a chance to catch up, and I can see what's going on in Chokecherry, and we can find a home for the Meyer family. Christina can let us know where to look tomorrow."

"That sounds good. I'll give her a call this evening. Tomorrow, you can tell me what's bothering you."

Abby laughed. Her mother was certainly direct, and she might as well tell her and get her opinion. "Sounds good."

"Now, let's go see what your dad is up to and if he needs anything. Jason will be gone by now. He's never here in the afternoon." She drove up the driveway to the farmhouse. "He's always back at his parents helping them by now."

"That makes a long day for him," Abby said.

"He's used to it. He's saving up money for school, so he's happy to get in the extra time, and your father can't get the haying done by himself. It works out well."

They got out of the car and walked up the front steps. "Isn't Jason getting old for college?"

"He decided to go last year and starts at the end of August, so yes, he's a little bit older than most students. His young sister had a baby yesterday, so the whole household dynamics are shifting. He's determined to go to school and get his degree though."

"Good for him. He's going after what he wants." Abby wished she knew what she wanted. She was glad she had the time at her parents' to decide. It was nice to be able to think at

the end of the day here at her parents' house. After work at home
there was Mark, and she was usually tired after her nursing shift
at the hospital. She breathed a sigh of contentment.

CHAPTER 5

Madison looked down at the little bundle of baby in her arms and tears threatened. She held them back with effort. Chloe was the sweetest little baby girl. How could she give her up for adoption when the time came? She knew she only had a few more days before someone would come and snatch the baby away from her. Tears slid down her cheeks.

Her mother came into the room and immediately rushed over to hug Madison. "Honey, it's going to be all right. You will be okay."

Madison tugged a tissue from the box on the stand beside the bed and wiped her cheeks and nose. "What if they're not good to her?"

"We'll make sure that whoever adopts her is a good family."

Her mother's assurance only partly mollified her. "Nobody will love her as much as I do." She sniffed and blew her nose.

Her mother patted her on the arm and gave baby Chloe a kiss on the top of her head. "You're right, honey, but you know you can't keep her. We'll agree to an open adoption, so you can see her. If someone wants to adopt and keep it a closed adoption, we'll just refuse. You'll see. It will work out."

Madison adjusted Chloe's little pink booties and sighed. Her mother was right. She couldn't keep Chloe, as much as she wanted to. Chloe's father wanted nothing to do with her or the baby. He had given up his rights, and Madison was too young to give the baby a good home by herself. She still needed to finish high school. She couldn't expect her parents to give up their life to help her, even though they probably would. It was better for Chloe to have two loving parents.

"I know," she whispered. She would spend as much time with Chloe as she could, and if anything seemed off about the couple who wanted to adopt her, Madison would just refuse. She was Chloe's mother and needed to do what was best for her baby.

Madison looked at her own mother. She had been supportive of Madison from the first she'd heard of the pregnancy. Madison knew how lucky she had been. Her father was still trying to adjust to the situation and was embarrassed by the whole thing, but he had stood by her too. He hadn't visited her in the hospital, but Madison knew he was busy on the farm. Her brother, Jason, had hugged her and told her it would be all right when he gave her and her mother a ride to the hospital. He had come by once to see the baby, but she knew he was busy with the haying for their family and their neighbors, Frank and Nina.

CHAPTER 6

Mark spent a lot of time working while Abby was gone. He missed her but knew she needed to see her parents. She had only seen them once since Samantha and Amy's funeral, and she was close to her parents.

He also knew there was something bothering Abby. She hadn't told him outright, but they'd been married for enough years that he knew when she was trying to work something out in her mind. She would do that first, usually, and then she would talk to him. He didn't think it was about having a baby. They'd given up trying, and she'd been resigned to the fact that it just wasn't going to happen for them. They had both wanted children. He took a deep breath and let it out. He had even hoped for twins. Since Abby and Samantha were twins, he thought there might be a chance. After several years and no pregnancy, they'd both given up.

While Abby concentrated on her patients, Mark concentrated on moving up in his firm's technology department. He loved coding, so it was no hardship. He thought Abby loved her job at the hospital, but maybe she was looking for something different. It was so hard to let her visit her parents knowing she was struggling with something but not knowing what it was.

He got himself a cup of black coffee and went back to his computer. The project they'd been working on for months was winding down, and he'd be happy to move on to something different. The late hours would end for a while until the next project.

He was looking forward to going to Chokecherry Valley for a few days. He got along well with his in-laws, and he missed Abby. He missed the way they used to talk about everything. He hadn't realized they were growing apart until this trip. It was time for them to start talking again. About everything.

Whatever Abby was dealing with, they would deal with it together. He made a pact with himself to be more aware of their relationship in the future. Starting now.

CHAPTER 7

When Abby and her mother returned to the farm, they pulled into the driveway as Jason was leaving. As their vehicles met side by side, Abby and Jason stopped and each rolled down their windows.

"Hi, Jason," Abby said. "It's good to see you again."

Jason smiled. "I'm sorry to say that I was too young to remember you, but it's good to meet you. Abby? Right?"

"That's right. We'll be running into each other again here at the farm. I'll even help with chores if you need something done."

"That's good to know." He looked across to the passenger seat. "Hi, Nina."

"Hi, Jason. Thanks for coming over and helping. Do you want something to eat before you leave? Or I can wrap something up for you to take?"

"That's okay. I saw some banana bread on the counter and helped myself to that and some milk. I better get home because I'm sure Mom has something cooked."

"Sure. How are Madison and the baby? Has she named her yet?"

Jason's smile widened. "They're fine. The baby's name is Chloe. She's a cute thing. I didn't realize I'd get such a kick out of having a little niece. I've only seen her a little bit because I'm always out in the field, though. They should both be home from the hospital this afternoon. I have too much to do to spend much time with her, though Madison could use the support right now while she decides what to do."

"Well, don't worry about us. If you need to take time off to help her, just let us know," Abby said. "I can do some fieldwork, though you might have to give me a quick refresher before you leave me alone."

Jason grinned. "I'm sure you'd do a fine job and remember how to hay. You just go in a circle or oblong. I didn't realize Frank had you in the field when you were growing up."

"Oh, well we were. My sister and I." She was surprised that she didn't feel more grief at the mention of her sister. She was just remembering the good times they had out in the field. "Sometimes we took turns working in the field. Of course, sometimes we also complained about it." She laughed. "We were normal kids."

"Very normal," Nina said. "You go along Jason. Say hi to your family for us, and we'll come see Chloe and Madison when they get out of the hospital."

"Thanks. I know Madison is afraid of what everyone thinks of her, so that would be kind of you."

"Of course, we'll stand by her," Nina said.

They said their goodbyes, and Jason took off for his second job at home.

As Abby parked the car in front of the farmhouse, she said, "What's going on with Madison that's she's concerned?"

"She's only seventeen." Nina got out of the car, and so did Abby.

Abby was beginning to understand the reason why Jason was so concerned about his sister. "She's still in high school and not married?"

"Right."

"Is she keeping the baby?" Abby asked. The thought crossed her mind that here was a baby who might need a home, but she and Mark had not talked about adopting. Would he be interested? She felt further away from Mark than ever before. They really needed to communicate with each other.

"I don't know. This is the first time Jason has said anything, and I haven't talked to her parents about the subject. They've brought it up, but I didn't push the issue. I've asked them how she's doing when I'm visiting, but it's been just a brief update whenever I said anything. I don't think the boyfriend is in the picture any longer, but I don't know if Madison will keep the baby or put it up for adoption."

"That would be a hard decision for anyone."

They had been walking as they talked and arrived in the kitchen, where Nina started getting lunch ready.

"What can I do to help you with lunch?" Abby asked.

"We're having meatloaf sandwiches, and I have to take one out to your father if he doesn't come in soon." She looked at her smart watch. "He told me this morning that if he wasn't here by one, to bring it out to him."

"I'll go if he isn't back. It's the field Jason started, isn't it?"

"Yes, out east of the house."

"It will give me a chance to get out and see the countryside. I might even take a half-hour drive around, and then I can come back, and we go driving to see the places you think might work for the Meyer family."

"And we can talk about what's bothering you," her mother said as she sliced the meatloaf and stuck it between two slices of bread.

"That too."

They had their own lunch, and Abby's father didn't come home, so she left to drive out to the field. She enjoyed looking out into the vastness of the prairie. There were few trees, and she could see fields for miles around. A few houses dotted the landscape, but otherwise it was fields, roads, and grass. She loved it.

She had missed the quiet when she moved to Houston, but she'd also loved the bustle of a big city. The closest she could come to a nursing job in North Dakota near Chokecherry Valley was in Bismarck. There were two big hospitals there, and she intended to check out the job vacancies there while she was staying at her parents' house. Nurses were in high demand, so she wasn't concerned about openings. She was just curious, and she hadn't talked to Mark yet, she reminded herself.

Her dad was approaching the end of the field where she parked. She got out of the vehicle with his food and went to greet him while watching the mower leave a freshly-cut row of hay behind it. He stopped about fifty feet from her and walked over.

"I was just starting to get hungry."

She handed him the sandwich wrapped in plastic and a thermos of lemonade. "Here I am. We went to Mom's Community Helpers meeting and then had our own lunch."

"So, I'm last." He grinned at her and then took a big bite of his sandwich.

"You wouldn't want us to starve, would you?" she teased him.

He swallowed and took a drink from the thermos. "Of course not. Then I'd have to get my own food."

"Do you want to sit while you're eating?"

"No. I'm fine. I'll be sitting on the mower for a while once I get back on it. I think we're going to have to do something about the seat. I don't remember it being so uncomfortable before."

Abby started to open her mouth, but her dad beat her to it.

"And you can keep quiet about my age, Missy." He grinned again.

"Wouldn't think of saying anything about that, Dad." She smiled back at him.

"So, what did Melissa assign you two to do this morning at the meeting?"

"We're supposed to find a place for the Meyer family to stay until they can either rebuild or find somewhere else to live permanently."

"That's going to be tough around here."

"That's what Mom said. We're going to get Christina to help us."

"She knows the most about the other communities around here, so that's a good choice." Her dad finished his lunch in silence, while Abby looked around at the countryside, feeling a sense of rightness and peace.

Her dad crumpled up the wrapping from the sandwich and handed it to her. "I'll let you throw this away. I'll keep the thermos. Tell your mom the lemonade is really good."

"I will."

He lifted his cap and set it back on his head. "I'll see you this evening. I'm probably going to finish this field, so it might be later."

"That's fine. If you want me to help with the haying, let me know. I'll see you later."

<h1 style="text-align:center">CHAPTER 8</h1>

When she got back to the farmhouse, her mom was ready to look at houses for the Meyers. She had called Christina and agreed to pick her up at 3:00 p.m. Until then, they had a few hours to look at three houses her mom thought might be possibilities.

"Brooke is going to come with us when we pick up Christina," her mom said as Abby drove the pickup out of the driveway. "I hope that's okay with you."

"Sure," Abby agreed. "I love children." She hesitated before she added, "I miss Amy. She had such a sweet disposition. I always envied Samantha for having her and not taking care of her better."

Her mother looked out the window on the passenger side, so Abby couldn't see her face. "I miss her too. I always loved buying her purple clothes, because her face would light up with joy." Her voice wobbled.

Abby reached over and squeezed her mother's hand. "You were a wonderful grandmother to her. Maybe you'll be getting some more grandchildren if Paul and Hannah get married."

"I'd love that," said Nina.

Abby looked over at her mom. "I'd like another niece or nephew too. We'll see."

She broke the silence after a moment. "Which direction first?"

Her mom wiped a tear from her eye and said, "Let's go east. There's an old farmhouse out that way that might work. The only problem is that no one's lived in it for a year or so. If it's habitable, we're going to have to get a few cats to take care of the rodents and do some other upkeep. I haven't been out that way for about six months. The owners live in Bismarck and come out occasionally to check it out, but we'll see what it looks like."

"What if we can't get inside?"

"I called one of the owners while you were taking your dad his lunch, and he told me a little secret to get into the house when it's locked." She smiled. "He was a little bit wild in his younger days. But now, from what I can tell, he's settled down with a wife and two kids and a steady job."

"That's good. I'm glad we can get into the house."

When they drove up the driveway, Abby was a little concerned about what they would find inside of the house. The outside of the medium-sized A-frame had peeling paint, the grass was overgrown, and the sidewalk had chipped cement.

"Well," her mother said. "We'll just have to see the inside before deciding."

Nina carefully walked along the cement steps and reached for the front doorknob. It turned but didn't open. She walked to the side of the house and found a little gnome stuck into the dirt. She pulled and tugged it out of the dirt. She turned it upside down, and there was a piece of duct tape covering a hollowed-out hole. She pulled at the edge of the tape, and a key dropped out of the hole. She left the gnome where she'd found it.

When they stepped into the house, Abby put her hand over her nose. "Well, you were right about the rodents."

She looked around at the bare living room. The carpet was stained with droppings and footprints from someone walking through the house in the winter or perhaps other wet weather. She looked up at the ceiling to see that it looked intact and okay to live with after a fresh coat of paint. The walls could use some paint too, but otherwise looked okay. There was no warping of the drywall that she could see.

They moved into the kitchen, and it looked similarly intact. It was dated, but not in bad shape with a little sprucing up. "This doesn't look too bad down here."

Her mother nodded. "No, so far, so good. Let's check out the bathroom and then the bedrooms upstairs."

The rest of the house was livable, but there were only two bedrooms and the only bathroom was downstairs. The upstairs just had the bedrooms. They inspected the ceiling, and there didn't appear to be any leaks that they could see.

They relocked the front door and replaced the key.

"This one would work if we can't find anything bigger. They could split the kids' bedroom into two rooms. It's pretty big. The house is about five miles from Chokecherry Valley, and the plows come out this way in the winter. I'm guessing the busing for school would be okay."

"Sounds like it would be okay, but we've just started looking." Abby pulled out of the driveway, and they went to look at the other two properties they knew about. Just from glancing at the outside, they knew that neither one would work. One was just too small, and the other one had a hole in the roof they could see from the road.

Her mother looked at her smart watch. "We have just enough time to pick up Christina and Brooke."

Abby remembered the way to their place, even though it had been years since she'd been there. "Why is Brooke staying with Christina? Is there something wrong with Kym that Brooke isn't with her?"

"When Kym got her divorce, she and her ex-husband basically dumped Brooke. It's sad. Christina is looking at adopting Brooke, so Kym can't come back later and take her away. Christina thinks Brooke has had enough trauma in her young life."

"That's sad about Kym, but it's a good thing Christina loves Brooke so much she'd adopt her."

"She feels she might be too old, but she said she loves Brooke and will do anything she can for her."

"That's great." Abby was thinking about Brooke and about Jason's niece, Chloe. Two little girls who needed a permanent home. Her throat closed with longing. Why couldn't she and Mark have a little girl of their own? Why was it so hard? She didn't know why God had made it impossible for her to get pregnant. At first, she and Mark hadn't been concerned, but as time went on and nothing happened, they both got tested. There seemed to be no reason for the lack of pregnancy. They just didn't have any children. She shut off the thoughts as she pulled into Christina's driveway.

Brooke and Christina were sitting on the front step with Brooke's car seat beside them. The white house behind them had dark green shutters. The place looked like someone had recently painted the exterior. It was a beautiful summer day, with the birds singing and the sun shining.

Christina stood up as Brooke came running over to Abby. "We're going to ride with you."

Abby smiled down at her. "That's terrific. We'll be going for a long drive. Are you ready?"

"Grandma said I could bring my book and my tablet to play with in the pickup. Is that okay?" Brooke asked anxiously.

"That's perfect. It will give you something to do when we're busy talking."

"I need my car seat. I'm too little to sit in a pickup without it."

"Your grandma is bringing it over. You get to sit in the back seat."

"Will you sit with me?"

"Sure. My mom can drive, and your grandma can sit in front, and they can talk while we talk."

"I don't talk much," Brooke said.

Abby was charmed by the little girl. She was a mixture of shyness, sweetness, and seriousness. "You just look at your book and tablet, and if you talk, I'll talk. Otherwise, I'll just listen to your grandma and my mom."

Brooke smiled back at her. "Okay."

They settled in the back seat, with Brooke in her car seat, and Abby beside her. Christina and Nina took their places in the front seat.

Christina started directing Nina to the first house to look at. The afternoon was warm but not overly hot, as long as they didn't sit in the car without the air-conditioning. Abby felt herself relax and started enjoying the day. Since it was the end of June, there were plenty of wildflowers to see among the grasses lining the road. She saw some sunflowers, wild prairie roses, and even a few bluebells.

Abby had become so used to Houston and people everywhere, that this quiet was a welcome change. Her thoughts about moving out of Houston returned. It wasn't that she wanted to move back to Chokecherry Valley where she grew up, but she did want to live in a smaller city than Houston. She thought about finding a nursing job in Bismarck. Her brother-in-law Paul worked at one of the hospitals, and he seemed to like it.

She thought about Paul and what her mom and dad had told her about his living with them for a few months. It sounded like he'd had a bad time after his wife and daughter's deaths. Even though she was mad at Paul for the lifestyle he and Sam had lived, she felt sorry for him. She missed her twin, and she could only imagine what Paul was going through with both his wife and daughter gone at the same time. Abby knew she'd have to get over her anger at Paul. Her mom had already invited him and his girlfriend, Hannah, over for supper tomorrow night. She was not looking forward to it.

She wondered what Hannah was like. Her own sister had been outgoing and always wanted to wear the latest styles and had her hair perfect. Except when she was drunk. Abby winced.

"Are you okay?" Brooke asked. "You made a funny noise."

Abby looked over and saw Brooke watching her with serious eyes and puckered lips. Abby smiled at her. "I'm fine. Just clearing my throat."

"Oh. I do that when I have a cold." The little girl watched her solemnly. "Do you have a cold?"

"No, I don't. Just a tickle in my throat."

Brooke put her hand to her throat and moved her fingers along her neck. "I can't tickle my throat."

Abby laughed, and it felt good. "You can't tickle your own throat. It just happens."

"Oh."

"We're here," Christina announced from the front seat.

Abby unbuckled Brooke from her car seat, and then opened her own door to get out of the vehicle.

Brooke climbed over the car seat and out the same door as Abby. They stood there looking around.

Abby thought the house seemed in better shape than the ones she had looked at with her mother earlier.

"Well," Christina said. "A little work on the outside might be necessary. It doesn't look too bad. Now for the inside."

The owners of the big, rambling ranch house had left the front door unlocked. It looked like certain parts of the house had been added at different times, but the L-shaped house appeared to be in pretty good shape except for the need for a coat or two of paint. The roof looked fairly new, and the front door looked like it had been replaced recently.

They went inside, with Christina holding Brooke back while Nina and Abby took the lead. The entryway was a mudroom with a sink and a place to hang coats and put boots or shoes.

"Nina, why don't you and Abby go see if we have any visitors here before I bring Brooke in any further?" Christina said.

Abby led her mother out of the mudroom into the kitchen. There didn't seem to be any animals or rodents that Abby could detect. She didn't smell any disuse either. She wondered how long the house had been uninhabited. She and her mother made a quick tour through the house and determined it was okay for Brooke. They rejoined Christina, and Nina nodded. "No problems."

Christina took Brooke by the shoulders and squatted down. "Don't touch anything, honey. We're just looking, okay?"

"Okay." Brooke had her serious face on again, and Abby felt her heart tug. The little girl needed a lot more fun in her life. Did she have any kids her own age to play with during the day?

They began to view the house and walked through the living room, downstairs bathroom, and kitchen. It all looked outdated but was in good shape otherwise. The upstairs was the same. There were three bedrooms and a bathroom. It actually seemed like the place would work for the family to move into until they had their bearings and decided if they wanted to stay in Chokecherry Valley or move elsewhere.

Nina was smiling at Christina when they met up in the kitchen again a short time later. "This certainly looks like it should work for them. What do you think?"

"I agree. We can get some volunteers to paint the outside of the house. The inside will need a thorough cleaning, but it's livable otherwise. I'll call the owners and see what kind of a deal I can make for the Meyer family to rent for six months. That's the time frame they gave me when I suggested we help them find a place."

"We need to check out the electrical and plumbing before we move any further. Let's have Frank figure out that part and who to call if he can't do it himself."

"I'll give you the owners' information when we get back to the pickup, and he can talk to them. If it's all okay, I'll bring the Meyer family out here to take a look and see what they think," Christina said.

"Sounds good to me."

Abby looked down at Brooke. "Let's get you back into your car seat and back home. You look like you could use a snack."

"I'm hungry," Brooke agreed.

"I have some juice and crackers in my bag in the pickup. You can look in there for them, Abby. I don't have any secrets in that bag." Christina smiled, and her face relaxed for the first time that day.

Abby realized how Christina was just as solemn as Brooke, and she wondered if caring for Brooke was taking a toll on Christina.

When Brooke was settled with her juice box and crackers, Abby joined her mom and Christina outside the house where they were studying the front steps.

"Just doing one last look before we head home," her mom said.

"Would you like me to watch Brooke for you tomorrow when you bring the Meyer family out here? I could take her over and meet Jason's new niece. I'd like to see the baby too," Abby told them.

"That's a good idea," Nina said. "I know that Madison is worried about what everyone thinks, and she could use some younger company. I'll call her mom and see if Madison is up for company. I know she was just getting out of the hospital today."

"We won't stay long," Abby said. "I just thought Brooke might like to see a little baby. Most kids like to see someone smaller than them."

Christina patted Abby's arm. "Thank you. That's a good idea. Since Brooke and I have been together this last year, she hasn't seen many kids. I intend to do something about that, but I seem to keep getting pulled into these projects, and my health isn't what it used to be."

"I'll be happy to watch Brooke anytime you want help while I'm here for the next few weeks. My husband, Mark, will be coming to stay part of next week, but he won't mind. He loves children too."

The drive back to Christina's house passed quickly. Brooke fell asleep in her car seat, and Nina and Christina talked quietly in the front seat. Abby wondered about Madison's baby. What had Jason meant by not getting to see his niece for very long. Was Madison giving her baby up for adoption? Abby really needed to talk to Mark when she got back to her parents' farmhouse.

"That was a productive day," Nina said when they were on their own again driving back to the farm. "Two options for the Meyer family, though I think they'll choose that second house. The first was just too small, unless they have no other option."

"I agree. It's nice of you to help out with this, Mom. You and Dad always help others. It's a good lesson you taught us growing up. I don't feel like I help people much anymore, though."

"Of course you do. There's your work at the hospital. I'm sure you've helped hundreds of people."

"It seems so impersonal."

"I'm sure they feel like you care when you're treating them."

"I try to make them feel better, but then they leave. It's in and out. I want someone to take care of all the time."

Nina laughed. "Maybe. But once you're taking care of someone all the time, you might get tired of it."

Abby laughed too. "You're right. But I still want it. Mark and I have been trying to have a baby for years, and it just hasn't happened. I had finally given up on the idea."

"Is that why you came to stay at Chokecherry for two weeks?"

"Partly. Of course, I wanted to spend more time with you and Dad, but lately, I just needed to get away from Houston. Let's say I'm doing both at the same time. It is so peaceful out on the farm with you and Dad, though. I'm glad I came here instead of going to some hotel or bed-and-breakfast to think."

"I'm glad you came, too."

Nina was pulling into the driveway when Abby asked the question her mind had been trying to brush aside all day. She felt like a bad person for obsessing about Madison and her baby. "Do you think Madison is going to give her baby up for adoption? You know her parents, Gary and Patricia. Have they said anything?"

Nina put the pickup gear shift into park and shut off the engine. She looked at Abby. "Patricia mentioned adoption, but I have no idea what Madison thinks of the idea since she had the baby. I don't know if Patricia has talked to her about it. Sometimes when someone has a child though, and they hold that baby in their arms, they don't want to give it up. I don't want to discourage you, but you might want to take this slow. I don't want you to be hurt if you set your heart on adopting and Madison isn't interested."

Abby looked down at her hands where she was twisting them in her lap. "I've wanted a baby for so long. I feel bad thinking about Madison's baby when she must be going through a very bad time trying to decide what to do."

She looked back up at her mother. "But if this is God giving me a baby, I don't want to miss the opportunity. Mark and I haven't even discussed adoption. I know we should have, but it's only recently we've come to the realization that we're not going to have our own child. We just haven't had the adoption discussion. And when I came to Chokecherry Valley, I wasn't even really thinking about adopting. I had just left my job in Houston. Something I haven't told Mark about either. There are just so many thoughts in my mind, decisions I need to make. A baby wasn't among those decisions."

Abby grimaced. "I guess a baby is now at the top of my discussion list with Mark. I need to call him tonight and talk to him."

"It sounds like the two of you have a lot to discuss."

Abby groaned. "I really wanted to talk to him in person, but if Madison is seriously considering giving up the baby, I need to talk to Mark now and not wait. I guess a phone conversation is going to have to do for now."

"Let's eat supper, and then you can talk to him. I'll take care of Dad's meal whenever he gets in from the field. It'll be okay."

"Thanks, Mom."

Abby wasn't looking forward to the conversation with Mark. She had really wanted to get her thoughts in order, and then talk to him in person, but that didn't seem to be the way this was going to happen. She would just have to go with the flow and take things with Mark one thing at a time. Was this God's timing? It was certainly different than hers would have been. She smiled wryly. Things happened when they happened. She should know that by now.

She dialed the number and listened to it ring. After two rings, Mark picked up.

"Hi, Honey," Mark said. "I miss you."

"I miss you too." Abby suddenly felt tears coming and sniffed.

Mark must have noticed, because he said, "Are you okay?"

She sniffed again. "Sorry. I'm just so happy to hear your voice, and I wish you were here. So much has happened that I don't even know where to start."

"What? You've only been there a day and a half. What on earth could have happened in such a short amount of time? Are your parents okay?"

"Yes, they are doing well. Dad's out in the field right now, and Mom's downstairs reading a book. She's finally relaxing a little while she waits for Dad to come back."

"That's good. I'm nearly done with that project. We're finishing earlier than planned. I'm mostly working from home the next few days, and I'll actually have the weekend off. I think I'll go golfing. What's going on there that's keeping you so busy?"

Abby wished she could see Mark's face. His brown eyes would be so full of love and understanding, and that's what she needed right now. She didn't want him so far away. "Mom and Dad have a hired hand. He comes early in the morning and is gone by noon. His name is Jason, and his family lives next door.”

“You mean the next farm over?” Mark asked. He came from country roots also and knew next door didn’t mean the same thing as it did in the city.

“That’s right. He’s a few years younger than me, so I never really knew him growing up. He has a sister Madison who is seventeen. She just had a baby.” Abby stopped there with the story. She wasn’t sure how to broach a possible adoption with Mark.

“Is she going to keep the baby?” He asked immediately with no hesitation. Almost as if he knew that’s what she wanted to know.

“I don’t know. Mom says adoption has been mentioned. What do you think about us adopting a baby, Mark? I know we never talked about it, and we should have at least brought it up. I don’t know how you feel about it, and I should know. We’ve been trying for years to have a baby, and it’s just not happening. I wasn’t thinking about adoption when I came here. I had other things on my mind, but now I can’t stop thinking about that little girl and what might become of her. I want to adopt. If not her, then another baby. What do you think about all this?”

There was a long pause, and Abby gave him time. It was a lot to take in.

“First,” Mark said, “I think we should have done a face-to-face chat on our phones for this conversation, since we couldn’t have it in person.”

“I never thought of that, but you’re right.” Abby frowned. Of course Mark would think of the technological solution. It would have been better than just a phone conversation.

“Second, I’m coming to Chokecherry Valley as soon as I can get my ticket changed. I think we need to be together for this discussion.”

“Oh, Mark.” She started crying.

“It’s okay, honey. It’s going to be fine. We’ll work this out.”

The tears slowed, and she got up from the bed where she'd been sitting to get a tissue. "Just a second. I need to wipe my eyes." She set down the phone, wiped her eyes and nose, and went back to the phone. "I'm back."

"Are you okay?"

"I'm so happy you're coming here, but don't you have to go into the office?"

"Like I said. Things are winding down. I can do everything from home, so I can do it from the farm."

"That's great. I can't wait to see you. Text me when you have the new flight, and I'll come pick you up."

"That won't be necessary. I think we're going to need our own vehicles to get around. I'll rent something when I get to Bismarck."

That sounded promising. Maybe he wanted to go see the baby and was seriously thinking about adoption. "Do you need time to think about adoption, Mark? Am I being too pushy?"

She heard Mark sigh.

"I've thought about it for a while, but you didn't seem to be planning any further than having our own baby, so I was waiting for you to be ready. It seems like you're ready now."

"I am. I don't know what will happen with Madison's baby, but I am willing to adopt."

"Then I think we should both do some more thinking on the subject, and I'll be there in the next day or two so we can talk together. Do you think you can keep busy during that time?"

"Definitely. There's a family who lost their house and belongings in a fire. We're getting a house ready for them to move into, and Mom's friend Christina is taking care of her four-year-old granddaughter, Brooke. She's so cute. I'm going to be watching her some of the time when she can't be with Christina and Mom, because of the work they're doing."

Mark laughed. "Sounds like you have plenty to keep you occupied."

"I might even take Brooke over to see Madison's baby. Are you okay with that?"

"That's fine, Abby. Do what makes you happy. We'll work it all out when I get there."

When they hung up a few minutes later, Abby was happier and more settled. Mark seemed okay with adopting a baby. If not Madison's, at least he would consider another baby.

She wondered how long Mark had been thinking about adoption, waiting for her to be ready. He was definitely a keeper in the husband department. She smiled, but it didn't last long. She still hadn't told Mark she had quit her job at the Houston hospital and wanted to find something different. A lot would depend on how things went with Madison and her baby. That could change their whole life plan. Maybe if they didn't live in Houston, she could stay home with the baby for a while before going back to work.

She was happy he was coming to Chokecherry sooner than planned. They'd have more time together to talk about a lot of things they probably should have discussed already. It didn't do any good to push hard topics aside. They were always still there waiting to be dealt with sooner or later.

She went downstairs to tell her mom that Mark was going to be visiting sooner than planned. She knew her mom would be happy for her.

The next morning Abby got up early to help her mom in the garden. The June day promised to be hot, and they wanted to get out and weed as early as possible. The summer breeze brought the scent of lilacs. There were some late-blooming purple lilacs on the bushes near the garden. Her mother had also planted some marigolds, petunias, and pansies that she got at the grocery store. She said that she couldn't wait for the flowers to grow and bloom. She wanted the plants already started, so they would bloom earlier in the season.

They worked on the carrot and radish patch and planned to get the onions and beans done before they went to visit Madison and her baby, Chloe. Nina had called Patricia the evening before and asked if they were up for company. Patricia said it would be a good idea, since Madison seemed to be sinking into some kind of depression and needed something to focus on besides deciding what to do about the baby. Christina had agreed to visit and bring Brooke with her. She thought the four-year-old would help lighten the atmosphere.

Abby changed into shorts and a white T-shirt to visit Madison and Patricia. She slipped on sneakers and was ready to go. She was trying to decide whether or not to mention to Madison and Patricia that she and Mark wanted to adopt a baby. She just couldn't decide what to say and chose to wait and see if there was a good opportunity. Mark would be angry at her if she said anything without him present, but she didn't really want to wait. She felt an urgent need to speak up and tell Madison she was interested in adopting Chloe.

Abby was driving, and she glanced at her mom before looking back out at the road. She had told her mom about part of the conversation she'd had with Mark. "Did you mention to Patricia that Mark and I might be interested in adopting a baby?"

"No. I really think it's best for you and Mark to bring it up with Madison. Patricia did say that Madison was considering adoption but also said that since the baby was born, it's hard to talk to Madison. She's depressed and tired. I'm sure her hormones are fluctuating. It's hard being a new mother. Plus, she's young and trying to make a hard decision."

"I agree. It must be difficult." Abby wondered what it would be like to have her own child. It looked as if that wasn't God's plan for her, so she'd never know about fluctuating hormones. If she got to adopt, maybe she'd at least know what it was like to be a mother. She had hope for the first time in a long time.

It was around 10:00 a.m. when they drove into the Allmen's yard. Christina was just pulling into the driveway too. Brooke was waving eagerly at Abby, and she waved back.

"Brooke is really taken with you," Nina said.

Abby smiled at her mom. "I love that little girl. She is so sweet. I bet she'll make Madison feel better."

They all went up to the doorway together, where Patricia stood to greet them. Somewhere in the bustle of entering the house, Abby found that Brooke had slipped her hand into Abby's hand. It was a good thing that Nina was the one carrying the quilt she'd made for the baby, and she also carried the two jars of chokecherry jelly that she'd brought over for Patricia.

"Are you excited to see the little baby?" Abby asked Brooke.

"Yes. Grandma said her name is Chloe, and I might get to hold her if Madison lets me," Brooke said proudly.

"That would be nice."

"There she is," Brooke said.

Madison was sitting on the couch with Chloe in her lap. There was a blanket, pacifier, and some baby toys scattered on the sofa on either side of her. She smiled at them all, but Abby noticed the tired droop to her eyelids. They would have to keep this visit short. She felt a twinge of disappointment that she wouldn't get to speak with Madison alone and see if she was still considering giving the baby up for adoption. She chastised herself for thinking more about her own wants than Madison's needs. But Chloe was so cute. Abby couldn't believe the possibility that this baby might be her own daughter if Madison would give her up for adoption.

Chloe had her eyes at half-mast and seemed content.

Brooke tugged on Abby's hand. "Can I hold her now?"

Abby looked at Madison. "Hi. I'm Abby. I saw your brother the other day when he came over to help my dad, Frank, with the haying."

Madison smiled shyly. "Hi. Jason mentioned seeing you. I remember you from when you lived at your parents' house."

"Brooke would like to hold the baby. Are you okay with that?" Behind her, she was aware that Patricia was talking quietly with Christina and her mom.

"Sure." Madison struggled to sit on the edge of the couch. She pushed the baby toys and other things off to the side and gestured to Brooke. "Why don't you come sit here on the couch, so you can hold the baby." She smiled as Brooke got up onto the couch and held out her arms.

"Why don't we just set Chloe in your lap?" Abby sat on the couch, with Brooke between her and Madison.

Madison set the baby in Brooke's lap and held Chloe's head, while Brooke rested one hand on Chloe's tummy.

"Look, Grandma," Brooke said to Christina. "I'm holding Chloe."

The baby's eyes seemed to open wider as she stared at Brooke.

"See. She's looking at me."

Everyone in the room laughed to see the two together.

"I need to get a picture of this," Christina said, pulling her phone out of her jean's pocket. She snapped a few pictures, and then said to Brooke. "I think it might be someone else's turn to hold Chloe."

Brooke frowned, but then smiled when Abby said, "How about me? You can stay here next to me while I hold her."

Madison withdrew her arm from under Chloe's head when she was assured that Abby had a good grip on the baby. She flexed her arm. "She is heavier than she looks."

Abby stared down at Chloe. She was such a cute little thing in her pink onesie and with her serene expression. Chloe closed her eyes and sighed.

"She does that all the time," Madison said. "The first time she sighed, I was worried. She kept doing it, and then I got used to it."

"She's very cute. You're doing a wonderful job," Abby told her.

"Thank you."

Abby thought she detected a note of tears in Madison's words, but other than biting her lip, Madison didn't say anything else.

The other women had been watching and then gone back to talking about the Community Helpers project for the Meyer family.

"They decided to take that house we looked at yesterday," Christina said. "Melissa is getting volunteers to paint and clean."

"Frank had the volunteer electricians and plumbers out there yesterday, and everything looked fine to them," Nina said.

"Well, that's one thing off our to-do list, but there is a lot more to getting them set up," Christina agreed.

"Did the flyers get put up for donations? I can help with that. Madison and I could drive around and put some of them up," Patricia volunteered.

"I'd like to do that," Madison said. "I need to get out of the house for a bit. Besides the hospital, I haven't been anywhere for a while."

"Do you want to take Chloe with us?" Patricia asked.

Madison shrugged. "Sure. Why not?"

"Okay. That sounds like fun," Patricia said. "I'll call Melissa and see what's going on with that, and she'll let us know what to do."

Abby looked at the other women. "Who's next?" she asked, even though she wanted to keep holding Chloe. She could hold her all day.

Christina took the baby from Abbey, and Brooke followed her grandmother around the living room as Christina cooed and swayed with the baby as she paced the living room.

"Do you want to go outside, Madison?" Abby asked. "It's a really beautiful day."

Madison got up. "I'd love to. Mom said the yard looks summery today with the birds singing on the lawn by the bird feeder. I haven't had the energy since I got home from the hospital, but it would be great to get outside for a bit."

"Well, I think you have plenty of babysitters right now," Abby said as they went out the front door together and left the other women with Chloe.

Madison blinked as she stepped outside. "It's bright. Yeah. I don't like to leave Chloe with my mom too much. She's done so much already."

Abby heard the tears in the teen's voice again. Her mom was right. Lots of hormones and emotions going on with Madison. "Let's sit on those chairs." Abby pointed to two chairs that were close enough to the bird feeders for them to watch if they remained still so they wouldn't scare the birds.

They sat down, and Madison sighed. "I wish…"

Abby waited, but she didn't continue. "I'm only going to be here for two weeks, and then I'll be gone. If you want to talk about something I can keep it to myself. I won't tell my mom, so you don't need to worry that it'll get back to your mom."

"I just feel like such a burden to my mom. She's helping me take care of Chloe, and she doesn't complain, but it just makes me feel guilty that I'm adding more work for her." Madison took a deep breath and let it out.

"Your mom seems to be doing fine," Abby said. "She loves you and only wants to help you."

Madison started crying, and Abby got up and placed a hand around Madison's shoulders. "It's okay. I heard you might give Chloe up for adoption."

Madison only cried harder.

Abby just patted her on the shoulder as Madison pulled some tissues out of her pocket. The fact that she was prepared with tissues gave Abby a clue as to how often the tears came.

Maybe if she came straight to the point about adoption, it would help Madison talk about the situation. "What's bothering you about adoption?"

"I want to keep Chloe," she blurted out. "I just don't want to burden Mom if I keep Chloe, and I know it will be a lot of extra work for her, and I don't know how it would work. I don't want to give her up. She's mine." The tears continued, and Abby just let her cry. Eventually, the tears stopped, and Madison just sat there breathing heavily.

Abby moved away. "I'm going to let you sit here for a few minutes while I go keep the others in the house for a little bit. How about I come back in ten minutes and see how you are?"

"Thank you," Madison looked up at her. "I don't want them to know."

"Okay. I won't tell anyone, but I would suggest that you let your mom know. I think she'll be on your side. She loves Chloe too. She would probably be happy to help you raise her."

Madison shrugged and looked down. "I don't know," she whispered.

Abby patted her on the shoulder and went back into the house, her own heart hurting for herself and for Madison. It looked like Chloe was not going to be the baby for her and Mark. She really thought that Chloe should be staying with Madison, which was a good thing for both of them.

CHAPTER 11

When Abby and her mom arrived back at the farm after their visit with Madison and Patricia, there was an SUV parked in the driveway. "Do you know who is here?"

Her mom shook her head. "The vehicle doesn't look familiar."

Abby noticed a rental sticker. "It's Mark. He's here already. Why didn't he text me that he'd be here so soon?"

"Have you looked at your phone lately?"

Abby pulled her phone out of the holder in the front of the pickup. "I guess I left it here in the pickup when we went into Patricia's house."

She looked at the incoming texts and saw she'd missed a few from Mark. He must have texted earlier that morning when she was sleeping, and then again when he arrived in Bismarck. She didn't know how she missed the early morning text. She couldn't remember if she'd even looked at her phone that morning. She thought it was a habit to at least glance at it, but she couldn't remember.

Mark came out of the house to meet them.

"Hi, Nina," he said to her mom.

"Hi, Mark." She gave him a hug and then said, "I'm going into the house. You two can talk."

"Thank you." He watched until the door closed behind her, and then he turned to Abby. "Hi, Honey."

She hugged him, and he hugged her back. "It's so good to see you. I didn't expect you so soon, and I must have forgotten to look at my phone this morning."

He continued to hold her. "Could that be because you were going to see that little baby?"

She looked up at him from the shelter of his arms and saw he was smiling. She did get wrapped up in things and forget. She nodded. "I think so. I really wanted her to be the one. When you said you were ready to adopt, it just seemed like it was meant to be."

She stepped out of his embrace and took his hand. "I'm happy you came early. I'm kind of bummed right now."

"What's going on?"

She led him over to the front steps. "Let's sit down, and I'll fill you in."

They sat down on the top step, and he took her hand in his. "What's up?"

"Mom and I just came back from visiting Madison and her baby, Chloe. Madison's mom, Patricia, was there. So were Christina and her four-year-old granddaughter, Brooke. We spent some time visiting, and then just Madison and I went outside to talk. I meant to bring up that you and I were interested in adopting, but before I could say anything, she burst into tears and told me she wants to keep the baby. Of course, I couldn't say anything at that point, so we talked a little bit, and I told her to tell her mom that she wanted to keep the baby. Madison is afraid it's too much of a burden for her family to help her."

Mark leaned over and kissed her on the top of her head. "I'm sorry. What do you think is going to happen?"

"I think she's going to keep the baby. I think once she tells her mom, Patricia will do what she can to help Madison. I don't think Chloe is the baby for us."

Mark gave her a hug. "We've just started talking about adopting. Maybe it's just too soon. We'll find a little one to add to our family. I know you're disappointed now, but let's not give up hope already."

"You're right. I can get rather impatient."

Mark laughed. "How about very impatient?"

Abby laughed too. "Let's not start an argument right away. You just got here. Let's wait until later."

Mark squeezed her hand and got up, pulling her with him. "Let's go find your mom and get some food. I'm hungry."

"Me too. It's been a long morning."

CHAPTER 12

Abby spent the rest of the day helping her mom in the garden and catching up on household chores. Mark worked remotely on his work project trying to finish it up by the weekend.

The next morning, Friday, Mark continued working, and Abby and her mom went to Chokecherry Valley to St. Anne's Church to see the secretary, Melissa. She had the plans for the Meyer family.

Abby planned to go shopping with Mark in Bismarck after lunch. They were going to buy supplies for the Meyer family, and she needed to know what they should be getting to help out the family. She knew one of the other Community Helpers members had already taken the family shopping, so she wanted to know what the best things to buy would be.

She was looking forward to getting into Bismarck and spending the day with Mark. Between his work and her helping her mother and working on the Community Helpers project, she hadn't seen much of him since he arrived. They planned to eat lunch with her parents and then go to the city for shopping.

She was also happy to be busy with Mark, because she was nervous about seeing Paul and his girlfriend that evening. Her mother had invited them for supper. Abby wasn't sure how she felt about her brother-in-law dating so soon after Sam's death. He deserved to be happy, but she still held a grudge about how much drinking Paul had done with Sam during the early part of their marriage before Paul got clean. She knew intellectually the accident that killed Sam wasn't Paul's fault, but she still had a lot of mixed feelings that she couldn't seem to sort out over the whole ordeal.

She wasn't sure why she was still holding a grudge against him. He had had a problem with drinking, which he had gotten help for. He tried to get Sam to accept help, but she didn't. That was what Abby was having a hard time understanding. Why didn't Sam get help? She had a good husband and a lovely little girl. Why didn't she get help and stop drinking? Abby knew her anger should be directed at Sam and not Paul, and she shouldn't really be angry anyway. It was sad that Sam didn't get help before it was too late, and she'd died in that accident.

Maybe it wasn't the drinking so much as the jealousy Abby was feeling over Sam's blessing at having Amy. She didn't understand why Sam was able to get pregnant, and she wasn't. That's what she was really angry about. She finally admitted it. She was angry and jealous that Sam had had no trouble having Amy, and she threw it all away by her drinking.

Somehow, she was going to have to learn how to live with her feelings. Maybe once she and Mark were able to adopt a child, some of her jealousy would disappear. She didn't want to be angry at Sam. She missed her. She'd missed her for a long time even before she died. That was the other part of the equation. She missed the Sam she'd grown up with before the drinking started. And she blamed Paul for Sam starting to drink, and that wasn't fair to Paul. She'd come back to some circular thinking. It was time to go shopping with Mark.

She went into her bedroom and dressed in jeans and a button-down, short-sleeved shirt. She slipped some comfortable sandals on her feet, as they would be doing a lot of walking for the afternoon while they shopped. She stuffed the list from Melissa into her purse and headed downstairs to see if Mark was ready to leave.

Mark had finished working on his project, and since it was Friday, he said he wouldn't work anymore today or during the weekend unless a problem came up. Since they were shopping, and then having company that evening, he had needed to finish before they left.

When she got to the dining room, where he had set up for the morning, she saw he was on his phone.

"Right," he said into the phone. "Ten-thirty a.m., Monday. Tuesday's the Fourth of July, so we won't be doing anything that day."

He listened for another minute, and then said. "I'm taking off the Fourth and the rest of next week. You can call or text if there's a problem, and I'll work on it. Otherwise, I'm here in North Dakota spending time with my wife's family."

There was another pause. "Okay. Bye." He pressed the end button.

Abby had stood waiting for him to finish. "Was that your boss?"

"Yes. As you heard, there's a meeting Monday morning that I'll attend remotely. Then I'll finish up a few things and take vacation time. That should work out well. I'm done for today and this weekend."

"Good. Then we can leave in about fifteen minutes, if that's okay with you?" she asked.

"That's fine. Let me finish up one quick email, clean off the table, and we'll take off for the city."

"I'm going to tell Mom we're leaving and see if there's anything she needs us to pick up in Bismarck. I forgot to ask her earlier."

Abby found her mom sorting through some papers that were spread across the coffee table by the living room couch. "You look busy."

"Just trying to get a handle on all this paperwork Melissa gave me for the Meyer project. Thank goodness it's just copies, because I'm getting them all mixed up."

"I can help you tomorrow. Right now, Mark's finishing up a few things, and then we're leaving for Bismarck. Did you want me to bring you anything?"

"No, we're fine. Your dad and I did a little shopping the day we picked you up from the airport, so there's nothing more to do. I'm going to bake a pie for this evening and look at these papers. Your dad should be done with the haying in that field by four. I think he'll just stop there for the day."

"That sounds good."

"Your dad is really looking forward to seeing Paul and Hannah again. I know you have some reservations about Paul, but he was really good for Dad when he helped us this spring."

"I know, Mom. I'll be nice. I'm really trying to see his side of things. I just miss Sam and Amy, and I want someone to blame."

Her mother got up and hugged her. "You know in your heart who's to blame. Let's just let forgiveness be our focus, and remember the love and joy we had with Amy and Sam. We can't change anything."

Abby hugged her back. "I'm working on it, Mom. Like I said. I promise to be good this evening. I won't scream and yell at him."

"Good. I know you're going to like Hannah."

Abby thought about that and realized she really did want to like Hannah. None of what had happened involved her.

CHAPTER 13

It felt good to get out of her parents' house for a while. She enjoyed seeing them, but there were a lot of memories of Sam and Amy in all the rooms. She wasn't as fragile as she'd been when she was there for the funeral, but still. It was sometimes difficult when a memory caught her off guard.

She understood her mother's apprehension about Abby and Paul in the same room again. She hadn't seen him since the funeral, when she had screamed at him, Abby claimed that the accident was his fault. Paul hadn't even been in the vehicle when it crashed.

She smiled as Mark drove to Bismarck. It was good to spend some time alone with him. Before she'd come to Chokecherry Valley, he had been wrapped up in his project at work, and then as soon as he got to Chokecherry, they discussed adoption. This felt more relaxed.

"We've got a long list for today. Are you ready?" Abby asked.

"Definitely. It will feel good to be walking around instead of sitting at a desk or table all day long. What do we have to buy?"

"It's just a lot of household things. As much as we can fit into the SUV. I told Melissa we're donating everything we buy today. I hope that's okay with you." She didn't anticipate Mark objecting.

"Hey, that's great." He smiled at her before returning his attention to the road. "I'm glad you thought of it."

"Thanks for being so understanding. About everything."

"You mean the adoption too?"

"Yes. I told Mom we're considering it, and I'm sure she told Dad."

"That's okay. I expected that."

"I don't think Madison's baby is the one for us." Abby sighed. "I know that would have been too easy."

"Don't give up yet. She may change her mind. And we just started the process. It can take a long time."

"I know. I'm just happy we're talking about it. Would you be willing to adopt an older child?" She was thinking that she'd be okay with a young child instead of a baby, but what would Mark think?

"That might be harder to do. They already might have known their mom or dad. I'm not sure about that. I'd have to think about it. I'm not totally opposed to adopting a child, but a lot would depend on the circumstances of the child."

They talked of other things after that and enjoyed their time in Bismarck. They stopped midway through the afternoon and chatted over coffee. Abby felt like she was on a date with her husband. She still hadn't told him about leaving her job in Houston. Maybe on their way back to the farm she would tell him. She didn't want to ruin the rest of her afternoon with him.

In the end, she didn't say anything to Mark about her job. Adoptions could be expensive, and she might need to beg for her nursing job back in Houston until an adoption was finalized. She could manage staying at the job if she knew something good would come of it.

CHAPTER 14

As the time for Paul and Hannah's arrival neared, Abby moved around the kitchen and fidgeted.

Nina finally put a hand on her arm. "Calm down. It's just Paul and Hannah. It will be okay."

"I know," Abby said. "But I have to apologize to Paul for the nasty things I said to him at the funeral. Screaming at him at the graveside. I can't believe I did that." She squeezed her eyes shut and then opened them. "What was I thinking?"

"We all do things we wish we could undo. Paul will understand. Just tell him you're not angry with him anymore, and he'll forgive you. I think you'll find that Samantha's and Amy's deaths have changed him a lot."

"I would expect they would change him. I hope for the better." Abby regretted that last bit but couldn't take it back.

"You've always had a grudge against him since he and Samantha married. Maybe it's time you thought about why that is." Her mother held up her hand before Abby could say anything. "And no, it wasn't his drinking that upset you so much. Just think about it."

"It was his drinking. I think it led to Sam drinking more." She saw her mother was going to say something, and she beat her to it. "But I will consider there is another reason and think about it. Maybe then I can get past it."

"Maybe you can. And if you need help, I'll tell you why you were so mad at him," her mother said irrepressibly.

Abby laughed. "I'll let you know when I want to know."

Nina nodded. "You do that."

They continued setting the table. Mark was answering some work emails in their bedroom and then would return to the kitchen. Frank had gone to get another chair from the living room to set around the table. He'd stopped haying around 4:30 p.m. and come back to the house to clean up. He said he was going to take the evening off to visit with Paul and Hannah.

That was something new for Abby to hear. Her father didn't usually stop until it was too dark to see. Her dad was slowing down some and taking time off. It was nice to see. Jason must be getting a lot done during the time he was here to help, too. She was happy to see that her parents were managing the farm and doing okay. She knew it was hard work, and she worried about them.

Abby was looking forward to helping in the garden again tomorrow. Since it was Saturday, she anticipated that Mark would be able to help her. He had said he wouldn't work the weekend, which meant he'd check his email occasionally, but otherwise was free.

She smiled. The one thing about her job was if she wasn't at the hospital, there wasn't anything she could do from a distance. It had been great so far this week to be done with work. She couldn't wait until she could do something else, but for now, she was content with letting the situation ride until the adoption plans could be put in motion.

If Madison really wanted to keep her baby, then Abby and Mark could sign up in Houston for places that handled adoptions. She smiled. Why hadn't she thought of adoption sooner? She and Mark had been so set on having their own baby.

Well, she had anyway. Mark must have been thinking about it for a while based on his response when she brought it up. He said he'd been waiting for her to come to the same conclusion. Would she have considered it sooner if he'd brought it up? Maybe not. Maybe she still would have been consumed with the idea of them having their own.

"Abby? Abby?" Nina said.

"What?" She realized she'd been standing in the middle of the kitchen, in the way of her mom and dad, who were trying to set the table and get things out of the oven. Her dad had returned to help while she was standing there pondering the future.

"I asked if you would put butter on the table for the corn and buns."

"Sure." She got the butter out of the fridge and found a bowl to put it in.

"You were thinking hard," her mother said.

"Just about adoption," Abby said, as Mark wandered into the room.

He smiled at her.

Her dad looked over at her. "Your mom told me what happened with Madison today. I'm sorry."

"That's okay, Dad. I saw Madison with little Chloe, and they're meant to be together. Mark and I will find our own little bundle of joy. We'll sign up at adoption agencies when we get back to Houston assuming Madison decides to keep Chloe. It will work out. We just started talking about the process and need to fill out tons of forms. I've heard it can take a while." She smiled at Mark. "We've waited this long. A little longer won't hurt us, but I am anxious to begin the process."

"Me too," Mark said.

They heard a knock on the door, and Abby took a deep breath and let it out. Mark squeezed her hand. "You'll do fine."

They all trooped into the entryway. Mark and Abby stayed back a little way, because there wasn't enough space for all of them. Nina and Frank exchanged hugs with Paul and Hannah. Abby found it interesting that her dad greeted Paul with a hug. It used to be a handshake. Things really had changed.

"Hi, Paul." Abby greeted him but couldn't reach him due to her parents being between them.

"Hello to you two." He smiled at Abby and Mark. "This is my friend Hannah."

They greeted Hannah, and she smiled at them. "It's good to meet you."

Hannah looked right at home with Frank and Nina, and Abby knew she was looking at a future in-law. Abby liked her on sight. She seemed calm and peaceful. Just what Paul needed, Abby realized. Samantha hadn't been calm or peaceful. She'd always been a go-getter.

"Let's move into the kitchen, where there's more room," Nina said.

They all began moving into the kitchen, and Paul asked Frank about the haying. Abby knew Paul had helped Frank with the spring planting and the calving. She also knew Paul had grown up on a farm. His parents had died when he was in college, right before Paul met Samantha. Maybe that was why he took up drinking, although drinking was a usual rite of passage for most teenagers in the state of North Dakota. She briefly thought of her mother telling her to think of another reason Abby might be angry at Paul other than his drinking, but now wasn't the time.

Her mother had directed Paul, Hannah, and Mark to sit at the table. "I think Frank, Abby, and I take up enough room moving around here, so the rest of you just sit and relax."

"Thank you," Hannah said. "We've been sitting and relaxing for the last hour on the drive out here, though, so we would certainly be happy to help."

Nina waved her hand at them. "It's okay. You can help clean up after the meal if you want."

Abby knew that wasn't just to pacify the guests. They'd be helping with dishes if Nina said so.

They soon had everything on the table, said the before-meal prayer, and passed the food around.

"What's happening out here at Chokecherry Valley?" Paul asked. "What are we missing?"

"The Community Helpers group is getting things together for a family who lost everything in a fire. Abby and Mark were out shopping for the family earlier today."

"Oh, we'd like to help too." Paul looked at Hannah. "Do you have plans tomorrow?"

"Nothing that I can't change."

Paul looked back at Nina. "We could help tomorrow, since it's Saturday. I don't work, and Hannah just volunteered."

Hannah laughed at him. "You're lucky I knew why you asked. I'm willing to help, or I would have told you my plans couldn't change."

She looked at Nina. "I'd love to help. What needs to be done yet?"

"Melissa is keeping track of everything. She's the church secretary at St. Anne's Church and the secretary for the Community Helpers group. The Community Helpers group isn't a Catholic group. It's just a bunch of women from around the area who get together, and those who have the time work on various projects."

"That's okay," Hannah said. "I'm glad it's various faiths getting together to work and help others."

"I'll check with Melissa after we eat and see what needs to be done tomorrow. I think right now they're getting the house ready. It needs to be painted and some handyman things done inside to make it livable. It's in pretty good shape, so most things are minor and can be done by anyone."

"Hannah paints. I'm sure she could wield a paintbrush." Paul smiled at her.

"I paint pictures on canvas. Not houses." She laughed. "But sure, if the house needs to be painted, give me a paintbrush, and I'll do boring up-and-down and side-to-side strokes."

They all laughed with her.

Abby decided then that she really liked Hannah. "Well, if they're going to help out, I guess we should volunteer. Right, Mark?"

Mark groaned. "I was waiting for you to say that." Then he grinned. "I'm not going to be outdone by Hannah. If she can pretend to paint, so can I."

Abby looked from her mom to her dad. "Did you have something we need to do around here first before we go over there?"

Nina shooed her away with her hand. "You go help them. Your dad and I will be just fine."

Abby looked at her dad.

"Definitely. Go help them," Frank said.

"Okay."

"Like I said, I'll check with Melissa, and see what she says. I'm guessing there will be quite a number of people there tomorrow working on the project," Nina said.

"We can unload the SUV over there with what we bought today," Abby told Mark.

He just nodded.

Abby was happy Mark was so good-natured. He'd spent the last few months working night and day on his work project,

and now during his vacation, she was putting him to work
instead of letting him relax. He didn't seem to mind, though.

CHAPTER 15

After they'd finished eating, and everyone helped put away the food and do the dishes, they moved into the living room.

Abby was wondering when she might get Paul alone to apologize, when he asked if she would show him the garden. That made her nervous. When had he ever sought her attention deliberately?

"I helped Nina plant the garden this spring. I need to see how things are growing," he told her as they walked outside.

They took the three steps down from the front door and went around the back of the house where the garden was. It was a gorgeous evening for the last day in June. The birds were chirping. She could hear frogs croaking down by the stream that ran through part of the land.

She twisted her hands together as she stood by the garden. The scent of marigolds and the last of the lilacs perfumed the air.

Paul was walking up and down the rows, inspecting the garden. "Looks pretty good, if I do say so myself." He looked up and smiled at her. "I see you and Nina have gotten some of the weeding done. If I have time this weekend when we're not working at the Community Helpers project, I'll come out here and do some more. I find it relaxing."

Abby gaped at him. "You're so different." She was chagrined at her words but could only stand there stunned.

He stood where he was in the middle of the garden. "I hope so, Abby. I'm sorry for the way I behaved. Before and after Sam's death. I loved her, and I know you did too. We both lost someone precious to us when she died. I understand why you yelled at me at the cemetery. I deserved it. While Sam chose to drink, I didn't do much to dissuade her. I yelled at her a lot, which didn't do a lot of good. I should have taken Amy away from her, and maybe at least Amy would be alive. But I didn't.

She loved Amy so much, I could never have taken her away
from her mother." He cleared his throat. "Now they're both
gone. In heaven is my belief."

Abby couldn't think of anything to say, and then the
words came. "It's not your fault, Paul. I know that I blamed you
at the cemetery that day, but it was my grief lashing out at you. I
blamed you for many years for my sister's drinking, but the truth
is more complicated than that. You drank, but then you stopped.
First, I blamed you for drinking with her, and then I blamed you
when you didn't force her to stop drinking after you stopped.
The truth is, Sam chose to drink. The disease of alcoholism had
her wrapped around in circles, and she couldn't get out. I don't
know why she didn't try. Or maybe she did try, but she never
told us because it didn't work."

"She loved Amy," said Paul. "If she could have done it
for anybody, she would have done it for her, but she didn't.
Sometimes, people just don't know the right steps to take. That's
the way it was for her."

They stood silently for a few minutes, and Abby realized
something else. She knew what her mother was talking about
when she said that the drinking wasn't the only reason Abby was
angry at Paul. "I felt you took her away from me. That's the
other reason I was angry. I blamed you that she never came to
Houston to visit. I know it wasn't your fault. Sam made her own
decisions."

"If it helps you to know, I suggested many times we
should visit you in Houston, but she said no. She felt like you
had your life together and she didn't."

Abby laughed bitterly at that. "I should have come out
here and talked some sense into her. She had some of what I
wanted, and I had some of what she wanted. I wasted time being
angry at her too. I guess I just pretended it was only you I was
mad at, but the truth is, I was jealous of both of you.

"I felt you took my sister away. And then she got
pregnant easily and had a baby. I wanted a child so bad, and she
had no problem, and then drank her life away."

"Are you still angry at me, Abby? Because if you are, I'll
make some excuse for tomorrow, so we aren't working in the

same area of the house. Or I can come a different day when you're not there."

Abby thought about it. She realized that by talking to Paul, a lot of her angry feelings toward him were gone. So was the jealousy that had been eating away at her. She felt calmer over what had happened. Now, she mostly felt sadness in the pit of her stomach. She'd always miss Sam and Amy.

She took a few steps toward Paul. "We can all work together tomorrow. I'm not mad any longer. You did the best you could. I miss them both, but I'm sure you do too."

"I miss them every day, but I'm lucky to have Hannah now."

"How about a hug to seal the deal?" she asked.

Paul held out his arms, and she took the few remaining steps to his side. His hug was warm and comforting. "Thank you," he said. "I really want us to be friends."

She stepped away and smiled at him. "I believe we are," she said softly. "I hope for the best with you and Hannah. You deserve happiness, Paul. Thank you for bringing me out to the garden tonight, so we could talk this through."

"You're welcome. I'm happy too. I hope you and Mark have a child. You would make a great mother." He started walking down the row out of the garden, and she followed.

CHAPTER 16

The next day, Frank headed out to the field. Jason wasn't coming over because he had agreed to do some of the plumbing repairs at the Meyer family house.

Abby and Mark drove over to the Meyers' house-in-progress in their SUV, and Nina drove separately. Their vehicles were both loaded with new items for the family along with cleaning supplies and other things Melissa had requested. Nina had found a few outside decorations that she and Hannah had discussed the night before, and Hannah had said she could repaint the garden gnomes, turtles, and some other things for the Meyers so they would have some decorations in their front yard.

Nina had talked to Melissa the night before as planned, and Melissa had told them she'd hand out assignments when they arrived.

As Abby got out of the SUV she looked around at the flurry of activity. There were at least ten people already working on the outside, and she wondered how many were inside. There were cars and pickups lined up along the roadside, and Mark had parked along the road too. They left all their things in the vehicle until they knew what Melissa had planned.

Melissa stood at the door to the house. It was propped open so that people could come and go easily. She directed Abby into the house, through the kitchen, and into the living room. "How about you join Hannah and Christina in painting the living room," she suggested to Abby and Nina. "They got here just a little bit ago and are just starting."

Hannah and Christina said hello, and Brooke came running up to Abby. "Will you help us?"

Abby squatted down and gave the little girl a hug. "Of course. We're going to paint. What are you going to do?"

"I get to paint too." She pointed to a little can of paint that was open, and a little mini brush. "It's just my size."

Abby's heart swelled with love for the little girl. "It sure is. You'll do a great job."

She stood up and looked back at Mark. "I guess I'm painting. Do you want to check with Melissa about your job?"

Mark shrugged. "She already told me I'm in the back with some other guys clearing out the backyard. It's full of dead things and leaves and branches." He shuddered, and then broke into a big grin. "What fun. I can't look at my computer all day." He left.

She laughed. "He's been looking for a break from that laptop for weeks. This will be good for him, but he's going to be sore at the end of the day."

Christina laughed with her. "We're all going to be sore at the end of the day."

They started taping so the window frames wouldn't get paint on them, and then continued taping around other borders. Hannah took the light-switch covers off with a screwdriver and grunted every once in a while when she came to a screw that refused to budge.

"Why don't you leave those really hard ones, and we'll get one of the guys to take them off. They can do it in a second. It will save you some energy," Abby said.

"Then I'd have to admit I'm a poor, weak woman," Hannah argued.

"No, you won't. We'll grab one of those guys doing the electricity or plumbing. They don't know us. Mark and Paul are in the backyard, and they'll never know."

"That's true," Hannah grinned. "You've sold me on the idea."

The women worked companionably and joked and laughed. Brooke floated from person to person, interrupting with some innocent question and then going back to drawing pictures on her corner of the wall. Some of the volunteers brought them sandwiches and bottles of water for lunch, and the men took a break and joined them in the bare living room.

"Wow, you've made progress," Mark said when he came in.

Everything they didn't want painted had the edges taped, and the switch plates had all been removed. They had started painting one of the walls a creamy beige. Abby had started on one side, and Nina had started on the other.

Hannah had said she'd paint up by the ceiling, so she had climbed the ladder by the opposite wall and painted a section while Christina stayed by the ladder and made sure it was stable. Then they'd move it a little more. It was slow going, but they had a start.

Lunch was brief, and they all started back in on their assigned tasks. The women in the living room wanted to get the room painted before the end of the day. The men had decided they wanted to get the backyard cleaned before they left, so they were all in a hurry to continue.

When the day was done, the volunteer teams had most of the house painted and most of the exterior cleaned up. Melissa thought they might be able to get the outside of the house painted and the rest of the landscaping done the next weekend. They were lucky the roof didn't need to be redone.

Some of the volunteers said they could come in Monday and finish up the inside painting. The flooring was getting installed on Wednesday, the day after the Fourth of July, so nothing could be done inside on that day. And nobody planned to work on the Fourth of July as there was a parade in a neighboring town, and a lot of people had company and fireworks planned for that day. They were lucky the year had been wet enough that they could shoot off fireworks in the county.

CHAPTER 17

Abby went to church at St. Anne's with her parents on Sunday morning. After supper Thursday evening, Nina had already invited Paul and Hannah to join them at the house after church. At church, she invited Christina and Brooke to also join them. They all met for brunch.

Paul and Hannah had brought an assortment of blueberry, raspberry, and banana muffins. They'd also brought all the ingredients and insisted they were cooking the omelets and hash browns for the brunch. Abby tried to join them in the kitchen, but she was sent back to the living room to talk with Christina and play with Brooke.

In the living room, Mark sat talking to Frank, while Abby played on the floor with Brooke and her toy cars. Abby listened in to the conversation her mom was having with Christina.

It was a pleasant morning, and Abby knew she was going to miss the whole bunch of them when she returned to Houston. Her home was going to be very quiet compared to her parents' constant activity. She and Mark had let work become their whole way of life. Either she was on shift at the hospital or Mark was working on his computer. They hadn't connected in a long time. She realized that situation needed to change.

There was no reason for her not to have talked to Mark about her quitting her job. The fact that she hadn't told Mark yet indicated a fault in their marriage that needed to be corrected, especially if they were going to raise a child together. She wasn't sure why she feared him knowing about her leaving her job. Maybe she thought he would try to convince her to continue working there even though she was so unhappy. She didn't know. The sooner she talked about it with him, the sooner it would be clear in her head.

Mark might appreciate that she was considering a different job. Maybe she'd get a job at a clinic working for a

203

physician. She'd only be working weekdays, because most clinics were closed on the weekend. She smiled at the thought.

"Can I play on the piano?" Brooke pointed to the piano that was along one wall in the living room.

"It's kind of noisy," Abby told her, thinking of everybody else in the room talking.

"That's okay," Nina told her. She must have overheard Brooke's request. "We won't be disturbed."

Abby knew her mom missed hearing Sam play. Sam had been the musician in the family. Abby had given up learning the piano. She just didn't have the patience for it.

She helped Brooke get up on the piano stool, and then she opened the lid. Brooke made lots of noise, and the adults in the room indulgently listened to her pound away. After about five minutes, the newness wore off, and Brooke quit. Abby closed the piano lid.

Instead of getting down, Brooke wanted to look at the pictures on the top of the piano. Abby went and sat in a wing chair across from the couch where her mom and Christina were sitting. Brooke had then climbed down from the piano bench and leaned against the chair's arm where Abby sat. The women were all having a conversation when Brooke interrupted.

"I talked to that girl," she said.

Abby looked down at her. "What girl?"

"The one in the picture on the piano."

Abby got up and followed Brooke back over to the piano. There were some pictures of her and Sam when they were small, and there were a few pictures of Amy sitting at the piano. "Which little girl?"

Brooke pointed to one of the pictures of Amy. "That little girl. She told me I'm going to get a new mommy and daddy."

Christina gasped. "When did she tell you that?" She got up from the couch and hurried over to Brooke. She scrunched on her haunches looking at her.

"When we were at Madison's house looking at the baby."

The adults looked at each other wide-eyed.

"I don't think that's true, Brooke. That little girl wasn't at Madison's house. You know what I said about telling stories," Christina said. She looked at the others. "Brooke has a vivid imagination."

"It's okay," Nina said, though her voice was tight, and her face was white. "We understand."

Brooke looked at Christina uncertainly. "Did I do something wrong?"

"No, honey. Of course not. You just go ahead and play now. I need to talk to Nina."

Mark came to the rescue. "I can take her outside if you want. She can play until brunch is ready," he said to Christina.

"Let's go outside, Brooke," he said to her. "I'm sure there must be something interesting growing in the garden."

"Yay! I get to go outside." Brooke skipped out of the room, and Mark followed.

A moment of silence descended on the room once she was gone. Then Christina collapsed on the couch and leaned back. "Wow. I'm so sorry she brought up Amy. I'm sure it must be hard to hear about her. Brooke didn't really understand what she was saying."

"It's okay," Nina said. She hesitated for a moment. "Can I tell you a family secret, Christina? This needs to stay between us."

Christina straightened up on the couch and took a deep breath. "Of course, I'll keep whatever you have to say a secret. I don't usually go blabbing things to others."

Nina patted her hand. "I didn't mean to hurt your feelings, but this is kind of different and might be hard to understand. It involves Paul, and I think he should be the one to tell you. I'm just going to go talk to him for a minute."

She left the room to talk to Paul.

Abby sat there wondering what it was that Paul had to do with Brooke's pretend game of talking to Amy. Little kids always had imaginary friends, and Brooke just saw the picture and wanted to pretend she and Amy had talked. It really sounded as if Brooke wanted to be part of a family with a mother and father. The picture she had pointed at was a family picture of Sam, Paul, and Amy.

Nina came back into the room, with Paul and Hannah behind her. They were smiling, so obviously Paul wasn't upset by what Nina told them. Abby noticed Paul and Hannah were holding hands. Hannah must be a great support to Paul, based on his reaction.

Paul went directly over to Christina, and he and Hannah settled on the couch beside her. "I hope you're okay, Christina. That must have been a shock to hear Brooke mention a mom and dad."

"It was. You see, her parents divorced and neither wants her. They left her with me two years ago and haven't once been back to see her. They're just traveling and seeing the world and each doing their own thing. Neither one has barely asked about her at all. I hardly know where they are. Once in a while, one of them might call and that's it. I'm considering adopting her myself or seeing if there's a couple who would be interested in adopting her. When I heard her say she would have a new mom and dad…well…it almost seemed like someone else would be adopting her. But I know she couldn't have talked to Amy. It's all confusing."

"We'll get to Amy in a minute, but I do want to know if you really want to adopt Brooke. If you do, I think you should get it done and sealed before either of her parents change their mind. Obviously, they're not fit parents if they really don't want Brooke. She deserves better than that."

"I've put it off, thinking they'll be back." She looked down at her hands, twisting them in her lap. "I have to admit my daughter and son-in-law just don't care. That's hard, because Brooke is such a sweet little girl. I will move forward with adoption after the Fourth of July. You're right, I shouldn't put it off. Physically my arthritis is starting to act up, and I wish her to have two parents, but I don't know how to go about finding someone who would love her as much as I do. I should just go forward and adopt her. I know she wants a dad, but I guess that's something I can't give her."

Paul squeezed her hands and let go. "It might work out yet. You never know, but we'll leave that for a few days. Let's talk about what she said about Amy." He looked around the room. "It might be true that she talked to Amy."

Abby felt the room spin and then right itself. Her mom and dad didn't look surprised, she noticed. Christina looked puzzled.

"I saw Amy myself right after she died," Paul said. "I know it's hard to believe, but whenever I was in extreme distress, she would come and talk to me. Although I was shocked when she appeared, her presence was always a great source of comfort for me. I believe God sent her from Heaven to comfort me."

Abby had thought he was calm about sharing the information until she saw how tightly he was now holding Hannah's hand.

"I haven't seen her for quite a while. I guess she had someone else she needed to comfort. Brooke." He paused and looked at Christina. "I don't know if you'll believe me, but Amy probably did talk to Brooke. As far as what that means when she told her she'd have a new mommy and daddy, I don't know. I saw Amy several times after her death. Seeing her, and knowing she was okay, helped me get through these months since her and Samantha's deaths. I'm sure you'll need to think about what I've said, and what you believe, but that was my experience."

Paul looked at Abby. "I was going to tell you the other night when I was here, but we got sidetracked. You know now." Paul stood up and looked at Christina. "Let me know if you have questions, but as Nina said, I'd appreciate this conversation be kept confidential for obvious reasons. Other people probably won't understand."

"Brunch will be ready in about ten minutes. I'll let you finish your conversation, and then you can join us in the kitchen whenever you're ready," Paul said before returning to the kitchen.

There was silence when he was gone.

Finally, Christina broke the silence that had settled when Paul and Hannah left the room. "I don't know what to think."

Frank and Nina looked at each other and then both laughed. Nina said, "We don't either. Paul told us this summer what he experienced. We find it hard to believe, but whatever happened, it helped him. He'll never get over missing Amy, nor will we. But it helped him to know she seems okay, and she says she's in heaven. We believe that, so we just accept it. You do what you have to do, Christina. Just know Frank and I will help you however we can with Brooke. If you decide to adopt her officially, we'll definitely help you in whatever way we can."

Abby didn't know what to think. Paul really seemed to believe what he said, and he was normally very pragmatic. She couldn't believe he'd been having conversations with Amy. She was also stunned by the realization of what Brooke's parents had done. They'd just left their little girl. From what Christina said, they didn't seem to want Brooke. How could they not want that sweet little girl?

The rest of the visit proceeded with lots of laughter. Since Hannah and Paul had made the brunch, Mark and Abby cleaned up. Christina had taken Brooke home right after they finished eating, so she could have her nap. The rest of them played cards until late afternoon, and then Paul and Hannah went back to Bismarck.

CHAPTER 18

Abby waited impatiently for the evening meal to be over. She'd been thinking about Brooke and wanted to talk to Mark, but there was the meal to get ready and the outside chores to be done.

Sunday was generally quiet around the farm, but there were still chickens, cows, and calves to be fed. Mark had gone with her dad to take care of them, and she and her mom straightened out the house. They were going back to the Meyers' house tomorrow to help with whatever they could.

Finally, Abby suggested a walk with Mark so they could talk. Her parents were settled in front of the television and were quite happy to relax, she could tell.

Abby applied bug spray and handed the bottle to Mark as they stood on the porch of the house. "Let's stick to the road. Hopefully, there will be fewer bugs."

"Sounds good," Mark said, after he'd sprayed himself and followed her down the steps. "This might be a short walk, if they're as bad as I think they're going to be."

Abby agreed. She could hear the buzzing of insects as they walked down the driveway.

"I know what you're going to say," Mark said as they walked. "You want to talk about Brooke."

"You're right. How could her parents just dump her on Christina and not check on her? I don't understand how anyone can do that."

"Not everyone is cut out to be a parent."

Abby stopped short and stared at him. "Are you saying it's okay that they just abandoned her?"

He put up his hands to placate her. "No. That's not what I meant at all. I'm agreeing with you. They obviously don't want to be parents. They haven't grown up, and Christina's doing a marvelous job with Brooke. She's a sweet little girl."

Abby relaxed her shoulders. "She is, isn't she? That was nice of you to take her outside while we talked. Dad filled you in on what Paul said, didn't he?"

"Yes. He took me aside while the rest of you were busy."

"I kind of thought so, since you weren't surprised when I said Brooke's parents had abandoned her."

Abby couldn't hold back her eagerness any longer. "What if we adopted her, Mark? Her parents don't want her. Christina isn't sure she can take care of her by herself, though she will if there's no other good choice for Brooke."

Mark didn't say anything right away. She could tell he was thinking about it. "I just don't know, Abby. When we talked about adopting, we were thinking of a baby. I know we mentioned in passing an older child, but now that that might be a possibility, I see lots of problems."

Abby was disappointed that he wasn't as excited as her. "I just feel like it might be a sign, since we're here when Brooke said she saw Amy, and Amy mentioned Brooke getting a new mommy and daddy."

"Do you really believe she saw Amy?"

Abby shrugged. "I don't know. I don't think it matters."

"You love Amy. What do you mean, you don't think it matters?"

"I think what matters is what Brooke thinks. She believes she's going to get a new family. We could be that family."

"What about Brooke seeing her grandmother? We rarely see your parents. We'd be taking her back to Houston with us. She wouldn't get to see Christina very often.

Abby hadn't considered that. "We could move back to Chokecherry Valley," she said impulsively.

Mark swatted at a mosquito on his sleeve, and then reached toward Abby as they stood in the driveway. "As much as we need to talk about this, I don't think this is the place. There are too many bugs out here tonight." He brushed a fly off her arm. "We're going to get eaten alive. Let's wait until we get back inside."

"Do we keep this to ourselves or mention it to mom and dad?" she asked, disappointed that Mark hadn't immediately jumped on the idea of adopting Brooke. She realized that she had felt the urge to adopt Chloe only a few days ago. Maybe it was time to slow down and think instead of rushing forward.

"You can talk to them about us wanting to adopt, but I think we should tell them not to mention anything to Christina or Madison. I really don't want to talk with anyone else about it until we talk about it more ourselves and decide what we want to do."

"That's fine with me," Abby said. A little more time was just what they needed. Madison and Christina each needed to decide what they wanted to do.

Mark reached out and drew her to him in a hug. "I know what you want, honey. A bigger family. I do too. I just think we need to really think about this and do the right thing. We just found out this morning that Brooke might need a new family, although Christina will do a wonderful job alone. I'm not worried about Brooke. We just need to consider what would happen if we did decide to adopt. Is that the right thing for Brooke? And us? We need to think about it."

Abby snuggled up to him. He smelled of fabric softener and bug spray. "You're right. I need to curb my impatience and make the right decision for all of us."

"It's one of your lovable qualities. I love your enthusiasm."

She looked up at him, and he kissed her on the lips. "And I love you," she said.

"Ditto."

***

When they got back to their room later, Abby realized Mark hadn't said anything in response to her suggestion that they move back to Chokecherry Valley. She wasn't sure if he'd purposely avoided the topic or if the adoption discussion had taken precedence.

They were getting ready for bed, but Abby planned to read for a while, and Mark planned to look at work emails. Abby waited until Mark had closed the laptop and put it on the floor beside the bed. She'd sporadically flipped pages of her book, not actually reading a thing, while he'd read his emails. She placed the bookmark where she had stopped reading earlier and closed the book.

"How about a game of rummy?" Mark asked. "It's too early for bed."

Abby scooted up to sit straighter against the headboard. "I was going to talk to you about something."

Mark walked over and sat against the headboard next to her. "What about?"

She didn't blame him for the note of uncertainty in his voice. A lot had happened since she had come to Chokecherry Valley. Or a lot of things that had lain dormant had come to the surface. "It's about the comment I made earlier about moving to Chokecherry Valley."

Mark looked at her, his forehead crinkled in concentration. "I thought you just said that because you wanted to adopt Brooke. I didn't realize you were serious."

Abby looked down at her pajama bottoms and folded part of the material between her fingers before smoothing it out again. "I don't know about the moving to Chokecherry Valley part. I quit my job in Houston. It isn't the right place for me anymore."

"You quit? When?" he asked quietly.

She looked at him and could tell he was upset by his clenched hands. "The day before I left Houston."

"And you are just telling me now? We have a big problem, Abby, and a baby isn't going to fix that problem."

"What do you mean by that?" The sadness in his eyes tugged at her heart. He didn't seem angry. He seemed hurt, which she had expected when she first started keeping the secret.

"We don't talk anymore about things, and we need to do that. I don't care that you quit your job if you were unhappy with it. I care that we didn't discuss it either before you quit or right after."

Abby knew she should have said something sooner. "I agree we don't talk enough. I'm tired of shift work. I'd like to go to work and come home at basically the same time every day.

With you working on IT projects, there are some weeks that we rarely see each other. I don't want us turning into strangers."

Mark reached over and pulled her close to his side and kept his arm around her. She laid her head on his shoulder. "I don't want us turning into strangers either. We need to communicate with each other, though, or we won't have a marriage. Have you looked at other jobs yet?"

"No. We've been kind of busy, and I've just been thinking about it a lot. I guess I wanted to hear what you had to say before I started looking."

"Right." He laughed.

"What does that mean?" She looked up at him.

"It means as soon as you had a little energy back, you would have looked no matter what I said." He hugged her close. "Which you know would be all right with me."

She laughed too and snuggled back beside him. "You're right. I'm glad you agree, but I would have started looking for a different job. In Houston."

"In Houston. But now we're here in Chokecherry Valley, and we might adopt a child from here. And so, you're now thinking about maybe moving here?"

He said it as a question.

"Yes. If we were able to adopt either Madison's baby or Brooke, it would be hard to separate them from their loved ones. But it's also a huge step to move from Houston to Chokecherry Valley. I think I'd rather move to Bismarck if we move to North Dakota. It's a bigger place, and I wouldn't have any trouble finding a job. And if the adoption originated in Chokecherry Valley and we lived in Bismarck, we'd still be close enough for visits."

"No, you wouldn't have trouble finding work. I think we could move anywhere, and there would be a nursing job available."

"I think so too."

"I don't think we can make a decision about moving until the situation with Madison's baby or Brooke is sorted out. If we did adopt one of those children, we'd have to think seriously about what to do. Right now, it's just kind of a 'what if' scenario."

"I know." Abby was content that Mark hadn't seemed upset by the conversation. He hadn't said no right away, which was a good sign. "I think you could find a job or telecommute to Houston if you wanted."

"I agree. But of course, I haven't looked or thought about it until today." He laughed, looking down at her. "You keep my life interesting, Abby. I don't know what I'd do without you."

"Your life would be simpler," she replied.

"But boring. Very boring looking at the computer all day long."

"That's right."

He took her by the shoulders and looked into her eyes. "You need to tell me what's going on, Abby. Whether you want to adopt a child or get a different job, we need to communicate with each other. Agreed?"

"Agreed." She knew she needed to be more open with him. Samantha's death had caused her to close herself off, and she needed to get past that to keep her marriage strong.

CHAPTER 19

Monday passed quickly as the volunteers put the final touches on the Meyers' new farmhouse. Abby and Mark unloaded their SUV of the things they'd bought the previous week and made another trip to Bismarck for a few more necessities.

Tuesday morning, Abby woke up excited for the Fourth of July celebration. She always liked fireworks, but she was also looking forward to the picnic after the parade. A lot of her graduating class would attend the picnic, and she wanted to catch up with them.

There was also the additional excitement of seeing Madison and Chloe and finding out if Madison had made a final decision about adoption. She was sure Madison would have spoken to her mother by now about wanting to keep the baby, but there was still a chance she would give the baby up. Abby had wanted to quiz Jason when he came over for haying, but she'd left him alone. It wouldn't be fair to put him on the spot.

At the community Fourth of July picnic, Abby and Mark went through the food line. Her parents had already gotten their own food and joined some friends of theirs at a table.

Abby was trying to decide between potato salad and coleslaw when she realized Madison and Patricia were seated with Brooke and Christina, and there was room at their picnic table for Mark and her. She thrust her plate at Mark.

"Can you get me some potato salad and a hamburger with ketchup?" she asked. "I'm going to save us a seat over there." She pointed to the group she wanted to join.

Mark agreed, and she took off to join the others. "Hi," she greeted them all.

They looked up from their plates and smiled.

"Do you want to sit with us?" Christina asked.

"We'd love to. Mark's getting some food for me. He should be here soon." She gestured toward the food-laden tables.

"It's good," Madison said shyly.

"I see you're without Chloe today. Is she home with a babysitter?" Abby asked.

"Jason had some time off and wanted to watch her. He said he doesn't get enough time to spend with his niece since he's always working, and this would be a good opportunity. I felt funny leaving her, as I haven't done that before, but I keep my phone handy."

Abby noticed the pink-encased phone sitting on the table near Madison. "I'm sure Jason is a fine babysitter. I know he's a lot older than you because he was in school with my brother-in-law, who is twenty-nine."

"Yes, he is older and a good uncle," Patricia agreed. "We'll only be here for a short time and then be back home." She patted Madison on the back.

Abby knew she couldn't ask Madison her plans in front of everyone. She bit back a sigh and greeted Mark enthusiastically when he brought her plate of food and set it in front of her. "Thank you," she said.

He smiled and sat down beside her. "Hi. It's great to see all of you again," he said to the group as he scooped up some of the coleslaw on his plate.

They all greeted him, and there was happy silence as they all continued eating.

Brooke had been intently coloring during the greetings, but now she slid off the picnic table bench and brought her picture over to Abby. She held it up for inspection. "Look what I drew."

Abby put her fork down and took the picture from Brooke. "It's lovely. Do you want to tell me about it?"

Brooke shifted back and forth from one foot to the other as she pointed out different colors on the paper. "That's a tree, and some flowers, and that's grass."

"It's lovely," Abby told her, reaching to hand the picture back to Brooke.

"You can keep it," Brooke said. "I'll make another one for Grandma."

"Thank you." Abby was touched by the gesture. "I'll put this one up on my wall."

Brooke skipped back to her place at the table and started another picture.

Mark patted Abby on the shoulder. "She really likes you," he whispered.

Abby smiled at him. "I like her too."

They all had a pleasant conversation, and then Madison got up to leave. "I really need to get back to Chloe and give Jason some time to do whatever he wants."

Abby stood up. She felt this might be her chance to talk to Madison alone. "Do you mind if we talk for a minute?"

Madison looked at her mom.

Patricia smiled and waved with her hand. "I'll meet you at the pickup in a little bit."

Abby waited until they were in the parking lot before she said anything. When Madison stopped by a blue pickup, she looked at Abby. "Thank you for talking to me the other day when I was so upset. I really needed to talk, and you were so kind."

Abby smiled at her, though she was trembling inside with nerves. "You're welcome. Did you talk to your mom and make a decision?"

"I did talk to Mom. It really helped." Madison wore a big smile now. "I'm going to keep Chloe, and Mom said she would help. She was really supportive. She said we would make it work out somehow."

Abby hid her disappointment. She knew this could happen, but she still had hopes that maybe Chloe would be the baby for her and Mark. That wasn't possible any longer. "That's good, Madison. I'm glad it all worked out."

She heard someone approaching and looked to see Patricia coming their way. "There's your mom."

"Did you get to talk?" Patricia asked them.

"Yes," Abby said. "Thank you. If you have time, why don't you all come over to the house before I leave for Houston next Tuesday. Mom would love to chat with you," she said to Patricia.

“We’d enjoy that. With taking care of Chloe and trying to get the Meyer house completed, we haven’t had much down time to visit, but we’ll make time,” Patricia said.

“That sounds good. See you soon.” Abby stepped out of the way and stood in the parking lot after they’d driven away. Their decision had saddened her, and it made her realize that much more how deeply she wanted a baby of her own. She needed to have patience. She and Mark had just started looking, and they wouldn’t find a baby overnight. She went back to join the others and tried to enjoy the rest of the day with her family.

CHAPTER 20

That evening Abby and Mark sat on some folding chairs they had brought to the fireworks display. The fireworks were being set off in a clearing near the town, and the whole town had gathered around with chairs and blankets to sit on and watch the display. Abby's parents had joined them, and the four of them sat chatting and enjoying the warm night as they waited for the display to start.

Abby looked at the group of people around them and smiled. In the week she'd been back to Chokecherry Valley, she'd reconnected with old friends and made new ones. She felt lucky.

She snuggled her chair closer to Mark and took his hand. He patted it, and then held it firmly in his. She treasured the feeling of closeness. They had talked more and gotten closer during this trip, and she knew that would help their relationship long-term and when they found the right baby to adopt.

She noticed Christina and Brooke, and they were looking her way, so she waved at them. She caught a glimpse of a woman behind them and squeezed Mark's hand tightly.

"Look behind Christina and Brooke," she whispered.

He turned his head toward them and waved because they were still looking toward their direction.

"Behind them," Abby gasped. "That woman looks like Samantha."

Mark turned further and looked around. "I don't see anyone behind them that looks like her. I just see a bunch of teenage boys."

Abby stared at the area behind Christina and Brooke. She saw the boys too, but she also saw the woman. The woman was pointing at Brooke. And then she disappeared. Abby jumped up from her chair. She needed to find that woman. She hurried through the groups of people to Christina and Brooke and looked around, but the woman was gone. Her heart was beating fast, and she was near tears.

Mark was just behind her, and she turned around and fell into his arms. "It looked just like her. She was pointing at Brooke."

He held her close. "Do you want to stay and watch the fireworks, or should we leave?"

"I want to leave." She felt close to tears and didn't want to break down in front of everyone. She missed Samantha, even though they'd had their differences.

She felt a tug on her short pants and looked down to see Brooke standing there, grinning widely up at her.

"Hi," Brooke said. "We're waiting to watch the fireworks. Do you want to sit with me?"

Abby pulled herself together enough to answer. "We're already sitting over there with my parents." She pointed over to them. They were both staring at her and Mark, probably wondering why they had suddenly left.

Brooke patted her hand. "They can come over here too."

Abby smiled down at her and looked around. "There really isn't room here. There are already lots of people. We'll go back to our chairs and talk to you after the fireworks."

She and Mark and her parents had set their chairs a little further away at the edge of the crowd. Abby was glad for that now. She just wanted to sit down and have Mark hold her hand again.

Brooke had turned to talk to Christina, and soon she was back. "Grandma said we can sit over there with you since there's more room."

Abby looked at Mark, and he shrugged, leaving it up to her. Abby dredged up a smile. "Sure. We'll help you move your things."

Soon Christina and Brooke were settled beside Abby and Mark. Her parents accepted the change in company with a smile.

When the fireworks started, there were lots of oohing and aahing from the spectators. Brooke jumped up and down with excitement. The noise didn't seem to bother her, and she kept commenting on how high the fireworks shot into the sky.

Abby found herself enjoying the show in spite of her spinning thoughts. She knew there was no way Samantha had been in the crowd, but the woman had looked so much like her, and then she'd just disappeared. Abby shivered, and Mark noticed.

"Are you cold? Do we need to pull out a sweater?"

Abby looked at the others to make sure they weren't listening. Everyone was distracted by the fireworks. "No. I was just thinking about that woman."

"You know it couldn't be your sister, right?" Mark looked worried.

"I know. It was just so strange. And she pointed right at Brooke."

Brooke, hearing her name, looked up at them from her place on the blanket where she was now sitting. She'd worn herself out. "Will you be my mommy and daddy?" she asked.

Christina took Brooke's hand and frowned at her. "Honey. Why did you ask them that?"

Brooke pulled her hand away. "A lady told me tonight that I was getting a new mommy and daddy, and I like Abby and him." She looked shyly at Mark.

It was the first time Abby had seen her act shy since she met Brooke at the church that first morning.

Christina shrugged helplessly as an awkward silence fell on the group.

Mark broke the silence. "Let's talk about that tomorrow morning, okay." He leaned down and patted Brooke's hand. "It's late, and we all need to get some sleep."

Abby was glad for the respite. She needed to get away from all these people. She stood and folded her chair. "It looks like the fireworks are over. I'm tired."

They gathered their things and said goodnight. Abby saw Mark speak to Christina for a few minutes, but she didn't hear what he said. She was too tired and strung out to care. She just wanted to get back to her parents' house and calm down.

CHAPTER 21

Abby had showered and hurried into her pajamas. She now sat with her back against the headboard in their bedroom at her parents' house. Mark was taking his shower, and she was glad to be alone for a few minutes.

Had she seen her sister at the fireworks? Or had it just been her imagination? The picture was so vivid. And the woman had pointed right at Brooke. And then Brooke had asked her and Mark to be her parents. What did it mean?

Mark came out of the bathroom in his pajama bottoms and joined her. He leaned against the headboard and pulled her to him, and she relaxed against him.

"Quite a night," he said.

"That's for sure." She snuggled closer.

He took in a big breath and let it go. She looked up at him. "Are you feeling tense?"

He leaned down and kissed her forehead. "I have a confession to make."

She could feel him tense up again and sat up. She felt she was going to need to have this conversation face-to-face.

"I saw her," Mark said.

"Saw who?"

"The woman you saw. She looked just like Samantha. Just like you said. And I saw her point at Brooke." He dropped his gaze and then looked at her again. "I'm sorry I said I didn't see her. I was afraid."

"Afraid?"

"Remember when Brooke told us she spoke to a little girl, and that girl looked like Amy? And she said she was getting a new mommy and daddy. It was hard to believe. Kids have imaginary friends all the time. But then tonight…" He shrugged. "The woman was pointing at Brooke, and I knew what that meant, and I was afraid I couldn't do it."

Abby's stomach was flipping at what her husband was saying. He'd seen the woman too. She was beginning to think it really was her sister, Samantha. Samantha coming to her to let her know that Abby would be Brooke's new mother. She felt a moment of joy at the thought, but she and Mark had to sort this out. "Afraid you couldn't do what?"

"Raise a child. What if I'm not very good at it? Everything keeps pointing at Brooke being the child for us to adopt. I thought we'd adopt a baby and learn together. Brooke already has a grandmother, and a mother who doesn't want her. She's already learned so much, and we're coming into her life in the middle of things."

Abby reached out and hugged Mark. "She already loves us, Mark. That's the biggest hurdle. She wants a mom and dad, and she wants us."

She took his hand and squeezed it. "Do you want to adopt her? Don't say it just for me. Say if for yourself and for Brooke too. Only if you want to."

He smiled. A smile that took over his whole face. "I really want to adopt her. For me, and for you—and for her. I love her already. She's the sweetest little girl."

CHAPTER 22

September had come to Chokecherry Valley, and it was a warm fall day. Leaves were starting to turn bright yellow and red and orange.

Abby and Mark had moved to Bismarck in August, but today was a special day. They were at Frank and Nina's house spreading balloons throughout the living room. Abby had baked a chocolate cake with chocolate frosting because that was what Brooke had requested. There was only one candle on the cake, and writing that said, "Welcome Home." Beside the cake, a glass unicorn from Abby's parents and a stuffed elephant from Mark and Abby sat on the table with two cards. Abby was getting nervous.

"I hope she likes it," Abby said to her mom.

Her mom gave her a big hug. "She loves you and Mark. I bet she doesn't stop talking from the moment she runs in the front door."

Mark and Frank joined them in the kitchen.

"We're ready," Mark gave Abby a big grin. He had come to terms with adopting Brooke and his fear of not being a perfect dad. Love was all that mattered.

The four of them looked at each other as they heard the sound of an engine coming up the driveway. Christina and Brooke had arrived.

"Show time," Frank said.

They all laughed nervously as they went to the front door to greet their new family.

Abby opened the door, and Brooke came running in. She headed straight for Mark. "Are you my new daddy?" she asked.

He picked her up in his arms and smiled at her. "Today's the day. The paperwork is official. I'm your dad."

He reached out his hand to Abby and drew her into the circle of his embrace. "And Abby is your new mom."

Brooke leaned toward Abby and put her little hands on Abby's cheeks. "I love you, Mommy," she said.

"I love you too, Brooke," Abby choked out her response and held back her happy tears as she kissed Brooke on the cheek. She had a child and a husband and a new job in Bismarck.

In the background, unseen by the others in the room, stood Samantha. Happy tears streamed down her face as she watched her twin sister get the child she had always wanted. Samantha knew that Abby had been jealous of her pregnancy and Amy's birth, yet had also been heartbroken at their deaths.

The addition of Brooke to Abby's family would help heal the wound of being unable to have her own children. And Abby and Mark would help heal Brooke's wound of being abandoned. Brooke would bring so much love to their family, all with God's blessing.

~ ~ ~

CHOKECHERRY VALLEY LOVE
LOVE
Book 3

ACKNOWLEDGMENTS

Special thanks to the excellent editor, Krista Venero at Mountains Wanted Publishing & Indie Author Services for great suggestions. She helped create a better book than I could have envisioned on my own.

Thank you to the book cover artist at Sunset Rose Books for an amazing cover.

Considerable thanks to my family who have encouraged me in my writing journey.

Thank you to Sally, Ruth, and Amy, great friends who are also great at running book ideas and cover designs past. I couldn't have finished this book without your help.

Special thanks to Connie Victoria Volk for helping by editing and making suggestions for a stronger book. She writes her own books. www.connievolk.com

CHAPTER 1

Wednesday Ashley hurried into the almost full classroom and her heart started beating even faster in her ears. She should have taken Oral Communications when she was a freshman, but she'd put it off because she hated to speak in front of others.

In addition to her fear of speaking, she preferred getting to class early to choose a desk in the back of the room. Today, she'd been delayed after her previous class by a classmate who wanted to talk, and she had a hard time getting away from her heartbreaking story. Ashley's choices came down to a desk in the center of one row in the middle of the room or the desk in the front row next to a guy whose feet splayed way out in front of him. He was tall, or else the slumped posture made him seem that way. He appeared to be sleeping.

Oh, well. She sat next to him as the noise level around her continued at a steady rhythm of books slapping on desks, along with laughter and voices. At least the sleeper wouldn't be snickering with friends or looking at his phone during the upcoming lecture. She pulled out her notebook and hung her backpack on her chair.

A minute later, the instructor walked into the room and stood behind the podium. She'd never had Dr. Williams as a teacher, but she'd heard he ran a strict but fair class. The sudden decrease in noise level showed most of the students had listened to the stories from prior students.

Dr. Williams looked at the sleeping guy next to her. She didn't know what possessed her, but she reached out and jabbed him in the arm with her finger.

He startled awake and looked around. Then, with a sheepish grin, he sat up straight and eyed the teacher. "Sorry." His voice came out gravelly and deep.

Ashley found herself intrigued by his immediate way of taking responsibility and she might turn out to like the guy. His

228

dark hair emphasized his brown eyes, and they looked clear, if dazed. They weren't red, which meant he probably wasn't sleeping off a late night due to drinking.

She noticed his age because he was an older student like herself. At twenty-seven, she was one of the oldest students in most of the classes she took. In addition, freshmen usually took Oral Communications to get it over with, which especially highlighted the difference in age between her and the other students in this class. Her advisor for her psychology undergraduate degree had pointed out the class each semester they met to go over her schedule.

Dr. Williams looked at her and asked, "Do you know him?"

"No," she murmured.

"Well, if he drifts off again, you have my permission to poke him." He nodded at her and then the guy. He pulled a stack of papers out of his briefcase. He handed the stack to the girl at the end of the front row. "Please pass these around."

As the papers were being handed down the row, Dr. Williams said, "You'll need the first book for the four speeches you'll give in the class. Below that, you'll find the suggested reading for additional help with any of the speeches. I don't care how you get the book. Beg, borrow, but don't steal."

Ashley began to like Dr. William's sly humor.

"Seriously," he continued, "if you can't find a copy of any of this information, please let me know. I want everyone to have a fair chance at passing this class. Please write your name and your email on a sheet of paper and leave it on my desk on your way out. I usually don't bring paper to class. I send everything by email."

After that, she missed most of the following lecture on the different speeches, and it turned out to be the longest thirty minutes Ashley spent in a long time. The harder she tried to pay attention to the instructor, the more she wanted to talk to the guy next to her and find out his story.

When Dr. Williams dismissed class, she grabbed her notebook and backpack and quickly slid from her desk to hurry out of the room. She didn't realize the guy who sat next to her was following her until he said, "Hey, wait."

She glanced behind her and met his gaze. For a second, she stopped, stunned by the brown of his eyes, and then forced herself to continue out the door. "Sorry, we can't hold up traffic here."

When she got into the hallway, she moved along the corridor away from the door. "I don't have much time," she said. "I have an appointment."

"I wanted to thank you. Dr. Williams found my nap amusing, but I don't imagine he would have if you hadn't done the finger jab to my shoulder." He smiled at her.

She found his grin as fascinating as his brown eyes. She couldn't believe how attracted she was to him, and she didn't even know his name—which she should find out, and then get going. "He did seem amused. I do have to get to an appointment. Maybe we can talk more before class on Friday. Would that work for you?"

"Sounds great. I'm Jason."

"Hi, Jason. I'm Ashley. See you Friday. I have to run." She forced herself to turn away from him and hurried down the hallway to the outside door. She was going to be late if she didn't run when she got outside.

***

The cool fall afternoon felt good after the heated classroom. Early September could be any temperature between freezing and a hundred degrees. Today was in the low sixties. No need for a jacket if she didn't linger too long, and if she stood in the sun, the temperature was perfect. She loved the sixties and low seventies, and September and October were her favorite months.

Ashley met with her class advisor, who kept her fully engaged. They discussed her forty-hour clinical observation at St. Gertrude's Medical Center, where she'd observe in the Social Work Department and then the Mental Health Unit every afternoon starting at 1:00 p.m. Because she could only get in four hours a day, the time at St. Gertrude's Medical Center would actually take two weeks instead of one week. Her oldest brother, Paul, worked as a physician there, and she wondered if she'd run into him at work.

The hours were meant to give undergraduate students a chance to observe those experiencing psychological issues, so she could decide what area she wanted to specialize in after graduation. She knew she needed to get a master's degree, and there were other educational requirements if she continued on the path to becoming a psychologist. She tried not to think of the long road ahead to get her Ph.D. She'd already signed up for the master's program, so she could sign up for classes next semester if she continued.

She didn't have time to consider anything else until she was back outside in the sunshine. As she walked toward her car to go home for a quick lunch before work, she smiled.

She'd see Jason again Friday morning, but they weren't going to have much time to talk before class. She had her Special Topics in Psychology class right before Oral Communications and didn't have much time to get from one classroom to the other. She already regretted taking the Special Topics class. She didn't need the two credits. She'd signed up because the topic was sibling relationships, and her relationships with her brothers needed help.

She got home and prepared a lunch of chicken and carrot sticks before texting Jill. She and Jill could talk about it, and she'd get a clearer idea if she should drop the class or continue as planned. She didn't want to wait until her roommate got home for the evening.

"Met an interesting guy," she texted. She sat on the couch in her living room, her plate in her lap. If Jill was free at all, she'd respond to Ashley's provocative text.

Sure enough, as Ashley finished her meal, her cell rang.

"Where? Who?" Jill demanded.

Ashley laughed. "I figured you'd be calling."

"I need all the information, which can't be done by texting, now can it, girlfriend?" Jill asked.

"Well, it would be a rather lengthy text."

"Spill it. I'm eating lunch as we speak, and I only have a half hour."

"I went to the Oral Communications class. Still dreading it, by the way. I got there at the last minute because I was talking to someone, and time got away from me."

Jill laughed. "Why does that always happen to you? No, don't answer. Go on with the story."

"There were two desks left. One in the middle of the class where I would have to crawl over everyone, or one in the front row by this guy who was asleep."

"You took the one by the sleeping guy, I take it."

"Who's telling this story?" Ashley asked, but she smiled.

"You. Too slow. Time's passing."

"Then let me finish so you can go back to work, and I can get to my job. Anyway, the teacher came in and looked at the guy, and I got this sudden urge to wake him up, so maybe he'd avoid the wrath of the instructor. I poked him in the arm, and he jerked awake and looked around. Dr. Williams, the instructor, found it humorous and assured me, if Jason fell asleep again, I could repeat the jab."

"You know his name?" Jill asked.

Of course Jill would notice that piece of information. "We had a brief conversation in the hallway after class and exchanged names. I had to get to an appointment with my advisor."

"Is Jason cute?"

"Yeah, kind of. I mean he's not gorgeous or anything, but he is attractive. He's an older student too. I have reservations. Why was he sleeping? I hope it wasn't because of a hangover. You know I couldn't deal with that," Ashley said.

"Yeah. Because of your brother, but he's sober now, isn't he?" Jill asked.

"I think so." Her mind wandered to her brothers, whom she missed.

"Ashley? Are you there?" Jill asked.

"Sorry. I was remembering. I better let you go. I do need to talk to you about my brothers and that class, but your lunchtime is probably up by now. Thanks for listening."

"What are you going to do?"

Ashley laughed. "What do you think? I'm going to stay in the class, and we'll see what happens with everything. Jason will be my incentive since my class with him is right after the sibling class. We'll talk more when you get home this evening and have time."

"Good for you. I've heard Paul has a new girlfriend. Hannah works in fundraising at the hospital. She's probably a softening influence. It'll all work out. See you after work."

Hopefully Jill was right about Paul's attitude change, and time had softened his demeanor. Ashley hung up and looked around the room. Life was going to be interesting in the next few months.

Her brother, Alex, would be getting out of prison soon. The past would be raked up, and her sister-in-law could use support. Ashley always liked Courtney, but Courtney told her the best thing to do was stay away from them and not be tainted by Alex's actions.

Ashley shouldn't have listened to their advice, even if Courtney and Alex wanted her to stay far away. Because of it, she'd missed spending time with both of them since Alex went to prison for embezzlement. She regretted the missed time, as she could never get it back. She had to remind herself she was two years older now and knew more about life in general than she had back then.

CHAPTER 2

Jason got home in time for lunch. He walked into the kitchen and looked over his mother's shoulder as she stood holding a spoon over a pot. Chicken and dumplings. His favorite. He gave her a quick hug. "Looks good, Mom."

She patted his arm with her free hand. "Thanks."

"I'm going to change out of these school duds and into my farm clothes. Then I can help you with anything you need." He headed upstairs to his room, whistling tunelessly. He thought of Ashley. She was cute with her short curly dark hair. He'd been surprised when she woke him in class.

He'd never fallen asleep in class before, but they pushed hard on the farm to get harvest done, and he hadn't gotten a lot of sleep lately. It wouldn't happen again because he realized thinking of Ashley gave him energy. Sitting next to her would be the jolt he needed to keep awake during class.

He bounded down the stairs and into the kitchen. "What can I do?" he asked his mom.

She put a potholder in the center of the table, which was already set with dishes and silverware. "You can set the pot from the stove right here. I'll get the salad and dressing out of the fridge."

His sister, Madison, joined them in the kitchen. She carried Chloe, Jason's niece, who sucked on a pacifier. After he set the pan on the potholder on the table, he gently rubbed the side of Chloe's cheek. He saw the smile behind the pacifier. She lifted her arms to him, and he took her from Madison.

"Thanks," Madison said. "She's only a few months old, but it feels like she's gained a ton since her birth. I already fed her, so here." She handed Jason a towel for his shoulder. "She's been spitting up when she burps, so good luck."

He smiled at Chloe. "You wouldn't spit up all over your uncle, would you?"

He sat down at the table and shifted Chloe to one arm. His mom and Madison joined him. They said the blessing and started passing food back and forth. "Dad out in the field yet?" he asked.

"Yes. When you're done eating, he said he'd come in and eat."

"Sounds good. I appreciate he's letting me take this class. I have to take one class on campus every semester. I wish it wasn't right in the middle of the morning. At least the online classes are on my own time."

His mother waved her hand as if it were a magic wand. "You've put in so many hours helping here on the farm. Long past the time we expected to have help, so don't worry about it. You deserve to get your degree and move on with your life."

Jason didn't know why, but it made him feel guilty. When he finished his degree, he'd be leaving the farm instead of taking it over and letting his father retire. Maybe not right away, but eventually, depending on job possibilities. His parents supported whatever path he chose. Until now, he hadn't known what he wanted to do. Right now, they were all concentrating on Madison and little Chloe. He would do his part on the farm, plus help their neighbor Frank as much as possible. Then maybe when he got his associate degree, he'd be able to start his own business and take some electrician classes.

"You look far away. Did something happen in class?" Madison asked him.

Of course she would notice. He smiled. "Now don't get upset, Mom. Everything is okay. The teacher found it amusing."

His mom's hand, holding a forkful of chicken, paused on its way to her mouth before she continued the motion and went back to eating. "I'm sure it's fine if you say so."

He caught the doubt in her voice. "Don't worry. I fell asleep before class, and my classmate poked me awake in time for the lecture. Like I said, the teacher thought her jabbing me was funny."

Madison's eyes lit up. "Was the girl cute?"

Jason's face flushed, but he had a dark tan from working outside over the summer, so he hoped she didn't notice. "She was okay."

His sister stared at him and smiled as if she knew a secret. "Okay."

That was all she said but he knew she'd caught on that he found Ashley attractive.

His mother wasn't quite ready to drop the subject. "Are you sure the teacher was okay with it?"

"He's fine. Don't worry, Mom. It's not going to happen again."

She frowned. "You're trying to do too much. I knew it when you said you wanted to go to school. We should hire someone to help around the farm."

He mentally kicked himself for bringing up the story. It wasn't a disaster. "Mom, everything's fine. Harvest will be done tomorrow, and that's always a busy time. I won't be falling asleep again."

He got up and kissed the top of her head. "Don't worry. All's well. I need to get out to the field."

Madison got up to take Chloe from him.

"You finish lunch." Jason pointed Madison back to the table. "I'll lay her down on her blanket on the floor. She'll be fine for a few more minutes. I'll keep checking on her until I leave."

He spread Chloe's blanket and a few toys on the living room floor and laid a contented Chloe in the middle of it.

He started gathering what he needed to take to the field, checking on her every few minutes. She fought against sleep, and he smiled. Her lids would fall, and she forced them open.

He was ready after pulling out two bottles of water and a cola from the fridge. "She's all yours. She looks like she'll be asleep in a few minutes."

Madison scooped up the last of the food on her plate. "I should change her quickly then and let her sleep." She took her dishes to the sink. "I'll do dishes, Mom. Let me get Chloe settled first."

"Thanks, dear."

"See you later, Jason," Madison called from where she sat on the floor changing the baby.

He waved on his way out.

CHAPTER 3

Ashley spent the rest of the day interning at the mental health unit at St. Gertrude's Medical Center, so she had no time for thoughts of Jason or her brothers intruding at odd moments. During her first week at work, she concentrated on learning the rules and regulations of the hospital.

By the end of the day, she slouched on the couch after eating dinner. Her roommate, Jill, hadn't come home yet from her nursing job, so Ashley enjoyed the peace of having the place to herself. She liked these free moments in the evening. She got to relax for a short time before she started studying.

She searched the internet for the books she needed on sibling relationships and for her speech class on Friday and ordered them in both digital and paperback formats. She ordered the extra books too but just in digital format.

Thank goodness the Special Topics class only met for an hour on Monday and Friday. Oral Communications met Monday, Wednesday, and Friday. That might give her a chance to talk to Jason on Wednesday.

She looked at the first type of speech she needed to give. Informative. They had to give two informative speeches and two persuasive speeches total. There were also other types of speeches, although they didn't have to do anything vocal for them, just study them for exams.

Jill arrived home just as Ashley was going to open the digital book on speeches. She was happy to be interrupted.

"What are you reading?" Jill asked as she stepped out of her slip-on shoes. She left them in the entryway and padded into the kitchen.

The open floor plan gave Ashley a good look at Jill's frowning face as she pulled a spoon out of the drawer.

"I was just opening a book about speeches. Did something bad happen at work?" Ashley asked her.

"Just tired." Jill reached into the fridge and pulled out a yogurt. She closed the door. "It was a long shift. Short of other nurses to help, as usual. I wish we had a full staff."

"Do you want to sit and watch a movie or something?"

"I want to talk more about your classes and Jason." Jill took a seat on the recliner and lifted the footrest.

Ashley sprawled out on the couch across from her and set her tablet on the floor by the couch. "If it'll take your mind off work, I'm happy to discuss classes. I'm so conflicted about this semester. I can't believe I'm going to graduate in December with my bachelor's degree in psychology. I wanted to be a psychologist, but now I don't know. Maybe that's not what I want to do."

Jill stopped spooning up yogurt and stared at Ashley. "You what? After four years of studying, you're changing your mind? Didn't you have any idea before now that you were on the wrong track?"

Ashley sat up. "You believe I'm on the wrong track?"

"No. I was repeating what you said." She started eating again.

"I've still got a lot of school to go, and clinicals, and certification exams. And on and on. It suddenly doesn't feel like the right thing anymore." Ashley didn't know how to explain the uncertainty that she'd been feeling since summer. She knew she was going to at least get her bachelor's degree. After that—she didn't know.

"Are you just feeling overwhelmed? If you were done in December and could practice as a psychologist, would you feel the same way? Is it all the work needed yet?" Jill asked.

"No. I don't know why, but I've changed and don't think it's for me." She'd been lost for an answer for a while now.

"You must have gone into the program for some reason. Why did you want to become a psychologist in the first place?"

"I wanted to help people with dyslexia. I had a friend who got help with some of the newer treatments and ways of reading with dyslexia, and she was so excited. I guess I wanted to help people like her have a better life. I didn't want to specialize."

"Speech therapists and teachers can help once there's a diagnosis. Do either of those sound like something you want to do?" Jill asked.

"No."

They sat there silently for a while.

Jill finished her yogurt and set the container on the coffee table between them. "What does this Jason look like?"

Ashley smiled at her. "I wondered how long it would take you to get to that subject."

"Well, the future discussion isn't moving along, so I thought I'd see about this guy."

"He's got dark hair and brown eyes. He has a wonderful smile." She felt her own smile growing. "His name is all I know because we didn't have time to get better acquainted before I had to meet with my advisor."

"And you're going to see him in class for the whole semester. He might be a good resource to help you get over your fear of speaking."

Ashley blushed and cringed. She hadn't even considered that. "I can't give a speech in front of him. Oh, no. What am I going to do? I can't quit the class. It's required to graduate."

Jill laughed gently. "If he likes you, you can practice speeches together. It will help to have a friend in the classroom when you give the speech," she encouraged.

"I'd rather make a fool of myself in front of a bunch of strangers."

"Me too. People I won't ever see again. Anyway, what about your other class that discusses sibling relationships? Are you staying in that class?"

"Yes. I signed up because I want to figure out how to mend fences with my brothers. It's been two years since I talked to either one of them. We need to reunite. Now that Paul is alone since his wife and child died, he would probably like to get together again, even if he is dating. I'm hoping he wants to get together again. And Alex gets out of prison the first of December."

She didn't like the estrangement. The situation with both of them felt so complicated. Jason was interesting, and if she wanted a relationship with any guy, she needed to address her abandonment issues brought on by interactions she'd had with her parents and siblings. It had been a long time since she found a guy attractive.

"I want to drop the sibling class, but I'm hoping there will be information I learn to help my relationships with Paul and Alex."

Jill was quiet for a minute, and then she said softly, "You deliberately signed up because of the subject matter. That's a sign that you're on the right track, and it's time, Ashley. Maybe God wants you to try and mend your relationships with them."

"Maybe. There's a lot to forgive."

"There always is. Life isn't perfect. People aren't perfect. Maybe consider it?" Jill suggested.

"I'm thinking. Believe me, I'm thinking," Ashley said.

"Good. You saw Paul from a distance at the funeral. You made the first move."

"You're right. It was hard to attend, but he'd just lost his wife and daughter in a car accident. I needed to go no matter how difficult our relationship is. He smiled at me, like he was glad to see me. He didn't approach me. He left that up to me."

"He probably appreciated that you went to the funeral," Jill said.

"Probably." Ashley remembered the sweet smile on his face when he'd seen her. And deep down, she knew she missed him. She wanted Paul and Alex back in her life. They had great times growing up. And then life happened. She also missed Alex's wife, Courtney. If nothing else, she should have stood by her and helped her through the last few years. She felt guilty about not being there for her, even though that had been Courtney and Alex's choice, not hers.

Jill yawned and got up. She picked up her yogurt container. "I'm going to read in bed for a while."

"You'll probably fall asleep before you get a page read."

"Probably." She went into the kitchen and threw away the container. Before she started walking down the hallway to the bedroom, she stopped at the foot of the couch. "If you want to talk more about the future and school, let me know. Just think about what you want to do, and what you like to do. You'll come up with your answer."

Ashley looked down at her hands twisting in her lap. She'd been thinking about it for months and hadn't come up with an idea. She had four months to arrive at an answer. Sooner would be better. She yelled toward where Jill had disappeared down the hallway, "And, by the way, I know you. Something happened at work. When you're ready, I'm here to listen to you too."

***

Friday, she woke up half nervous and half excited to see Jason again. First she had to get through her Special Topics in Psychology class on sibling relationships.

Dr. Athena moved to the center of the room. "I see we lost a few classmates from last time. I'm assuming the rest of you are here because the subject is of interest to you, or you couldn't find another class to replace this one." Her eyes twinkled.

Ashley wanted to stand up and say, "Not me. I want to know everything about siblings."

"You had the assignment on Wednesday and a chance to get the books needed for the class. I'm sure there are a few of you who have read the readings, and a few of you who haven't."

The class laughed.

"Just a reminder that we will only be meeting on Fridays and Mondays from now on. When we met on Wednesday, it was to replace the day before Thanksgiving. For today's class, you'll be given a reprieve if you haven't read the assignment but don't expect a repeat. I'm guessing there may be a few in the class who don't have any siblings. Please raise your hand if you don't have any?"

Four people raised their hands.

"Thank you. You can lower your hands. I assume the rest of the class has siblings. I believe you'll find, even if you didn't grow up with siblings, parts of this class may pertain to your other relationships, such as friendships. Especially if you have a

242

large group of friends. If that's not the case, don't worry. You won't be graded on how applicable the subject of siblings is to your life.

"I'll be assigning four papers for you to write. Your grade will be based on those papers. Today's topic is birth order and how that affects our choices in life. I gave you the first chapter to read for class today. Who wants to volunteer where they are in birth order in their family and how it has affected you?" Dr. Athena asked.

There was a pause, and then a young woman raised her hand. She looked to be about twenty, and Ashley was impressed by the number of piercings in her nose. "I'm in the middle of a family of six. I'm the peacemaker. Sometimes I hate that position. I feel like I get lost in the middle of everything. My parents love us all, but I'm not the oldest, and I'm not the youngest, and they seem to get the most attention." She suddenly flushed red.

Then she lifted her head proudly. "I guess that shows how jealous I am of them at times, but I usually get along with them."

"Thank you for sharing your experience," Dr. Athena said. "That is a common phenomenon in families. There's usually a favorite or two in a large family. Parents are people, which we forget. They have their own personalities and mesh better with some of their children. That doesn't mean they don't love us. It means their relationship may be smoother and appear to have less angst with it."

A young guy in a blue hoodie and jeans raised his hand. His dark hair had enough curls in it to make it a little ruffled. His brown eyes were serious. "I'm the oldest in a family with three children. Do I think I'm my parents' favorite? Well, my mother's favorite. Not so much my dad's. We don't agree with each other on a lot of things, but my mother would probably do anything for me.

"It makes me feel guilty. Like I don't deserve her love. I mean, I make mistakes, but instead of telling her something she should know, I feel like I have to hide it, or she won't love me anymore. She's blinded by love sometimes, but my dad can see when I've done something wrong. He probably can read my emotions better because he doesn't love me like my mom does."

He paused. "I guess that didn't come out right. My dad loves me, just not with the closed-eye love like Mom."

Dr. Athena nodded. "That's another complication in sibling relationships and in parent-child relationships. Gender plays a part too. Birth order doesn't always affect the way a family operates. A child can connect with a parent because of habits or hobbies in common. A lack of things in common doesn't doom a relationship, however. In fact, it doesn't matter if a parent and child have anything in common or not. It's more dependent on if they accept their differences, but realize they're in the same family, and that's enough."

"One thing I want to emphasize while we're discussing this subject. Because someone doesn't fit into the general mold we're discussing doesn't mean there's anything wrong with them. We're all different. Even if ten of you are from a family of three, there will be all manner of differences in how your family may look. Please remember, we're generalizing here, so don't go home and feel like something's wrong with you because your situation is different. Different makes the world go around. What if we were all alike? How boring for us all.

"Thank you all for participating. You have the assignment for next Monday. Also, a reminder about Monday for those of you who haven't read the syllabus. Bring paper and a pen or pencil on Monday. You'll be writing a short essay during class. I will be bringing a paper shredder in case you decide you don't want to take the paper with you and want it destroyed. I know. Old-school.

"Class dismissed."

***

Ashley made it to her next class about five minutes early, as the class right before hers ended. She saw Jason standing in the hallway along with a few other early arrivals. She went over to him. He looked cute in his worn jeans and short-sleeved black t-shirt.

244

"Hi," he said. "I'm awake this time."

She laughed. "It's hard to take a nap in the hallway, especially when another class is charging out of the classroom."

By that time, the classroom had emptied. They followed the other students who had been standing in the hallway into the room. Jason sat in the same seat he had on Wednesday. Ashley sat next to him again.

He pulled his notebook and the speech book out of his backpack, and then turned to her. "First, thanks for getting me out of trouble last class. I can't believe I fell asleep."

"Oh, it was nothing. A spur-of-the-moment impulse on my part. Dr. Williams focused on you. Before I knew it, my finger flew out, and you were awake."

"All by itself?" He smiled.

"All by itself." She returned his smile. He had a nice one. "How come you were asleep anyway? You don't look like the partying type."

He took a deep breath and let it out. "I'm not. I work on a farm, and we were working long hours to get the harvest in. When I finally sat down, I guess I drifted off."

"You look more rested today." She cringed when she said it. "Sorry. That came out wrong."

He laughed. "I know what you mean. We're finished with getting the grain out of the field. Now it's a matter of repairs and catching up on everything else. At least we don't have to worry about the weather anymore. We can move slower and get more rest."

"It must be hard to run a farm and go to school. You said 'we.' Who does that include?"

"My father and me. We have a small farm, and we help our neighbor, Frank. He's got fewer acres. I think he's getting ready to retire."

"Do you have any siblings?" Ashley asked as Dr. Williams came into the classroom.

"One younger sister. You?"

"Two brothers." She was relieved that class was about to start because she didn't have time to discuss her brothers right now. "Looks like Dr. Williams is about ready."

"Do you want to meet for coffee sometime?" Jason asked.

"I'd like that." Her heart beat a little faster at the idea of getting to know him better.

He handed her a piece of paper. "Here's my phone number. Text if you want to set something up. I guess we better pay attention to the instructor now." He flashed her another smile and then faced forward.

Ashley tucked the piece of paper with the number into her jeans pocket. The ten minutes before class had passed quickly.

Next up, Dr. Williams. She was nervous during the class as she anticipated seeing Jason again sometime for coffee and having to give a speech.

She wasn't sure what he meant by writing his phone number down before they'd even gotten into the classroom. Did women fall all over themselves for him all the time? She'd find out more when they had coffee.

Ashley looked at her watch. 10:50 a.m. The time had passed quickly. She didn't realize they were there for the full class. She assumed Dr. Williams dismissed them early. She'd even managed to ignore Jason part of the time.

He gathered up his things. "Well, I'm done with classes for the day. How about you?"

"I have to work at one o'clock, but I'm free until then."

"Want to get an early lunch?" He stood there with his backpack over his shoulder and his arms crossed, as if waiting for a rejection.

Wow. Her heartbeat fluttered crazily. They were having lunch with their coffee now? Jason had surprised her, but it only took her a moment to respond. "Sounds good. I have to eat before work anyway. Did you have a specific place in mind?"

He dropped his arms to his sides and smiled. "There's a burger place a few blocks away. They have salads too, if you prefer."

"Sure. It's nice outside. It was somewhere around sixty-eight degrees right before class started. Do you want to walk?"

"Sure." She gathered her folder and notebook and stuck them in her backpack where her tablet and purse already resided.

They headed out of the building, into the sunshine. Suddenly Ashley couldn't think of a thing to say, and either Jason had the same problem or didn't feel the need for conversation.

She looked at him out of the corner of her eye. He smiled as he walked and didn't seem concerned about the silence. "What did you think of class today?" she asked.

He looked over at her. "It's interesting, isn't it? I have to admit, I'm nervous about speaking in front of everyone."

She was surprised and relieved. She wasn't the only person scared to get up in front of everyone. "I would never have guessed that. You come across as very self-assured and calm. No one would know you aren't. Unfortunately, I turn beet red, and there's no hiding the fact that I'm scared stiff."

"Would you like to get together and practice our speeches with each other?" he asked.

"That sounds like a good idea. I can have you and Jill critique them for me."

"Who is Jill?"

"My friend and roommate. We've known each other since I moved to Bismarck." She didn't have time to get into the complicated situation with her youth, so she changed the subject. Since family was on her mind, she'd ask about his. "Tell me about your sister."

"We get along great. She's a lot younger than me. I'm twenty-nine, and she's turning eighteen soon. I got to be her babysitter when Mom and Dad had things to do, which happened often when she was a baby. I was twelve when she was born."

"Wow. That's a big difference. I have two older brothers, Alex and Paul." She quickly changed the subject back to him. "What was it like living on a farm?"

"I did chores around the farm. Of course, Dad and Mom did any driving when it came to fieldwork. I was about fourteen when they let me run the tractor around the field for simple things."

"That sounds young." Ashley pictured a fourteen-year-old Jason, listening to music as he circled a field in a tractor. She didn't have much experience with farm life. She'd lived in Chokecherry Valley off and on, but their house was on the edge of town, and she hadn't had any friends. Her parents weren't farmers. They had family money. She'd spent most of her high school years in Bismarck, staying with her grandmother while her parents jetted around the world. "Where is the farm located?"

"The farm is just outside Chokecherry Valley. I live with my parents and my sister, Madison, and her daughter, Chloe. It's busy out there. Do you know where Chokecherry Valley is?"

"Yes. I grew up there until I turned thirteen. Maybe you know my brothers. They went to high school around there, but I stayed in Bismarck with my grandmother. Paul and Alex Richmond?" Ashley remembered the few times she'd been out to visit Paul's in-laws who lived outside of town by Chokecherry Valley. "My brother Paul's parents-in-law live on a farm out in Chokecherry Valley too. Frank and Nina."

"Oh, they're our neighbors. Your brothers are Paul and Alex? I know you mentioned them, but I didn't put it together," Jason said. "I know Paul, mostly from the summer planting season this year when he helped Frank and Nina. They're our next-door neighbors in the country. I know Alex too, as he was a year younger than me at school. And, of course, I saw him around town, until—"

"Until Alex went to jail." She knew the moment he said he was from Chokecherry Valley that he would know what happened with her brother. It was a small town. Ashley knew Paul stayed close to Frank and Nina's farm when he'd worked there over the spring and summer. She hadn't realized Jason's family were their neighbors.

"Right. We don't need to talk about Alex right now," he said easily, as if he were dismissing the weather as a subject. "It helped having Paul there during the spring planting season this year. There's a lot to do, and my parents and Nina and Frank aren't getting any younger. I work for Frank when Paul isn't there."

"That must keep you busy."

"Yes, it does." He stopped in front of the burger place. "Here we are. Are you hungry?"

"Very hungry. I only ate a banana for breakfast. I was in a hurry." She didn't tell him she always rushed around in the mornings. She dragged herself out of bed, and then always ran out of time before she needed to leave the house.

They seated themselves at a small booth in the red-and-white-checked deco restaurant. Ashley didn't even scan the menu, leaving it where the server placed it. She knew what she wanted. She noticed Jason didn't look either.

"Do you know what you want?" Ashley asked him.

He nodded. "I come here a lot. If I have time between classes, this is where I go."

Ashley looked around at the classic diner. There were booths around the perimeter and tables in the center of the room. All of them were covered with red-and-white-checkered tablecloths. Black-and-white pictures hung on the walls.

The waitress came and took their order. A Reuben sandwich for Jason, and a hamburger and fries for Ashley.

"I kind of pictured you as a salad person," Jason said.

Ashley laughed. "I eat my vegetables. Usually. I need protein to get through the rest of the afternoon, and, I'll be honest, a potato in any form is my favorite food."

He had a nice laugh. Soft and low. "What about you? We've talked about my farm work, and you know I go to school. What keeps you busy?"

The waitress set their drinks on the table and left.

Ashley took a sip of her water. "I'm a senior. I'll graduate at the end of December because I took a few extra classes in the past few years to graduate a semester early. I was going to become a psychologist, so my major is psychology. I'm thinking about changing my career path. I'm not sure if I want to become a psychologist. In the afternoons, I have a clinical observation class at St. Gertrude's Medical Center for a few weeks to see what the work would be like."

"That should help you decide if you want to continue studying psychology, shouldn't it?"

"I hope so. I feel directionless now. Is that even a word?" She laughed to lighten the mood. "Enough about me. You sound busy with farmwork and school."

Jason shrugged. "I'm used to it, and I love farmwork."

"What's your major?"

"I'm just starting an associate degree. As much as I love farming, there's not a lot of money in small farms. School won't be as difficult to fit into my schedule during winter. There's not as much to do on the farm. We have a few cattle, and you can't do fieldwork in frozen ground covered by snow. Spring might be complicated, but we can hire someone to help for a short time. Fortunately, this degree is a two-year program. I only have to take a few general classes, like this speech class and an English class. Otherwise, the classes all pertain to business. I'd like to be an electrician, but I want to have the business degree first. Then I'll probably get an electrician's certification."

Their food arrived while Jason talked, and Ashley dug into her burger immediately. Time passed quickly, and she was going to have to eat and run like usual to get to the hospital. "It sounds like a good fit, if it's what you're interested in doing."

Jason took a bite of his food, chewed, and swallowed before he answered, "I'm more excited by the electrician part, but business knowledge is necessary." He grinned wryly. "Besides, it will come in useful no matter what happens."

"Sorry I'm eating fast, but I've got to get going," Ashley told him.

"Don't worry. We can meet up again." His cheeks reddened, and he paused. "I mean, if you're interested?"

She'd heard the question at the end of his sentence, so she stuck a fry in her mouth to give herself time. Did she want to get together with Jason? She wasn't experienced in relationships with guys. Should she tell him? Or let things happen as they happened?

She liked Jason, and he seemed nice. He was worth the time to see if they could be friends. "Sure. I'd like that."

"Great," he said. "I guess it's time for us to get going."

"Yes. You have to get back to the farm, and I have to get to the hospital." She felt let down at the idea of leaving. She reminded herself she'd see him in class, and they agreed to get together again. She wanted to see where the situation went.

Ashley and Jason walked to her car first. When he saw her safely inside the driver's seat, he left for his own vehicle. Ashley drove home and quickly changed into her work clothes, a light blue sweater and a pair of navy pants and blue loafers. She'd noticed it was generally cold in the counseling rooms in the afternoon, despite the weather being warm for September. Maybe because they were on the north side of the building.

By the time she arrived at work, she had little time to get from the parking lot to the office. She glanced at her phone.

Jill had texted, "How was class?" with added red heart emojis. She was for sure going to push a relationship with Jason.

Ashley texted back, "Great. Class was good. Lunch with Jason. Just walking into the office for work. Want delivery pizza after work? If yes, text me when you're ready to leave work, and I'll order it. I know I'll be done before you. Gotta go!"

She put the phone on silent and stuck it in her pocket as she went in to meet with her supervisor to talk through the afternoon schedule of patients.

CHAPTER 4

Ashley looked at the phone as it rang. She'd been busy cleaning the apartment while Jill worked all weekend. Why was Paul calling her? They hadn't talked for years. Not since he told her to leave his house and never come back. He and Samantha were drunk at the time.

She let it go to voicemail. It looked like God was trying to tell her the time had come to put the past behind her, to forgive her brothers and have an adult relationship with them. Otherwise, why would He have given her the urge to sign up for a class about siblings, and now Paul was calling her out of the blue?

She listened to his voicemail.

"I can understand why you probably don't want to talk with me. It won't help my case to say I was plastered that night. I only remember bits and pieces. That was my life before I got sober. I've been sober now for two years, and I'd like to repair our relationship, or start over, or whatever you want. Please give me a call if you can find it in your heart to talk to me," Paul said. The voicemail clicked off.

She sank down on the couch with the feather duster in one hand and her phone in the other. When she realized she was gripping them, she set them both on the coffee table and leaned back onto the couch cushions.

It was good to hear from Paul. He sounded like the older brother she knew before alcohol took over his life. She felt like crying. She knew when the class she signed up for involved the topic of siblings, she was ready to connect with one or both of her brothers. She believed it would be in her time frame. The moment had come, but she wasn't as ready as she'd hoped.

She needed someone to talk to about all of it. Jill wouldn't be available until after work, which was hours away. Maybe Jason would have time. She had no idea what he'd planned for today, other than working on the farm. And why would he come to mind? She'd only met him a few days ago.

She should call Paul and talk to him. She sat there, not making a move to call him back. What if she called him, and then it all fell apart again? Could she handle that? She was older and stronger mentally now. Yes, she could handle it. She'd take it slow.

Right now, she needed to calm down. She got her camera to take pictures. That always took her mind off her problems. There were lovely autumn trees with gorgeous colors she noticed when driving to work and school. The leaves wouldn't stay on the trees much longer.

She put away her cleaning supplies, ate a tuna sandwich, and drank a glass of water. After changing into jeans and a bright yellow t-shirt, she gathered her camera and a couple of bottles of water and left the apartment.

She drove to a park she'd noticed yesterday near her apartment. Today was Saturday, and parents brought their kids to the parks on the weekend, so she didn't expect it to be as quiet as yesterday. She was right. Fortunately, the trees were on the opposite side of the park from the playground equipment. She could take pictures without constant questions from the children and querying looks from parents.

A lovely maple in a glorious red shade glinted in the sun, and she focused mostly on that tree. Then she moved on to other yellow and gold trees. After that, she backed away and did wide panoramas of large sections of the trees.

She felt calmer after taking the pictures, and when she returned to her car, she decided to phone Paul right then. Parked at the curb with the trees between her and the playground, it would be hard for anyone to see what she did. Not that there was anything wrong with it. She was always paranoid at playgrounds after one mother accused her of taking pictures of her daughter—which she hadn't been doing.

One of the curvy slides was beautiful, and she'd been considering how it would make a good background for a picture. She hadn't even noticed the girl, who had been playing on the swing a distance away. Fortunately, they were the only ones at the park when the mother started screaming at her to leave the playground, or she'd call the police.

Putting the memory aside, she set her camera on the passenger seat and pulled her phone out of her back pocket. Before she talked herself out of it, she pushed the return call button for Paul on her phone and listened to it ring.

"Hello," he answered.

"Hi, Paul. It's Ashley." Her voice shook slightly, and she clenched her free hand into a fist.

"Thanks so much for calling me back. It means a lot to me. As I said in my message, I'm sorry for the things I said, and I don't expect forgiveness, but I have to try."

His eager voice sounded sincere. "Why now, Paul? I mean, it's been a few years since our fight. Why do you want to talk now?"

"It's time. One of us has to take the first step. You were gracious enough to come to the funeral. It meant everything to me to see you there. I was so alone when they died."

"Is that why you're calling me now?" Annoyance crept into her voice. "Because you're alone?" She felt bad for him, but she wasn't going to fill some hole in his life after what he said to her.

"No. No." She heard him take a deep breath.

"I'm not alone," he said. "I have Frank and Nina, Hannah, and other friends. I'm doing fine, and I realized I needed to make amends to you and Alex. And I want you in my life too. I know this is a lot to take in, but we're family. Our parents dumped us, and we didn't know what to do. Now, it's time to take a look at our family and try and salvage what we can. Family is important."

Family is important, she repeated to herself silently. It would be nice to be a family with Alex and Paul again. If they were like they were when they were growing up. Not if they were going to be the adult versions she'd known. She hoped they'd both grown up since their experiences.

"Are you there?" Paul asked.

"Yes. I was remembering when we were younger." She heard the wistfulness in her voice. "We three took care of each other while Mom and Dad traveled around the world."

"Until I started drinking and partying in high school. You went to stay with Grandma," Paul said. "I'm sorry. I'm not proud of how I behaved. I feel maybe that led to what Alex did. If I had been paying attention, maybe he would have come to me and asked for help."

She felt compelled to dispute his idea for some reason. "Alex was a grown man. He was twenty-seven and knew what he was doing was wrong. You can't take the blame."

"He'll need help now. He and Courtney both will. I plan to approach him when he's out of jail. I don't know what he thinks either, since he continually told me not to visit him in prison or go see Courtney," he explained. "Would you consider getting together to talk? I'd like to see you again."

"I was hurt, Paul. I'm going to have to think about this and pray." She wanted to see him, but she was suddenly afraid of additional hurt, so she backed out of immediately saying yes. "I will say it's likely I'll get together with you, but I need time to adjust now that we've talked. I'll give you a call when I'm ready."

"Thank you. I appreciate it. I'll wait to hear from you. Bye, Ashley."

She pushed the end button with a sweaty finger. The part of her heart that tightened whenever she started getting close to someone loosened its grip. Would reuniting with Paul and Alex open her heart to other relationships?

CHAPTER 5

Amy stroked Baby Chloe's cheek where the tears leaked from her eyes as she lay in the crib. After a few minutes, Chloe quit crying and stared at Amy, fascinated by the light surrounding the seven-year-old.

Amy knew that light came from God because she'd come down from Heaven to comfort the child. For some reason, God had sent her to this baby. She must have something to do with Amy's father, Paul, who still lived on Earth. Whenever someone from her dad or her mother's family needed help, God would send Amy or her mother, Samantha, from Heaven to help them.

Amy whispered, "You're okay. See? There's nothing to cry about. I'm here, and God's here. We'll take care of you."

There might have been a smile on the baby's face behind her pacifier. She settled down and quit crying.

Amy kept stroking her face and then her arm. She could hear Madison crying outside, and then a vehicle drove up the gravel road. She knew it was time to leave. Someone else had come to help Chloe.

Amy heard the baby start crying when she disappeared, but she knew it would only be a few minutes before someone took care of her again.

CHAPTER 6

Jason arrived home at his parents' farm in Chokecherry Valley to find his sister sitting on the top step of the house sobbing hysterically. He jumped out of his vehicle and ran to her. "What's wrong?"

"It's Chloe." She sniffled, swiped her nose with a tissue, then started sobbing again. "She wouldn't stop crying."

"Are Mom or Dad home?"

"No. They left for a while."

Jason cringed. "You left her alone in the house?"

He didn't wait for an answer and ran into the house. The minute he opened the front door, he heard Chloe crying. He had no idea how long they'd both been crying. This was not good.

He picked the baby up from her crib, crooning to her as he gently swayed, "Shh. It's okay. It's okay, Chloe."

She hiccupped a few times, and then sighed. She looked up at him in a sleepy way. Her lashes were wet, and she had a snotty nose. He found a tissue and wiped her nose gently to keep her from starting to cry again. He walked slowly into the kitchen, swaying and murmuring quietly to her. He found a bottle in the fridge and warmed it up in the microwave.

At least he knew how to do all this. He'd babysat Chloe often enough to know where to find everything and how to take care of her. When he gathered what he needed, he took Chloe into her bedroom and sat in the rocker, holding her.

She latched on to the bottle and sucked greedily as Jason gently rocked. He leaned back against the headrest and closed his eyes. What happened? He was concerned about Madison, but Chloe came first. He would talk to Madison when he settled the baby in her crib after she'd eaten and fallen asleep.

Madison had been having a hard time in the past few months since Chloe was born. He didn't remember a time when it had been this bad. He said a prayer for Chloe and Madison:

God, please let me know what to say and what to do to help this situation.

He hadn't been praying enough lately, and it looked like things around him were starting to fall apart. It shouldn't take bad things happening before he prayed, but sometimes he lapsed without the reminder he needed God.

When Chloe finished the bottle, he burped her, changed her diaper, and walked around her room, swaying again. She looked up at him with her adorable brown baby eyes, and he was smitten. Had been since the first day he'd held her. She didn't look like she planned to sleep any time soon. She must have already napped.

He looked at the clock hanging on the wall, a simple pink plastic frame around the digits. 2:00 p.m. It didn't tell him anything of Chloe's schedule from the morning until now. He would ask Madison to come into the house, and he'd talk to her while he held Chloe.

He hadn't heard Madison crying since he came into the house, so maybe she'd gotten herself somewhat together. He walked over to the outside door and opened it. He leaned against it, keeping it open. Madison looked up from where she sat twisting her tissues in her hands.

Her look of relief hit him in the stomach. Something needed to be done. He didn't want to be the one to do it, but Madison listened to him more than she did to their parents. A teenager thing, he knew.

"You got her to stop crying. Thank you. I didn't know what to do anymore. The counselor said…"

A wary look passed through her eyes as she stopped talking, and he was afraid he knew where this was going. Madison had been seeing a counselor since Chloe's birth, and the rest of the family went along to one of the sessions to be given information about her diagnosis.

The counselor explained postpartum depression to them, and what Madison should do in certain circumstances. Their family tried not to leave her alone with the baby, but obviously something happened, and their parents had to leave.

"Let's go in the house and get comfortable. I'll take care of Chloe for a while." He kept leaning against the door until Madison came inside.

She went into the living room and sat with her feet curled beneath her on the couch. A pink bunny-patterned blanket covered the floor, and a few toys lay scattered on the soft surface.

Jason grabbed a soft gray stuffed elephant from the floor and settled in the recliner with Chloe.

"She needs to eat," Madison said quietly, picking at her fingernail polish and avoiding Jason's gaze.

Jason gathered his patience and spoke evenly, "I've fed her, changed her, and she's okay. What about you?"

"You hate me, don't you? I'm a bad mother." She blinked rapidly.

He sensed another bout of weeping, which he didn't want to deal with. He leaned forward in the recliner, keeping Chloe comfortably in front of him. "I don't hate you," he said softly. "I love you as much as I love Chloe. We need to talk about today and what to do."

As his last words registered, she looked up. "You love me?"

He smiled at her. "Of course. This is a tough time for you. You feel unlovable, and it doesn't help that Chloe's father took off and left you to take care of her alone."

"Alone, except for you and Mom and Dad."

"Where are Mom and Dad?"

"They went into Chokecherry Valley to help someone who broke her hip. She needed a ride."

Jason realized they'd need two people to help her.

"I was okay alone."

He almost laughed at the irony but kept his mouth shut. Sure, she was okay. That was why he came home to mayhem.

"Okay," she said. "It didn't last. She wouldn't quit crying, and I panicked. I left her in her crib and went outside. That's what the counselor told me to do if I felt like I couldn't deal with her calmly. I was afraid I'd drop her or something. I was crying as hard as her. I hoped if I put her in her crib, she might quit crying.”

“How long ago did all this happen?” He worried about what they were going to do about this situation.

“About a half hour. When I went outside, she quit crying within a few minutes. I believed I could get it together enough to go in and feed her. Every time I got up to go inside, I’d remember what a bad mother I was and start crying again. She seemed okay. I only heard her start crying again when you drove up the driveway.”

He rested against the back of the recliner again, trying to appear relaxed. “I’m going to say something, and I want you to listen to me, Madison. I know it’s going to make you mad, but I think you know more needs to be done. This can’t happen again.”

“I know. I don’t know what to do.” Madison started picking at her fingernails again and sniffling. A box of tissues sat on the end table beside her, and she grabbed a few.

“You’ve gone over the scenarios with the counselor. You know what your choices are.”

She nodded, wiped her nose, and sat up. She made direct eye contact with him for the first time since he’d arrived. “You’re right. I’m her mother. I need to do what’s best for her. The counselor doesn’t know how long this depression will last, and I hoped I’d be fine by now. I’m not. I trust you, Jason, or I wouldn’t say this.

“I’ve thought about giving her up for adoption again, but I can’t take that step. And I know it would be a permanent solution to what is going to be a short-term problem. I know when I say short-term, it could be six months. In the scheme of things, six months isn’t long compared to her entire childhood. I’ve decided to start medication.”

“When did you decide to do that? I don’t want you to make a rash decision, and then when we get to the doctor’s office, you change your mind.” She’d already done that several times in the past two months they’d been dealing with this.

“I’m not changing my mind this time. Chloe is my responsibility. I need to be here for her. I wasn’t today, and none of the rest of you were either." She held up her hand when he started to speak.

"That's not an accusation. That's life. Things come up. I don't blame anyone except myself. I should have started on medication right away. I kept telling myself, tomorrow I'll be fine. And then I'd wake up the next day, and I wasn't fine. I'd think, okay, this will be slow, but I'll see progress. I'm not seeing any progress in getting better. I believed taking pills made me a weak person, but it doesn't. Postpartum depression is a disease like any other disease. It needs treatment," she said.

"I'm proud of you for considering all of this," Jason said, getting up from the recliner. He knelt in front of Madison with Chloe nestled in his left arm and gave his sister a hug with his right arm. "You'll get through this. I know you will."

She hugged him back, being careful not to squish Chloe between them. "Thank you. You've been a rock. I couldn't have done this without your help."

"You're welcome, anytime. Next time, try and remember to call me. Promise?"

"I promise." She smiled. It was brief, but it was there.

"Okay." He got up.

"Can I hold Chloe?" she asked tentatively.

"Of course." He handed the baby over to Madison. "Have you eaten lunch yet?"

"No." She played with Chloe's fingers, and the baby cooed.

"I'll get you something. Food will help you feel better too."

He went into the kitchen to get her a sandwich, hoping the conversation would be a turning point. He was sorry it took a total meltdown, and no one to help her, but the ending turned out okay. Thank goodness. Thank you, God.

CHAPTER 7

Ashley joined Jill on the couch that evening where they set out a pepperoni pizza and soft drinks for dinner. They planned on watching a movie, but Jill's questioning about Jason hindered making a movie choice.

"Are you two dating?" Jill asked.

"I wouldn't call it dating. We ate lunch together after class today. That's not a date, is it?" Ashley liked Jason, but she couldn't convince herself their lunch constituted a date. It was a spur-of-the-moment idea, and she'd been hungry. And he was cute. Maybe it was a date. Especially since they'd agreed to meet for lunch after class again.

Jill turned to look at her. "What would you do if he asked you out?"

"I don't know." She got up and escaped to the kitchen area, which was part of the open floor plan, to get more napkins. They were out, so she grabbed the pen off the counter and wrote "napkins" on the grocery list posted on the fridge.

She searched for the paper towels and finally found them in one of the cabinets. She tore a few off the roll as she walked back into the living room area.

Jill's gaze remained focused on her.

Ashley couldn't escape this inquisition. The whole subject made her nervous. "I plan on going out with him on a date. There. Are you happy?" She placed the towels on the coffee table with their dinner and put her hands on her hips.

Jill grinned. "Ecstatic."

"I have work and school to finish. Then I need to figure out if I'm continuing with school or finding a job. With only an undergraduate degree in psychology, my options in that field are limited. Most jobs in the field require a master's degree at minimum, plus certifications. I don't have time for a man, but

I'll make time if Jason is interested. Now, let's choose a movie and eat. I'm starving."

She grabbed one of the two plates and put a slice of pizza on it. Then she grabbed her soda, popped the top and took a long drink. As she took a bite of pizza, she ignored Jill's stare. Next, she took the remote and changed the channel to a cozy mystery movie she knew Jill would find interesting.

Jill started getting her own dinner. "You know, you're going to have to deal with your past eventually. Not everyone is like your brothers. Or your parents."

"A recovered alcoholic and an embezzler. They're great examples. Oh, and my parents basically deserted us when we were growing up, leaving us with whoever would take us, while they traveled around the world."

"Well, Paul is sober now, right? He got his act together, and he told you he's been sober for two years. He didn't go back to drinking despite his wife and daughter's deaths. You have to give him credit for that. He's dating Hannah, who is wonderful," Jill said.

"I forgot you would know Hannah from the hospital."

"I don't know her. She hasn't done fundraising for our unit, but other people say she's great. Your brother did give a speech at the fundraiser for the NICU and impressed a lot of people."

"So, he got it together. Although we had a brief conversation, we aren't talking regularly yet. I know it looks like Paul and I are on track to being closer, but underneath my desire to reconcile, I am still so mad at him. I can't seem to get over the anger and hurt."

"Well, maybe this class will help you to mend fences. And Alex is getting out of jail soon. He'll probably need your support, along with his wife. Everyone makes mistakes. Aren't there things about your life you regret?" Jill paused and ate a few bites. "Weren't there any good times with your brothers when you were kids?"

Ashley remembered how her brothers stood up for her in school when someone teased her. That had mostly been Paul because Alex was oblivious. They stuck together at whoever's house their parents dumped them at when they traveled.

"There were good times. I'm hopeful this class will help me navigate a new relationship with them. I admit it. I am trying. With my brothers and with Jason. I'm so used to closing myself off in case I get hurt that it's hard to change old habits." She smiled at Jill. "Now let's eat and enjoy our pizza. It's getting cold."

"Glad you're making up with your brothers. And at least you're trying with Jason. When you have your first real date with him, you will let me know, won't you?" She grinned at Ashley.

"Funny." Ashley smiled at her and turned up the volume of the television slightly to hear over her own chewing. The subject was over for now with Jill, but it would come up again. She didn't want to think about Jason or her brothers any more this evening. She wanted to sink herself into watching the movie and forget her fear of rejection and hurt for a few hours. She was dealing with her feelings as much as she could, but the day had been emotional. She needed a break.

CHAPTER 8

Jason studied while waiting for his parents to return. When he'd finished making lunch for Madison, he suggested she take a nap. Then he called their neighbor Nina to see if she could babysit Chloe.

Nina was more than happy to take the baby for a few hours, so he loaded up the diaper bag with everything she might need. He peeked in at Madison, who had fallen into an exhausted sleep. He left a note for her in case she woke while he was gone.

Once he left Chloe with Nina, he returned home, changed into his work clothes, and did the chores on the farm. He picked up Chloe and now sat at the table studying.

Madison continued sleeping. That concerned him. She was either sleep-deprived or oversleeping. She needed to get on postpartum medication sooner rather than later, and he planned to discuss it with his parents when they returned. The therapist already suggested it, but Madison hadn't wanted to go on any medication. Her change of heart might be temporary, even after today's events. They needed to call the clinic and get the medication before she changed her mind.

He realized her mood swings made it hard for her to make an informed decision, but maybe with the support of the whole family, she would now take meds. She'd tried to deal with the depression for the two months since Chloe was born. That should be long enough to know medication was necessary.

He needed to remember it was her body and her choice, even if he didn't always agree with her decision. His would stand by her, help her take care of Chloe and wait it out.

Today showed him she couldn't be left alone with Chloe any longer until she recovered. The coordination of the effort to help would take everyone's time. With the harvest over, and the farmwork not as busy, it would be possible to focus on Madison.

His father arrived home, and Jason only had time to greet him before Madison came out of her bedroom.

She still looked half asleep, but her face muscles seemed more relaxed, and her eyes were clear. "Where's Mom?"

Their dad plopped down on the recliner in the living room and tossed a smile in Chloe's direction, and the baby quietly sucked on her finger as she lay on the blanket in the middle of the floor. "Your mom stayed at the hospital. The lady who fell didn't have any relatives or other friends who could stay with her, so your mom said she'd stay overnight until the lady's daughter arrived in the morning."

Jason's talk with his parents about Madison looked like it would be a conversation with his dad, him, and Madison. One phone call would be necessary to get the prescription anyway.

CHAPTER 9

Ashley started the homework due on Friday for her sibling class. Monday would be Labor Day, so there were no classes.

According to the instructions Dr. Athena gave them, they were to write three letters. One of the letters would be from her perspective to a sibling, and one would be from her sibling's perspective to her. The third letter excluded all the assumptions the other two letters contained, to boil it down to facts instead of assuming what the other person meant. She wasn't sure if it would be easier to write to Paul or Alex, but she chose Paul.

Dr. Athena promised not to share the letters in class without permission. She didn't plan to let her letters be read out loud.

Dear Paul,

I haven't talked to you in a long time, except for that brief phone call. I was hurt by the things you said in the past. As my big brother, I've always looked up to you and thought you loved me. Of course, just because I believed that doesn't mean you wouldn't hurt me.

I guess, where love is involved, there's always going to be some hurt. If we didn't care, it wouldn't matter what the other person said. The day you told me I was just your little sister and didn't have any right to state my opinion about your drinking hurt. Yes, it was your business, but it was my business too. Both you and Samantha drank too much, which hurt Amy. Someone needed to speak up for her, and I did.

You were right, in a way. I have no right to tell you how to run your own life. Then you went on to tell me what a pain it was to raise me, since Mom and Dad were never around to do it. That hurt the most. I felt in the way. So, I quit visiting you, Samantha and Amy. I know you were drunk when you said it, but did it make it any less true? Was being drunk the only way I'd hear the truth from you?

In hindsight, avoiding visiting you afterward was a major mistake, as I missed time with Amy. And time with you when you got sober. Of course, Samantha never managed to kick the habit, and that was sad.

I always thought of you, Alex, and myself as a unit. A group helping each other through the dysfunction of living, or not living, with traveling parents. When they dumped us on various relatives and friends and went around the world on their travels, I thought at least we had each other. If they split us up, I think I would have fallen apart.

Maybe I depended on you too much, but I needed someone, and Alex wasn't much older than me.

I'm angry and hurt and lonely. I miss my time with my older brother: you. Maybe if I get this all out on paper, it will help me find the courage to visit you like you now want. It took hours to talk myself into going to Amy and Samantha's funeral. Even the brief wave from you that day was a relief and gave me hope. You smiled. Of course, it was a sad day, so a sad smile, but at least it was a smile.

You said you're staying sober. I don't think I can visit you if you're not. I heard you were dating Hannah. I've heard about her at the hospital. I haven't met her yet. We don't have anything to do with each other at the hospital. I don't think I could go up to her and ask about you.

I know I should gather my courage and have a few more phone calls or get together with you to find out what's going on in your life. I'm sure it's been difficult for you since their deaths. Will you insult me again? I don't think I could handle that.

Sincerely (with love),
Ashley

Ashley didn't reread the letter after she wrote it but stuck it in her school folder. She'd read it later. Her hands shook, and her mouth felt dry. She went to the kitchen and grabbed a glass of water, dropping a few ice cubes into it before taking a deep drink.

This class was going to be emotional. Maybe she shouldn't have signed up for it. She decided not to second-guess her decision any longer. She'd signed up. She was going to finish. Enough with the indecision.

She had two more letters to write. The one from Paul's point of view would probably be shorter. She'd have to write about his perspective, which might make her angrier, but she might feel less vulnerable than the first letter she'd written.

She refilled her water glass and went back to the couch. Pulling out her class notebook, she opened it to a clean page and picked up her pen from the coffee table. She leaned back against the couch and started writing.

Dear Ashley,

She paused and wondered, what would Paul say? She hadn't talked to him since he became sober, except for his brief phone call when he apologized. She'd have to guess for this letter. Maybe the point of the exercise was not knowing what other people thought and assuming their feelings and motives without proof.

I got tired of taking care of you and Alex without Mom and Dad's help. I always felt inadequate. It wasn't that I didn't love you. I really did. I still do. I was overwhelmed. Overwhelmed with a drinking wife and a child who wasn't getting what she needed from me or her mom.

When we fought, I guess it boiled over and spilled out. I didn't mean the awful things I said. Sometimes I remember our argument. I want to take it back, but I can't. That's the thing about saying what you're thinking at the time. It's out there, never to be returned, and people get hurt. People whom we love get hurt.

I've missed seeing you and talking to you. I've missed seeing you and Amy chatting away, aunt to niece.

We had an unusual upbringing. You seemed to be doing the best of the three of us with Mom and Dad gone. At least that's how it looked. Alex struggled. Maybe he told me more because we were closer in age. I felt totally unable to get you through your teen years, but I tried. You were at Grandma's for those five years. It was a long time without you. That's when a mom or dad is needed. I faltered and started drinking. I guess that's when I left the two of you alone too much.

I hope we can get together and be a family again.

Love,
Paul

The letter from Paul's point of view was harder to write. She stuck the letter in her folder with the other one. Deciding she was done with that part of the assignment for now, she grabbed her glass of water from the coffee table and took a drink.

The next part of the assignment was to find a reference from the textbook pertaining to her situation with her sibling. She needed to find a reference about fighting siblings or reconciliation, or something similar. She'd enjoy her water and then look it up to see what it said.

Dr. Athena ran her class in an unusual way. It was certainly different than her other instructors. It would be interesting to see how it would play out when everyone was reading a different part of the textbook.

CHAPTER 10

By the time Jason talked to his dad that Friday, the clinic was already closed. An on-call doctor could help, but Madison wanted her own doctor to write the prescription. That meant waiting until Tuesday morning because of Labor Day on Monday.

They'd have to wait three more days to get medication for her. Hopefully, she continued to agree she needed the medication by the time Tuesday arrived. She could change her mind one hundred times in the next few days. Who knew what would happen on Tuesday?

He decided to try and convince Madison her doctor would have noted in her chart exactly what medication she would prescribe. The only thing the on-call staff needed to do was look at the chart and prescribe whatever her regular doctor suggested. That might be the best thing to do.

He wanted to talk to his parents without Madison overhearing them. They needed to discuss who would be most likely to convince her not to wait until Tuesday. There was a better way to get through the days until her depression lifted.

After breakfast, his chance came. Madison took Chloe into her bedroom to change her diaper, and Jason suggested to his mother they take a walk in the beautiful fall day. The leaves were starting to change color, and the morning temperature was especially comfortable.

He peeked into Madison's room. "Mom and I are taking a walk. Chloe will like the falling leaves, so I'll take her along. Are you okay with that?"

"Sure," Madison said.

He picked Chloe up from the crib and told Madison she should yell out the door if she needed something. "We'll be back soon."

When he and his mom were outside, he said, "We need to talk about Madison. Let's go find Dad and have a conversation."

Patricia glanced sideways at him. "What happened yesterday while we were gone?"

"Madison had a major meltdown. I came home to find her crying on the outside step and Chloe crying in her crib. I settled Chloe down, and then Madison. I told her to take a nap, and I left Chloe with Nina while I did chores. Later I went back and picked up Chloe again.

"I talked to Madison, and she agreed to take medication but wants to wait for her own doctor to prescribe them. She won't be back in the office until Tuesday. The on-call staff can prescribe the medicine based on her chart, but Madison says she wants to wait," Jason said.

They found his dad working on a seeding machine, getting it ready for the next spring planting.

"I told Mom about Madison agreeing to take the medication but wanting to wait until her own doctor is back in the office. I don't think we should wait," Jason said.

His dad frowned at him. "What are we supposed to do? She can be stubborn. I'm not sure we should push her now she's agreed. What do you think?" He lifted his ball cap up and scratched at his balding head before putting it back on.

His mother put her hand on his arm. "We can't wait. I agree with Jason. After yesterday, we can't leave her alone with Chloe either. She could fall apart again anytime. How are we going to manage? We could take Nina into our confidence. She can help with Chloe, but we need to get Madison well. It's going to take a while even on the medication."

His dad looked at her. "Maybe you should tell her your story."

His mom shook her head before he finished his sentence. "She doesn't need to know."

"Why not? It would help her feel like she isn't alone. She probably believes no one understands. And why does it matter to you now? It's nothing to be ashamed about, is it?"

Jason had no idea what his parents were discussing.

"No." She didn't sound convinced.

"Just think about it." His dad took her hand and held it, then pulled her closer and hugged her.

Jason rarely saw physical displays from his parents. That hug, and the secret she wanted to keep, reminded him his parents had pasts he knew nothing about. "Who should talk to her?" He was sorry to break up the moment, but Madison would start wondering what was going on soon.

"I'll talk to her," his mother said. She slipped out of her husband's embrace. Then she leaned forward and kissed him. "You're right. She needs to know. Why don't you stay out here and tell Jason? I'll go talk to Madison."

His dad smiled gently at her and nodded. Jason watched his mother walk slowly back to the house. When she left them, he turned to his dad.

"Let's get to work on this seeder," his dad said.

"What do you want me to do?"

"Hold that end steady while I work on this end." He grabbed a wrench and started twisting while Jason held the end of the steel steady. He should have brought a pair of gloves outside with him to help keep a grip. He held Chloe and only had one hand free. He could feel the steel digging into his hands.

Jason tapped his hand on the steel, and his dad stopped what he was doing. "I need to get gloves, Dad. If we're going to work on this, I'll need to take Chloe back to the house. I don't want to interrupt Mom and Madison." He let go of his end. Chloe was looking around, contented to be held in his arms.

"I don't need help. I was trying to decide how to tell you." He took a deep breath and let it out. "Your mom had postpartum depression after Madison was born. She had a tough time, and she didn't want to take medication either. She never did.

"We made it through, but I wish she'd taken the medication. It's a disease that hasn't been understood for years. While she was lucky enough to have a good doctor, it was difficult being isolated on the farm, in addition to being depressed. They've come a long way in treatment and understanding, but there are people who consider you're weak if you get treatment. Believe me, there's nothing weak about your mother."

Jason walked over and patted his dad on the shoulder. It was the most serious thing his dad had said in a long time. When Jason was younger, he got a few lectures on cars and girls and respecting other people, but this was more personal. "Thanks for telling me, Dad. I certainly won't spread it around. That's up to Mom. I'm sure it will help Madison to know Mom understands what's happening to her."

"To a certain extent, it'll help. Madison has to live with those dark feelings, and that's hard. I hope she tries the medication. We'll have to see what happens and be there for her."

His dad took off his ball cap and wiped the sweat off his forehead. Then he put the cap back on his head and picked up the wrench.

"You know I'll do anything I can." He hugged his dad, and his dad hugged him back. "Thanks for telling me. Since you don't need my help, I'm going to take Chloe for a walk while Mom and Madison talk. I'll be back in a while."

His dad nodded and then started tapping with the wrench.

Jason got the feeling his dad wasn't doing anything. He walked in the direction of the creek. He always went there to think. He wanted to call Ashley and talk to her. Something about the sibling class she was taking—or anything. How had she done with her sibling relationship letters? Maybe it would help him sort it out if he put his own feelings about Madison on paper.

He wandered around the farm for a good half hour, enjoying the nice temperature and the free time. He rarely spent time wandering these days. There was always work to be done.

The leaves were starting to look golden on the maple trees. Chloe giggled at the falling leaves and jerked in his arms when one of them hit her on the nose, but then she smiled again at the fluttering colorful leaves.

The stream near their wheatfield trickled softly. He could cross it this time of year because the water was shallow in most spots. He knew where he could cross, but he didn't want to chance slipping with Chloe in his arms. He stood there, watching the water slowly meander along.

He took his phone out of his pocket to check for messages. None. His friends ignored him over the summer when he was busy on the farm. He should get in touch with them again. Maybe going out with them would take his mind off Ashley for a while.

Brad would be a good person to call. He helped his dad on their farm too, and he was probably ready for company. Maybe they could go out for the evening. Hopefully his parents would be able to watch over Madison and Chloe.

Even if Madison decided to take medication, they'd been told it would take at least three weeks to see any changes and know if it helped at all. Then there would be possible adjustments in dosage. He thought about his mom suffering from the same depression. She probably didn't want Madison to feel bad because it didn't sound like his mom had postpartum depression after his birth. She'd kept her secret all these years.

CHAPTER 11

Ashley was deep into reading fiction books for fun. She rarely had the chance in the past few years, as she was usually studying or working. She found after writing the first draft of the letters to Paul and from Paul, she needed to get out of her own head.

She chose a cozy mystery she checked out from the library online. She knew if she'd gone to the library to check out a book, she'd wander around the shelves and bring home more books than she'd have time to read. Her mind wandered too much during the first few chapters. She worried about her relationship with her brothers and wondered what Jason was doing today.

She finally got immersed in the story and was deep into guessing the guilty party of the murder. Her phone rang, and she almost ignored it. She was so wrapped up in the book. One look at the call log changed her mind.

"Hi, Jason," she said as she scrambled to hold the phone and set her tablet down beside her on the couch.

"Hi. What are you up to?" His voice sounded different from his usual calm tones.

"Reading a book. What's going on with you? You sound upset," Ashley said.

"I am upset. Madison won't take meds until Tuesday, and she's a mess. I don't know how we got to this point."

"Since you called and told me this, I'm assuming you're open to talking about what's going on with her."

"Well, I needed someone to talk to, and since you've taken those psychology courses, I thought I'd talk to you," he said.

She felt her heart stutter. He called because she knew a little psychology? She wasn't very knowledgeable in the situation with his sister. He was one of the few guys she had gone out with in a long time, and it had only been coffee and lunch. She believed he liked her.

"I'm sorry. That didn't come out right. I meant I really wanted to talk to you, and I'm using the fact you might know more than me to call you. I would talk to you anyway. Do you still want to talk to me after my failed attempt at conversation?"

He sounded like he meant he would call her even if she couldn't help him. "You know I can't give out advice. I'm just an undergrad, and I haven't even met your sister," Ashley said.

"How about this: I'm a guy calling to talk to my friend about my sister? Does that work? Because that's what this is. There's nothing you can do anyway. She has her own therapist, and her own pigheadedness." The frustration in his voice rang through clearly.

"Yes. We can talk as friends." She relaxed a little. He really wanted to talk to her as a friend, not because of her psychology background.

"I came home to find my sister sitting on the front step of the house having a major meltdown. It's postpartum depression. She refused medication in the past. I thought she changed her mind and planned to try them. Then Mom talked to her and shared her own experience. She didn't take medications because of the stigma back then. She hid her illness. My sister said if Mom got by without them, she didn't need them either. I wanted her to at least try them."

"No luck, hmm. Your Mom meant well," Ashley said.

"She tried to get Madison to take the medication and not wait. Mom said if she had to do it over again, she would have tried. I don't know why my sister is so opposed to them; except she said it would make her feel weak to take them. To top it off, she starts her senior year Tuesday after Labor Day, which means more pressure for her with homework and getting to school every day," Jason said. "Mom cried after her talk with Madison because her story changed my sister's mind again on the medication."

"I have a feeling your sister will change her mind again pretty quickly. She'll probably only make it to school for a few days, and then find it too strenuous for her. You might need to suggest she take classes at home. I would hope the school would be open to that plan. She can get rest throughout the day," Ashley tried to reassure him.

"I hoped her going to school would be a good thing. She sleeps a lot already because of her depression. However, it's hard to know how much sleep she's getting because she sleeps at odd times and is awake in the middle of the night." Jason sounded desperate.

Ashley wondered if she dare broach the subject but decided it couldn't hurt. "Do you pray, Jason?" She didn't wait for him to answer. "Maybe this is a time to ask God for help. Ask Him to help you do the best thing for your sister."

Silence descended on the other end of the phone, and she waited. There was no way to know his feelings until he voiced something one way or another. He hadn't hung up on her, anyway.

"You've got a good idea," he finally said. "I do go to church, but I have to say, my daily prayer life isn't consistent."

Ashley's shoulders relaxed. He didn't sound mad. "Mine either. I even avoid church. I guess I'm mad at God for giving me the family I have, so I stay away. The class I'm taking about siblings is harder than I anticipated. We're not exactly reconciled at the moment."

"Writing these letters for class is bringing up bad feelings?" Jason asked.

"It's bringing those feelings to the front of my mind. I've been busy trying to get my psychology degree, so I've been able to avoid thinking about the situation for years. I considered quitting the class. Then I decided to stick it out. I guess I want my brothers back in my life. Dr. Athena might have the answers I need." She hoped. Her parents were off jetting around the world, and she'd probably never have a real relationship with them. Her brothers were another story. They had been close once. They could be again.

"I haven't even started my homework on the speech we need to write. I've been too busy dealing with Madison's issues." His laugh was bitter. "I'm sorry. I'm sounding whiny. I'm tired, and we don't have a solution for my sister. Until we find one, this situation is going to continue. At least harvest is over, and there's not as much to do around the farm," Jason said.

"You're going to have homework. Madison is going to have homework and spells of depression, so you feel overwhelmed," Ashley said sympathetically.

"Exactly. You know, you're going to make a great therapist if you continue on with classes. If you don't, you'll always be a great friend to talk to. Thanks for listening. I'm done with my moping."

"You're welcome to call any time you need someone to listen." She was getting more comfortable with the idea of a friendship with Jason. Jill would be happy about her taking more chances in her relationships.

She and Jason were certainly starting out with some complex situations. His sister's depression, and Ashley's family dysfunction. That was life.

What did God want her to do? Probably help Jason when possible. Besides, that wasn't difficult since she liked him.

"I'll be taking you up on the calls. Mainly because I like talking to you," Jason said.

Ashley felt warmth flood her face and was glad he couldn't see her blush. "Thank you."

"I'm looking forward to our next coffee lunch date," he said.

She cleared her throat. "Me too."

"Talk to you soon."

She could hardly say goodbye through the lump in her throat. Nerves jangled as she hung up the phone. She was not good with relationships. Hiding herself away for years hadn't been healthy. Plus, it made the learning curve steep, but Jason was worth it.

CHAPTER 12

The weekend passed quickly for Ashley. After spending Saturday cleaning and reading, she slept soundly. Sunday, she and Jill attended the ten a.m. church service and went out for brunch. Then Jill worked the evening shift.

Ashley took her two letters out of the homework folder and reworded them as much as she could. She read the assigned book passages.

Labor Day came too soon. She spent her last free day before going back to work taking photographs of the autumn leaves and other pretty views around the city. She enjoyed landscape photos. When she was younger, she liked taking pictures of people and their facial expressions. Now she preferred taking pictures of scenery.

The brilliant blue sky shone, and the birds chirped insistently. She spent a lot of time thinking about Jason and Paul. She couldn't continue to let her abandonment issues run her life.

So, her parents left her with other people and signed their parental rights over to her grandmother when she was a teenager. One of her brothers had a snit when he was drunk. The other brother and his wife tried to save her reputation by keeping her out of their lives once he went to jail. When she summed it up, she realized that all of it had shaped her. Yes, it was hard, but it wasn't the worst thing to happen.

She needed to decide if she was going to continue with school or start job hunting. She hadn't signed up for any classes or even applied to the master's in psychology program. That should have told her something right there. She wasn't committed to the plan she had when she started school. She groaned. She had no plans at all.

She did know she wanted to be closer to her brothers. Since one lived in Bismarck, and one lived in Chokecherry Valley, her best option would be to stay in North Dakota. If she decided to work, the job market would probably be best in Bismarck unless she moved west to Dickinson.

To start on her plan to get closer to her brothers again, the first step would be to see Courtney. With Alex getting out of prison in December, Courtney would need all the friends she could get. If she planned to patch up her differences with her brothers, she might as well visit her sister-in-law.

***

Ashley hadn't seen Courtney for two years. When Alex went to prison for embezzlement, Ashley's visit with Courtney hadn't gone well. Courtney told her she didn't need sympathy or pity. She had no idea how Courtney would react when Ashley arrived at their house in Chokecherry Valley. When she'd called to tell her she was coming to visit, there had been no answer. She'd tried visiting when Alex first went to prison, but Courtney refused to come to the door. This time, Ashley wasn't taking no for an answer.

On the hour drive out to Chokecherry Valley that afternoon, Ashley considered Alex's situation. She'd wanted to go visit her brother in prison, but Alex didn't want any visitors. Ashley didn't understand why not. She had even gone to the prison, only to have Alex refuse to see her.

She hadn't been judgmental when he was on trial. All the proof against him seemed to be solid, and Alex hadn't fought at all. Ashley didn't understand that either. Alex hadn't put up much of a defense. When he could have hired a better lawyer, he didn't. She volunteered to help pay, and both Alex and Courtney adamantly told her to stay out of it. They knew what they were doing.

The whole situation confused her. Alex and Courtney weren't big spenders, and Ashley's parents gave all their children plenty of money to live on and go to school. Alex's job at the bank paid well. She suspected they kept important parts of the situation between the two of them.

281

The turnoff from the highway to Chokecherry Valley came closer, and her hands got sweaty on the steering wheel. She breathed faster. She prayed for calm and peace.

The worst that could happen had already happened. Courtney and Alex turned her away two years ago. Courtney might do the same again today, but Ashley was two years older and more mature now than she'd been on her last visit. She'd insist on a good reason from Courtney not to stay in touch.

Courtney had a big family, and Ashley knew she hadn't cut them off. She hadn't seen Courtney for so long, maybe she hid from her own family too. It was time for the truth.

Ashley planned to contact Paul anyway, and if Courtney turned her away again, she would bring Paul with her next time. One thing she knew: she wouldn't give up easily this time. She missed her brothers and Courtney. With Samantha's and Amy's deaths, she realized how short life could be.

Courtney and Alex lived at the end of Main Street on five acres of land, so they were slightly set apart from the town. The house had been owned by Ashley's parents. When they gave money to all their children, Alex wanted the house. Ashley and Paul were intent on getting out of Chokecherry Valley and going to college.

Ashley had always wanted to major in psychology. She wasn't sure Paul had always wanted to be a doctor. Alex had been content to get his four-year bachelor's degree in business and was fortunate that he happened to graduate just when the previous bank manager retired.

Alex and Courtney met in college and got married right after graduation. Alex worked at the bank for three years before the charge of embezzlement derailed their life. Ashley couldn't believe it when she heard about it. The amount of money was small, and Alex didn't need it.

Their parents settled a lot of money on each of them before they went off to travel around the world. She always thought of it as guilty conscience money. She needed it to live, so she hadn't turned the gift down. She dreamed of paying them back in full and totally divorcing herself from her parents. The whole situation irritated her.

She pulled up in front of Alex and Courtney's house. She expected Courtney to be home because it was a holiday, but she no longer knew if Courtney worked or not. If she changed her job to retail, or something similar, she might not have the day off. With Alex's reputation in shreds, Courtney's life must have imploded. Ashley didn't know what happened, and it made her mad.

She got out of the vehicle and approached the front door. The white house looked well-kept on the outside. A wrap-around veranda with a porch swing on each side of the front door sported colorful red and navy pillows and cushions. The curtains were open in the front window and the kitchen.

She knew from growing up in the house, the kitchen was on the left, and the living room on the right when you entered. Alex did minimal remodeling. He removed the wall between the kitchen and the living room to make it all one space. Otherwise, he left the structure alone.

Ashley walked up the stairs to the front door and knocked. While she waited, she looked back down Main Street. The grocery store and a small café were open for business. There weren't many other businesses along the street. Most people went to a few of the bigger towns in the area for anything else, such as medical care or more shopping variety. The bar, bank, and a gas station were the only other businesses. The bank and bar looked closed now, probably because of Labor Day.

She waited another five minutes and then sat on one of the porch swings, gently swinging. It felt good to be back in Chokecherry Valley. It had been great to move out of town to go to school, but time had passed. She felt nostalgic for the times she had lived in the house with Paul and Alex during weekends when her grandmother needed a break.

Obviously, Courtney wasn't home. Ashley had peeked into the garage, which was empty, and no vehicles were parked in front of the house. Ashley looked down Main Street again. Should she ask at one of the open businesses? Courtney might even be working at one of them. Or maybe she went to her parents' house in Bismarck for the long weekend.

She had decided to go back to her vehicle when she heard a car headed her way from the back of the house, not from Main Street.

The woman parked in the driveway. At first, Ashley didn't recognize the driver. From this distance, she noticed short, choppy purple hair, and the glint of the sun caught something glittery.

Ashley watched her sit in her vehicle for a minute. She realized it was Courtney, and she didn't hurry to get out of the car to talk to her. She hadn't shut off the engine either. Ashley hoped she wouldn't leave.

Finally, the engine died, and Courtney leaned over to the passenger seat. She straightened up again and opened the driver's door. She struggled to get out with her purse while juggling a pile of books in her hands.

Ashley stood up from the swing. "Would you like help with those books?"

Courtney stared at her for a moment before answering, "Sure."

Ashley moved forward and took some of them from her, and Courtney managed the rest. Looking at the top title, she realized they were library books. She didn't know Courtney liked to read. She looked up. "I wasn't sure I'd get to see you today. I'm glad I waited."

"I told you I didn't want to see you." Courtney walked to the front door, rummaged in her purse, and eventually pulled out a key. She stuck it in the lock and turned it, then opened the door. She turned to Ashley, reaching out for the books. "Thank you."

Ashley hung on to the books. "I'll bring them inside."

"Not necessary. You can set them on the porch swing," she said in a dull monotone.

Ashley didn't like the lack of life in her voice. "No. I'm coming in. I imagine you can call someone to chase me off, but I plan to talk to you today. I drove an hour here, and I'll be driving an hour home. I waited on your porch. I'm not leaving until we've discussed this situation.

"Alex is getting out of jail soon, and I plan to visit him. I shouldn't have listened to you before when you told me not to visit, but I was too young to know better. Well, I know better now. Life is short, and I'm not leaving until we discuss this." She took a deep breath and then let it out. The long speech had been brewing ever since her decision to visit.

Courtney must have realized the futility of arguing. She didn't say anything, but when she went into the house, she left the door open. Ashley took it as an invitation to enter, which she did quickly before Courtney changed her mind.

From the entryway, Ashley looked around curiously at her childhood home. Alex and Courtney hadn't changed much since they purchased the home from Paul and Ashley. The floor plan was still an open living room, dining room, and kitchen.

They took out the carpet and replaced it with wood floors. The walls were all painted a soft creamy white instead of the light blue color her mother favored at one time. Her mother had gotten into a country vibe and hung gingham curtains in the kitchen. Ashley changed them in her senior year to a lacy cream panel over a cream blind. Courtney and Alex must have liked them because they were still there.

She realized while she'd been taking stock of the room, her sister-in-law was watching her. "You want to sit down and get comfortable?" Courtney asked, settling herself on the plush blue couch where she dumped the books and her purse.

Ashley added the books she'd been carrying onto the pile on the couch and took a seat on the matching chair across from Courtney. Now she'd cornered her, she didn't know quite how to build the bridge back to some sort of relationship. "How are you doing?"

"Well, people talk to me when they walk into the grocery store now. They used to totally ignore me."

"Why didn't you move? You know I would have helped you, and so would Paul."

Courtney's expression hardened. "You would have, but Paul…" She shrugged.

Ashley nodded. "Yes, I suppose it wouldn't have worked." She decided to keep her own feelings about how Paul treated her to herself. "I would have shared an apartment with you and helped you find a job."

"I know." Her face softened. "Listen, Ashley. I get what you want. I have a big family. I know how it works. There are things about the situation Alex and I didn't share with anyone. We made the decision together to keep you from being in the middle of it. You were going to school and had a dream to be a psychologist. Alex and I didn't want to ruin your life too."

Ashley's heart pounded uncomfortably fast. "I wanted to talk to him."

"He didn't let you visit him in prison, did he?"

"No. He refused to see me."

"He did it to protect you."

Ashley felt tears welling. Finding out Courtney and Alex discussed how to exclude her from their lives hurt, even if they believed it was for her own good. "I wish you two would have included me in that discussion."

"I'm pretty sure we knew what you would say."

Ashley blinked, and then sniffed.

Courtney got her a tissue from the kitchen. "I'm sorry we hurt you, but you don't know what it's been like around here in Chokecherry Valley since they convicted Alex."

Ashley wiped her nose and, taking a deep breath, sat up straight. "I could have handled it."

Courtney shook her head. "It's difficult. Plus, that's not the point. Alex didn't want you to have to handle it. He and I made the decision for him to plead guilty. He didn't want you to suffer for his actions. He was glad you were away at school and wouldn't be in Chokecherry Valley. The farther away you were, the better he assumed it would be for you."

"What about you? You were left alone to manage it," Ashley said.

"I wasn't. You know I have a big family. They came and hung around with me until the talk died down to a dull roar, and I was an occasional footnote in the gossip."

Ashley felt a pang of longing when Courtney said her family helped her through the last few years. Paul and Alex basically deserted her, and she'd been on her own. It was the reason she couldn't readily open herself up to a relationship. At her age, she felt she should have had at least a boyfriend or two, but she didn't trust them not to leave her. Meeting Jason opened her eyes to missed possibilities.

Her parents left her and her brothers to the kindness of others. They'd never been warm and loving. Ashley longed for a family, but not like her family. She wanted a close one like Courtney's family.

It amazed her she could envy her sister-in-law, who dealt with Alex's actions at the bank and the poor reputation he'd created. It couldn't have been easy to stay in the town and work.

"I have my job. It's only me and the owner. She's kind to me and frowns at anyone making rude comments. They pretty much leave me alone. It's okay, Ashley. Alex will be home soon," Courtney said.

Ashley thought Courtney's voice held a hint of tears, but she had built a shell around herself, so it was hard to tell. She stood up. "I'm going to go now. You seem to have everything you need. I want you to know, I would have been here for you. I'm available for you now."

Courtney stood too, and they looked at each other across the coffee table. "I know. But Alex—"

Ashley interrupted with a smile. "He said no. Got it. I'm a few years older now, and this time I'm not listening." She walked to the door. "I'll be back to see you soon."

She walked down the steps and over to her car, smiling to herself. She made progress in patching up part of the relationship between herself and Courtney. They'd at least had a conversation in the house instead of on the front step.

CHAPTER 13

Jason emerged from the grocery store and saw Ashley come out of the Richmonds' house. He hadn't realized she knew anyone in Chokecherry Valley when they'd first met. Now he knew Paul and Alex were her brothers, he figured she was visiting Courtney. He knew Alex was still in prison. As soon as he got out, the news would be all over town.

If she'd been a child in Chokecherry Valley, how had he never known her before he saw her in class? This was a small town. He must have met her when they were young, and it hadn't registered. Her explanation of being with her grandmother in Bismarck during high school explained why he didn't know her from those years.

He ducked back into the grocery store. As much as he wanted to talk to her, he needed to get back to the farm.

"Is there something you need, Jason?" Betty asked.

He looked back at the owner, who ran the store today. "No. I'm fine." His face flushed. He glanced out the glass window, watching as Ashley backed out of the driveway. He looked at Betty again. "I have a feeling I forgot something. Thought if I stepped back inside, I might remember."

"Anything coming to you?" Betty glanced out the window too. Without waiting for him to answer, she asked, "Do you know the woman coming out of Courtney's house? She looks familiar to me."

He shook his head, then changed his mind. "Ashley Richmond. She's in one of my college classes."

"Oh. That's Ashley? Alex's sister. I suppose she came to talk to Courtney since Alex is getting out of jail soon."

Jason nodded. He didn't want to discuss Ashley. He needed to get back to watch Chloe and Madison so his mom could do what she needed to do. He had lots of homework because last night he spent too much of his time thinking about Ashley.

At least Betty wasn't a gossip. She didn't push any further conversation on him.

"Well, if I've forgotten something, I can't remember what it is." He smiled at Betty, and she smiled back.

"I'll see you soon." He walked back outside to his vehicle, wondering if Betty was watching him leave. It didn't matter. He couldn't feel any more foolish than he already did.

The puzzle of Ashley and why he didn't recognize her from Chokecherry Valley would remain a mystery. He had other things to take care of this weekend.

Madison seemed to be doing better since the family banded together to make sure she got her rest and got breaks from taking care of Chloe. Jason didn't mind the extra work if Madison improved.

His trepidation centered around what would happen once school started on Tuesday. It was Madison's senior year, and she decided to go to school instead of trying to get her G.E.D. online. He hoped her getting out of the house and seeing other people throughout the day would help her mood. It concerned him that having to get up every day and get to school, do homework, and take care of Chloe all together might prove too much for her. She might get more depressed.

He'd talked to their mom about it, and she'd advised waiting for the end of the first week of school to see what happened. At least the school week only lasted four days because of Labor Day.

He hoped it wouldn't matter. Maybe he worried for nothing, but he felt Madison would crash with one more thing added to her plate. Maybe he should be more positive about the situation. Time would tell.

When he opened the front door of their farmhouse, the smell of freshly baked cookies greeted him. He looked at the counter. Chocolate peanut butter. His favorite.

His mom came into the room carrying her purse. "Nina and I are going over to the Millers to see if they need anything before winter comes. We want to make sure they're doing okay in their new home."

"We did hurry to put things together when they had that fire. Let me know if you and Nina need help with anything. I'm sure Dad and I can do any repairs or find someone who can."

His mom settled her purse in the crook of her arm and leaned over to pat his hand, which rested on the counter near the cookies. "I know, dear. You're always so kind. What did your dad and I do to deserve such great kids and a wonderful grandchild?"

"I don't know—and I'm not sure what I did to deserve chocolate peanut butter cookies either."

The glint in his mother's eyes should have warned him. "They're not for you."

He frowned at her as she headed toward the door to leave. With her hand on the knob, she turned and smiled at him. "Just kidding. Help yourself."

He smiled back, and then turned to scoop up a few cookies. He heard her laughter as she closed the door behind her. His mother had a great sense of humor. It had been a long time since he'd heard her laughing, he realized, which meant she was worried. Worried and stressed.

Something needed to change. If Madison couldn't handle school, he'd talk her into online schooling and medication. At least she could try it. He should probably research the medication angle. Maybe it wouldn't be good for Madison.

Ashley might know. Other than calling her, when would he have time to get together with her? As much as he wanted to date her, now wasn't a good time. She would continue with more classes or look for a job. Maybe even move away, depending on what she decided she wanted for her future.

He was trying to take a full load of classes, work on the farm, and take care of Madison and Chloe. His mother was already stressed out and worried. As much as he liked Ashley, he shouldn't add one more thing to his life. As much as he argued with himself, he knew what he was going to do: spend as much time with Ashley as possible. They'd work it out.

CHAPTER 14

Ashley arrived at class early on Wednesday. She hoped Jason would be there, and she could talk to him. He walked into class with Dr. Williams, so she had no chance to ask him how his long weekend had gone or how Madison made it through. She'd spent way too much time over the weekend thinking about him and hoping they could get together after class again today.

He smiled and said hello to her as he sat down, and then Dr. Williams started the class. He went over some extra information about different types of speeches and mentioned there was a sign-up sheet for the students to choose a date to give their speeches.

"We have time for three speeches per class, so we can discuss the presentation after each speech."

She planned to write her first speech as quickly as possible and practice once in front of Jason. Then she would sign up for the first opening that would reasonably give her time to be ready. Hopefully, she would have a few minutes to talk to Jason about when he would be available to practice their speeches. If not, she could text him and ask.

She sent a sideways look at him, but he was concentrating on Dr. Williams. She started listening too, and it helped take her mind off her own churning thoughts.

When class ended, Jason quickly got his stuff together and said a quick goodbye. "Busy day with Chloe since Madison is in school," he explained. "I'll call you when I get a minute."

She gathered her own things as he walked out the classroom door. Well. She'd worried all weekend about being nervous at lunch with him today, and he didn't have time.

She told herself not to be hurt. It wasn't his fault he needed to watch Chloe, but Ashley was disappointed. She had wanted to have lunch with him, even if it made her nervous.

She had enough to keep herself busy for the day. She got home, ate quickly, and went to work. Being at work reminded her she needed to set up a meeting with Paul.

She wondered if she'd seen Paul's girlfriend at work yet. Since she didn't know what the woman looked like, it was hard to know. She was kind of surprised she hadn't run into Paul in the hallway either, but they were in different parts of the large building. She'd only been at work for a few afternoons too. Different hallways, stairways, and elevators to use. He probably stayed in his department seeing patients and eating lunch in his office or their staff lounge.

She wanted to see him from a distance first. Maybe she should go over to his side of the building and skulk around. She laughed at the idea. That was ridiculous. The best thing to do would be call him and set up a time to meet. Getting together with him as soon as possible would calm the butterflies flipping around in her stomach. She hoped.

Telling him how hurt she felt by how he treated her two years ago and setting some parameters for future times she saw him would go a long way toward showing her where she stood with him. If they were going to get closer, she needed to follow through and get courageous.

CHAPTER 15

Ashley called Paul on her break at work. Their conversation was stilted but cordial. They set up a time to meet for dinner that evening. She hadn't expected him to be free right away, but his eagerness to see her was a good sign. She wanted to get together with him but assumed she'd have a little more time to get used to the idea. It was better she didn't have time to ruminate.

She chose a quiet bistro she loved. It would be a good place to talk.

She saw Jill for a few minutes between work and going out to meet Paul. Work had kept her busy, but now her stomach cramped at the idea of seeing him.

Jill looked her over when she came out of the bedroom. "You look nice in your pink blouse and jeans, but you're pale. Are you okay?"

"I'm fine. Just nervous about seeing Paul, you know?" She gripped her purse in one hand and rubbed her head with the other.

"He's your brother, and he wants to mend your relationship. He'll be on his best behavior," Jill tried to reassure her.

"You're right. I need to remember him from when we were younger and not when he drank. He lost his wife and daughter. I imagine that has made him more sympathetic. I don't want to get hurt again if he suddenly changes."

"You don't have to give your whole heart over to him today, silly." Jill slung her leg over the couch arm and lay back on the couch.

Ashley envied her. She wanted to forget meeting Paul and join Jill for a relaxing night of movies and popcorn.

"Hey, look at it this way: it'll take your mind off what's-his-name from your class." Jill grinned at her.

"Funny. You know what his name is." Jill did have a point. If she kept busy talking to Paul, she wouldn't wonder if Jason would have time for lunch after their next class. She knew he was busy with his sister and other things. She had to be patient and give him the space he needed to take care of his responsibilities.

***

She arrived at the bistro before Paul and sat at a table along one of the walls. She liked it there better than one of the tables in the middle of the room. The waiter arranged two menus and asked for her drink order.

"I'll have water for now. Thank you."

He left, and Paul arrived soon after, his face lit up with a smile. "Hi, there," he said as he took his seat.

She smiled back. She wasn't ready to hug him yet. "Hi. It's good to see you."

He looked much better than at the funeral. He appeared less weary and less uptight than she'd seen him in years. Even when he drank, he had a stressed look around his mouth and eyes. Like everything in life was difficult.

"Let's order first, and then talk," he suggested.

She liked the idea. Maybe her nerves would settle while he looked at the menu.

"What's good to eat here?" Paul asked.

"Pretty much everything. I've never had a bad meal. I'm having a shrimp salad."

Paul smiled again. "You always did like seafood."

She laughed. "You used to call me a fish. I never did learn how to swim."

He laughed too. "I'm going to have the chicken alfredo with broccoli."

"I've eaten it, and it's good here." The small talk and his easy manner calmed her down, she realized. Whatever happened after Samantha's and Amy's deaths relaxed him in a way she'd never seen before. Even when they were children moving from place to place, he'd been high-strung.

294

"I never told you in person. I'm sorry about Samantha and Amy."

They were interrupted by the waiter bringing the bread and olive oil dip with seasoning. When the waiter left with Paul's drink order and their meal order, Paul acknowledged her words. "Thank you. I appreciated you coming to the funeral. It meant the world to me."

He took a piece of bread but didn't dip it in the oil or take a bite. He looked at it for a minute and then set it on his plate. He looked over at her. "I'm sorry for what I said when I was drunk that day. It was inexcusable, but I hope someday you can forgive me. I know you came to the funeral and agreed to meet me this evening, but I don't know if we can ever have the sibling relationship I want. I don't know what you want, and I'm not going to put you on the spot by asking you. I appreciate any time you can spend with me."

As Ashley listened to him, he sounded sincere. He left it up to her whether she wanted to talk to him or not. She knew she wouldn't have come this evening if she didn't want to see him or talk to him again.

The waiter came by again with a tray holding their main courses, a water pitcher, and Paul's glass of water. After he placed everything on the table and refilled Ashley's water glass, he left them alone again.

Ashley used the time to plan what she wanted to say. "You'll always be my brother, Paul. That's never going to change. Yes, I was hurt when you said I was a nuisance, and you'd rather not see me again.

"Maybe I didn't have the right to talk to you about Samantha the way I did, but I couldn't ignore the fact she and you were both drinking to excess while taking care of Amy. I felt you should do something, and you brushed me off. Rudely. I was concerned about Amy." She didn't add that it had resulted in tragedy in the end. Her brother knew all too well.

The smile left his face, and she saw the deep grooves of grief in his features. He had lost weight, which enhanced those grooves. The smile hid the extent of his pain.

"You were right, and I paid the price. I'm not going to hide behind excuses. When I got sober two years ago, I should have taken further action to protect Amy. I didn't."

"I'm sorry that happened," Ashley said. "I forgive you, Paul. I really do. I've considered getting in contact with you a lot in the past year, but I didn't have the guts. I'm glad you called. I do want to spend time with you too."

His face relaxed again. "I'm glad. I've missed you. I didn't realize until I heard your voice on the phone the other day just how much." He picked up his fork to start eating.

While they both needed to let the matter settle for a while and gradually form a new relationship, she had one more thing to say. "Paul, I need to tell you, if you start drinking again, I'll do what I can to help. However, I won't put up with you treating me badly again."

"Understood," he said.

She picked up her fork and started on her salad. They ate in silence for a while. She was surprised she had an appetite, but with the initial conversation behind them, she relaxed.

When Paul took a drink of his water and cleared his throat, Ashley almost laughed. He always cleared his throat when he had something important to say. She hoped it was about something good.

He put his fork back on his plate. "I met someone at the hospital. Her name is Hannah, and she makes me happy."

"Great, Paul. I'm glad for you." She didn't tell him she'd heard rumors.

"We're dating right now, but I did buy her an engagement ring this summer. I told her about it and asked her to let me know when she was ready. She wants to wait until a year has passed since Samantha and Amy went to Heaven."

What astonished Ashley the most about Paul's words was his use of "heaven." She hadn't realized he believed in God. She wanted to talk to him about the subject, but they were already covering a lot of ground this evening.

"Congratulations." She lifted her water glass in a toast to him. "Here's to your wonderful news."

"Thanks. I can't wait until it's formal, and my ring is on her finger."

"Did you know I'm working at the hospital where you work?" Ashley asked. "I'm taking a clinical observation course to view potential job opportunities in the field."

"I heard the rumors. That was another reason I wanted to get together with you. We didn't need to have our first meeting in a long time to happen in the hospital corridor," Paul said.

"Good point." She finished her salad and pushed her plate away. "I'm also starting to have second reconsider whether I really want to become a psychologist. The problem is, I don't have another occupation in mind."

The waiter stopped by to replenish their water and ask if they wanted anything else. They both refused dessert, and he left again.

"That must be difficult. You always knew what you wanted to do." Paul's face crinkled in concern.

"I thought I did. Sometimes life changes when we least expect it." She thought of her career but also of Paul's life.

"That's for sure. I'd really like to help you if you want to discuss other careers or anything else, Ashley. Just getting together this evening has shown me that I really missed you. I'd like to start getting together on a regular basis. Are you okay with that? I want to make up for lost time," Paul said.

Again, he left the choice to her. "You don't have to let me make the decisions about getting together, Paul. I said I forgive you, and I do. There might be some lingering hurt, but eventually that will go away. Life is short. Let's become the family we never were before. Yes, you and Alex and I hung out together, but we were young. We didn't know what was going on half the time. Let's build something better than what our parents left us to muddle around in."

Paul's smile lit up his face again. "I love your idea. Of course, we have two new people involved. I have Hannah, and Alex has Courtney. Maybe you have someone else too?"

She almost mentioned Jason, but it was too soon. She'd only known him a week and hadn't talked to him since their lunch the previous week. She felt like keeping their new relationship to herself for a while yet. She smiled back at Paul. "You never know when someone will pop up in my life. Five is a good number to start with for our family for now."

She frowned. "However, convincing Courtney and Alex to join in this family effort might be difficult. Alex told me not to visit him in prison, and Courtney basically threw me out of the house when I went to visit her after Alex was first imprisoned. I went there this past weekend and told her I wasn't staying away any longer. She grudgingly let me in, and we talked for a while."

"I tried to visit Alex too, and the same thing happened to me. He said to stay away. He didn't want to contaminate me or you with his misdeeds."

Ashley twisted the napkin on her lap. "I find it difficult to believe Alex embezzled that money. He didn't need it. Mom and Dad gave him and Courtney enough to live on, and his job at the bank paid well. It always felt strange to me, but he pled guilty. Didn't you find it strange?"

"Yes. Money never seemed important to him, and the amount was low compared to the settlement we all got from Mom and Dad. I mean, if you're going to steal, do it on a grand scale."

Ashley knew Paul was the one who did things on a grand scale. He was always all in. Alex had been the cautious one.

"Maybe he did it to see if he would get caught, and that's why he kept the amount low. I don't understand the whole situation," Paul said.

Ashley had been about to take a sip of water but set her glass down. "You don't imagine he did it just as a game?"

"He does have a bit of a sense of humor, but embezzling is going a little too far and not his usual idea of a joke. He didn't realize he'd go to prison for it. I bet if we got him to tell the truth, he'd say he assumed he'd have to pay the money back, do community service, and that would be all."

"They did decide to send him to prison. What about Courtney? Wouldn't he have wanted to protect her from the scorn of all the people in Chokecherry Valley? She lived with their sneers and vandalism all this time," Ashley said.

"He probably talked it over with her once the situation got dire, and she agreed with our banishment. He wouldn't have done that to her if she hadn't felt the same way. Courtney's tough."

Ashley shook her head and kept twisting the napkin in her hands. "If we're right, Alex should have gotten a better attorney."

"Well, when he's out of prison, I can pester him until I know the truth."

"And what good would that do? Alex did it for a purpose. It's his life and Courtney's. They must have a powerful reason for their actions."

"Oh, I have no doubt."

Ashley had doubts, but she didn't mention them to Paul. There was no reason big enough for Alex to spend two years in prison without fighting a little harder for a lighter sentence. At least he could have appealed.

"Well, I'm going to visit Courtney again this weekend. I'll be there as many weekends as I can until Alex gets home in December, which is just a few months away. I know Courtney has family, but one more person on her side can't hurt," Ashley said.

"I'm going to stop by their place the day after Alex gets out of prison. They'll need his first day home to themselves, but I'm not waiting longer than a day. If Alex hadn't refused to see me when I went to visit him at the prison, I would have gone there on a regular basis. Now, he can't stop me."

"Me either. Do you want to pick me up, and I'll go with you, or do you want to go alone?"

"Let's go together." Paul picked up his water glass and lifted it in the air. "Here's to our new closer-knit family."

She raised her glass to him too.

CHAPTER 16

Jason woke up Friday with the feeling the situation with Madison was working out the way the family hoped. They hadn't left her alone with Chloe, and both of them appeared calmer. There was less crying. Madison seemed more engaged with Chloe, without getting overwhelmed.

Madison had gone to school for three days now and hadn't said much about it when she got home. He hoped that meant everyone treated her okay.

He showered and dressed for classes. He looked forward to seeing Ashley in class. Now that Madison spent all day in school, he could stretch out class to include lunch again. He knew his mom would watch Chloe for the extra hour it would take him to get home, as it would be a few days a week. Especially if he told her why he was late.

Did he want to tell his family about Ashley? He kept changing his mind about telling them. They would work extra hard to let him have time with her, and he didn't want them to go out of their way. The situation with Madison might be okay now, but it had only been a week since they'd made the changes. She hadn't recovered from her depression, and until then, he couldn't add a further burden on his parents.

He would tell them he was meeting a friend for lunch. In a way, Ashley's small window of time for lunch worked to his benefit. He didn't have to be the one to always hurry away from her. He already decided he wanted to see her more often, and he was trying hard not to be frustrated by the other demands on his time. From the moment when she poked him in the shoulder, and he looked up to see her smiling, he wanted to get to know her.

Humming a tune as he left the bedroom, he noticed Madison's door remained closed. He looked at the watch on his wrist. She would be late to school if she didn't get up soon. He knocked on her door.

Madison didn't answer. He knocked again. "You're going to be late."

As he listened, he heard the crib creak, but he got no response from Madison. He opened the door and poked his head into the room. Madison's bed was empty.

Chloe lay in her crib, sucking her fingers, her eyes sleepy in her sweet face as she looked at him. He went to pick her up and saw her pajamas were wet. He rubbed her cheek with his finger. "I might need to get your mom or grandma to change you."

He smiled at her, and she gurgled back. He went to find Madison or his mom.

His mom sat at the kitchen table eating toast slathered with chokecherry jelly and cereal. "Good morning."

"Good morning, honey." She looked at his clothes. "All ready to leave?"

"Yes. Chloe needs a diaper change. If you don't have time, I'll do it, but I don't want to get these clothes wet. I don't have time to change again for school."

"I'll do it. Wasn't Madison there?"

"No. She must have left for school. I didn't hear her leaving. Did you?"

His mom shook her head. "That's strange. I've been in the kitchen all morning. I should have seen her. She must have left early, but I don't understand why she would do that."

She got up and rummaged around through the papers and other items on the counter. "I don't see a note."

"No note on the fridge either," Jason said. "Why would she leave so early?" He didn't like the flutter in his stomach. She wouldn't leave early enough to miss their mom. Unless she had something to hide. The thought did nothing for the state of his stomach.

"I'll go check for her car." Jason went outside and around the corner of the house where they usually parked their vehicles. They were all there. He stood there a moment, not wanting to break the news to his mother. This was not good. He tried to call Madison on her cell but didn't get an answer.

He went back into the house. "All the vehicles are here. Maybe she got a ride from a friend." He tried her phone again and walked into her bedroom. He didn't hear it ringing in the house either.

His mother finished her breakfast and stood by the sink. "We would have heard a vehicle drive up to the house. We'll need to call the school to see if she's there." She took a deep breath as if to say something more. Instead, she pursed her lips together. "My cell phone is in the bedroom. I'll be back in a minute."

"I'll go change Chloe. At least she's been content to lay in her crib this morning, but she'll need to be fed." He got Chloe changed and dressed, then picked up her blanket and a few toys and laid her on the floor in the living room. She waved her arms and smiled, satisfied with life, which was a blessing. He expected her to be crying by now. Maybe Madison fed her before she left. He'd find out soon.

He heard his mom talking on the phone but not the words. She took longer than he expected, which didn't bode well. He knew his dad had started taking his phone with him wherever he went, even if he only went to the barn. If Mom called Dad after the school, then Madison hadn't shown up at school this morning.

He finished making Chloe's bottle. He went back to the living room, picked her up, and held her in the crook of his arm as he started feeding her. She sucked greedily, so it was hard to tell if Madison fed her or not. That didn't give him any clue as to when she left the house.

His mother came from her bedroom and stood there looking at him and Chloe. He said it for her: "She didn't go to school."

"No." She plopped down on the rocker next to the couch where Jason sat. "I don't even know if she has any friends anymore. We'll have to call around. Madison will hate that."

Jason nodded.

"I called Nina. She'll watch Chloe for us while we figure out what to do. I said we'd drop her off in about a half hour."

"That'll work. I'll skip class today. It's a good thing most of my classes are online. When I'm done feeding Chloe, I'll change into other clothes, drop Chloe off at Nina's, and then go looking on a few of the paths out here where she usually walks. Maybe she twisted an ankle or something." He tried to be upbeat and not mention worst-case scenarios.

"I talked to your dad. He'll be done with chores soon and then come back to the house."

He burped Chloe, then he reassured his mom, "We'll find her."

Her expression was doubtful. The lines on her forehead and around her mouth deepened.

"Yes, we will."

He saw her shake off her lethargy. "Yes, we will," she repeated.

He got up and set Chloe in her lap. "Here. Hold your granddaughter for a few minutes while I go change." He smiled at his mom and dropped the burp cloth on top of Chloe's lap. He went to his room and shut the door. He said a few prayers to God to keep his sister safe as he changed his clothes.

Where could his sister be? Why hadn't she left a note? Why had she skipped school? What was going on in her mind? No answers came.

His mom must have told Nina the whole story because when he dropped Chloe at her house, she gave him a hug and said, "You'll find her. She probably needed to get away for a walk and lost track of time."

He thanked her and went home to start searching. His mom was on the phone again, and his dad, who was pacing back and forth, said she started calling around the neighborhood to see if anyone knew anything. He left them to it and started his own search of the paths on their property.

As soon as his mom finished making calls, he fully expected she and his dad would be out scouring the countryside too. He tried to keep his thoughts from going in one particular direction. He didn't want to come across his sister's body. He wanted to find her alive, but he knew what depression could do.

He took the easy paths first, the ones without many trees or vegetation. He took a quick walk around the farm. Then he went to the east and started up and down the paths his family made working and playing on the farm. Trees surrounded both sides of one path. He hoped she hadn't gone off the path in that part of the valley because it would be hard to see her if she went too far into the trees.

Close to noon, he started on the more complicated path, hurrying along the winding dirt road, more concerned than ever about Madison. He'd brought along water and took a few swigs from one of the bottles. The morning had been cool, but the sun was higher in the September sky, and it was getting warmer.

The trees along the route offered some shade. He looked first to his left and then to his right, trying to scan the ditches and look into the trees, so he wouldn't miss anything in his rush to find her. It would help if he knew what his sister was wearing. She probably had on her dark blue hoodie and jeans, but he couldn't depend on it. He walked slowly, and then he heard something that didn't blend into the usual country sounds.

He stood still for a minute, listening. The sound came again. A sniffle. He thought the noise came from his right but couldn't be sure. He started along the path again, looking more often to his right but also scanning the left.

Then he saw her a few feet ahead of him sitting against a tree. She must have heard his feet on the dusty path because she looked up as he approached.

Her forlorn look and red eyes tugged at his heart as she sniffled again. Her drawn face looked like it belonged to an old woman who had given up all hope.

"I couldn't do it," she said, holding up a steak knife.

He saw blood on her left wrist then, and his heart stopped for a second before starting to race. "Good." That was all he said before he walked over and sat beside her. He took the knife and set it farther away from her before pulling her into a hug.

She cuddled up to him. "It felt like the only thing to do."

"I suppose it did, but I'm glad you didn't do it. We all love you."

"I know," she said. "But I can't feel it. I can't feel anything. I don't have any energy, any belief that everything is going to work out. I don't have any friends at school. They all ignore me. I'm stuck at home with Chloe. I can't go out. But I don't want to go out. Who would I go anywhere with?" She started crying. "I thought I was done crying."

Jason wanted to point out that if Madison wanted to go somewhere, she could, but he knew what she meant. She felt stuck, and she couldn't see past this moment when the depression had such a hold on her.

"You need to get help."

They sat there silently for a time, then Jason pulled his phone out of his pocket and the other water bottle he brought along. "Here. Have some water. I need to call Mom and Dad and tell them you're okay."

She didn't object. She was listless, letting him take the lead.

Jason called his dad and told him he'd found Madison, and she was okay. He wouldn't go into the fact that Madison really wasn't okay. She wasn't in immediate danger now that he was with her. He told his dad they'd be back in about fifteen minutes and suggested his dad tell his mom to make eggs and bacon for Madison's breakfast to keep her busy.

Between her making breakfast and calling back all the people she'd talked to earlier, he figured they had plenty of time to get back to the house, but his dad might come out to meet them. He'd deliberately not told his parents where to find them, so as not to overwhelm Madison.

They couldn't go on this way any longer. She needed help. Maybe even inpatient treatment. They couldn't watch over her twenty-four-seven, and she needed that now. They would be headed to the emergency room in Bismarck as soon as Madison ate and showered.

CHAPTER 17

Samantha watched them walk back to the house. She spent a good part of the morning convincing Madison not to take her life. The teenager left the house around five that morning, and God sent Samantha.

Samantha knew of Jason's new relationship with Ashley. She'd noticed that God sent her to Earth to help anyone known to Paul's family who needed help. Usually that included pregnant women. Since Samantha had been at Chloe's birth, it seemed Madison also fell under Samantha's care.

Of course, Madison couldn't see her, but Samantha wrestled against the depression gripping Madison's mind.

Samantha had her own memories of depression from when she lived on Earth. She knew where the mind could go in the darkest moments. She'd felt worthless. Felt Amy deserved a better mother. Paul deserved a better wife. Her twin sister deserved a better twin. And on and on.

Her mind had gone in circles until she didn't feel much at all. She understood Madison. She was glad she could help in any way possible.

CHAPTER 18

Ashley got to class before Jason. She didn't realize how much she wanted to talk to him until she got there, and he wasn't there. When class started, and he hadn't appeared, she didn't know what to think. Had something bad happened with Madison? Jason had been so concerned on the phone the other day. And the way he had hurried out of class Wednesday to get home to be with Chloe showed how dependable he was with his responsibilities.

Her mind wasn't on the class. When it ended, she drove through a fast-food restaurant and took the food home to eat. She sent Jason a quick text to ask if everything was okay. He responded that he would fill her in when he had a chance. That reply worried her more.

When she arrived at work, the receptionist told her she and her supervisor were going to interview a patient who came to the emergency room.

As her supervisor, Dr. Beth Thorn knew Ashley wanted to work with younger patients. This seventeen-year-old would provide much-needed experience for her. Ashley hadn't told anyone from the school about her possible change in career. She'd only told Jason, Jill, and Paul.

They walked down the hallway talking about other things, not wanting to violate patient confidentiality. There wasn't much known about the girl at this point anyway. The father called and said they brought her in because of a suicide attempt, but that was the extent of their knowledge.

When they arrived in the emergency department, the receptionist admitted them to the locked patient area. A nurse came over to talk to them. Her name tag said Sarah.

"Hi, Dr. Thorn and Ashley. We can go into this area here, where no one can hear us talking, and I'll fill you in." She led them into a small office with a window looking out into the emergency room area.

She pulled up a chart on the computer on the desk. There were two chairs in the room, and Dr. Thorn and Ashley sat down.

"Madison is the girl's name. Her vitals are stable. She's in good physical condition and has a three-month-old baby."

"I understand she's seventeen," Dr. Thorn said. "Is the baby's father in the picture?"

"Doesn't appear to be. Her parents and an older brother brought her in. They look like a supportive family. They told me they've been taking turns staying with Madison, so she's never alone with the baby. Apparently, Madison has been to their local doctor, who diagnosed her with postpartum depression. The doctor recommended medication, but Madison refused."

At the mention of Madison, Ashley started to get a bad feeling. Was the patient Jason's sister? Her name was Madison. She had a baby, and she was seventeen.

Sarah continued, "One day, the brother found Madison on the front step crying, and the baby in the house crying. They started taking turns making sure someone always stayed with her. This morning she slipped out of the house before anyone was up and went out to the woods near their house. She took a knife with her to slit her wrist but couldn't go through with it. She's got a slight knife mark on her wrist, but that's as far as she got."

"Anything else we need to know?" Dr. Thorn asked.

"That's about the extent of it. I'll leave her in your capable hands. Dr. Wright said he will admit her if you think it's advisable."

"I'm already thinking that's going to be necessary. You can start searching for a bed for her and let Dr. Wright know we would like her admitted. I'll give you the go ahead when we're ready," Dr. Thorn said.

"She's in Room 5 now," Sarah told them.

She left them as they exited the small office, and Dr. Thorn headed in the direction of Room 5. Ashley followed behind and wondered what to do about the situation.

Dr. Thorn pulled the curtain back and held it for Ashley, who took one look into the room and stopped. Jason stood in the room with Madison. She was right. Madison was Jason's sister. She threw a smile in his direction, and then said, "Dr. Thorn, I need to see you out in the hallway for a minute. It's necessary."

Dr. Thorn looked at her strangely, and then followed her out of the room with a murmured excuse to the family. They moved far enough away from the room so they couldn't be heard.

"I know Madison's brother, Jason. I didn't realize at first when we talked to the nurse that he was her brother. Is that a conflict of interest?"

Dr. Thorn frowned. "How well do you know him?"

"We met in class last week. We went out for coffee after the first class and lunch after the second class. Other than that, a few phone conversations."

"You like him," Dr. Thorn said it as if it were fact, not a question.

Ashley's face heated. "Yes."

"Well, this is awkward." She stood there for a minute. "You can remain for the intake if the family approves. That's all you were going to do as an observer anyway. Someone else will be the counselor for her case. We'll ask them if you can stay in the room before we go any further."

"Okay."

They headed back into the exam room. Dr. Thorn took charge. "I'm sorry about the interruption. Ashley tells me she has known Jason for about a week from a class at school."

At this information, Madison lifted her head. Probably because the first part of this conversation wasn't about her. She looked at Jason.

He flushed as he became the focus of the group. "That's true. We met last week."

"There's a question of conflict of interest. I told Ashley if you were all okay with her staying for the intake, she could, and Madison will have someone else assigned to her for counseling. The intake will be the questions I'll ask right now, and the decisions we make for treatment now. After that, someone else will take over. Madison, it's up to you. We want to do what you want."

Madison smiled shyly at Ashley, and she smiled back. "It's up to you," Ashley told her. "Please do whatever you're comfortable with."

"You can stay." There was no hesitation in her voice.

"Okay." Dr. Thorn took over again. "We have six people in this small room. Again, Madison, who from your family would you like to remain here? If it's everyone, we'll have to move to a different location."

"How about my mom?" She looked at her dad and brother. "Mom can tell you everything. I'm fine with that, but Dr. Thorn is right. This is a little overwhelming to have so many people listening."

"Okay. We have a plan." Dr. Thorn stuck her head outside the curtain. "Do we have someone who can escort a few people to the waiting area?" she asked Sarah.

"Sure. I can do it." She stepped over to the curtained area. "Who's coming to the waiting area?"

"We are," Jason and his dad said in unison. They each gave Madison a hug.

"I'll call you as soon as I get a chance." Jason smiled at Ashley as he passed her on his way out of the room.

She nodded at him as he and his father followed the nurse to the waiting area.

Ashley appreciated the time it took to settle the room for the four of them. She had gotten over her shock of finding out the patient was Jason's sister and could concentrate on her job.

CHAPTER 19

Madison's mother had been looking at Ashley since she'd heard Jason and Ashley knew each other. It made Ashley nervous, but she pretended not to notice. Fortunately, as soon as Dr. Thorn started talking to Madison, her mother's attention returned to her daughter.

Ashley watched Dr. Thorn talk to Madison, who sat on the small gurney with the top of the bed raised. Dr. Thorn asked if she could sit at the foot of the bed, and Madison nodded. Ashley stood in the far corner to be out of the way as she observed.

Having gotten the preliminaries out of the way, Dr. Thorn asked, "Do you still feel like hurting yourself?"

Madison hung her head and whispered, "No."

"What are you feeling right now?"

Madison avoided eye contact. "I don't want to live, but I don't plan to do anything about it."

"Good." Dr. Thorn patted Madison's jean-covered leg. "What should we do in the meantime, so you can start feeling better?"

"I'd like to go home and continue on the way it's been." She peeked at Dr. Thorn through her bangs.

Her mom cleared her throat, and Dr. Thorn held up a hand to stop her from saying anything. "Is that working?"

"Well…"

"How old is your baby?"

"Almost three months old." She straightened a little on the bed, and a smile crossed her face.

"You love your baby, don't you?" Dr. Thorn asked.

"Yes. And I know some people hurt their babies when they have postpartum depression, but I would never do that. I would leave… I have left when I get too impatient with her."

"What's changed now? How are things going to be different? You've tried to change your feelings. Has that worked?" Dr. Thorn asked matter-of-factly. Her voice held no condemnation, just an inquiring neutral tone not likely to cause Madison to shut down.

Madison sat quietly for a few minutes. "I guess nothing has changed. I don't care what happens to me. I feel numb, and there's this darkness around me. Like the lights aren't on in this room. Does that make sense?"

"Perfect sense," Dr. Thorn assured her. "Normal for depression. But it's not normal to live every day feeling like that."

"Well, my mom got over her postpartum depression on her own. I thought if I waited long enough, mine would go away too."

Dr. Thorn turned her gaze in Madison's mom's direction. "You had postpartum depression too?"

"Yes. It lasted about a year. They didn't have as many treatments, and it wasn't understood or talked about much at that time." She looked at Madison. "You can trust Dr. Thorn. She seems sensitive to your feelings. If I had it to do over again, I would have tried treatment. I wish I had. I want that for you, but it's your choice."

Ashley appreciated how they treated Madison like the adult she nearly was. She was old enough to make her own decisions, but Ashley also wanted to shout, "You need to be an inpatient because you want to die, and you need to be on medication." She kept her mouth shut and waited to hear what Dr. Thorn would say next.

"What do you think of what your mother said?" Dr. Thorn asked.

"She's right. I didn't know it took her a year to get better. I don't want to wait that long."

Ashley heard Madison's mother let out a small breath.

"I believe we can find a medication that will help you. Would you be willing to try one?" Dr. Thorn asked.

"Yes, but I'm scared of side effects." Her vulnerability was obvious.

"What if you stay at the hospital a few days while we start you on a medication? The side effects usually show up early in treatment. The medication takes a longer time to help the depression. We can talk more once we know if you have side effects. We'll keep you informed what the side effects are, so you can decide what you want to do. You're making the right decision."

She stood up. "I'm going to go talk to the nurse about a room for you to stay in for a few days. Why don't you talk to your mom for a bit, and then I'll be back to see if you have any more questions?"

Madison nodded.

Ashley followed Dr. Thorn out of the exam room, and they went to the nurses' station. "You didn't give her a chance to say no to staying here."

"I know. I didn't want her to say no because we would have to commit her, and I didn't want to put her through that. At least she feels like she has some say in her treatment, but she's suicidal. She says she won't do anything, but she says she doesn't want to live. If something happened that stressed her more than she already is, who knows what decision she'd make. I don't want it to come to that."

Ashley watched Dr. Thorn talk to Dr. Wright about Madison's condition. As a psychologist, Dr. Thorn couldn't admit a patient to the hospital. Dr. Wright agreed Madison needed to be admitted and signed off on an order for admission to the Mental Health Unit.

Dr. Thorn finished her own charting of Madison's intake evaluation on the computer. They went back to Madison's curtained alcove and asked if there were any questions. The women both shook their heads.

"Okay. I'll get your medical plan together and come up to your room later to talk it over with you. Ashley will escort you to the room you'll be staying in as soon as the nurse comes by with your room number. We only let one person visit at a time. Your mother can go with you until you're settled."

Madison's mom stood up and patted her shoulder. "Thank you, Dr. Thorn."

"You're welcome." She left.

Ashley stood there as they turned in her direction. She smiled her reassurance, relieved when she heard the curtain being opened again. The nurse appeared and walked over to cut off the armband Madison already had on her wrist and put a new one on. She noticed Madison turned her hand downward, so they couldn't see the knife cut.

"I'll be going along with you," the nurse said. "My name is Sarah. If you didn't remember from before, that's okay. We'll stop by and pick up your brother and dad from the waiting room. They can go with us part of the way."

Madison smiled at that plan. She seemed close to her family.

Ashley pushed down a twinge of jealousy. She was getting together with Paul again, and soon Alex and Courtney. She should be thankful for her life, not envying a depressed girl who had a lot of courage.

They stopped at the waiting room, and Ashley motioned for the two men to join them. "Let's wait until we get into the hallway, and then we'll talk," Ashley said. Jason took a quick look at her before he focused on Madison.

They left the emergency room waiting area, and Sarah led them through the hallways. "Okay. We're going to the fourth floor. It's quiet in these hallways now with fewer people, so you can discuss what you want. Madison, do you want to say something?"

"I'm going to stay here for a few nights." She looked at Jason and then her dad. "The doctor said she'd start me on medication, and she'd tell me what to expect with side effects."

"Are you scared?" Jason asked.

"Yes, but I know this is the best thing to do." She looked down at her feet as they continued to walk down the hallway. "I scared myself this morning. I don't want to do that again."

Jason pulled her into an awkward hug because they were walking when he did it. "You'll be fine. We'll check on you often. You'll be home and feeling better before you know it." He let her go, and they continued on their way.

By the time Madison said a tearful goodbye to her dad and Jason and settled into her room with her mother, Ashley felt drained. Madison's mom could stay an hour, and then she'd have to leave. Ashley was glad she didn't have to be there for their parting.

They all thanked Sarah, who was ready to go back to the emergency room.

Ashley walked with Jason and his dad to the exit. She felt awkward and couldn't think of anything to say in front of Jason's dad. She was glad Jason had already mentioned calling her as soon as he could. She wanted to be a comfort to him.

"She's in good hands," Ashley told Jason and his dad at the hospital exit.

"You're right," Jason agreed. "Dr. Thorn seemed understanding."

"She is." Ashley nodded.

His dad shook her hand, and they both said goodbye.

Ashley returned to her office and found out that Dr. Thorn had already assigned a counselor for Madison and filled her in on the situation.

CHAPTER 20

Ashley arrived home to find the house empty and remembered Jill had the night shift. She took the time alone to regroup. When Jason didn't show up for class, she didn't know what to believe.

Then she was assigned her first patient to observe the process of admission, only to find out she happened to be Jason's sister. What were the odds? She felt bad for their whole family, but she liked how close they all seemed to each other.

Would Jason have more time or less now that Madison was an inpatient for a while? Dr. Thorn suggested Madison's stay would be a few days, but Ashley knew it would probably be closer to two weeks. It would take at least three weeks for the medication to have any effect, and since Madison planned to take her own life, they would keep her in the hospital if they could convince her to stay. She hated that the family might have to commit Madison if she decided to leave the hospital before she was ready.

The family appeared close, but committing a person to the psychiatric unit could create long-term animosity and conflict. She didn't want that for Madison or her family. She knew Jason figured high in the equation. She wondered how soon he would have a chance to call her. He probably had a lot of homework tonight and was taking turns with his parents watching Chloe. She would text him tomorrow if he didn't call her by the afternoon. It could be a simple *how are you?* text.

Ashley fixed herself a grilled cheese sandwich and considered calling Courtney. She wanted to stop by and visit her again when she had the time. Last weekend had turned out well, and she wanted to continue visiting before winter weather made the roads tougher to drive on due to ice or snow.

The pleasant September weather wouldn't last long. The changing colors on the leaves would make it a pretty drive to Chokecherry Valley, whether she saw Courtney or not.

Should she ask Paul to go with her? Or would Courtney feel they were plotting against her and Alex's directive? Ashley decided she'd go alone. When Alex was out of prison, they could drive down together. She texted Courtney she'd like to visit, and Courtney texted back to confirm it was okay.

The next day, the drive was as pretty as she expected. The leaves of some trees were green, but there were also many yellows, reds, and oranges. She felt a sense of peace wash through her as she thanked God for the beautiful day.

She started thinking about her brothers the closer she got to Chokecherry Valley. She didn't want to hold a grudge against them. She would find some passages on forgiveness in the Bible and study them. With God's help, she could get past these feelings of anger and hurt.

She should also send a text to Jason to ask how Madison was doing. She could check with him and see if he had time to get together and practice their speeches for class. She wanted an excuse to contact him and talk to him. Maybe she'd call him instead of text. She'd decide after she talked to Courtney.

She arrived at Courtney's house about one o'clock Saturday. When she knocked on the door, she didn't have long to wait for it to be opened.

Courtney smiled at her in welcome. "Come in."

Looked like Courtney had gotten the message that Ashley wasn't going to be put off any longer. They were family, and they were going to spend time together like a real family. Fights and all. She smiled.

Courtney settled on the couch. "Have a seat. Do you want anything to drink?"

"No, I'm fine. I drank a soda on the way here. I do appreciate that you are letting me visit."

Courtney laughed, and her face lit up. "Like I had a chance against you once you made up your mind. Did anyone ever tell you you're tenacious?"

"A time or two. I did respect your request to leave you alone for two years. I was younger then, and I didn't know any better. Hopefully I've learned a lesson about how little time we all have."

"You're being philosophical today."

"Can't help it," Ashley said. "I've been taking a class about sibling relationships, and here I am. Trying to be supportive."

Courtney settled back against the couch and grabbed a throw pillow, which she held on her lap. "I know, Ashley. Probably more than you realize. I have five siblings. I can't imagine not seeing one of them for two years. You held out longer than I expected. Alex and I weren't fair to you. I regret that."

An apology? Ashley certainly hadn't expected one. She'd always gotten along with her sister-in-law and been crushed when she was ignored. They'd said it was for her own good. She didn't agree.

"We didn't want to taint you with Alex's mistakes. You were off at college, and we felt you'd be better off concentrating on your dream job and forgetting about us."

"Forget? Yes, I'm going to forget my brother I've grown up with and lived with, who I was close to, and who I confided in because Mom and Dad dumped us wherever they could. Yes. I was going to forget him. And you. I considered us friends, and while I know Alex was the driving force in the decision to cut me off, you went along with it." She took a deep breath then stood and paced. "I guess I needed to get that off my chest."

Courtney smiled in a gentle way, not sneering. "We deserve that and more. We were young too, and it was the wrong decision we made. We assumed you'd have Paul."

Ashley laughed bitterly. "Yes. That turned out well too." Then she plopped down on the recliner. "Paul and I are patching up our relationship."

"Seems like this class you're taking is bringing out your feelings and resolving some things."

"Well, I am studying psychology. I suppose I should get my own life together."

They sat in silence for a while.

"I'm glad you're back, Ashley. I missed you." Her expression showed a mixture of regret and sympathy.

"I missed you too. I wanted to be there for you and Alex." Ashley knew she sounded whiny.

"We know. Alex withdrew in prison. He didn't want to see anyone he knew except me. He felt my own family would support me, and they did. I missed you though. You were a big part of our life, and then you were gone. You don't know how much I wanted to open the door when you started pounding on it back then."

"I thought you found it easy to ignore me." Ashley heard the bitterness in her own voice.

Courtney frowned. "No, it wasn't easy. I almost went against Alex, but then I knew he'd ask me, and I didn't want to lie to him. He'd already been lied to by too many people."

"What do you mean?"

"Nothing important." Courtney shrugged it off. "It was tough for him being a bank manager. I don't know what he's going to do when he gets out of prison. He'll definitely be making a career change. Obviously, no bank is going to hire him."

"No, probably not." Ashley hesitated, and then jumped in, "If you two need financial help, let me know."

Courtney started to interrupt.

"No, let me finish, and then I'll bring it up once to Alex. After that, I won't bug you about it. I have enough to share. If this has left you short of money, I'll help. The offer is always there, but I won't bring it up again. You don't have to squirm."

Courtney stilled at her words. "We're fine, but we appreciate it. I'm speaking for Alex too. I know he'd agree."

"Okay. New subject. Do you have to work today?" Ashley asked.

"No, I'm off. Next weekend I do have to work. You might not want to make the drive."

They laughed together.

"I'll call before coming, unless you stop seeing me. Then I'll be the persistent knocker on your front door again," Ashley said.

"Not necessary. We're past that."

Ashley stood up. "I think so too. Well, I won't keep you any longer. Next time we'll talk about books or something lighter. Enough of the serious subjects."

"Sounds good." Courtney followed her to the door. "Thank you, Ashley."

Ashley waved from the front step. "Sure."

She looked down the street at the grocery store and the other small businesses. Maybe she'd stop and get a few items from the store, and then she could go straight home from here. She moved her car the short distance to the front of the grocery store, parking behind a pickup. It was an old blue farm pickup and brought back memories of riding in the bed of one during her younger years.

She got out of her car, and as she got to the door of the grocery store, it opened. Jason stood there. She stepped back to let him outside.

"Wow. Another surprise sighting," Ashley said.

"Do you want to talk for a minute or are you in a hurry to do your shopping and get back to Bismarck?" he asked, holding the door open.

"I can talk." She smiled at him. "I have plenty of time."

He smiled back and let the door close behind him. He went over to the old pickup with his groceries. After putting the bags onto the passenger seat, he closed the door. "Were you visiting Courtney?"

"Yes. We've come to an understanding, and I think we'll be close again. It looks like the class I'm taking is helping me move forward." She pointed to the house at the end of Main Street.

"Oh, right. Of course." He nodded. "I'm glad it's working out for you. I like Courtney and Alex. I always got along with him too. No judgment here." He stared straight at her.

"Thanks for saying that. I appreciate it." Ashley wasn't sure what to say next. She had so many questions and not a lot of time. He must need to get back home. "How did Madison do overnight?"

"Okay, I guess. We only get to see her for two hours in the evening because there are activities during the day. Of course, that's during the weekdays. The activities, I mean. And you probably already know this because that's your area at the hospital." He put his hands in the pockets of his jeans. "That was crazy running into you at the hospital yesterday. I never expected it."

"You don't need to worry I'm going to share any information about Madison with anyone. You and I can't even talk about what happened in the emergency room unless Madison signs a release or brings it up. They assigned another therapist to treat her anyway. Maybe you already met her. I'll be happy to listen to your side of things. Of course, it's all up to you," Ashley assured him.

"She hasn't been in the hospital long enough for anything to change. I guess we'll wait and see. Mom did get an update from the doctor this morning over the phone, and it looks like Madison did okay overnight. She starts the medication today, and we're hoping the first one works. I looked up information online, and it said sometimes they have to try a few different pills before they find the right one, and then they have to try different doses." His lips drooped, and he suddenly looked tired. "It's a long process, isn't it?"

"Yes. I'm sorry, Jason. I wish Madison had decided to get help earlier. She didn't, and so we go from here. She's in a good place."

He straightened his shoulders. "Yes, she is. What did I miss in class on Friday, besides you?"

"Well, you got to see me anyway." She smiled at him. "Just more information on the different types of speeches. Nothing that isn't in the books. There's a signup sheet for when you want to give your first speech. Three different people give speeches per day with discussion after each speech." Her lips twisted. "I really don't want to give one. I wish there was some way out of this class." She sighed.

"Do you still want to get together to practice your speech?" Jason asked.

She felt another smile cross her lips. "I'd like that. Do you have time?"

"I'll make the time. How about tomorrow? I'm going to be in Bismarck to visit Madison, and we can get together after that. Would that work?"

"Definitely. I don't have anything except homework the rest of today. If we meet tomorrow, it will force me to write the speech. I want to give it in class as soon as possible and get it over with," she said.

"Sounds good." He moved away from the passenger door. "I'll text you and check if the time works for you once I know when I'm visiting Madison."

"Sounds good." She took a step toward the store.

"We go to church every Sunday morning, so I know it won't be until after lunch. I must admit, I don't read the Bible otherwise. I do pray and beg God for things to change."

Ashley smiled. "Me too. I should start thanking Him for more things He's given me and include them along with all the asking."

He laughed. "Good idea. I'll adopt your philosophy too."

"Well, I should let you get going. You probably have things you need to get into the fridge, and I should get my groceries and start back to Bismarck."

"Yes. I'm on babysitting duty when I get home." He went around to the driver's side of the vehicle and looked over the top of the cab. "I'll text or call to check about meeting tomorrow when I know the time."

"Sounds good." Ashley went into the grocery store and looked around for the few things she needed. It felt good to talk to Jason, even for a short visit. Her heart sang. She'd see him tomorrow. It almost made writing the speech palatable. Almost.

CHAPTER 21

Saturday afternoon, Ashley worked on writing her speech. She often found herself daydreaming about Jason and how he'd looked in Chokecherry Valley that morning. Finally finishing the speech, she picked up her tablet to read her library book.

When Jill returned home from work, Ashley was happy to be distracted by conversation with her.

Ashley prepared a salad for both of them, and they sat at the table eating. "Do you want to tell me what's bothering you?"

"Your decision, or lack of a career decision, has got me thinking about my own future," Jill said. "I'm not sure I want to work on the Labor and Delivery floor any longer. You know I can't have children, and that's making it harder to be happy for other mothers every day. And on the days when a mother loses her child, I come close to falling apart."

Ashley reached across the table and gave her friend's hand a comforting squeeze. "I always wondered how you did it."

"I wasn't going to let my feelings win. I love babies, but now it's too much. Other options are available for nursing jobs, and my plan is to transfer to another department. Telemetry and the Kidney Dialysis Unit both have openings. I'm leaning toward Telemetry. I'm pretty good with broken hearts." She smiled at her own weak joke.

Ashley smiled back at her. "Especially mine. Look what you did for me. Made me face my fears with my brother and nudged me into a relationship with Jason."

"Oh, please!"

Ashley was relieved to see Jill's eyes light up.

"I knew you were crazy about that guy from the moment you first mentioned him. Even over the phone, your voice got all trembly when you mentioned Jason."

Ashley flushed. "Glad you found that amusing."

"I didn't. I found it sweet and nice. I worry about you, you know. That's what best friends are for."

"I worry about you too. I'm glad you told me what's been bothering you. Try out Telemetry. If you don't like it, there's always another department. You know the hospital is so short of nurses, you have your choice of departments."

"You're right," Jill agreed. "Now, I'm going to have a relaxing evening with my book."

They took care of the dishes and settled in the living room, each reading her own book.

***

Sunday morning, Ashley's mind kept wandering to Jason and the tired look on his face outside the Chokecherry Valley grocery store. She wished she could do something, but only time would help the situation. At least Madison was getting the help she needed.

Jason showed up about 3:00 p.m. to practice their speeches. Jill was working again, so they had the place to themselves. Ashley was happy to have the privacy. She didn't want to practice in front of two people at once. As she told Jason, she'd already had trouble just speaking in front of Jill last night when she went through her speech with her.

They settled across from each other in the living room. Ashley sat in the chair across from the couch where Jason sprawled in his usual slumped position. Maybe he was uncomfortable with his height. Or he was tired from everything that had happened, and that was how he sat when he was relaxed.

She wished she felt as relaxed as he looked. "Do you want to go first?"

"Sure." He sat up and took the backpack off the couch where he'd dropped it when he sat down. He searched inside and brought out a notebook. "I wrote it out instead of putting it on my tablet. I'll enter it into the computer and print out a nice copy when I have the final version worked out."

"I do that too. I like to cross things out on paper and make little notes, and then rewrite it again." She settled back against the stuffed chair. Since he was going first, she could take a normal breath.

"Okay. Let's stay sitting for the first time through. Here goes." He read the speech without looking at her once. When he finished, he folded the paper in half.

"That was good," Ashley said. "In fact, it only needs a few minor tweaks, and you'll be ready."

He finally looked up. "What do I need to change?"

She found the slight flush on his cheeks cute but kept that opinion to herself. Her face was going to be fiery red when she finished her own speech. He probably wouldn't think her cute at that point. "You've got it down pretty well."

She picked up a pen from the coffee table that was positioned between them and reached out her hand. "Give me your speech, and I'll show you the two places you hesitated."

He handed it to her.

She leaned forward, set the paper on the coffee table and made a few marks on the paper. "Look here."

He leaned forward, so their heads were close together. She found the closeness distracting but told herself to focus.

"You see this spot here?" She pointed to a pen mark by one of the sentences. "If you take out this word, it flows better. Same thing at this other place." She had crossed out another word.

He read both sentences out loud with the changes she'd suggested. "You're right. It sounds better." He read the whole speech from his seat on the couch, looking up a time or two to get her reaction.

She smiled at him. When he finished, she said, "Perfect."

"Now you," he said.

She took a deep breath and let it out slowly as she picked up her paper from the coffee table. She'd been working on the speech all morning since she got home from church and believed it sounded okay when she read it.

She followed Jason's example of sitting down through the first reading. He made one comment of a change when she was finished. She made the change and read it through again.

"Perfect," he said.

She laughed. "Okay. I guess we have our reading down. Now we need to actually stand up and do this. Along with some eye contact and inflection."

He smiled at her. "I guess so."

It helped her that he had some doubts about his speech too, which wasn't really fair. She should be hoping that he was calm. The saying "Misery loves company" came to mind.

They practiced for another hour, and then both had enough. She'd turned red a time or two, but she could remember most of the speech without her paper by the time they were finished. The instructor was allowing them to use their paper or tablet as a crutch for the first speech. After that, they had to memorize all the other ones.

"We're ready for next week," Jason said as he stood at her front door to leave. "If you want to practice before next week, we can do it over the phone. There are plenty of times when I'm watching Chloe, and she's asleep, so I can do other things."

"That sounds good. Same here," Ashley said. "You can also practice more with me if you want to do that."

They said goodbye, and Ashley stood by the door for a minute after he left. The apartment suddenly felt lonely without him there.

***

Jason managed to have lunch with Ashley the next few times after their class met. They enjoyed getting together, but they hadn't found an evening when they were both free for a date.

They each gave their speeches and did a passable job. Both flushed red and stumbled, but overall, Jason said he was happy with his own performance. Ashley just wanted to get through the

326

class, and as long as she passed, she didn't care how high a grade she received.

She got out of bed early on Monday, excited to see Jason at class. She hoped he would have time to have lunch with her, but she kept her expectations low.

When she arrived at the classroom, he was already sitting at his desk. He smiled brightly at her. "Hi."

"Hi. How's it going?" she asked as she settled at the desk beside his.

"Great. We had a good weekend."

Dr. Williams walked into the room, and she didn't feel she should talk about anything personal in front of him or the other students.

After class, she took a longer time than she needed to get her stuff together. She hoped Jason would ask her to join him for lunch.

Instead, he walked her out of the classroom and stopped on the sidewalk by the entrance to the building. "I'm sorry I can't get together today. It's my turn to watch Chloe."

"I'm sorry too." She certainly felt let down, and his eyes were shadowed with fatigue as they stood there for a minute.

"My parents had something they had to do today, so I have to get home," Jason said.

"That's understandable, Jason. You've all had a rough time. I know you'll make it through this. I pray for you and your family," she said, feeling shy at telling him.

He grinned down at her. "Thank you. That's the best news I've heard besides Madison coming home soon. I better get going. I'll see you on Wednesday."

"Bye." She watched him walk down a different sidewalk from the way she went. Obviously, Madison's condition still concerned him, so it was good that she was still in the hospital. Ashley walked along the path to her car. The bright sky and beautiful September colors lifted her mood. She considered what work might bring today. The people they saw in the clinic interested her, but could she deal with people's problems day after day?

She supposed, given the fact her parents had been largely absent, even when they were in the same house, she would find a career helping other people appealing. Especially since she'd been lonely.

Her upbringing kept her from trusting others and from getting close to them. She was always afraid they would leave her. Paul hadn't helped when he'd told her to get out of his life. Alex basically did the same thing when he went to prison. She hoped to quickly change his mind when he returned home.

Courtney was someone she hoped she could reconnect with now the ice was broken over the prison thing. Jill had been in her life since Ashley had started living at her grandmother's house. It was nice having one close friend who understood her.

She should try to set up more times to see both Courtney and Paul. She'd have time to make and hopefully keep friends now that she was nearly done with school. She'd call Paul first to meet up with him again.

She finished work for the day, went home and called Paul. They planned to meet the next evening. He asked if he could bring Hannah. Since Ashley didn't have anything personal to talk about with Paul, she agreed. She wanted to meet Hannah anyway.

***

Tuesday arrived, and Ashley did housework in the morning before she went to work. She got an hour of homework done for her class on Wednesday. Work passed quickly, and before she knew it, it was time to meet Paul and Hannah.

She wasn't as nervous as she had been when she saw Paul again for the first time. As long as his mood stayed stable this evening, which it should since he wasn't drinking, she was okay. He would be on his best behavior for her to meet Hannah.

They agreed to go to the same bistro where they met previously. It might become their spot.

She'd dressed in black jeans, black ankle boots, and a long-sleeved light blue sweater. Once the sun disappeared from

328

the sky, it would be chilly outside. The sky darkened as she headed out of her apartment.

She was the first to arrive, and the waiter led her to a table. She faced the entrance, so she could see her brother and his girlfriend arrive. The waiter was setting out three menus and filling her water glass when Paul came in with Hannah.

Hannah was average height with shoulder-length blond hair. Her bright smile showed a happy young woman, the kind of woman Paul needed in his life. A moment of jealousy struck Ashley before she pushed it away. Maybe someday she'd meet someone who made her that happy. She ignored the memory of Jason's face as it popped into her head.

"Ashley, this is Hannah. Hannah, Ashley." Paul waited until they shook hands and then helped Hannah remove her lightweight coat. She wore a pink sweater that gave her face a glow in the dimly lit restaurant.

"I'm excited to meet you, Ashley. Paul has talked a lot about you and the adventures you and Alex had when you were growing up," Hannah said.

"Well, he wasn't as happy about them when we were younger." Ashley grinned. "I admit I instigated most of our escapades. Poor Alex. He didn't want me to leave him behind, even when I started getting into girly stuff like makeup. He refused to try the makeup—except one time. We did have a picture of him wearing blush and mascara and one of mom's dresses, but he might have gotten rid of it by now.

"Most of the time when we stayed in Chokecherry Valley, I liked to climb trees. When I stayed at my grandmother's house here in Bismarck, I was quieter. I read a lot." She didn't add that she didn't want to upset her grandmother and get sent back to Chokecherry Valley. She wanted to stay in high school in Bismarck, so she behaved herself. She realized now she'd stifled her real inclinations by doing that. She'd built a habit of pushing away her more adventurous side.

"Hey there." Paul touched her hand.

"Sorry." Ashley smiled at them. "I was having a few memories."

"That's okay," Hannah said. "I paint pictures for fun, and, sometimes, I'll miss whole boatloads of information Paul shares. I'm busy imagining how the landscape would look better with a certain lighting."

"Oh, that's wonderful you paint pictures. I always thought it looked fun. I'm not creative. I tried to draw for a while, but the drawings didn't look like anything when I finished them."

"Oh, I don't do very well. My proportions can get all out of whack. Like I said, it's fun."

Paul reached over and squeezed Hannah's hand. "It doesn't matter as long as you like doing it."

"Have you painted a picture of Paul?" Ashley asked Hannah.

Hannah laughed. "I tried once when he napped on the couch. I drew a picture first because I didn't want to wake him up by dragging out all my painting supplies. He wouldn't let me do it if he knew, so I kind of snuck into the room and drew him with pencil and paper. It looked like a man, but not much like Paul."

"It was wonderful. I keep it on my fridge," Paul said.

"Like a child's drawing," Hannah said wryly but didn't look upset. "Paul told me you're almost finished with your bachelor's degree in psychology."

"Yes. I have two classes this semester along with a two-week long clinic observation class. I'm excited to be nearly finished. I'm tired of studying every night, but at least I don't have much homework in the classes I'm taking now."

"What classes are you taking?" Hannah asked.

Ashley decided to avoid mentioning the class that focused on siblings. "I'm taking Oral Communications. It's a freshman-level class I should have taken a long time ago, but I put it off."

"You always hated to speak up in a group," Paul said.

"Yes. That hasn't changed at all. I'm still scared to get up in front of the class. Oh, here comes the waiter. Do you know what you want?" Ashley asked, relieved to change the subject.

"What's good?" Hannah asked.

"Pretty much anything on the menu. I don't think you'll be disappointed."

After they ordered, there was a lull in the conversation. Ashley didn't find it awkward at all. Hannah seemed like a nice woman, and she was happy for Paul. There appeared to be a real closeness and contentment between the two, something she never noticed in Paul's marriage with Samantha.

With Samantha, there had always been sly digs against Paul. Little barbs and arrows flew through the air. Their discontent had been exacerbated by both of them drinking.

The conversation flowed with general information on each of their jobs, and once the waiter delivered their food, they all dug in with gusto.

"You're right," Hannah said after a few minutes of silence while they all ate. "This is excellent. I'm coming here more often."

Ashley was relieved Hannah liked the restaurant choice. She was always nervous when she chose the place to eat. "I'm glad."

Paul put down his fork. "I was going to wait until after we finished eating, but I can't wait any longer."

Ashley had taken another bite. She was afraid the food would get stuck in her throat when her mouth suddenly went dry. What did Paul want to say?

He glanced at Hannah. "What do you think?"

She put down her fork too. "Sure. Go ahead." She smiled at Ashley.

Ashley breathed a sigh of relief when she realized where this was going. Paul had mentioned that he already bought Hannah a ring. Hannah must have finally decided it was time to accept his proposal. She smiled back at Hannah and then looked at Paul. "What's up?"

"Hannah has agreed to marry me."

"Congratulations to both of you. I couldn't be happier." She picked up her water glass and gestured to the two of them. "I guess we're going to toast with our water?"

They did. There were laughs and more smiles all around, and they picked up their forks again.

"I didn't see a ring on your finger, Hannah," Ashley said.

Hannah's grin got bigger. "Oh, you looked," she teased Ashley.

"Of course. My brother wants me to meet his girlfriend and can't even wait a week?" Ashley laughed at Paul's sheepish expression. "I looked."

Hannah dug in her purse and unzipped a side pocket. She pulled out the diamond ring with a silver band and handed it to Ashley.

Ashley looked at the beautiful square cut with smaller diamonds around it. "It's gorgeous."

"Thank you." Hannah put it on her finger. She looked momentarily shy, like she wasn't used to showing it off.

"Have you worn it to work yet?" Ashley asked.

"No. Paul and I agreed to show you first, and then I'd wear it."

Ashley felt the hint of tears in her eyes. "That's sweet." Her face was starting to hurt from all the smiling she'd done that evening. "When we're finished and standing up, you're both getting big hugs from me."

When the meal was over, she didn't forget.

CHAPTER 22

The next few weeks sped by for Jason. He spent time watching Chloe, taking his classes online and in person, doing homework, and visiting Madison at the hospital when it was his turn. He was amazed they'd managed to keep her in the hospital for two weeks.

She wanted to come home the day after they admitted her, but gradually her pleas to come home diminished. They all somehow convinced her to stay until she started feeling better. God must have had something to do with it because it was a miracle she stayed. The doctor hoped for one more week before they released her.

On the last day of September, Jason realized he could ask Ashley to have lunch with him after class. He didn't have to get home immediately for a change. They talked before and after class, but he was always in a hurry to get home to help.

They hadn't even had time to practice their second speeches. He knew she was signed up the same day he was, because they had coordinated it in class. They were scheduled for next week.

He felt bad about always rushing away after class, but he'd told her he was busy. She knew about Madison and Chloe. He didn't know if she understood the time those commitments took. Did she think he wasn't interested in her any longer?

There was only one way to find out. He dressed casually but more neatly than usual before he headed for class. He parked in the parking lot he knew Ashley used. It would give him more time to talk her into lunch if he needed to persuade her.

When Ashley walked into the classroom, Jason made sure to send her a bright smile. He babbled away nervously. Ashley gave him a curious look, and then class started.

He felt foolish. No doubt she thought he had lost it. He hadn't given her a chance to say anything or respond in any way.

Class seemed to drag on for longer than fifty minutes. When it was finally over, he grabbed his stuff and stood by Ashley's desk while she stuck her notebook into a folder and put on her jacket. He forced himself to concentrate. "Are you busy today?"

She eyed him closely. "Don't you have to get home and take care of Chloe or something?"

"Not today. I finally have a break. I assume you have to get to work, but I wondered if you have time for a quick lunch before you have to leave." He spoke quickly, trying to get the words out before she left.

She looked at him for a minute and smiled. "It sounds like you want to go to lunch today. I have time. In fact, I have all afternoon. I finished the clinical observation at St. Gertrude's. I just have to put together a paper for the class. Let's go to the place we went to before. They had fast service."

He let her go before him as they left the classroom. He couldn't hide the big smile on his face as he followed her. His pulse slowed down to a more normal rate. She'd agreed, and she'd smiled. She didn't seem mad at him for how long it had taken him to meet with her.

They stepped outside, and she rummaged in her purse for her sunglasses. "How is Madison doing?"

"Great. We were lucky. The first antidepressant looks like it's working. We're hoping she'll agree to stay at the hospital one more week, and then she'll be home again. It feels like she's been gone forever."

"That's great, Jason. I'm glad for her and for you too."

"She sounded more like her old self when I visited a few days ago. I didn't realize how much I missed her being happy."

"Life has been rather chaotic for you lately, hasn't it?" Ashley asked sympathetically as they reached the parking lot. Jason shrugged and nodded. "Pretty much a mess. I'll meet you at the restaurant, so we can both leave from there."

"See you in a few minutes." Jason waited until she'd backed out of her spot and followed behind her in his own vehicle to the restaurant.

Once they were seated and ordered, Ashley asked, "Will Madison be able to settle in once she gets home?"

"I'm concerned about her regressing, but I'm taking it one day at a time. Something I've learned to do more lately than ever before," he said.

The waitress set down their order and asked if they needed anything else. Ashley shook her head. When they assured her they had everything, she left. Ashley started eating immediately.

Jason scooped up his own burger and took a bite. He should try harder to see Ashley in the evening sometime when they could have a real date. Sure, he'd been concentrating on family things, but come on. He could find the time.

"Is something wrong?" Ashley stared at him in concern as she finished her salad.

He picked up his burger again. "Sorry. I zoned out there for a minute." He took another bite of his burger to give himself time. She wouldn't expect him to talk with his mouth full.

"I said life might return to a more normal pace for you once Madison is discharged from the hospital. You won't be running to Bismarck in the evenings to visit her," Ashley said.

He swallowed and answered, "Maybe there would be another reason to come to Bismarck in the evenings. Maybe if you're free some evening, we could go to a movie or something."

She pushed her plate over to the side and leaned forward. Her eyes sparkled. "Are you asking me for a date?"

"Yes. I want to date you. I'm getting old, Ashley. I'm not into playing games. I could pretend I don't like you or play hard to get, or whatever people do these days. However, I'm a straightforward guy. Life has been complicated with a lot of things since we met, so it took me a while to get my act together. Now that I've realized I want to spend more time with you, I don't want to waste time. So, yes, I'm asking you out."

"Okay. The answer is yes. I'd like to go out with you too. I find your honesty refreshing." She looked down at the table as he picked up his burger again.

"I have something else to ask you." She looked up at him again. "I have been left and abandoned a lot in my life. I'm nearing thirty also, and I'm not into games either. I'm finally getting my relationships with one of my brothers and my sister-in-law back on track. I can't handle a relationship with someone who runs hot and cold."

"Like I have." His food sat heavy in his stomach. "I believed you understood how busy I was with Madison, Chloe, homework, and farmwork."

"I understand, but sometimes I need the words. You can call. You can text. You can send me an old-fashioned letter. Somehow, you need to communicate why you're busy. I don't want to wonder when you're going to get back around to me since you have all those other commitments. Am I making sense?" She leaned back and crossed her arms over her chest.

"Yes. I promise to be more forthcoming from now on," Jason said.

"That's all I ask." She smiled at him. "On the topic of dating, let me know when you have a free evening, and we'll plan our date. Either call me, or we'll have lunch again after class and discuss details." She patted his free hand where it lay on the table.

"Let's plan now," he said.

They agreed on a date for the following Tuesday. They were going out to eat.

CHAPTER 23

The doctor discharged Madison from the hospital over the weekend, and everyone used the time to adjust to her return home. She spent most of her time holding Chloe. The family continued to keep an eye on her.

Jason tried hard to trust Madison enough to leave her alone, but he couldn't let go yet. Neither could his parents. He noticed there was always someone around, and they scheduled it so Madison wasn't left alone. It looked like it would take time.

They tiptoed around the situation and tried not to make it obvious to Madison. She would probably notice at some point. For now, she seemed blissfully unaware as she took care of Chloe and enjoyed being home.

They talked briefly about whether she would return to school in a week, but she hadn't decided. She also had the choice to study at home for the G.E.D. high school certificate.

Jason hoped that would be the route she took. In one way, he saw how it would be easier for her, but she'd have no reason to leave the house on a regular basis, which was the one downside to studying online. She needed to make friends somehow.

She continued twice-a-week therapy with the counselor she'd had at the hospital. Once they were sure Madison was stable, they would transfer her care to a local therapist. Maybe then he could relax his vigilance.

***

Ashley looked around her and Jill's apartment Saturday. The place needed a thorough cleaning. She'd focused on studying and getting through the week and wasn't used to having an entire Saturday free.

As a psychology major, she found it ironic she was so unsure of herself with interpersonal relationships. She didn't have a lot of self-confidence in her appeal but should follow the advice she gave to others: practice liking yourself.

Jason seemed comfortable with himself. Well, most of the time. She had made him nervous before he declared he wanted to date her. She found that endearing. It was nice to know she wasn't the only shy one when it came to dating. Plus, speaking probably wasn't going to be his favorite thing to do either.

Ashley industriously cleaned the apartment during the morning but decided the afternoon was too beautiful outside to not enjoy it. She got out her camera and headed on her favorite scenic drive. She found a stream about five miles out of town she liked to take pictures of in different seasons.

Most of the leaves had fallen from the trees since mid-October arrived. In a few months, the ground might be covered with snow. The stream usually froze by mid-December because it was shallow.

She parked off to the side of the road, keeping her flashers on to alert other motorists. Since she'd been coming here for about four years, she'd never seen another vehicle drive by.

Ashley found it strange her parents never associated with the other families in Chokecherry Valley. Her mother inherited the house on Main Street from her parents but only visited Chokecherry Valley on occasion. Her parents had lived in Bismarck since Ashley's mom went to high school.

Ashley didn't have any idea why her father agreed to sell their Bismarck home and settle in Chokecherry Valley, making it their home base. Maybe they decided, since they were traveling most of the time, there was no need to make friends in Chokecherry Valley.

She realized now how their decision cut her off from being close with the other people in Chokecherry Valley. She'd visited Alex and Courtney occasionally, but since Alex went to prison after three years of being married, she hadn't been there until her recent visits with Courtney.

Alex would have a hard time coming back to the house in Chokecherry Valley when he got out of prison. As the previous bank manager, he must have known a lot of people in town, and they'd all know what he'd done. Courtney's job definitely brought her into contact with most of the residents of Chokecherry Valley. What could Alex do for a job? No one was going to hire an ex-con in a small town.

She took her pictures and started driving back to Bismarck. She wanted to go see Jason, but she knew now wasn't the time. Madison needed to settle into a routine with her family.

She waited until she got home and then texted Jason. "How are you?"

She tried not to keep looking at her phone, wondering if she missed the chime of an answering text. In the meantime, she pulled out the book she'd checked out from the library days ago. She'd try to read again.

About fifteen minutes later, she got a response. "Doing well. Madison's settled. She's playing with Chloe," Jason texted. "I'm nervous about her."

"That's normal. Soon you'll be more relaxed about the whole situation," Ashley responded. "What are you doing?"

"Did chores, now I'm watching them have fun while I try to study. I'm working on my next speech. I hope you want to get together again and practice."

Ashley felt warmth slide through her veins. "I'd like that. You got me through the first one. Since we have to memorize the next one, I'll need even more practice."

"Me too. We'll have to get together a lot." He laughed. "Can you tell I want to spend time with you?"

He didn't wait for her to answer. "I do want to spend a lot of time with you."

"That's good. Me too." She found it easier to say it over text than in person.

"Okay. It's a plan. I need to get back to my homework."

"I have to finish my paper, so I can be done with that clinical observation class. Can't wait to see you."

"Same here," he texted. "See you Monday."

"See you then."

She put away her phone and picked up her book. She finally got into it about a half hour later when she stopped thinking about Jason every other minute.

CHAPTER 24

Ashley dressed in black pants and a black sweater with a three-strand golden chain necklace for her date with Jason. Her calmness surprised her. They'd been in class together now for almost two months. Besides that time and their meetings for lunch, this wasn't the first time she'd be alone with him. It would be the first time they'd be alone at her place without the distraction of homework. He might want a kiss. She didn't know if she was ready for that intimacy yet. She'd decide how she felt if the time came. She pushed it out of her mind.

Jason arrived on time, and she didn't make him wait. Opening the door, she took a deep breath at the sight of him. He wore his usual jeans and had chosen a button-down, open-necked shirt instead of his usual t-shirt. His hair looked recently combed, and whatever cologne he used smelled citrusy.

She felt more in this moment than she'd felt for him the whole time they'd been sitting beside each other in class. She knew everything had now changed between them. He was going to be in her thoughts constantly, as if he weren't already a big part of them.

"Hi," he said, smiling at her and shifting from foot to foot. "It's great to see you all dressed up. Not that you don't always look good. You do, but— I'm expressing myself very badly. You look nice."

"It's fine, Jason. Thank you." She smiled back at him, noting his nervousness. "You look quite handsome." She was floored by her feelings for him. She finally got her act together and invited him into the apartment, glad she'd done a thorough cleaning over the weekend.

He pulled his hand from behind his back and held out a beautiful bouquet of yellow and orange mums and other fall flowers in a gorgeous crystal vase. "These are for you."

She noticed his hand trembled as he waited for her to take it from him. Her smile widened. "Thank you. They're gorgeous. Choose a seat if you want or wander around. I'll put these on the coffee table here, so we can all enjoy them."

"All?" he asked, looking around the room. He didn't sit down either.

She suddenly felt short beside him. "My roommate, Jill, would be the other one enjoying them. She's visiting her mother this evening. She'll be home by nine at the latest. Her mother is getting older and doesn't stay up much past ten."

"I see."

Ashley wondered if Jason took that as a warning she wouldn't be alone tonight if he wanted more than a kiss in the hallway. He didn't seem like that kind of man, but they hadn't had any intimate moments since they met. Practicing speeches didn't count. She'd been more nervous about them than spending time with Jason. Until now. They'd always been in a hurry to get to their next commitment.

"Are you ready to go?" he asked.

"Sure." She grabbed her black beaded purse from the couch. The mild late October evening didn't require a coat yet. "Where are we going?"

"I found this wonderful Italian place. Do you want to go there? If you prefer somewhere else, that's fine with me," he said.

"No. Italian sounds good."

He led the way to her front door and opened it for her. She stepped through and then waited for him to step out into the hallway, so she could lock the door. Once they reached his car, he opened the front passenger door and closed the door once she leaned back against the seat.

While she strapped on her seatbelt, she got an even better feeling for Jason. He certainly had manners. It didn't look put on for her benefit either. He probably held doors for his sister and mother too.

When he pulled out of the parking spot, he said, "The restaurant is about ten minutes away."

She laughed. "Most things are only ten to twenty minutes away. Except the colleges. Both are a little farther, depending on traffic. It's nice to live in the middle of town."

"I like the size of Bismarck," he said. "Have you come up with a plan yet after you graduate in December? Is it more school or a job?"

"I've given it a lot of reflection. I still haven't made up my mind and have another month before I need to sign up for next semester's classes. If I continue. At least I've already been accepted for the program, so it's my choice. If I decide I'm done with school, I'll job hunt. If the right job comes up here in town, I'll stay. If not, then I'd consider moving. I don't know what I'd do for a job. I guess I'd look at the openings and see what interests me.

"It's just not like me not to have a plan. I'm a planner by nature. A lot depends on what happens with my family situation."

"Meaning?" he asked.

"I'm starting to get to know Paul again after a separation, and Alex…I guess I don't have to tell you what happened with Alex, since you live in Chokecherry Valley."

"When we're seated at the restaurant, I'd like to hear all about it, Ashley. Gossip isn't always accurate, and I hope you're okay with telling me what's going on with your family."
He laughed. "You already know half of what's going on in my family, since you've met Madison and my parents."

"Yes. I can't believe that happened in the emergency room. I don't know anything about your parents though."

He parked in the restaurant's lot.

"And," she smiled at him when he looked over at her to see what she wanted to say, "you haven't shown me any pictures of Baby Chloe. As a proud uncle, I know you have at least one."

He grinned back at her. "We'll be hunched over my phone and ignoring the food all night if you want to see pictures of her."

He got out and opened the door for her again, even though she could have been out of the car before he walked over to her. She knew it would please him to be helpful, so she waited. It made her feel taken care of, which she enjoyed. No one had waited on her since her grandmother, and only on special occasions when Ashley was a teenager.

When they were seated at their dimly lit table, Ashley looked around. "I like it."

The room felt small but appeared to have plenty of seating. The candles on the tables and the lower lighting made it seem cozy. Her mouth started watering at the wonderful smells of garlic and oregano wafting around the room.

"What's good?" she asked Jason.

"I'm a fan of their lasagna. Do you have a specific Italian food you usually eat? It's all good here." He set his menu to the side. "Don't hurry on my account. I already know what I want."

He sat there quietly while she perused the menu. He seemed relaxed. She realized she liked that quality about him the best. She knew that was an exterior view. He had not been so calm about Madison, and Ashley had seen him agitated on a few other occasions. Even then, he appeared dependable.

She should wait to start cataloging his good qualities until after she decided what to order. She'd never been this distracted by a man before. When she was a teenager, she'd swooned over boys, but she had been too busy pursuing a career lately.

The waiter arrived with their waters. When he asked what they'd like to drink, Jason ordered a soda. He asked her if she wanted wine with her meal. She shook her head and ordered coffee. They both ordered the lasagna, and the waiter left.

Ashley said, "Let's see a few of those pictures before the food comes."

He pulled out his phone, and with a few swipes, brought up a cute picture of Chloe smiling up at him with big brown eyes and held it out for her to see.

"Oh, she's so cute. She has your beautiful eyes." Ashley felt her face flush, and she suddenly felt shy.

Jason smiled gently. "Thank you."

He handed her his phone. "Keep scrolling. Most of the pictures are family."

She looked through them, occasionally stopping to ask him to identify the people she didn't know. He had pictures of his mother, father, Madison, and Chloe. She recognized Paul's in-laws, Nina and Frank, and remembered they were Jason's neighbors. Ashley looked closely at all the pictures. She had a feeling she'd be seeing Jason's parents at their house soon.

She handed his phone back as the waiter brought their food. "You have a lovely family."

"Thank you."

They settled their plates and took a few bites. It was hot and delicious. "I want to keep eating," Ashley said, "but it's too hot. I need it to cool off for a minute. I've already burnt the roof of my mouth." She put some food on her fork and held it away from the rest of the plate to let it cool, so she could eat. She didn't want to stop. "I can't believe I've never eaten here before tonight."

"You've been busy. I'm happy I got to bring you here first." He grinned at her.

"Me too." She went back to eating little bites until her food cooled enough to take another bite.

They talked about work and school during the rest of their meal. Once they finished and refused dessert, they settled back to get to know each other.

"How were your meetings with Paul?" Jason asked.

"We've gotten together a few times lately. I met his fiancée, Hannah. She's nice. I'm looking forward to having her in the family."

Jason looked surprised. "Have they made it formal then?"

"Yes. I guess they just got engaged. It's news to most people."

He twisted his water glass back and forth. "She came out and visited him a few times at Frank and Nina's house during the summer. She seemed pleasant, but I didn't talk to her much more than to say hello in passing."

"We should probably keep it to ourselves until Paul has a chance to tell Alex and Courtney," Ashley said.

"I heard Alex will be coming home soon. When is that?"

Ashley didn't sense any distaste in Jason's voice. She'd wondered if he would bring up her younger brother. "He's being released December first. Paul and I will give him and Courtney a few days to settle in, and then we'll visit. I'm worried about his reception in town. Do you know how people are going to treat him?"

He paused before answering, and she was relieved he took the time to consider it through.

"For the most part, it's water under the bridge. In the end, what he did didn't affect a lot of people. The only problem is there are people who believe his boss, Steve Hanson, might not have had a cancer relapse if he hadn't had to deal with the disgrace of being the one who hired Alex."

"What do you think? Obviously, I want to know if there will be any awkwardness between you and Alex."

Jason's response could be a deal breaker.

"I'm totally okay with it. He's gone to prison and paid the price. I don't know the details, and it's not my place to judge."

"What about what they're saying about Steve Hanson?"

He pushed his water glass away. "I happen to know Steve had cancer before the embezzlement happened. His course of treatment worked, and he recovered from the cancer. Alex isn't to blame for the relapse. Cancer is unpredictable."

"That's good. It would about kill Alex to think what he did caused someone else that kind of pain."

"You were close with Alex?" he asked.

"Yes. Up until he went to jail. Then he and Courtney, in their infinite wisdom, refused all visits from me and Paul." She couldn't hide the bitterness she continued to feel over their actions.

"I'm sorry. That must have hurt." Jason's voice was soft and comforting.

"It did. It was another rejection. It's recently I found out they did it to save me from the anticipated fallout from Alex's actions. I wish they'd let me make up my own mind. I was certainly old enough to decide for myself. Besides, I don't live in Chokecherry Valley, so it wouldn't have been difficult for me."

Jason sat there quietly for a minute. "You may be underestimating people's reaction at the time to what Alex did. Yes, it's been two years since it happened. At the time, there were nasty things being said about him. If you heard them, you would have felt the need to correct their impression, and that wouldn't have done anyone any good. You might have said things you regretted in the heat of the moment, and you can never take back what's said."

"Well, I wanted to defend him," Ashley said stubbornly.

He smiled. "You seemed like such a softy, but you have a tough center. Alex knew. He did what he believed best."

"Well, I have something to say to you. I expect, if we continue our friendship, you'll allow me to make my own decisions." She clenched her fist on the table.

Jason's expression turned serious. "Definitely. You're a grown woman. Your choices are your own."

Her fist unclenched. She smiled at him. "You're a smart man."

"And about Alex. I've always liked him. I'll continue to be pleasant and courteous to him when I see him. Unless he turned into a bad guy while he was in prison."

She laughed. "I'm sure he hasn't changed."

The rest of their conversation was less serious, and they finally left the restaurant. The drive back to Ashley's apartment passed silently. With a flutter of nervousness in her stomach, she wondered if he would kiss her goodnight. She snuck a peek at him. His mouth was set in a firm line of concentration as he pulled the car up to her apartment entrance.

"Do you want to come in for a while? I'm sure Jill won't care. She's probably home by now."

He turned toward her where she sat in the passenger seat. "I do want to meet Jill sometime, but it's been a long day. Do you mind if I take a rain check?"

She felt her heart sink. He wanted to leave. "Sure. Some other time."

He reached out with his hand and touched her cheek. "I'd like to kiss you."

She took a deep breath, surprised at his openness. She was ready for that kiss.

"But," he continued, "It's too soon."

"Too soon?" she protested. "We've known each other for two months. That's acceptable for one small kiss."

He smiled at her.

She could get sidetracked by his smile easily, but she wanted a kiss.

He leaned forward, leaving his hand against her cheek. He placed a kiss on her forehead.

She pushed his hand away from her face but laughed. "Okay. Fine. On date two, we are going to kiss."

"How do you know there will be another date?"

"Because you like me, and you respect me. And I like you." She reached up and patted his cheek with her hand, then removed it from his face and opened the car door before he could react. "Let me know when you're free for our second date." She laughed again and slipped out of the car.

She knew he watched until she got into the apartment building. She waved from the doorway before she closed the door and headed upstairs to update Jill on her first official date with Jason.

CHAPTER 25

Paul picked up Ashley the following Saturday morning. He'd changed his mind about waiting until Alex returned home before he visited Courtney. Ashley called Courtney and told her they were coming to visit, and Courtney didn't object. Paul wanted to visit Frank and Nina while they were there, so they agreed to lunch at their house.

Ashley wanted to fit in a quick stop at Jason's house to see his family again. She hoped having Paul with her would ease the atmosphere. She'd texted Jason they were going to be in Chokecherry to visit family and might stop by his house.

He sent back a quick text with a thumbs-up emoji.

Ashley smiled. He might think it wasn't a big deal, but she had no idea how his mother would feel. Would she want to clean the house, or was she laidback and took things as they came? Probably the latter. With Madison's ups and downs, she'd probably learned to let go of unimportant things, such as a spotless house.

It was nice to have company on the drive to Chokecherry. She'd brought along her camera to take a few pictures. Since it was November now, the trees had lost all their leaves. They hadn't had much snow yet, so the landscape had a stark brown look. The temperature was in the forties, wonderful for this time of year.

She and Paul talked about Hannah, Ashley's work, and a bit about Jason.

"He seems like a nice guy," Paul said. "I'm glad things are working out."

"It's early days yet," Ashley said. "We've only been out on one official date. We see each other in class three times a week and go to lunch afterwards."

She remembered the text she got from Jason yesterday. He'd set up another date for the coming week, and she looked forward to it. And the kiss he promised. This time it wouldn't be on the forehead either.

Paul laughed. "Sounds like more than one date to me. All those lunches." He glanced at her.

"That's what I thought too." She smiled back at him. "He's cautious. I'm cautious. There's no hurry either."

"No, there's not. Better to take time and be sure." Paul concentrated on the road. They turned off the highway and onto the gravel roads.

She wondered if he thought about Samantha, but she didn't say anything. It wasn't any of her business. Paul's first wife put them through a lot, but Paul hadn't been blameless. Now she was gone, and Paul had Hannah.

"Are you okay if I set up a lunch with Hannah sometime? I'd like to get to know her."

"No, I don't have a problem with that. In fact, it's a great idea."

"Good. We'll have a great time talking about you without you there."

"I'm sure you'll come up with plenty of stories from our youth." He pulled into Courtney's driveway.

Courtney sat on the rocker on the porch. She waved as they got out of the car.

"Isn't it chilly to be sitting out here today?" Ashley asked. Sure, forty was a good temperature for this time of year, but not warm enough to sit outside on the porch without a fire pit going.

"I came out about a minute ago. The house was too warm from the oven being on this morning. Hi, Paul." She stood up to go into the house with them.

"Hi. It's great to see you again." He didn't hesitate but went up to her on the porch and gave her a firm hug. "It's been too long, but I'll forgive you."

Courtney glanced over at Ashley. "You two are definitely from the same family. It's great to see you too, Paul. And you, Ashley."

They followed her into the house, and Ashley took a deep breath of the lovely scent wafting from the counter. "You made blueberry muffins."

"Yes. I'm in a baking mood, and since I had a warning you were going to make frequent visits now, I figured it would be a good thing to feed you once in a while." She sent Ashley a sly glance.

"Yes. I get it. I stormed the castle before, and I don't regret it a bit."

Courtney smiled. "I don't either. I'm going to blame these visits on you and Paul. Alex can blame you for breaking the guidelines we set up."

"Fair enough," Ashley said. "I'm happy to take the heat."

They ate muffins and laughed together. They left right before lunch and went to visit Paul's in-laws.

Nina and Frank had a surprise for them. They arrived to find Jason, Madison, and Chloe there also. Ashley was happy his parents hadn't come too. It was enough to see Jason and his sister and niece.

Before Ashley knew it, Madison hugged her, and then she found herself holding Chloe.

"Looking good," Paul whispered in her ear.

She would have jabbed her elbow into her brother's side if she had her hands free. She settled for a subtle glare. Then she was distracted by Chloe. The baby felt so soft and comfortable in her arms, and she had an epiphany. This was what she wanted to do. Take care of children. In a group and one at a time— preschoolers of all ages.

While she sat there holding Chloe, she started having visions of starting a daycare. She'd find a business place to rent and use some of the money her parents had given her to start the daycare. She knew she'd have to update any place she rented. She'd have to get certifications for the building and for herself and maybe take some more classes to run the daycare.

"Hey there," Jason said.

She jumped at the sound of his voice. "Hi."

"You were sure deep in thought," he said.

She glanced around and found that conversation around her continued, but she and Jason were getting a few looks from the others. She realized they believed they were being subtle. She smiled up at Jason. "Yes. I made up my mind about something. I'll tell you later."

He appeared ready to question her, but then he said, "Okay. Do you want to join the others in the kitchen or stay here?"

"I'd rather stay here with Chloe. She's so cute. I'll go see if the others in the kitchen want any help."

"You can take Chloe with you." Jason smiled at her. "Then all the women will be in the kitchen."

"That better be a joke because any man in my life better expect to be helping out in the kitchen," she warned.

"Oh, you don't need to worry about that. My mother has already trained me to make meals and clean up after myself," Jason said.

"That's good." Ashley got to her feet, still holding the baby. "I'm going to the kitchen now, only because I choose to." She flipped her curly hair back with the hand that wasn't holding Chloe.

"Don't worry. I'm sure Nina will have the men clean up after we eat. Plus, we'd all offer anyway. That's the way it is."

Ashley left to join those in the kitchen, leaving Jason in the living room. Nina was directing Madison on setting the table while she scooped mashed potatoes into a bowl and set out a plate of pork chops. A salad and several dressings followed. Once the food and place settings were ready, the men were called from the other room.

Ashley gave them credit. They asked if they could help with the meal, but Nina told them they were fine. They could help clean up after the meal, she told them. They hadn't protested. All of them were used to Nina's way, just as Jason had assured Ashley.

The lively lunch featured a lot of laughing and talking. Ashley sat by Jason, and Chloe lay in her car seat, happily playing with a hanging toy.

After they'd eaten, the men stayed in the kitchen and cleaned up after the meal. Ashley found herself sitting on the couch in the living room. There was a gorgeous corner fireplace. It wasn't lit now, but she could smell the recent smoke from it.

After Ashley talked to Nina for a while, Madison came into the room with Chloe. She walked over to Ashley. "Would you like to feed her?"

Ashley hadn't noticed the bottle in Madison's other hand. "Sure." She reached out for the baby.

Once Chloe settled in her arms, Madison handed her the bottle. "I changed her diaper, so she should be fine for a while."

Chloe latched on to the bottle, and Ashley stared at her in wonder. Her brown eyes were wide open and stayed focused on Ashley's gaze. "She's a beautiful baby."

Madison flushed. "I love her so much." She glanced at Nina. "Do you mind if I say something to Ashley?"

"No, that's fine." Nina started to get up, but Madison stopped her.

"You can stay. It's nothing private."

Nina nodded and settled back into her rocker.

Madison sat by Ashley on the couch and played with Chloe's little socked feet, avoiding eye contact. "I wanted to thank you for what you did the day I came into the emergency room. You were so kind to me. I was scared, and you were calm."

Ashley smiled at Madison and would have given her a hug if she hadn't had Chloe in her arms. "You're welcome. You deserve to be happy. I hope things are better for you now."

Madison looked up, her expression serious, and finally made eye contact. "Yes. I feel a lot more like myself. I even smile occasionally."

"Good. You'll be okay. You have a wonderful family, and it looks like Nina and Frank are good friends."

Madison looked at Nina. "They are wonderful. All the times they've taken care of Chloe have been so helpful. I know Mom is grateful too. We couldn't have done it without you and Frank helping."

Nina smiled back at her. "We love you and that little one. Any time you want us to watch her, we will."

Ashley looked down at the baby in her arms. "You're a special little person with all these people loving you."

"She's added another admirer," Jason said from the doorway.

She knew he'd arrived in the room because she'd felt a shift in the atmosphere. Oh, she was so in trouble with her feelings for Jason.

"Of course I'm an admirer. Who wouldn't be?" she cooed at the baby. She had fallen in love with Chloe the minute she held her. A feeling of warmth ran through her, and she realized that when she started her daycare, she'd be able to continue holding little babies, and playing with and teaching little children. It was the perfect answer to the question she'd been asking herself since the summer. Did she want to stay in psychology? The answer was no. She wanted to work with children but in a different capacity.

The other men came into the room behind Jason, and Paul said, "I t's about time to get back, Ashley. You'll have to say goodbye to your new love."

Ashley bent over the baby and softly said goodbye. She had a sneaking suspicion Paul meant Jason, but she ignored him. She'd give him a hard time on the drive back to Bismarck.

Madison reached over and expertly took Chloe from Ashley's arms then looked around the room. "I'm glad I got to see you today," she said shyly.

Everyone returned the sentiment.

Ashley hadn't had another moment alone with Jason since right before they'd eaten, but maybe that was best. They parted with the comment they'd see each other Monday in class. She knew they'd have lunch afterward. She was disappointed they hadn't talked much today, but she was looking forward to their next date and, hopefully, a kiss.

***

354

Soon Paul and Ashley were in the vehicle to go back to Bismarck. Paul drove.

"Can we stop at Courtney's again for ten minutes?" Ashley asked him as they left the farm's driveway.

He looked at her in surprise before looking back at the road. "Sure. Did you forget something?"

"No. I just want to ask her something. Since we're here, I may as well do it in person."

She knew he thought it a weird request, but he didn't comment any further other than to agree. She hoped Courtney was at home. If not, she would have to ask her the question on the phone.

They pulled into the driveway behind Courtney's vehicle. Ashley tensed up and reconsidered. Maybe she didn't want to ask Courtney in person.

"Looks like she's here," Paul said.

"Good." Ashley opened her door. "I'll be right back."

She hurried up to the front door, and Courtney opened it as Ashley reached out to knock.

"I didn't expect to see you again today." Courtney stepped aside to let her in. "Isn't Paul coming in?"

"No. I have a quick question and hoped I could ask you. Do you have a few minutes?"

"Sure."

They both stepped into the house, and Courtney closed the door. "Do you want to sit down?"

"No." Ashley twisted her hands together as they stood inside the front door. "I'll make this quick. How did you know you were in love with Alex?"

Courtney's mouth dropped open, and she stared at Ashley. Then a grin quickly came and went. "That's an interesting question. I won't leave you waiting for an answer. When things progress a little further in your relationship with Jason, I'll give you a hard time about this conversation." A grin appeared again. "I knew something was going on when I saw you talking to him outside the grocery store the other day."

"Courtney, I don't have time." She knew her face was flushed. She was glad it was winter, and when she stepped outside, Paul would attribute her red face to the cold air.

"I knew I was in love with Alex almost right away. We had a lot in common. I was attracted to him, and I felt in my heart he was a nice guy. We just clicked. Most things we did together were easy. Not that we have a perfect relationship. No one does. I wanted to impress him, but I didn't have to. Does that make sense?"

"Yes. Thank you." She turned back to the door, wanting to leave now that she had her answer.

Courtney didn't stop her. She opened the door for Ashley and said, "If you ever want to talk, feel free to call. I was lucky enough to have sisters, but a sister-in-law like you is the next best thing."

Tears came to Ashley's eyes, but she held them back. She reached out and hugged Courtney, who hugged her back. "Thanks," she choked out and hurried out the door.

When she got in the vehicle, she was grateful for the warmth. Paul had left the pickup running while she was talking to Courtney.

"Are you okay?" he asked as he backed out of the driveway and started driving down Main Street to exit town.

"I'm fine. Courtney gave me a hug before I left, and it made me emotional." She wasn't about to tell him what they talked about in the house.

"Okay." He drew out the second syllable, like he knew there was more, but he didn't press her.

She was grateful for his restraint. She had so much to pray about. Jason, for one. Her new realization that she was either falling in love with him or in love with him already. It was all so new to her. She had been so excited when she first saw him at Nina and Frank's house, but then really disappointed when she didn't get to spend any time alone with him. She wasn't sure of anything, except she wanted to spend all her time with him. She hoped he felt the same way she did.

Second on her mind was her new career in child care. She just knew that was what she wanted to do when she graduated. Holding Chloe had been eye-opening to her. The experience had suddenly made her realize how much she loved children. She didn't know where she'd start a daycare, but she finally had a direction. She had a lot of thinking to do.

She realized Paul had been quiet while she was doing all of this thinking. She looked over at him and caught his swift gaze.

"Still okay?" he asked with a wrinkle in his forehead and a concerned look in his eyes.

She smiled at him. "You can relax. I'm fine. It's nice of you to care."

"I do." He smiled back at her.

"I know. It's sweet." She leaned back in her seat and relaxed. "I was planning my career choices. I've decided I don't want to be a psychologist, but I do want to work with children."

"Hey, that's great. What career do you want with children?"

"I'm going to start a daycare, but I have a lot of research to do. How to be a certified daycare center, or whatever the proper term is. What I need to do with building code for rental places, and all that stuff. I'm excited." Her smile got bigger. It was such a relief to have a direction again.

"I can see that. You're practically bouncing on the seat, now that you're back in the present. I thought I'd have to yell in your ear when we got you home, so you'd come back to earth," Paul said.

"Not necessary. So, when do you want to get together again?" she asked.

"I'll have to look at my schedule when I get home. Hannah has me signed up for a few things."

"Glad she's keeping you busy," Ashley said, content to see the happy smile on Paul's face.

"Me too."

"If you're interested, how about coming over with Hannah on Thanksgiving Day? Or does she have family?" Ashley almost regretted asking. What did she know about cooking for a holiday?

"She's got a sister. I'll check with her about Thanksgiving and let you know."

CHAPTER 26

November passed quickly, and Jason and Ashley continued to get together after class for lunch and to practice their speeches. They were unable to find an evening or time for a second date. Finally, they decided to get together in the evening on Thanksgiving Day at Ashley's apartment. Jill was going to be out of town for the holiday.

Jason would spend the day with his family. Nina and Frank's daughter, Abigail, and son-in-law, Mark, were visiting Paul's in-laws. Courtney would be celebrating the day with her family. Paul and Hannah had agreed to come to Ashley's apartment for a dinner meal at 1:00 p.m.

Thanksgiving arrived quickly, and Ashley tried to get everything done in her small kitchen. Hannah agreed to bring a salad and dessert. Ashley had never cooked a turkey, and she began to perspire in the hot kitchen. She opened the window above the sink and started doubting she could pull off this meal. What had she been thinking?

She should have agreed with Paul and let him and Hannah host the meal. A knock on the door interrupted her anxious musings, and she looked at the clock on the stove. Who could that be on Thanksgiving Day? It was too early for Paul and Hannah.

She opened the door to find Hannah standing on the other side with a big smile on her face. "May I come in?"

Ashley's heart sank, although she couldn't help but smile back at Hannah. "Certainly."

She stepped back and let Hannah in. "You can set those on the island," she said to Hannah when she realized Hannah was carrying her meal offerings.

Hannah set a pumpkin pie on the island and put a bowl of pasta salad in the fridge, along with whipped cream. "I know I'm early, so don't panic. Paul and I discussed it, and we decided I might be able to help you. We knew if we called, you'd say you had it all handled."

Ashley stood there for a minute; her feelings all jumbled. She'd been so stressed this morning and now realized she had family who cared. She burst into tears.

Hannah came over, put her arms around her and hugged her hard. "It's okay. I know it's been tough for you for a long time, but you're not alone any longer."

Ashley leaned against her, and it took a while to stop crying. Eventually, as the soft wool of Hannah's coat finally penetrated her consciousness, she realized she hadn't even taken Hannah's coat. She pulled away. "I have to get some tissues. Why don't you take your coat off? It's stifling in here. You must be roasting faster than my turkey." She laughed. "I'll go change and wipe my nose."

She headed toward her bedroom but turned around in the hallway before she reached her door. Hannah was unbuttoning her coat. "Thank you. I guess I needed that."

Hannah grinned at her. "We could all use a good cry now and then. I've done it plenty of times, believe me. Now, go do whatever you need to get ready. I'll be fine watching things here in the kitchen. When you get back, we'll settle down with a donut and something to drink."

"You brought donuts? Oh, Hannah. I love you. No wonder my brother proposed."

Hannah laughed. "Go."

After Ashley's rocky start to the day, she had fun with Hannah. Before Paul arrived, she and Hannah got to know more about each other. Ashley was pleased with Paul's choice. They had a lot in common.

Hannah cut off parts of the turkey and put them in a separate pan, so at least some of the turkey would cook in time. She helped peel potatoes and set the table.

Ashley had bought a beautiful autumn floral centerpiece. It all looked lovely once it was ready. There was a lot of eating and laughter during the day.

When they left, Ashley gave Paul a hug, which he returned wholeheartedly. "You made a wonderful choice," she told him. "Hannah's what you need."

"Thanks. I agree," Paul said.

Ashley turned to Hannah. "And thank you. For everything." They also hugged goodbye.
When they left, Paul's arm was around Hannah's shoulders.

Ashley looked around her apartment. They had helped clean up before they left. The apartment was ready for Jason's arrival. Hannah left the pie and whipped cream for her and Jason to have an evening snack. Ashley smiled. Hannah was so kind.

Ashley had an hour before Jason would arrive. She went into her bedroom and studied the clothes she wore. Would they work for an evening with Jason? This was their second official date. She studied the clothes in her closet, looking for something that made her feel good when she wore it.

She found an amber sweater and a pair of worn blue jeans. She debated on shoes. She finally decided to wear a pair of blue socks and forget shoes. She felt comfortable and stylish at the same time. She knew Jason probably wouldn't even notice. She combed her hair until it shone. She was ready.

She wandered around the apartment for the next half hour, unable to settle. He arrived about fifteen minutes late, but she didn't hold it against him. Judging holiday traffic was difficult, and Chokecherry Valley was about an hour away.

When he knocked, she took a deep breath and let it out. This was it. She felt it was a momentous occasion. She opened the door.

He smiled and held out a gorgeous red poinsettia in a pot. "Hello."

"Hi. Thank you. These are beautiful flowers." She set the pot on the island.

"It's for an early start to the Christmas season," Jason said.

"Let me take your coat." She was so happy to see him. She remembered what Courtney told her about falling in love.

He pulled off his black puffer coat, which she threw on a chair in the living room. At least she got that part right, and she didn't feel like crying since she'd gotten it out of her system with Hannah's help.

"Let's have a seat in the living room," she suggested.

He sat on the couch.

She chose a chair across from him, even though she wanted to snuggle up next to him. "How was your Thanksgiving?"

"Busy. Why is it that the same people who get together every day can be busier on Thanksgiving than a normal day?"

"Because you spend time together. Otherwise, you're all doing your own thing."

"True," Jason said.

"What did your family do today?" Ashley asked.

"We played games before we ate. Then my dad and I watched football until he fell asleep in his chair. Then I watched alone. Madison and Mom took a walk while I watched Chloe," Jason said.

"Madison seems to be doing well."

"Yes. I'm definitely happy with the way she's feeling. Is it weird that I keep waiting for something to go wrong?" he asked.

"No. It's normal. You had three months of chaos before she got help. It takes a while to get over that," Ashley assured him.

"You're right. What did you do today with Paul and Hannah?"

"We ate and talked and laughed. It's the first time I spent much time with Hannah—or Paul, in a long time. We had fun." She considered the day, pleased with the happiness she'd seen on their faces. "I'll ask Hannah out for lunch in the new year."

"That's great. I'm glad you two are connecting," Jason said.

"Yes. I'm really happy with Paul's choice. On a different subject, I realized Alex is returning home next week. His release date is December first," she said.

"How do you feel about that?"

"I'm so excited. It's going to be hard to wait until he's home a little while before I go and see him and Courtney."

"Things worked out for you and Paul. I'm sure it's going to be okay with Alex and Courtney."

"You're right." She decided that was enough talk about her brothers for today. "Do you want to do something tonight?" she asked.

"Sure," he agreed.

"What did you have in mind?"

"How about a movie here at your house?" Jason asked. "And you can come join me on the couch and snuggle while we watch."

She could feel his eyes practically drilling into her brain to see what she thought. "I'd love to do both."

Ashley grabbed the remote from the coffee table and plopped down right beside him. "I've been waiting for you to ask me to come over here." She was elated he'd suggested snuggling. She planned to make sure she got a kiss before he left. She wanted to ask him how he felt about her, but at the moment, she couldn't come up with a subtle way to do that. Maybe she'd be blunt if she didn't come up with subtle.

Without hesitating, he put his arm around her. She leaned into him.

"Before we start the movie, I'd like to tell you what I was thinking about when I was holding Chloe at Frank and Nina's house the other day." She didn't believe he was going to have any problem with her career change, but she felt the need to tell him right away. Mainly because she wanted to share her excitement.

"Is everything okay?" he asked with concern, his brow wrinkled in concentration.

She considered it as his "thinking face." "I want to start a daycare. I love little children and decided that would be the perfect place to start a career."

He hugged her closer. "That sounds perfect for you, Ashley. I'm so happy that you're happy with your choice."

"I am," she said, reveling in the feel of his arm tight around her.

"Great! I also have something to say to you, Ashley," he said with a tremor in his voice. He was focusing on her face and almost looked afraid. "I really like you a lot. I haven't had a lot of girlfriends in the past. Mostly because I never found someone who interested me enough to date for very long. I feel different about you. I like you a lot, and I'd really like it if we spent more time together. I'd like it if we would date exclusively. What do you think?"

She felt his hand shaking when he picked hers up and held it. She knew her own hand was trembling too, and her heart beat faster than she felt was healthy. "Yes. You're the only man I want to date." She looked up at him, willing him to kiss her now.

He leaned forward and kissed her on the lips. It seemed to go on forever until she felt dizzy. Then it ended too quickly. "Hey, why'd you stop?"

"I needed to breathe." He laughed. His expression relaxed.

She did notice he was breathless. Well, she was too. "The kiss was worth waiting for, but let's do it more often."

"Definitely."

They watched a movie, but she wasn't really paying attention and couldn't have described it when it was over. There had been a few more kisses during the movie, which hadn't helped her concentration.

When he was ready to leave, she got another kiss at the door. "See you tomorrow," he said as he held her in his arms.

"We don't have class tomorrow because of the holiday." She looked up at him with a smile and raised brows.

"I know." He smiled down at her. "But I need my Monday-Wednesday-Friday lunch with you. Any objections?"

"No. I could spend time with you every day. What about you?" She waited breathlessly for his answer.

His smile grew bigger than she'd ever seen, and when he gazed at her, the light in his brown eyes stole the rest of her heart. "I'd love to spend every day with you. We'll plan that out tomorrow when we see each other." He stole another quick kiss and left.

She leaned against the closed door. Her heart felt full. A Thanksgiving to remember forever.

~ ~

CHOKECHERRY VALLEY VALLEY
FAITH
Book 4

ACKNOWLEDGMENTS

Special thanks to the excellent editor, Krista Venero at Mountains Wanted Publishing & Indie Author Services for great suggestions. She helped create a better book than I could have envisioned on my own.

Thank you to the book cover artist at Sunset Rose Books for an amazing cover.

Considerable thanks to my family who have encouraged me in my writing journey.

Thank you to Sally, Ruth, and Amy, great friends who are also great at running book ideas and cover designs past. I couldn't have finished this book without your help.

Special thanks to Connie Victoria Volk for helping by editing and making suggestions for a stronger book. She writes her own books. www.connievolk.com

CHAPTER 1

Alex walked in between the two guards, his cuffed hands in front of him. At least his feet were no longer chained. He took a deep breath, trying to calm his racing heart. Courtney would be waiting. He was equal parts nervous and excited about seeing her again although she visited him only last week.

They reached the waiting area for visitors as they arrived at the prison. The guard asked the desk person for Alex's possessions and took the cuffs off his wrists. The person behind the desk handed him a small manila envelope and a Bible. He reached into the envelope, took out his wallet and stuffed it in his pants pocket, and put his wedding ring on his finger. He'd lost weight in prison, and the ring spun loosely around on his finger.

Sitting around for two years should have made him gain weight, but the lack of interesting food, his poor appetite, and increased anxiety had the opposite effect.

He looked up from his ring, and there stood Courtney. Underneath the red knit hat she wore, she flashed a brilliant smile at him, and he smiled back. It felt almost painful, his facial muscles unused to turning up instead of keeping firmly straight to hide his emotions.

What was she thinking behind her smile? They'd seen each other monthly in the two years he'd been in prison, and she'd stood by him. He suspected there were a lot of things she put up with in Chokecherry Valley she hadn't told him. Just like he kept secrets of what happened in prison from her. They didn't want to waste their time together when they met for the rare visits.

He hadn't wanted her to come more often, even though the prison allowed it. Every time she walked out of the visiting room, he kept himself from begging her to stay. He missed her so much when she left him there to go back to his empty cell.

"You're free to go, Mr. Richmond," the guard said.

"Thank you," Alex responded, keeping to his polite demeanor. He tried to treat the guards politely while in prison. There was no point in being angry at them.

Alex walked over to Courtney, who grabbed him in a tight hug. He held on to her for a bit before pulling away.

"Here's your puffer coat and a pair of gloves. I wasn't sure if you had any winter wear." She handed them to him.

"Perfect." He slid his arm into the sleeve of the black coat and slipped it on the rest of the way.

When he put on the gloves and picked up the Bible, she said, "Let's go."

He caught a glimpse of tears in her eyes as she turned away and walked around the other people waiting their turn at the counter. They reached the outside door. When he stepped outside, the sun shone brightly in the deep blue sky, brilliant and unlike anything he remembered. He blinked and took a deep breath of the frigid December air.

She hugged him quickly again and then let go. "We're over here." She led him to their vehicle, walking carefully on the icy pavement.

He took hesitant steps, as if he hadn't walked on ice for a long time. He kept expecting the prison door to re-open, and the guards to call him back, and put him in his cell again. This freedom was going to take getting used to. He also sensed Courtney struggling with how to treat him since his release.

"Do you want to drive?" she asked when they reached the vehicle and clicked the door locks open with the key fob.

He automatically headed for the passenger side. He laughed—a rusty, tentative laugh, but a laugh. "I haven't driven for two years. I'll practice when we get home, and there's less traffic. Plus, I haven't looked at my license. I assume it's in my wallet, but it might be out of date."

She nodded, opened the driver's side door, and got in.

The ride out of the exit gate was routine, however when they stopped at the guard's station to leave, Alex had the same fear of being returned to prison. It didn't feel like he was free yet. Everything seemed unreal. How long would it last until the outside world felt like the real world again?

He gripped the armrest every time Courtney took a turn. The closer they got to their house, the tighter he gripped the leather. He should be calmer the closer they got to Chokecherry Valley, but he wasn't sure what kind of reception would greet them. Were there going to be any local reporters or people who resented him for his actions?

Courtney kept glancing over at him.

"What?" he asked.

"You're jittery, aren't you?" Concern laced her voice.

"It's best you know sooner rather than later. I don't sleep well at night. I can't remember the last time I relaxed. I've become afraid of everything. I suppose it was bound to happen."

She didn't tell him it was his own fault because of his confession and consequent prison term. She reached over and touched his gloved hand. "We'll get through it. I'm glad you're home. I'll help you get better."

He relaxed slightly. That was one confession out of the way, and she'd taken it well. Hopefully, they could work through the problems that plagued him, because, being married to him, she had suffered the consequences too.

They reached home. Courtney avoided going through town and took the long way around to arrive behind their house. She parked, and they went in through the back door.

He stood there taking in the scent of home, while Courtney went to look out the windows to see if anyone noticed their arrival. "There's no one out there."

"Good." He walked down the hallway and into the open space of the living room, kitchen, and entryway. During his time away, she hadn't made any changes, and he was grateful for the familiarity of home.

He took off his gloves and his coat and hung them in the entry closet. He sank onto the couch and rested his head against the back. "It's great to be home."

"Do you want something to eat? I made chicken salad and cut up fruit before I left to pick you up. We could have sandwiches with the fruit."

"That sounds wonderful, but you know what I'd really like right now?" He stood up. "I'd like a long hot shower and some other clothes. Do you mind?"

"No, go ahead. I'll get lunch while you enjoy your shower. How about I give you time to get used to your privacy? I didn't move any of your things, so you can find what you need. If you're missing something, let me know."

"I got used to going without." He was glad for time to look around and get reacquainted with the place. He found clothes that might fit, but the pants would probably hang on him. He found a belt for the jeans.

He enjoyed every moment of the shower and felt better when he got into clean clothes. He dropped the ones he wore home from prison into the corner. He might throw them away.

He entered the kitchen in his stockinged feet. "Do you want help?"

"No. I'm fine. It's ready." She pointed to the plates on the table in the kitchen nook. It had a bench seat in the bay window and two chairs around the outer side.

"Good. I'm going to enjoy the great view while we eat." He sat down in one of the chairs, so he could look out the window."

"What would you like to drink?" she asked.

"I'll have water. I'm too jittery for coffee right now."

She got a glass out of the cupboard and filled it with water from the fridge. After she set it in front of him, she got her coffee mug from the counter and joined him at the table.

"I'm glad you're home, Alex. I know relaxing will be hard for you, but other than a few irate neighbors, it's calm around here."

She sounded like she understood, at least. For today, he'd let her wait on him. She wanted to take care of him. But tomorrow, he'd do his share. She would have to go to work, and he'd somehow have to find work. He'd have plenty of time to provide the meals.

He took a bite of his sandwich, enjoying the taste of something homemade and edible again. He gazed outside, finally feeling a small measure of peace. It would be okay.

Everything will work out had been his mantra for two long years. Maybe everything would finally be okay.

CHAPTER 2

Courtney found herself second-guessing everything she did. Alex was finally home. She wanted to cry and laugh and scream. Her emotions careened all over the place. On the outside, she tried to look calm. Alex needed that right now.

She was tired of being strong. It had been a long two years without him. She visited monthly, only to leave and come home alone to the house. It felt too big for one person. It was too big for two people.

The house had belonged to Alex's parents until they bought it from them when Alex got his job at the bank. His parents hadn't spent much time here, as they were roaming around the world on one long vacation.

Alex's sister, Ashley, and brother, Paul, approved of them buying the house. Both Ashley and Paul settled in Bismarck shortly after graduation from high school. They hadn't planned to come back to Chokecherry Valley, but now Ashley dated a local guy.

Alex set up guidelines when he went to prison. He refused to see either Paul or Ashley. He also told them not to visit Courtney in Chokecherry Valley. He didn't want his disgrace to rub off on them.

Ashley followed orders until a few months ago. She finally ignored his edicts and paid a surprise visit to Courtney. Ashley said she would support Courtney and Alex now that he was getting out of prison. Courtney could tell Ashley regretted not being around for Courtney sooner, but Courtney had her own family. She had three brothers and two sisters of her own, and her parents were supportive of Courtney and Alex.

She told them if they didn't support Alex too, she wouldn't see them. Her protective family reluctantly said they would treat Alex politely. She hoped they would. They didn't know the whole story, but if they did, they would understand. She hated secrets, but sometimes life forced them on her.

She cleaned up after lunch. There wasn't much to do. Alex settled on the navy-blue cloth couch and stared out the living room window. She could see him from where she tidied the kitchen and wondered what he was thinking. She finished wiping the table and then sat on the chair across from Alex.

His mouth turned up in a smile. "You're staring." He turned to look at her.

"How did you know?" Courtney asked.

His mouth flattened into a grim line. "You learn to read a room by feel when you're around the guys I was around."

She got up and went to sit beside him, taking his hand in hers. "I know this is going to take a while." She waved her free hand around the room. "You've got all the time in the world. I know you're not going to be happy sitting around for long. Have you thought about what you want to do with your time?"

"I'm hoping to get a job but don't have any idea if someone will hire me," Alex said.

Courtney put her arms around him and settled her head on his chest. "We'll work something out. At least we don't need the money."

"The irony of the whole embezzling charge." He slid an arm around her and let out an abrupt laugh.

"There's something I need to talk to you about. Do you want the news now or later?" Courtney asked.

"We may as well talk about whatever it is now. What else do we have to do today besides catch up?"

She nodded. "I know." There was no sense in keeping the news from him. "Steven Hanson is sick again."

He pulled away from her, and she lifted her head to see his expression. She might have to get used to the grim set of his mouth.

He looked down at her. "Same cancer?"

"Same cancer. Only worse this time. They say he might only have a few weeks left. It's metastasized."

"I should go visit him. I'm sure it's been hard on him and Barbara." He stood up and started pacing. "How can I visit them in secret? You know the whole town thinks I shouldn't go anywhere near him."

Courtney watched him. "I know, but he'll want to see you. You know that."

"Yes. I know. We'll have to figure something out."

"He's at home, which makes it easier and harder at the same time. At least they don't live on Main Street like us. Our car would be noticeable if we drove there. It would have been easier if he were in the hospital instead of having hospice at home," Courtney said.

"We'll figure something out." He plopped down on the couch beside her again, and this time, he took her hand. "I'm suddenly very tired."

"Want to go lie down?" she asked.

"No. I'll lean here against the couch. Do you mind staying with me?"

She looked around the living room. Her book was in the bedroom. She'd had a hard time sleeping last night, knowing she would be picking him up this morning. "I'm going to get my book, so if you fall asleep, I'll have something to do."

She got up and headed for the bedroom. It felt good to take a moment to get away from Alex. She didn't quite know how to treat him. Carefully? No. Just as if it were a normal day.

She picked up her book and returned to the living room. "I might fall asleep on your shoulder. It's been a long day, and it's only two o'clock."

She put her book beside her on the couch and settled back in his arms. She wanted to be close to him.

CHAPTER 3

Last night before bed, Alex had delicately told Courtney he needed to sleep alone for a while. He felt hot and flushed when he explained he was fine continuing the physical side of their relationship now, but he couldn't relax enough to sleep with her in the same bed.

He told her about his fear of hurting her in his sleep because he had always been careful to be half aware while in prison. He could lash out if someone touched him when he was asleep.

Courtney looked shocked but then understood. He didn't know what she felt. There were going to be minefields in their marriage until they worked them out.

He'd been gone two whole years. She'd been without him, and he'd been without her. They'd navigated their individual worlds alone. They were more independent and older than they'd been two years ago. They'd made the big decisions together while he was in prison, but the day-to-day problems, they'd negotiated alone.

"Wow," he said as he came into the kitchen and saw the table set in the kitchen nook. He'd heard Courtney get up earlier, but the luxury of staying in a nice soft bed kept him from getting up for a while. He lay there, enjoying the peace and quiet, and the sounds of Courtney in the kitchen. "You made waffles and omelets?"

Courtney smiled at him. "I know. We never ate like this for breakfast, but I thought you might be hungry for real food."

"It smells great. Yes, I am hungry for something not made in a big vat," Alex said.

"I have the whole week off, and I'm going to spoil you," Courtney said. "Have a seat."

Alex hugged her and then sat down at the table. "Okay. Today you can spoil me. Tomorrow we start taking care of each other. I know you didn't have it easy while I was gone. You don't need to pretend."

He saw tears glisten in her eyes before she turned back to the stove. "Okay. We'll take care of each other."

He could barely hear her and knew she fought for control. She dished up the food and delivered it to the table.

"What do you want to drink?" she asked. "There's orange juice, coffee, and water."

"Water. I can get it." He started up from his chair, and she put her hand on his shoulder. He felt her kiss the top of his head.

"I can tell spoiling you isn't going to be easy. I'll get your water, and then we'll do things together."

He breathed out a sigh of relief. "Thanks for understanding, Courtney. I feel guilty for the time you did everything. I want to be helpful."

"I know." She set the glass of water beside his plate and sat down across from him. "And I want to make things up to you for having to endure all you did for the past two years."

They looked at each other across the table, understanding passing between them. Life sucked for each of them in its own way. They had a long way to go for things to be easy between them again, but they'd get there. They'd promised to stick by each other during their marriage ceremony, and he knew Courtney took her vows as seriously as he did.

"Let's make a pact." He placed his hand palm up across the table in front of her, and she put her hand in his. "To many happy days together." He emphasized *together*.

"Together," she said and squeezed his hand. Then she pulled it away.

Her smile said her withdrawal wasn't a rejection. "Let's eat before it gets cold."

His sensible wife. He smiled at her and took a bite of his omelet. It tasted good after all this time. He was suddenly, almost overwhelmingly, happy. "This is terrific."

For the first time in a long time, he felt hungry, and he ate the omelet, two waffles and fruit. He would feel overly full when he was done because his stomach had shrunk, but he enjoyed the fresh meal. When he finished, he settled back in his chair and sipped his water.

Courtney wore a pleased look on her face. She'd been watching him eat. He could feel her eyes on his, but now she concentrated on her own food. She wasn't gulping it down like he had.

She finished up and settled back with her coffee. She must be tired. He had a feeling she hadn't slept well last night or the night before she picked him up.

"Let's make a plan," she said. "First, shopping for new clothes for you."

His heart started to race. "I don't want to be seen around here yet. I'm not ready." He gasped for air.

Courtney slid out of the booth under the window, pulled the other chair up close to him and grabbed his hands. "It's okay. I'm with you. We're not going into Chokecherry Valley."

He nodded, unable to speak.

"We're going to Bismarck. The place is big enough, we shouldn't run into anyone we know from here. We're only going to two places while we're there."

He could feel his heartbeat slowing as she talked.

"We'll go one place to get you clothes that don't fall off you. You only need some pants, underwear, a few belts, and new shoes. Not much. The shirts you have will work okay. They might be a little big for a while, but you'll put on a few pounds eating waffles and omelets every morning." She laughed.

His heart rate returned to normal although his hands tingled from nerves. And from Courtney's touch. Her hands were warm and comforting. He gave her a weak smile. "We are not having waffles and omelets every morning, unless I make them," he said, looking into her eyes.
She had such beautiful blue eyes.

"Hey. Don't go to sleep on me." She tugged on his hands.

"I'm not. I was thinking what beautiful eyes you have." He appreciated the blush rising on her cheeks.

She pulled away as if embarrassed. "Thank you. Now, you seem to be recovered. Let's go shopping. We're going out the back way, and we'll be gone before anyone sees us. The minute our shopping trip becomes too much for you to manage, let me know, and we'll come home."

A few of his nerves returned, but he kept his expression neutral. Eventually Courtney would catch on to what that look meant, but for now, he didn't want to worry her. She didn't know how bad his anxiety had gotten in prison, but she probably already had an idea. He also didn't want it to ruin the day.

"Okay." He put a cheerful note in his voice. "Let's do dishes and get out of here to buy my underwear."

She laughed like he knew she would.

"By the way, you said two stores. What other store do we need to go to?"

"Someplace where they have toiletries. You need a new razor and other things like that. I did pick out things for you but figured you might want to choose other things for yourself."

"Thanks. For everything." He hugged her.

They cleaned up and escaped out the back door. No one saw them leave as far as they knew. They agreed to have a fun day together and not talk about the looming problems they had to address at some point.

CHAPTER 4

Courtney circled around Alex for the next few days. They weren't comfortable living together. She thought, as soon as Alex came home, they would continue their life at ease with each other, even if they had other things happening outside the house.

It wasn't working that way at all. Alex was jumpy and hyper alert. She was unsure of everything he'd gone through in prison. Before he'd been imprisoned, she could have asked him what was going on. Since he'd returned home, she couldn't bridge the distance, almost like a wall separated them.

How long would this go on? She second guessed taking time off from work this week. Maybe it would have been better to let Alex readjust to being home without her.

Their trip to Bismarck to update Alex's wardrobe had been the easiest day so far. They had a common goal. They needed something else to keep them occupied in the next few days.

A light snow of about two inches fell overnight. Not a lot, but enough that it gave Alex something to do outside. He'd been almost giddy at going outside to shovel and sweep the sidewalk and driveway.

A few people drove by on their way to pick up items at the stores on Main Street. Alex pretended not to see them stare avidly out their vehicle windows at him. Word would spread throughout the neighborhood and surrounding area by nighttime that he was out of prison. Which was good. No sense in hiding.

She tidied up the kitchen and heard a vehicle pull into the driveway. She tensed. Who could it be? She didn't get many visitors.

Alex got up from the couch, where he had been reading his Bible, and looked out the window. "It's Paul and Ashley."

Courtney's mouth stretched into the first natural smile since Alex returned home, and her shoulders relaxed about four inches. "Ashley stopped by a few times in the past few months. I forgot to tell you."

Alex frowned. "We told her to stay away."

"We did," Courtney said as she headed for the front door. "Your sister has developed quite a backbone in the past six months. She refused to leave one day, so I finally let her in."

"I don't like it. They're not supposed to be involved." He continued frowning.

"You tell them then." She gestured toward the door.

He didn't move from his spot by the couch.

She opened the door. "Hi, Ashley."

Ashley swept her into a hug. "Hi. I brought Paul with me."

"I see. Hi, Paul."

"Hi," he said.

Courtney ushered them into the house. Ashley slid off her sneakers, which were wet from the snow. Paul tugged off his shoes too.

Courtney noticed Alex stood there staring at them from his place in front of the couch. She took their coats and hung them in the closet by the door.

They all looked at Alex, who finally spoke. "I told you—"

Ashley ran over to him before he could finish and pulled him into a tight embrace. Courtney could almost feel the rigidity of his frame from her place by Paul.

Alex finally lifted his arms and encircled Ashley in a big hug. Courtney let out the breath she'd been holding.

When Ashley and Alex let go, Ashley looked him in the face. "I know what you said. Well, that doesn't matter anymore. You're where I can see you, and you need company. You're not going to hide out in shame from your own family. Whatever happened is in the past. I left Courtney alone for too long, but that's over. You're stuck with Paul and me now. Get used to it."

Alex looked at her as if he'd never seen her before.

"You look surprised I'm not the doormat I used to be." Ashley grinned at him.

Alex looked over at Paul, who shrugged. "What can I say? She's got me talked into visiting you. I see her point."

"But what about your reputations?" Alex sounded doubtful.

"Who cares?" Ashley asked. "Paul's job is in Bismarck. They don't care. I'm in school. No one there cares either. We don't work here in Chokecherry Valley. Besides, you did the time. They better start getting over it."

Alex shrugged helplessly. "Well, it's complicated."

Paul came over and sat on one of the chairs across from the couch. "We always knew that. But you didn't tell us then, and you're not going to tell us now. So, I guess we'll pretend it's not complicated and love you anyway."

Courtney saw a shimmer of tears before Alex blinked and sat down on the couch.

"Okay. I guess I'm stuck with you." A big smile broke out on his face as he looked around the room.

Courtney relaxed even more. Finally, she had someone else to share the load. Reintegrating Alex into the neighborhood would be hard enough with his anxiety and the community's anger.

Paul settled back on his chair and stuck his black stockinged feet out in front of him. "You may as well know right away I have news. I got engaged last month. Her name is Hannah."

Alex got up and shook his hand before settling back on the couch. "That's great. Where did you meet her?"

"She works at the hospital too. She does fundraising, and I was involved in one of her fundraisers. We got to know each other, and now, here we are."

"I saw a picture of you online. You gave that kid a scholarship, which was nice of you to do."

Paul's face flushed bright red. "Yes. It was the least I could do for him, but the story is for another time."

Alex turned to Ashley. "How about you, Squirt? Or maybe I should change your nickname to Feisty."

Ashley laughed and sat down on the other cushioned chair beside Paul's seat. "If you want something, you have to go after it." She glanced at Courtney.

Courtney smiled at her and joined Alex on the couch. "Like you did to me. Camping on the front porch until I let you in."

"I'd had enough of the separation," Ashley said. "Besides, it was time to get this family back together."

"And what about the other person you come to see in Chokecherry Valley?" Courtney asked slyly.

"Oh, him." Ashley shrugged like it was no big deal.

Alex leaned toward her now. "Out with it. Who is this guy?"

Now Ashley's face turned red. "It's Jason. You know? The guy who lives by Paul's in-laws."

"You mean Jason Allmen?" Alex asked.

"That's him," Courtney said gleefully.

Ashley threw her a quick smile. "Okay. You've had your fun." She turned back to Alex. "So far we've been on one date, and he came to my apartment for a few hours Thanksgiving evening."

"And they have lunch after class a lot of times," Courtney added.

"That's where you met him? In class?" Alex asked.

"Yes. We were sitting beside each other, and things kind of happened. I never dreamt I'd seen him before, but I must have."

"You stayed with Grandma in Bismarck a lot of times and went to high school there. If you'd been here when you were that age, you probably would remember him," Paul said.

"Probably." Ashley shrugged and smiled. "I guess I've met him now."

Courtney suddenly jumped up from where she'd been sitting. "I'm sorry. I didn't even offer you anything to eat or drink. Can I get you something?"

Ashley and Paul both shook their heads.

"We're fine. We snacked on licorice and mixed nuts on the way here," Ashley said.

"You mean, you did," Paul teased her, then shook his head at Alex and Courtney. "She's kind of going through a licorice phase right now."

Ashley laughed but didn't argue.

Alex continued smiling, but Courtney could sense strain behind his smile now. She wasn't sure why. She couldn't read his moods like she used to. She almost sighed before realizing that wouldn't be the best thing to do around company. Even if the company was Alex's family. And hers.

She knew it was time for them to leave. Alex wasn't used to long social visits.

Paul leaned forward and clasped his hands between his knees. "Just so we're clear. Ashley and I will continue to visit. Sometimes together. Sometimes alone. Sometimes with Hannah or Jason, but you're not in prison anymore, and you're not alone anymore."

Alex lifted his hand to stop him.

"Don't worry. I'm not going to get all mushy on you. I just needed to say that. I couldn't get to you in prison because you could refuse." He looked Alex in the eyes. "Which is the only reason you didn't see me."

He leaned back again and looked up at Courtney, who hadn't sat down after her offer of refreshments. "And I shouldn't have listened to you. I'm glad Ashley forced her way back into your life, but we should have done it sooner, Ashley and I agree."

He looked uncomfortable then. "Of course, my life was in a bit of a mess there for a while. Maybe it's for the best." He stood up and walked over to Courtney.

"Can I give you a brotherly hug?" he asked.

"Of course." She hugged him back.

"I'm sorry we weren't here for you. Next time we visit, we'll keep the conversation light."

She smiled at him. "Sounds good."

Paul looked at Ashley. "We should head back and let these two have some privacy."

Ashley hugged Alex and Courtney when they stood up from the couch. "Okay, but we'll be back."

After they had their shoes and coats back on and were walking down the driveway, Alex yelled out the door at them, "And next time, bring a Christmas present."

He laughed at their twin expressions of surprise. And then they were grinning and waving back at him. He laughed and closed the front door.

Courtney stared at him, her mouth open. "Wow. Where'd that come from?"

"I finally realized I'm actually home. And it's December. And it's almost Christmas." He grinned at her and pulled her into a tight hug.

She relaxed into the hug and laid her head on his shoulder. Maybe everything would be okay. She pushed all thoughts away about all the steps necessary to a normal life. It could wait. Maybe if they concentrated on Christmas and took everything else as it came, it would work out.

CHAPTER 5

Alex woke up Monday morning when he heard the shower start. Courtney was getting ready to go to work. Their brief time alone was over, and he knew he needed to visit Barbara and Steven. He'd given him the job at the bank when Alex graduated from college. While he didn't owe him anything, he needed to see him before the cancer progressed any further, and it was too late to talk to him.

When Courtney returned from church yesterday, she gave Alex the update that Steven only had weeks to live. Alex knew there wasn't much time, but now that he was out of prison, he could act.

Courtney came into the bedroom wrapped in a bath towel to get her clothes from the closet. She took up residence in one of the guest rooms until they were comfortable with each other again. She told him to take his time, and he knew the decision was in his control. She was ready to be a married couple any time he said the word. He wondered how patient she would be.

She pulled clothes out of the closet and turned to look at him where he lay on the bed. "What are you doing today?"

"Going over to see Steven and Barbara. I think it would give him some peace."

"You're a nice man, Alex Richmond." Her words came out softly as she struggled to juggle her clothes and her towel.

He ducked his head. He wasn't used to good things being said about him. "Thank you. What time are you done with work?" He looked back up at her.

"Around 2:30 p.m."

"I'll be here waiting. We can take a walk before it gets dark outside. It's in the thirties today, and we won't have very many more days this warm."

"Sure. Sounds good. I'm going to grab a banana on my way to work, so you're on your own for breakfast." She left to dress and get to work.

He lay there a few more minutes before deciding he should get moving himself. From now on, he'd make breakfast for Courtney. She was the only one currently working, and his choice of job was limited by his stint in prison. It could take a long time before someone would hire him.

The idea didn't depress him as much as he believed it would. He didn't want to hang around for a long time with nothing to do, but the visit from Paul and Ashley lit a fire in him to make a great Christmas for them all.

He would check with Courtney when they took their walk and ask if she was willing to host his family and their significant others for Christmas Eve or Christmas Day.

She'd been understanding yesterday about church. He wanted to go, but if they did it in stages, it might be more manageable for Courtney. First, everyone would know he was out of prison. Next week when he attended church with her family, the initial gossip would have died down. He hoped.

And her family's response to his attendance would be intense. He knew they'd be polite to him in front of Courtney, but how would they treat him when she wasn't around? He had no idea.

Courtney's family went to church in Bismarck, so at least it wasn't the local Chokecherry Valley church. He had nothing against the church. In fact, he wanted to stop there and visit with the local pastor in the next few days. He was glad Courtney didn't have to put up with everyone's stares. But he was wrong. She'd already done that by working at the local grocery store.

He felt ashamed. She put up with the local animosity while he'd been in prison. How did she stand it? Her firm conviction everything would work out okay got her through the days. He hadn't wanted to suggest they sell the house and move where nobody knew them.

He'd plan one last Christmas in this house where he'd grown up, and then, in the new year, they could start fresh. They had the money. At least there was no problem with that aspect.

He wanted to contribute something to society since he'd been given a lot from his parents, and they had a beautiful house and food to eat.

He called Barbara, who answered with a delighted laugh. "I'm glad you're home," she said. "I've been waiting to hear from you."

"Thank you, Barbara. Courtney and I were trying to get a few things settled, but she's at work today. I was wondering what a suitable time would be to visit you and Steven."

"Anytime. Really. He sleeps a lot when he's not in pain. A visit from you might settle him down. He's asked about you a few times." There was a sudden catch in her voice.

"I know," he said softly. He'd lost one of his good friends to cancer in college and never got over seeing the results of the disease, especially at the end of Kevin's life. "I'll be over in about a half hour. I'll come the back way to keep gossip to a minimum. Hopefully, I'll be in and out before anyone passes on the news I'm visiting."

"Oh, Alex." Her voice held a note of sorrow. "It shouldn't be this way."

He took a deep breath. "I'm fine, Barbara. I'll be over soon. Don't worry. Things worked out for the best. I'll tell you all about it someday."

"Thanks, Alex. You're a good man."

"See you soon." He hung up and laughed. Well, two women in one day thought he was a good man.

He didn't know where he fell on the scale of goodness. Two years of being locked up and keeping to himself stunted his ability to look at people normally. He'd always been assessing the other prisoners for threats although a lot of them were as scared as he was. They had to keep up an attitude in prison to survive. He saw beneath the surface to the good in some of them who had been caught in circumstances and made poor choices.

He looked around the kitchen and living room, wondering what to do with himself for the next thirty minutes. Most of the time since he'd gotten out of prison, he felt like he was looking at himself from an outside lens. He wasn't comfortable anywhere anymore. His cell had been his peaceful place.

He finally got out the Bible he'd brought with him from prison. He sank down on the couch and held it in his hands without opening it. Just holding it grounded him somehow. He finally opened it to his favorite verse about God's peace surpassing all understanding and felt his shoulders relax as he read.

Twenty minutes later, his emotions under control, he put on his shoes and coat. He found the leather gloves Courtney insisted he buy and smiled. She'd convinced him to buy more than he intended that day, but they had fun. He had a feeling he'd need everything she thought he did.

He left through the rear door. He liked the slight cold breeze ruffling his dark hair as he took the back path to Steven and Barbara's house. There was only one house between them, and he hoped they weren't looking out their back window as he walked along the gravel road. It was for their sake, not his. He could handle it. He and Courtney agreed, if she heard anything he needed to know, she would text him from work.

He walked up to the Hansons' back door, which Barbara opened before he reached it.

"Hi." She gave him a tight hug, then released him, and took a long look at him. Something in his expression must have convinced her things were okay between them. She relaxed. "It's good to see you."

"You too." He smiled at her, removed his gloves, and took her hand in his. "I'm sorry."

Her smile faltered, and tears filled her eyes. "We hoped when he was in remission, it wouldn't return, but here we are."

This time he pulled her into a hug. She rested against him and then pulled away, wiped her tears with her hand, and pulled out a tissue to wipe her nose. "A word of warning. He's lost a lot of weight."

Alex nodded and followed her into the house. They were in the back hallway that led past the bedrooms and into the main living room. Steven's bed was close to the wall. He could look outside the front windows or turn his head to the other wall and see the fireplace.

Alex stuffed his gloves into his pockets and unzipped his coat, slipping it off as he walked over to the bed. This was not the six-foot husky man Alex had seen two years ago. His face was sunken, and his hands clenched the sheets. His eyes burned into Alex's as Alex approached the bed. Barbara disappeared into one of the other rooms to give them privacy.

"Hey there," Alex said.

"Hi." His voice was low but still held a hint of strength running through it. "Good to see you. I've been pestering Barbara to see when you were coming." He smiled in the direction his wife had gone. "She told me to be patient."

"Patience is not your main virtue," Alex kidded him.

He sighed. "Well, I've gotten better at it since I got sick. Can't do much more than wait now."

"Sorry it came back."

"I know you are, but you gave me everything you have, and I won't forget. Barbara won't forget either when I'm gone," he said.

"There's nothing that can be done? No more treatment options?" Alex asked.

"Nothing. I'm resigned and ready to go. I've had two more years with Barbara than I expected. I'm lucky. I've led a good life with only a few poor choices—one big one I pray both you and God forgive." He turned his head away and coughed.

It hurt Alex just listening to him. It was painful to see his friend and mentor lying there helpless.

When the coughing fit passed, and he turned back around, Alex said, "I've forgiven you, and if you've asked God for forgiveness, I know He's forgiven you too. I'm moving on with my life." He frowned. "Well, that was a poor choice of words."

Steven laughed, which made him cough again. "And I'm done moving."

"I am sorry." Alex wished there were a way out of this, but nothing would change the outcome.

"You have nothing to be sorry for. I'm the one who's sorry."

"It's over. Let's talk about something else."

"The kids have been here. Mary's finished with college, and Sarah graduates next year. I can't believe they're grown and going to start their lives already."

Alex wondered what Barbara was going to do when both girls were gone and Steven too. He'd have to figure out what he could do to help her. "That's great. They're both doing terrific, from what I've heard."

He smiled like the proud father he was. "I think so."

Barbara came into the room. "Do either of you need anything?"

Alex shook his head. "I'm fine."

Steven reached out his hand to Barbara, and she held it lightly. "Thank you for getting Alex over here."

"Oh, he called right away this morning." Barbara smiled fondly at Alex.

"Yes, you're my first stop, although my brother and sister came by on Saturday to visit. Courtney finally felt she could stop babysitting me yesterday and went to church with her family." He grinned at Steven. "Things are going quite well. Nothing to worry about, so you rest."

He turned to Barbara. "And you get some rest too. I'm only a short distance away. Feel free to call me any time you need something."

Alex pulled his cell out of his jacket pocket and asked Barbara what her number was. She gave it to him, and he punched in the numbers and called her. They could hear her phone ringing on the kitchen table. Alex hung up. "There. You have my number."

"Wow," Barbara laughed, "you didn't waste any time getting connected."

Alex shook his head. "That's Courtney. She had the phone ready for me from the moment I left the prison."

Steven winced at the word "prison," and Alex realized that wasn't a good topic. "I'm going to pay her back by texting her constantly." He smiled at them both.

"Somehow I don't believe she'll mind," Barbara said.

Alex reached for his coat, which he'd thrown on the chair when he came into the room. "I know this has been brief, but you need your rest, and I'll be by frequently."

"You come by anytime you want," Barbara said.

Steven nodded his agreement.

"The community might not be happy I'm visiting you." Alex knew he had to broach the subject.

"We don't care. I won't be here much longer," Steven said. "I prefer you to visit when you want. Those who complain don't matter."

Alex caught the pain in Barbara's eyes when Steven said he didn't have much longer. "Okay. I'll be back." He patted his hand, but before he could withdraw his own hand, Steven turned his over. With a strength Alex hadn't expected, he gripped Alex's hand.

"Thank you. I'll pay you back." He squeezed Alex's hand and then let go, his eyes burning into Alex's.

Alex nodded and followed Barbara to the back door.

"Thank you for giving him time," Barbara said. "He wanted to tell you he was sorry."

"I know. It's okay." He wanted to get out of there now. He was starting to feel the claustrophobia he'd felt when he first entered prison and knew he couldn't leave whenever he wanted.

He waved at Barbara, who watched him walk down the drive. Then he was out of her sight and took a deep breath of the fresh air. He didn't walk directly back to his house. There was a side path that didn't lead anywhere but toward some pastures. He wandered along it.

There'd probably been about four inches of snow covering the ground from previous snowfalls. Soon his shoes were full of snow, and he headed back home. He was going to have to find boots to wear if he was going to take walks off the cleared paths.

He thought about his visit with Steven, and he remembered how he'd looked when Alex went to prison. The chemo took a toll the first time, and he retired from the bank the day Alex pled guilty to embezzlement. Steven said he wanted to spend any time he had left with Barbara. They had all been happy when he'd been declared cancer-free six months later.

Then, a year later, the cancer returned. They fought against it for six months now, and from what he'd heard today, they'd reached the end of options. Alex shook his head. At least they had the past two years, even though some of the time had been fighting his illness. Alex was sure it didn't feel like enough time to them. He knew, if Courtney were sick, he would do anything to spend the end with her.

He texted Courtney to ask her when she'd be home for lunch. He was determined to make her lunch today and have something waiting for her when she got home.

He was looking through the cupboards and fridge to see what he could make when he heard the doorbell. The sudden sound made him jump. He couldn't imagine who was visiting, and did they want to see him? Or had they come to see Courtney?

He walked over to the door and opened it to see Mary Hanson standing on the front welcome mat.

"Hi," he smiled in welcome, "do you want to come in?"

He noticed she didn't smile back. In fact, her face set in a fierce frown.

"What are you doing?" she asked, ignoring his invitation to enter.

He was confused by her manner and tone. He always thought they were friends, even though five years separated them. He'd spent so much time at her parents' house, he felt like Mary and Sarah were like sisters to him. "What do you mean, what am I doing?"

"Visiting my dad like that."

His own lips turned downward at her words. "Of course I visited him and your mom. They wanted me to come over and see them. Were they upset I was there?" He was surprised that he misread the situation.

Mary stomped her foot on the mat. "No, they weren't upset. I'm upset. You need to stay away from them. You're not doing them any good by going over there."

"What do you mean? They were happy to see me," he repeated.

"Of course they were. They love you. But this is a small town. What happens when word gets around you were over there? They're going to be gossiping about my parents. They don't need that right now." Mary looked at him like he had the understanding of a kindergartner.

"Now I'm back in town, people are going to talk no matter what I do."

"Maybe you should leave town until my father dies then," she suggested with a hint of tears in her eyes. "This relapse is all your fault anyway. He was getting better. He was in remission, and then he started thinking about you coming back to Chokecherry Valley, and the cancer returned."

Alex looked at her for a long moment. He didn't quite know what to say to her charge. In fact, there was nothing he could say. The one thing he knew was Steven's impending death wasn't his fault, and Courtney knew it too.

However, other people in Chokecherry Valley would see things the same way Mary did. Without Steven disputing the allegation, that was the way it had to be. There was no way Alex was bringing him into this mess when he only had a few weeks to live.

"I'm sorry, Mary. I don't like hurting you, but your father and mother are more important right now. They want to see me. Until they tell me to quit coming over there, I need to respect their wishes." He held up his hand to stop her because he could see she was going to continue the argument.

"I don't want to hurt you. You've been hurt enough. If you talk to your parents about your feelings, please be gentle. If they don't want to see me, I'll stay away."

She turned away without another word and walked down the front steps and back down the street.

He closed the front door and went back to his perusal of the kitchen. Courtney would be home soon. As he made lunch, he pondered Mary's visit. What a mess. Maybe two years ago he and Courtney made the wrong choice. At the time, it seemed the right thing to do.

He pushed the thoughts away and smiled at Courtney as she came in the front door. He set two plates on the island. "Lunch is served."

She took off her boots on the entry rug and pulled off her coat and scarf before hanging them on the closet door by the entry. "Sounds good, whatever it is. It's nice to have someone cook."

He laughed. "Well, I didn't exactly cook. It's just a few turkey and cheese sandwiches, and I mixed up a simple lettuce salad."

"Good enough. I'm starving. We were busy at the grocery store today. People are already getting ready for Christmas baking. Butter, flour, and chocolate have been flying off the shelves." She sat on one of the counter stools.

"What do you want to drink?" he asked.

"Water." She took a big bite of the sandwich. "Yum. You put salad dressing on it."

He set a glass of ice water in front of her. "I tried to remember how you liked it."

"This is perfect." She helped herself to salad and poured French dressing on it.

Alex joined her at the island, sitting on the stool next to her, and started eating his own sandwich. He tried to decide if he should tell her about Mary's visit or wait until Courtney finished work for the day. Putting it off was probably the wrong way to go. Courtney might run into Mary yet today, and it wouldn't be fair to not warn her.

She happily ate her way through her food. He enjoyed her appetite and pleasure in the simple meal. He'd try and give her something warm in the coming days since the weather was turning colder. He'd make a list and go shopping.

"There are a few things we need to talk about." He set the rest of his sandwich on his plate. He'd deliberately waited for her to finish her sandwich, and she was almost done with her salad.

Her fork clattered to her plate, and she twisted around on her stool to look at him. "You sound serious."

He saw the fear in her eyes and hurried to dispel whatever caused that expression. "One subject is shopping." He smiled, "Relax and finish your salad."

She gave him a tentative curve of the lips and went back to eating.

He noticed she wasn't eating as heartily as before. Why did this have to be complicated? "I want to pick up groceries so I can make you hot meals to eat. You know? Casseroles, soup, lasagna…"

She put down her fork and pushed her plate away. She almost managed to finish the salad. She turned again to look at him. "Lasagna. My favorite."

"Homemade lasagna."

Her smile spread into a big grin. "You don't know how to cook. I used to do all that."

He was relieved to see the grin on her face. "You used to cook. I'm going to learn now."

She groaned, although the smile remained. "I'm going to be the guinea pig, aren't I?"

"Well," he paused, "I guess you could put it that way."

"I'm in," she said, sliding off the stool. "If you're going to cook, I'll try it all. I'm not saying I'll eat a full helping of everything, but I'll make the attempt."

He laughed. "Fair enough. My question is, do you want me to come to your workplace to get groceries, or would you rather I go to a neighboring town to buy the food? It doesn't matter to me."

She didn't hesitate. "You may as well come to the store where I work. We live on Main Street and can't hide away. My boss is supportive of me and won't care. I refuse to run away and hide."

"Okay." He stood up and gave her a gentle hug. "I'll shop there tomorrow."

She hugged him back. "I guess I need to get back to work. This was nice." She started toward the entryway to get her boots and coat.

He might as well rip off the Band-Aid. "One more thing. Mary came over and was upset I'd gone over there to visit this morning."

She paused in the act of putting the scarf around her neck. "Why was she upset?"

"She blames me for her dad's cancer coming back. Said he was in remission, and the thought of me getting out of prison caused him to get sick again."

She shook her head. "You know that's not true."

"Yeah, I do, but there's no easy answer. Steven and Barbara want to see me. Mary doesn't want me to go over there. This is getting complicated."

Courtney stared at him from her place on the entry rug. He walked over and gave her another hug. "Sorry. I needed to warn you."

She returned his hug again. "Hey. We knew this was going to get difficult. Thanks for the warning. Don't spend time worrying about it. Make up the grocery list. I'm looking forward to seeing what you make." She turned and opened the door.

He thought she would just leave but was surprised when she turned around and looked directly into his eyes. "I love you—don't forget. And put canned soup on the list so when you have cooking disasters, we can eat soup."

She laughed and closed the door on him. He knew his mouth was hanging open for a good five seconds before he shut it and laughed. That was Courtney. A good sense of humor when it was needed. In one sentence, she'd released a lot of his own worry over how this was affecting her. Obviously, she'd had two years of practice while he was gone.

He gave God thanks for being available for Courtney. He knew Courtney's family had also been supportive of her. He was going to have to face them eventually. Later.

CHAPTER 6

Alex got out a few recipe books from the drawer in the kitchen. His first foray into cooking would be learning to make lasagna. He wrote out the ingredients on a shopping list and added other items he missed eating while in prison. Realizing he hadn't asked Courtney what she wanted, he wrote a few items she liked in the past. He'd ask her on their afternoon walk to add any other food she wanted to the list.

When she got home, they took a pleasant walk. He told Courtney he was going to visit Steven again in the morning, and then he would stop at the store for the groceries he'd put on the list.

"I'll start looking around for a job in the afternoon," he said.

"Oh, there's no hurry." Courtney looked up with wide, startled eyes. "You just got home."

"I can't sit around doing nothing while you're out working. That isn't fair."

"You know I started working to have something to do while you were gone."

"You can quit if you want." He wasn't sure if she wanted to continue working or not.

She was silent for a while. "I'm not sure I want to quit. It's an easy job. My boss is nice. It gives me something to do."

"I can understand. I don't want to sit around either. There are too many memories I don't want to dwell on anymore. The past is in the past. I want to look forward to the future. I'm considering going back to college."

Again, there was a pause before Courtney responded, "I think it's great you want to go back to school, but you need to know. Finances are beginning to be an issue."

He stopped in the middle of the road where they were walking. The chill in the air spread throughout his body. What new problem was this? He wasn't sure he wanted to hear it, but there was no sense in avoiding the subject.

Courtney looked down at the ground. She didn't appear to want to talk about it either. Obviously, since he'd been home for days, and she hadn't brought it up.

"Let's go home and talk about this over some hot chocolate," he said.

She looked up at him and took the gloved hand he held out. They silently trod along the snow-covered ground.

He was busy wondering about the finances, but he had no idea what she was thinking.

They settled on the couch with the hot chocolate on the coffee table in front of them.

"Okay. I'm ready." He gave her a big smile. "We'll figure it out together."

She smiled. "It's nice to hear the word 'together.'"

"I realize you managed everything while I was gone. We need to start communicating about everything again," he said and felt her stiffen beside him.

"That sounds like a tall order." She withdrew to the other end of the couch and pulled her feet up in front of her, winding her arms around her knees. "We don't have enough money for you to go back to school," she said bluntly. "I did what I could, but the money went fast in the last few years.

"There was the help we gave to Steven and Barbara. That was a chunk. I've been living here and fixing things up as cheaply as I could without cutting corners. The heating bill, groceries, and other things have all gone up in price. The gas I used to go see my family. We remodeled the kitchen just before you went to prison. That took another big outlay, but we weren't concerned. You were still working, but we haven't had your income since then."

"It can't be that bad," Alex said.

"When are you going back to work?" For the first time since he got out of prison, he heard hostility in her voice.

"I don't know," he said, puzzled.

"I know you don't know. I don't know either. That's my point. We're only in our late twenties. We've got years to live.

I'll go over the accounts with you tomorrow and show you what we have. If you go back to school, we will use up what we're living on now. There won't be a lot of room for error. We'd be giving up our cushion. You need to find work before you decide to go back to school."

"How many other things are wrong you haven't told me?" He was starting to see she was used to taking responsibility for everything, and he'd let her. When she'd visited him, she hadn't told him anything about her home life, except the good stuff. And he hadn't asked questions either. He assumed since she hadn't brought up any problems, she wasn't having any.

"Did you see the egg stains on the siding on the front of the house? That happened this week," Courtney said.

"I didn't notice." He couldn't believe he missed the mess, but he scurried out of the house to hide from anyone whenever he left. He didn't stick around to inspect the outside of their home.

"You've been coming in the back door. They don't do anything back there. They want others to see what they've done."

"Do they leave you alone at work?" He was suddenly worried about her. Two years too late, he decided.

"Yes, my boss made it clear from the beginning if they treated me badly, they weren't welcome in her store, and a lot of them pretend I'm not there. But there are others who are kind and take the time to talk to me and ask me how I'm doing." She sniffled.

He reached toward her, and she moved to cuddle in his arms. "I'm sorry. You always seemed strong when you talked about what's happening," he said.

"There was nothing you could do. My sisters came and spent time with me, and we'd have little parties when they sensed I was getting down. They were good for me."

Thank goodness she had a big family who took care of her.

"From now on, let's talk about these things. I could clean the egg off the front siding tomorrow."

"People will see you," Courtney objected.

"When was the last time someone egged the house?"

"Not since right before you came home," she said.

"Word is out, and the community knows I'm home. There's no reason to hide anymore. My first official outing will be going to the grocery store tomorrow.

"I'll be seeing Steven and Barbara, but I'll still go the back way. Mary's already upset, so I hope we can keep those visits a secret at least. I guess the rest of people's responses we'll have to deal with as they happen."

"I guess," Courtney said.

"And school is out of the question for now. As a convicted felon, I don't know what's going to happen. We'll look at finances tomorrow and see what needs to be done. I do have a business degree. I should be able to set up some kind of budget."

"I've already done that." Her voice was sharp again.

He hugged her closer. "Sorry. Of course you have. We'll look at it together. I can get the full picture, and we'll see what kind of job an ex-convict can get."

She patted his leg. "Don't undersell yourself and don't use the word 'ex-convict' in front of me again. We both know what happened. You're a good guy. Don't forget what you did for your friends."

"I'll try. But you paid as big of a price as I did by helping them. Don't forget I know that too."

CHAPTER 7

Courtney walked to work the next morning in the bitter chilly air. The thermometer on the side of the house registered ten degrees outside. She wore a hat and wrapped a scarf around her lower face and neck. The wind stung her eyes. She was glad the store was only a block from her home.

She walked into the store and greeted Betty, "Good morning. How are you?"

Betty stood at the till, checking the bills and change in the drawer. "I'm good. It's a cold one out there, but at least it's not snowing. How are you and Alex doing?"

"Oh, you know. One step forward, one step back. Someday we'll get to two steps forward and one back."

She considered Betty a friend. Betty gave her a job and defended her decision to hire Courtney when people complained. She'd stood firm in her support, and Courtney appreciated it. Except for her family and Barbara, Betty was one of the few people who treated her kindly. Although some ignored her she preferred that to the sneering stares of others.

"He'll come around, and you'll get used to being together again. It takes adjustment time." Betty's plump cheeks were still rosy from the chill outside. Beneath her lovely white hair, her eyes were kind and understanding.

Courtney held back the tears. "Thank you. I'm going to get those shelves stocked from those boxes that came in yesterday." She hurried to the back of the store.

"Thanks, dear," Betty called after her retreating back.

Courtney took a few deep breaths, wiped her eyes, and concentrated on work. At least here, she was usually busy enough to put aside thoughts of her current relationship with Alex. They would work things out. She knew that. But it was still hard getting through this phase. She'd believed, once he was home, everything would go back to the way it had been before he left.

She started putting cans of various vegetables on the shelves, listening to Betty's soft voice whenever a customer came in and visited with her. It was getting close to lunchtime when she heard a familiar male voice.

"Hi, Betty," Alex said.

"Alex! It's good to see you." Courtney peeked around the corner of the shelf she finished stocking. She saw Betty walk over to Alex and give him a hug. "You've lost weight, but those eyes still have a lot of sparkle in them."

"Are you flirting with me?" Alex hugged her back.

"Not with that wife of yours working for me. She's a hard worker, and I don't want to lose her. Besides, you know me—no shenanigans."

Courtney started toward the front of the store. "Betty is immune to your charm."

Alex's smile widened as he saw her. "Thank goodness I have you then."

"Don't you forget." She smiled back. "Are you here to do the grocery shopping?"

"Yep." He put his gloves in his pocket and pulled out the list he had started the day before. "Anything specific you want before I start?"

She reached out for the list and looked it over. "This looks like an ambitious list. I'd add mint chocolate chip ice cream. No specific brand." She handed the list back to him.

"I'll get right on that," he said.

She watched him pull out a cart and start down one of the aisles.

"At least you're training him right from the start." Betty smiled. "Get the groceries."

"He said he wants to cook. I'll have him start doing laundry next week."

"I heard you," Alex called over his shoulder.

She and Betty laughed together.

Courtney returned to finish stocking the last shelf, then moved the empty boxes to the back room. The stockroom was full of empty boxes, and she just finished when she heard yelling out in the store. She rushed out to help Betty with the situation.

Van Hanson stood in front of Alex's cart. "You don't belong here. You should still be in prison. It's because of you Steven got sick again." He shoved the cart into Alex.

Alex stood there and didn't say anything.

Courtney didn't understand why he didn't defend himself.

There were a few other shoppers standing behind Van, nodding. "We don't want you here," Van's wife said.

Van walked around the cart to stand directly in front of Alex. Alex had his back against the shelves, and Courtney heard them rattle together as Van pushed Alex against them.

"Let's take this outside," Alex suggested. "It's not fair to Betty to ruin her store." He stepped to the side and started heading to the storeroom and the back door.

Betty took that moment to come running with a mop from the closet and jabbed Van in the back. When he turned around to see what was going on, Betty slipped between him and Alex. "That's enough," she said. "Alex, go."

Van took one step in his direction, but Betty wielded her broom once again and poked him in the mid-section. "Stay," she commanded.

As Van hesitated, Alex disappeared out the back door.

Courtney assumed he was running along the back path to their house. She turned to see the other shoppers staring at Betty.

Betty put down the mop and put her hands on her hips. "If you want to shop in my store, you'll be polite to all my customers." She emphasized "all." "Do not come in again if you can't be civil."

Van scowled at Courtney.

"And that includes Courtney, Van. This is your only warning. As for the rest of you, the same goes. Now get back to your shopping or get out of my store." She picked up the mop and marched back to the closet where it belonged.

Courtney heard the slam of the closet door and slipped over to an aisle devoid of customers. She wondered what Alex felt as he left. He wouldn't have liked leaving without giving

Van a fight, but he knew the best thing to do for Betty and Courtney was to leave without further violence. She loved that about him.

Courtney hauled the empty boxes out to the recycling dumpster, and Betty came out the back door.

"They're all gone, dear," Betty said.

Courtney nodded and headed back into the store. "Thank you for understanding. It was nice of you to stand up for us."

"It was the right thing to do. Next time, Alex can stay in the store, and I'll make the others leave." Betty stared at her with shrewd eyes. "Besides, I know more about two years ago than you might think."

Courtney's mouth dropped open.

"Some of us aren't as thick as the rest of people around here. Why don't you go and finish up the grocery shopping your husband started and take it on home? I can manage the store until one o'clock." She smiled.

Courtney gathered her wits and smiled back. There had been many times Betty stood up for her in the last two years. She never considered Betty knew more than the rest of the community, but she was Barbara's friend, which might explain her words. "Are you sure?"

"Yes. Go on with you. I believe your young man could use your support right now, and you could use his. Go."

Courtney walked over to the other woman and gave her a quick hug. "Thank you. For everything." She started walking toward Alex's abandoned cart. "And remember, if this gets too bad around here now that Alex is out of prison, I'll quit, and you can have some peace."

Betty made a shooing motion with her hands. "Not going to happen. It will all work out."

CHAPTER 8

Alex hustled out the back door and hurried along the path back home. Then he changed his mind. He would go for a walk. Despite the freezing wind blowing, he hardly noticed. He pulled up his collar around his ears. With that and his gloves, he was comfortable enough and close enough to the house to not be concerned.

He remembered the scene in the grocery store. Was that what Courtney put up with for the past two years? He'd ask her when she got home from work. If it was, and it was going to continue, he would convince her to quit. Van was belligerent, but Alex didn't believe he was dangerous to Courtney. There might be others in town who felt the same way but *were* a danger to Courtney and Betty.

He smiled at Betty's use of the mop. She was a fearless lady. She'd bucked public opinion by hiring Courtney, and she'd stood up for them in the store. His smile disappeared. She shouldn't have to protect them.

He would have stayed and fought Van if he'd had to protect Courtney and Betty, but they hadn't needed him. By leaving, he'd de-escalated the situation. He sighed. He knew this wasn't going to be easy.

"She'll be okay."

The girl's voice came from beside him, and he stopped abruptly. When he looked down, he saw his niece, Amy. Despite his concerns, a grin spread across his face. "I never thought I'd see you again."

She shrugged and grinned back at him. She was dressed in her usual print leggings and short-sleeved shirt. "You must have needed me because here I am. Besides, I have a message for you."

"I did need to see you. You're the only one I want to see right now."

Amy came to visit him in the prison on countless occasions. He believed he was hallucinating the first few times he saw her. She had died in a car accident, so her appearance in his cell was inexplicable. He quickly got the message she was there from Heaven to help him through his incarceration.

He would never have considered a seven-year-old as someone God would send to a prison, but Amy didn't have any fear or anxiety about the situation. He gradually relaxed his vigilance when she was around, realizing no one else could see her when she visited, and God protected her.

"I have a few messages for you," Amy said.

Obviously the cold didn't affect her. Alex figured God had a warm shield around her.

"Messages?" This was different. Usually, God sent her to comfort him when he felt depressed in prison. Just having another person who wasn't threatening near him calmed him down. Plus, the knowledge God loved him enough to send her brought him closer to God.

He'd started reading the Bible, making notes in the margins and memorizing scripture. Slowly, he saw Amy less and less. Probably because he had started feeling God's presence even when Amy wasn't around.

"What messages?" Alex asked.

"The first message is that, by Christmas, everything will have changed. You're near the end of this trial."

"What trial?" Alex turned back toward home because, even if Amy wasn't cold, he was freezing.

"What you're going through now. You'll know what to do soon to get out of the situation with all the townspeople." Amy skipped along, and Alex had to stop himself from telling her she was going to slip. She wouldn't slip. Or, if she did, she wouldn't be hurt. God would see to that.

He had no idea how anything could possibly change, and her message made no sense to him. In fact, Steven didn't have long to live, and when he died, the whole community would probably band together and start their house on fire.

Amy reached for his hand and squeezed. "God got you through prison, right?"

He felt a surge of courage rush through him. He squeezed her hand in return. "Right."

"I have to give you the other message and then go because Courtney's going to be here soon to talk to you."

He never questioned her knowledge of things to come anymore. She knew things he didn't. They stood in his backyard. "Okay. What's the other message?"

"It's time to talk to Courtney about becoming a pastor or missionary." Her clear gaze met his.

"But Courtney told me we didn't have any money for me to go back to school."

"Maybe that's true, but God will find a way. You know that," she half-scolded him and put her hands on her hips in mock outrage.

"Okay." He laughed and pulled her to him in a quick hug and let her go. She was precious to him, and he hadn't gotten to know her until he was in prison.

Paul and Samantha hadn't kept in touch before he went to prison, and he had to admit, he and Courtney hadn't reached out to them often either. When Paul lost Samantha and Amy in a car accident, Alex had already been in prison for over a year. Courtney told him the news about their death on one of her visits. Then Amy started coming from Heaven to visit him, and his whole life changed once again. He still needed to tell Courtney about Amy.

"Remember what I said. Everything will work out. Bye," she said and was gone.

CHAPTER 9

Courtney hurried home from the grocery store. The bags she carried were heavy, but she only wanted to make one trip. She struggled along under their weight. By the time she got home, her nose and cheeks felt frozen.

Alex jumped up from the couch and hurried to take the bags from her. "Why didn't you call me? I would have come down and helped carry them."

"I didn't want a repeat of this morning's fun." She heard the bitter note in her voice. She was tired of the whole thing. She wanted to stay home and rest, but someone had to make money, and it wasn't going to be Alex. Not here in Chokecherry Valley anyway. No one would hire him.

His head jerked up, and he stared at her. "I'm sorry you went through that. At least I got to leave."

"Oh, Betty let me hide in the back room until everyone was gone. Then she let me check out these groceries and bring them home. I'm here until one o'clock." She dumped the last bag on the counter beside the ones he'd already placed there.

While he started unloading groceries and putting them in the fridge and cupboard, she shed her coat and boots and stifled a sigh. She didn't want to go back to work. Just looking at Alex today irritated her. She knew it wasn't his fault, but he was the closest person on whom to unleash her frustrations. She didn't want to do that.

"Why don't you rest on the couch while I whip up something for lunch?" he asked. "You must be tired."

She didn't answer right away. She was close to telling him everything she felt. She collapsed on the couch and adjusted the throw pillow beneath her head. She closed her eyes and prayed for patience. She heard Alex moving around the kitchen, cupboards opening and closing, the suck of the fridge door opening and the quiet whoosh of it sealing shut.

She started to relax. She didn't like what happened this morning. "I think we're going to have to move to Bismarck." She hadn't meant to say it out loud, but she was glad she had. All movement stopped in the kitchen, and she opened her eyes and lifted her head.

Alex stood between the island and the fridge staring at her. "Why do you say that?"

She lay back down on the pillow and put her hand over her eyes. "Alex. They hate us."

"Not everyone."

A short laugh burst from her. "Right. Not everyone. But enough."

She removed her hand from her eyes and sat up on the couch. "Sit down." She pointed to the chair across from her.

He sat and leaned toward her, his elbows on his knees. "We can get through this."

"I don't want to anymore. Today showed me things won't change. Everyone…okay, not everyone, but a lot of people feel the way Van does. I can't continue to work this way, and Betty doesn't deserve the skirmishes that will continue to break out.

"I'm tired of not knowing when someone is going to come in and start shouting at me or turning down a different aisle to avoid me. I'm tired of eggs and tomatoes thrown at the house. I'm tired of not inviting my family here because I'm afraid of what's going to happen to them if someone decides to come and demonstrate on our lawn. I'm afraid, Alex. I'm tired of being tired and afraid."

She leaned back against the couch and watched him absorb all she said. She'd never told him how she felt, but today something in her had broken. Something that couldn't be put back together the same way.

"I didn't know you felt that way. You never said."

Alex looked like she'd struck him, and she felt sorry for him. "There are a lot of things we need to discuss that neither one of us has told the other."

"You're right. I have some things I should tell you too. About prison, and about this morning," Alex said.

"I hope they're good things because I don't think I'm in the mood to deal with any more problems today." She knew that was a selfish thing to say. What was he going to tell her about prison? She'd been afraid someone would kill him or beat him up or harm him in other ways while he was there. He had certainly calmed down since he'd come home a week ago, but he was still hyperalert, and she anticipated that could take years to go away, if it ever did.

"One thing is fantastic, and the other…well, it's fantastic in its own way too. Just more complicated," Alex said.

"I'll take the one fantastic, less complicated thing, and then you go back to making lunch while I digest your information and rest," she said. "The more complicated fantastic thing can wait for another day."

He looked uneasy but got up and returned to the kitchen.

What did he have to say that he couldn't tell her while looking at her? "Alex, speak. You're driving me crazy, and we've already had a rough morning. It's fantastic, right? That means good. So…"

He started to crack the eggs he set out on the counter. "Okay. Here goes." He refused to look at her and finished with the eggs. Then he chopped scallions. "When I was in prison, I saw my niece, Amy. She would come to me and keep me company in my cell."

Courtney tried to wrap her mind around what he'd said. His dead niece visited him in prison. His dead niece. "Um…"

He finally looked at her. As he took in her expression, his own face turned grim. "You believe I went crazy."

"Well…not exactly." But what? What did it mean?

"She was real." His voice was now firm. He quit lunch preparations and watched her reaction. "I really did see her, and she did come from Heaven to visit when I needed her. When I was at my lowest points, she was there. I know you're going to say I imagined her, but I didn't. In fact, I saw her again this morning on the back path when I left the grocery store."

"You saw her again," she spoke slowly. "This morning."

She studied his expression. Who was this man? Did she know him anymore? They'd been apart for two years. "And this is your fantastic news from prison?"

"Yes." His look was steady, but he stayed where he was.

Perhaps he sensed she needed the space to take this in. She did. It would take days. A moment later she realized she was also jealous. If he saw Amy, why hadn't God sent a comforter to her? Why him? She immediately felt ashamed.

"Well, I think it's fantastic. It proves there's a God and a Heaven. I didn't grow up in the kind of family you did. You had steady parents who took you to church and taught you about God. I'm happy for you. But I guess God decided I needed to learn about Him in a different way." He went back to getting the omelets ready for lunch. "I know you need time to absorb this. I know I did."

She sat there, listening to the butter sizzling in the pan. That was why Alex's omelets tasted good. He melted butter in the pan and then poured in the egg mixture. The omelets had a wonderful buttery crust around the outside. Why was she thinking of buttery crusts when Alex just told her he'd seen Amy?

"What did she say to you this morning?" Courtney asked.

"Does that mean you believe me?" Alex's eyes searched her face.

"I don't know, but if you believe it, I'll try. It's going to take me a while."

"Okay. If or when you want to know more, just ask me. It's not a secret from you. The idea takes getting used to, I know. It took me a long time to accept it."

She nodded. "What did she say this morning?"

"She said I would know soon what to do about the situation with the townspeople."

"Move away from here," Courtney announced.

Alex thought about that for a minute before turning back to the pan on the stove. "Perhaps. One thing, we can't leave before Steven's death. They need us."

"Agree. But you will consider moving, won't you?" Courtney asked.

Alex plated the omelets and set them on the island. "Yes, I will consider it. We can talk later about plans if you want."

He took a few muffins from the counter and placed them on another plate beside their omelets. "Come eat. The rest can wait, like you said."

She was suddenly hungry. Maybe her husband had a breakdown in prison. He seemed normal now. She didn't know what to believe. She wasn't going to solve it in the next hour. She'd eat lunch and then lie down. She did need to rest.

They were quiet throughout lunch, and Alex did dishes while she lay down. She fell asleep, thinking of sweet little Amy and wondering why her own life had gotten more complicated instead of less since Alex came home.

CHAPTER 10

Courtney woke up from her nap and found herself alone. She looked at the clock and was astonished to see she'd slept solid for three hours. She'd missed work. She never missed work.

She hurried into the main part of the house to ask Alex why he hadn't woken her. There was a note on the island that said he was visiting Steven and Barbara. He called Betty, and Betty said Courtney should take the rest of the day off. He ended the note with, "I love you."

She smiled. Their intimate relationship since his release from prison had been tenuous. It almost felt like they were new roommates circling each other, trying to figure out each other's likes and dislikes. It was strange because they'd been high school sweethearts. They'd known each other for years.

Until a two-year separation forced them to see each other in new ways. She supposed it might even be good for them not to take each other for granted. When she remembered his comments about Amy, she was concerned.

Suddenly she had an idea of who could help her. She found her cell phone on the coffee table and called Ashley. Ashley was at work, so she left a message, but that was okay. She asked her to call as soon as she could.

She was surprised when the phone rang ten minutes later, and the caller identification displayed Ashley's name.

"Hi," Courtney said. "How are you able to call during the day? Aren't you at work?"

"No. My clinical observation class is finished. I'm doing last-minute prepping for a speech I need to make. It's the final one, and I'll be so happy to finish the class.

"What's up? You never call me. I figure it must be important."

Courtney laughed. She and Ashley had their moments since Alex went to prison. They forbade Ashley to visit. They meant to keep the stigma of Alex's reputation from spreading to his family.

"Well, it's a question I have for you about Alex."

"Is something wrong with him?" Ashley's concern came through loud and clear in her panicked tone.

"No. At least I don't think so." How could she ask if Alex was having a breakdown? "Alex said he saw Amy when he was in prison. He said she came from Heaven and visited to comfort him when he was depressed. I'm concerned he's had a breakdown. He said he saw her again this morning after an incident at the grocery store."

"Really?"

"Yes, but the grocery store story can wait."

"Well, I know he's not going crazy," Ashley's voice was calm now, as if they were talking about nothing more important than the weather.

"How can you be sure?" Courtney asked.

"Because there have been other people who have seen Amy too."

"Who?" Courtney demanded.

"Just a minute. My doorbell's ringing."

Courtney sat on the couch, listening to the silence for what seemed like a long time. She heard the back door opening and Alex shedding his outerwear. She didn't want him to know she called Ashley about him. At least not yet.

Finally, she heard background noise on the other end of the phone, and then Ashley's voice. "I've got to go, but everything's okay. Paul and I will be coming out to see you and Alex this evening. I promise to explain then. We'll eat before we come, so no need to go to any effort."

Then silence, which was for the best because Alex joined her in the living room. "Hi. How are you feeling?"

"Much better. I needed the rest, but I wish you hadn't called Betty. I should have gone to work."

"You needed the break. Van must have stirred up some of the other residents because Betty had more complaints this afternoon." He joined her on the couch. "I'm sorry. I should have stayed home. We should sell this house as soon as something happens to Steven. It's almost over."

Courtney pushed her own problems aside. "How was he this afternoon?"

"Really weak. He hardly spoke. I did most of the talking, and that was with Barbara. Mary was there and glared at me the whole time, until Barbara told her to go to her room until I left."

"I bet that made her mad."

"She stomped off to her bedroom, but they both laughed and said she had always been a handful. Then they reminisced about her a bit. It seemed to make them happy." Alex looked thoughtful. "I guess I'd rather she be mad at me than them, so I'll try and visit when she's not there."

"Me too," Courtney said. "I'll call before I go over there."

The next few hours were quiet. Courtney found a book to read and settled deeper onto the couch although she found herself reading the same page over and over. Alex read his Bible and made them something to eat.

Courtney told him Ashley and Paul were visiting sometime that evening, but she wasn't sure when they were coming. Alex seemed excited at the idea. She was glad they were visiting but restless at the thought of Ashley bringing up Amy.

Courtney broke the unspoken rule of keeping Alex's secret, and she hadn't wasted any time in doing it. Trust was hard to come by, and this might be a big deal to Alex. She couldn't wait for Paul and Ashley to arrive, and she could get the evening over with.

They finally arrived around 7:30 p.m., and soon all of them gathered in the living room. Everyone refused anything to drink, but Courtney got herself a bottle of water from the fridge. Her mouth was dry, and she needed something to do with her hands, or she knew she'd be twisting the wedding band on her left hand the whole time they were there.

She debated about how to bring up the subject, as everyone did the initial greetings and talked about the lack of snow. They were discussing how cold it was supposed to be in the few weeks until Christmas when she broke into the conversation.

"I called Ashley today," Courtney said to Alex, who sat beside her on the couch. He turned his head in her direction, but she avoided his gaze. She looked at Ashley, who sat in the chair across from her. "We talked about Amy."

Paul looked at Ashley and then turned back to Courtney and Alex. "What's going on? Why did you call Ashley about Amy?"

Courtney couldn't look at Alex. She took a drink from her bottle of water.

Ashley broke the silence. "Alex saw Amy while he was in prison."

Paul's gaze focused on Alex. "You did?"

"I did." Alex's gaze was steady. He didn't appear upset at all. "I guess I can forgive Courtney for calling Ashley."

He reached over and took Courtney's free hand. "I told you I was fine."

"I know you did, but you have to admit it's weird."

"Yes, it was. But it's normal now. However, I also remember how it felt in the beginning before it became normal, so I understand your concern."

Alex turned to look at Paul and Ashley. "But you don't have to be concerned. Amy was a comfort. She'd bring messages to me from God, and her being there helped me. Of course, at first I was appalled she was in a prison seeing the other prisoners, but it didn't faze her at all. When I realized I was the only one who saw her, I relaxed a little. After a while, it became natural."

"I totally understand what you're talking about," Paul said. "The same thing happened to me."

Courtney dropped her bottle of water at the shock of his words. "How come I didn't know?"

They looked at her, and she blushed. Oh. Right. They'd forbidden Ashley and Paul to contact her or Alex in the past few years. Of course they weren't going to call up just to announce something hard to understand.

She picked up the bottle of water and went to the kitchen for a towel to soak up the excess spilled onto the wood floor. Then she settled back on the couch, waiting for the story.

"First of all," Ashley said, "you're no longer alone. You have us, and Hannah and Jason. Don't forget again," she admonished but smiled too. She gestured to Paul to continue.

"After Samantha and Amy died, I was in a bad state. By that time, I'd been sober only about a year. I was trying not to drink again, but the grief was nearly intolerable. Amy started appearing at my worst moments and helped me get through those times. She helped me stay sober.

"I know it seems strange a seven-year-old helped me stay sober and helped you in prison, but that's what happened. I think she also helped Ashley's boyfriend's family. Amy seems to be sent to Earth to help those who are depressed," Paul said. "I will tell you, when I first saw her, I went to the hospital and had brain scans and saw a psychiatrist." He laughed.

"Of course, the scans showed nothing. The psychiatrist helped me to deal with things, but I kept seeing Amy. Finally, I knew she was sent from God to help me and not a figment of my imagination. After that, I accepted the situation. Since Hannah and I have become closer, I see her less often. At some point, her part in helping me will be over, and I won't see her any longer." His face softened. "I appreciate those extra times I had with her. And I'm glad she's helping you."

Alex got up and hugged him.

Courtney didn't think she'd ever seen the two brothers hug before. Not even on her and Alex's wedding day. Of course, at the time, Paul had been drinking heavily and wasn't always easy to be around.

When they'd settled back down and the conversation resumed, Alex spoke up. "I guess I don't need any medical tests."

Courtney, who listened and watched the whole scene between the guys unfold, laughed. "I guess you're okay. At least in relation to Paul."

Paul laughed. "Right. If you want to consider me normal."

"Hannah thinks you're okay," Ashley finally inserted herself into the conversation.

"Have you ever seen Amy?" Courtney asked her.

"No. But I guess I didn't need as much help as my brothers."

"Hey now," they both objected in unison.

She smirked at them.

The gathering wound down, and Paul and Ashley drove back to Bismarck, as they both had to work the next day.

Courtney had to work too. If Betty let her. Was she out of a job? How could Betty handle this busy Christmas time by herself? Everyone was buying baking ingredients and other goodies for the holidays. She'd worry about that tomorrow.

CHAPTER 11

Alex lay awake after he'd said goodnight to Courtney. She was still sleeping in the guest bedroom. He felt like he was calming down enough to have her sleep with him, but he was taking it slow. He wanted it to be right.

The whole thing with his family tonight showed him Courtney didn't totally trust his mental health. Of course, he'd had his own doubts when he'd first seen Amy in prison, but he gradually learned God had a plan. Amy was the conduit.

He recalled Paul's story of seeing Amy after she died in the accident. They'd had the same experience. He'd felt closer to Paul and Ashley tonight for the first time in years. Even before he went to prison, he hadn't felt close to Paul.

Ashley was closer to him in age, and they had been closer than Paul was with either of them. The whole dynamics of their parents dropping them all off in various places played a role. He was glad Ashley at least had some stability while she lived with their grandmother in Bismarck.

He hadn't wanted to leave his friends in Chokecherry Valley, so he'd put up with being under the watchful eye of Steven and Barbara. Since they didn't have boys, they were pleased to be stand-in parents while his parents travelled.

Paul unraveled during that time. He'd started drinking too much and partying all the time. Strangely enough, he'd gotten away with it because his grades were always good. He'd made it through med school despite everything.

Then he'd married Samantha, and they'd both spent their evenings drinking and clubbing. Then one day, Paul had enough of the life. Alex decided something happened that woke Paul up to what they were doing to Amy. Maybe he felt like they were abandoning her the same way their parents abandoned them. Whatever happened, Paul had gotten sober.

Amy kept him sober after her death. It was an amazing story. He was glad he had his own experience with Amy, or he wouldn't have believed Paul's story. Courtney was having a hard time believing it all. He could tell from her decision to read in the guest room as soon as Paul and Ashley left.

She was probably lying awake too. As if the thought made her materialize, she was suddenly standing in the doorway.

"Can I come in?" she asked.

She must have assumed he was also awake. "Sure." He slid over to the other side of the bed and patted the empty space beside him.

She came in and sat down. "Are you mad at me?"

"Why would I be angry?"

"Because I told your family what you said. I know we should keep some secrets between us, but I was afraid for you. Ashley is taking psychology classes, and Paul is a doctor. I didn't think she'd tell Paul unless we asked her to, but then I didn't know Paul had the same experience with Amy you did. Anyway, I'm sorry."

He sat up against the headboard and stuffed the pillow behind his back. "I'm not sorry. It worked out for the best. If you hadn't called Ashley, I wouldn't have known about Paul and Amy. At least not for a while."

"You're right," he continued. "We should keep some things between us, but we've been apart for two years. You've learned to make your own decisions without consulting me on everything. That's okay." He stared up at the ceiling. "I wish there had been a different way to do things back then, but there wasn't."

She lay down beside him on the bed and cuddled close to him. "I missed you, but I'm not sorry. We did what was necessary. There's no going back."

He put his arm around her and pulled her closer. "What if you've lost your job?"

She laughed. "We'll manage somehow. We both know we might have to move to Bismarck after Christmas. It's becoming obvious this isn't possible for us to stay here."

"Well, before we leave, we'll enjoy the last bit of time we have here. If you can't work tomorrow, do you want to go with me to find a Christmas tree?"

"I'd love to. We can start decorating and put more cheer in the house," Courtney whispered.

"For me, the best cheer in the world is seeing your smile. But we'll decorate anyway."

"Also, if I can't go back to work, I'm going to bake. I feel the urge to make something. Let's invite your family here for Christmas. We'll have Paul and Hannah, and Ashley and Jason. If Jason isn't busy with his own family."

"Sounds good to me." Alex was pleased at the idea of hosting Christmas at the house. "One last Christmas here before it's sold. Although there isn't much to compare to in the past, since our parents weren't always around for Christmas."

"Oh, well. Less to live up to on my part then." She laughed.

He loved her husky, sweet laugh. Though, he wished their situation didn't make laughing such a rare event these days.

"Amy also told me it was time to become a pastor or do missionary-type work," Alex said. He hated to fling it out into the room, but he needed to say it.

At least Courtney didn't pull away from him. "Alex, honey. We talked about it. We don't have the money."

"How much money is it going to take? Maybe there's a stipend or some kind of fund for those who want to become a pastor. We have a house to sell. That should bring in money," Alex said.

"Which we need to use for food and shelter in Bismarck while I search for another job. You know it's not going to bring in much. Rural North Dakota real estate isn't big money." She patted his arm.

"There's got to be a way. God wants me to do this. Amy even said it was time." He knew it would work out, but how was he going to convince Courtney? She didn't see Amy.

He'd known this was his path in life for over a year. He'd just told her a short time ago, and she needed time to adjust to the idea. "Let's drop it for tonight and make plans after Christmas."

He could feel her relax against him.

"Yes. Let's get through Christmas, and then make plans."

CHAPTER 12

Alex woke up to the feel of Courtney's kiss against his cheek. She started doing that soon after he'd returned home. When he told her he might hit her in his sleep without knowing it was her, she learned to kiss him and step back quickly. He admired her considerate response and enjoyed the morning wake-up.

He promised to make breakfast in the mornings, but she only wanted something cooked about half the time. The rest of the time, she ate fruit and a boiled egg. She made her own toast, because she said he didn't know how to make toast without burning it. He had laughed. The toaster was temperamental, and he got distracted instead of watching it closely to make sure it didn't get stuck in the down position. He'd even set off the fire detector one morning.

Now he got up and joined her in the kitchen where she stood by the sink. It was one of those mornings where she didn't want a cooked meal. He sat down on a stool by the island.

"I'll go see Steven this morning while you're at work, and then, when I get home, I'll start doing the decorating inside. Where are the decorations?" he asked.

"They're either in the garage or in the attic. I didn't decorate last year, so they're probably dusty." She set her cup in the sink.

"Okay. I'll shake them off outside or in the garage. If they're in there. Is there something specific you want to help decorate?"

"Just the tree. I want to go with you to choose one and decorate it together." She walked around the island to his side and gave him a quick hug.

He hugged her back. "Okay. How about we go pick out a tree in the morning after church tomorrow and then ask Paul,

Hannah, and Ashley to help us decorate in the afternoon? Maybe Ashley would like Jason to come over."

"Sounds good." She had her boots and coat on and held her bag with her shoes and other things she might need. "You're not overdoing the people part? I thought you might want to spend more time without constant company."

"I'm fine. It depends on the company, and we've kept it to family and Steven's family."

"True."

He scuffed his bare foot against the floor while watching her pull her scarf a little tighter. "I have to admit I'm wondering how your family will treat me when we meet them for church tomorrow."

"There won't be any physical fights, if you're worried." She smiled wryly. "I can't promise there won't be scowls thrown your way."

"Well, I guess that's only to be expected."

"Mom and Dad will be pleasant and courteous. That's their way. They know I'll be mad at them and not visit if they aren't nice to you, so I guess we'll get through it. At least we're not going to visit their house before or after the service. We'll be in public the whole time." She opened the front door. "Try not to worry. It'll pass fast."

She was right. It shouldn't be a big deal, but he didn't want her at odds with her family. He jumped up from his stool and hurried over to the door. He just had to kiss her before she left for the day.

She leaned into his kiss, and he finally pulled back. He grinned at her, and she gave him a bemused look.

"Wow. You were holding out on me before," she said.

"I needed to know you still loved me," he said.

"And what happened this morning?"

"I know you talked to your family about me and reined them in. That was nice of you."

She left with another bemused shake of her head.

He finished his own breakfast, showered, and found the Christmas decorations in the garage. He left them in place, not wanting to get dirty before visiting Steven and Barbara. He'd move them into the house when he got home again.

He snuck across the back lane, mindful of the altercation in the grocery store the day before. Sarah opened the door when he knocked and motioned into the living room without greeting him.

Barbara sat on the chair beside the hospital bed. She held yarn and a knitting needle but wasn't knitting anything with them. There were only a few rows done, and it looked about the same as last time he visited.

Sarah sat in the recliner and picked up her book, ignoring him. Mary glared at him from where she sat in a chair across the room.

Glancing at her father, who was sleeping, she said, "You shouldn't have come."

"Mary!" Barbara's look held a warning.

"Well—"

Barbara interrupted her quietly, "If you have a problem, go into the other room for a while."

Mary sat there frowning for a few minutes longer. Eventually, she gave up and went into the other room, as they both ignored her.

Barbara and Alex carried on a quiet conversation without a lot of meaning. Steven could wake up at any time, and their talk was meant to be soothing. Alex was about ready to leave when he finally woke up. His gaze was hazy, and it took him a few minutes to orient himself.

"Hi," Alex said from the chair he sat in. He pulled one up next to Barbara.

"Alex." Steven's voice was soft and wispy. "It's good to see you."

"You too. We were talking about Christmas trees. I'm going with Courtney tomorrow to get one. The one you've got decorated there by the window is wonderful."

"Got it from Van," he whispered.

"Good plan. Courtney and I decided to get an artificial one. We'll be picking one out tomorrow," Alex said.

Steven reached out slowly.

"He wants you to take his hand," Barbara said.

Alex grasped his hand.

Steven looked him directly in the eyes and squeezed his hand. "Thank you. You've been a great friend."

Alex nodded. "You're welcome. Thank you for taking care of me when I was younger."

"Never been a better kid than you, except my kids." His eyes drifted closed.

Alex could feel tears forming and surreptitiously wiped them away. He stayed a little longer, but Steven remained asleep. Alex put his hand gently on his shoulder when he got up to leave.

Barbara trailed him to the back door. "It's almost time," she said quietly.

Alex nodded. "Want a hug?" he asked. "It's a tiny payment for all those hugs you gave me when I got hurt when I was younger." He knew this was a lot bigger hurt than any of the ones when he was young.

He gave her a big hug, and she pulled his head down to kiss him on the cheek. "You always were a good boy."

He left with more tears in his eyes and didn't bother to wipe them away. He somehow knew that this was the last time he'd be able to talk to Steven.

When he got home, Alex got out all the Christmas boxes from the garage. He needed something physical to do to keep himself busy. Nothing would take away the image of Steven in his hospital bed. As he gathered the decorations, he prayed for him and Barbara and their girls.

He opened the boxes on the far side of the living room to keep them out of the way. Courtney could help decide what she wanted to use from them. A lot of the decorations were from the Richmond family's Christmases. Ashley and Paul only took a few of the ornaments when they moved out, but he and Courtney made additions in their time together.

He started pulling out strands of garland and untwisting them. He realized what he needed to liven up the room was Christmas music. He got up and put his phone on the channel for Christmas carols.

He laid out all the garland in strips on the floor and was working on the string of lights for the tree when he heard the door open.

"Oh, wonderful," Courtney said when she saw what he'd done. "I'm excited to be celebrating Christmas with you this year."

Alex got up from the floor and walked over to give her a kiss. "Your lips and cheeks are cold."

She pushed him away slightly and unzipped her coat. "It's cold out there. You can warm me up later." She fluttered her lashes at him.

He laughed and moved away to give her room to get her boots and other outerwear off. "How about hot chocolate?"

"I'd love that."

When she finally settled on the couch, he brought her a cup of cocoa with a coaster and a snowman cut-out cookie on a plate.

"Christmas cookies? Did you bake?" She picked up the cookie, inspected the frosting and then took a huge bite. "Yummy," she said around the food in her mouth.

"Please," he objected with a grin, "no talking with food in your mouth. By the way, I can bake."

She swallowed and took a drink of her cocoa before putting the cup back on the coaster. "Perfect temperature. Sure, you can bake, but you didn't bake these."

"How do you know?" He plopped on the couch beside her.

"Because the icing is done neatly, and you slap the frosting on when you do cookies." She laughed.

"Well, there are a lot of cookies to frost. It takes forever if you are too careful where you put the icing," he said defensively.

"Which is why I know you didn't bake. The kitchen is still in one piece."

"You're right."

She finished the cookie and picked up her cup again, holding her hands around the mug. "In spite of that, I appreciate the snack."

"It should hold you over until we eat, but if not, there are more in the kitchen."

She jumped up, went over to the island, and grabbed another cookie. "I'm starving."

"We can eat earlier, if you want."

"Okay."

"How about in an hour…about five? If you get hungry this evening, you can have more cookies."

"You sound like you're talking to a toddler, promising sweets."

He shrugged. "If the shoe fits." He slid back down to the floor and started untangling light strands again.

"I'd throw a shoe at you if I still had one on. Yes," she said, "my heavy winter boot."

"Why don't you join me on the floor here instead?" Giving her a wink, he patted the floor beside him.

She swallowed the last of her cocoa and put the mug in the sink. "Good idea."

She joined him, and they companionably worked together. He heard her humming to the music and was content. For the first time since he returned, he felt like he was home.

They enjoyed an early meal and spent the rest of the evening putting up decorations and finishing the Christmas cookies Barbara sent home with him. They even watched part of a Christmas movie together, until Courtney fell asleep in his arms on the couch. He stayed awake, watching her sleep, and relishing the opportunity to hold her in his arms.

CHAPTER 13

When he awoke in the morning, he was on the couch alone and could hear the shower going in their bedroom. He had a crick in his neck from sleeping in an awkward position, but it was worth it.

For breakfast, he made a hashbrown, sausage, and egg casserole, which he stuck in the oven and went to take his own shower. Courtney had the next two days off, and yesterday must have gone okay at work. She hadn't said otherwise or looked stressed when she got home.

They enjoyed joking throughout breakfast, and then drove to Bismarck to pick up an artificial tree. Singing along to Christmas songs was the most fun he'd had since yesterday. Courtney had a lovely voice, but she didn't know the words to all the songs. What she didn't know, she made up. They laughed all the way to the store.

It didn't take them long to pick out the tree. A six-foot balsam fir. It already had fiber-optic lights. They could change the color of the lights or make them twinkle as the mood struck them once it was set up.

Courtney teased him about straightening out all the light strings and said he'd wasted his time. He shook his head at her and told her it had been relaxing.

They invited Ashley and Paul to come over in the afternoon to put up the tree and help decorate, and they agreed. Paul was bringing Hannah, whom Alex hadn't met yet. Ashley wasn't sure but mentioned Jason might join them for a short time. It all depended on the Christmas errands he had to do for his family since there were only a few weeks to finish up before Christmas.

Courtney and Alex took time to eat lunch in Bismarck and were ready to hang the rest of the strings of lights around the house when they got home. They had extra now that they didn't need them for the tree and agreed any they didn't use could be donated.

"I'd like to bake cookies before they get here. It'll make the house smell Christmassy," Courtney said.

"Sure. I'll help you with the frosting," Alex teased.

"I think not. You work on the lights. I'll do the cookies."

They were still joking with each other when their first guests arrived. Ashley, Paul, and Hannah arrived in a flurry of chilly air. When they'd all settled into the living room, Paul wandered over to the box with the tree in it. "Wow. Top of the line, man."

"You bet. We're going to put this up for years to come. It needed to be a sturdy tree," Courtney said before Alex could get a word in.

"It even has those cool fiber-optic lights," Hannah said. "I tried to talk Paul into them, but he insisted on the old-fashioned ones."

Alex was glad she was comfortable joining in the conversation. She looked like she'd fit right into the family. Of course, he'd only met her ten minutes ago, but Paul looked content in her company, even in the short amount of time Alex observed them.

"Old-fashioned is fine." Paul tapped her on the shoulder. "They still light up."

"But you don't have the option to change colors on the tree every few seconds," she teased him.

"Oh, ours has this lovely switch," Courtney said. "You can have several colors at once, or only white ones, or only blue ones, or—"

"We get the idea," Paul said dryly as Hannah sent him a triumphant look.

Ashley asked for a knife to open the box. "Let's get this thing up."

Courtney went into the kitchen to get one for her.

"Is Jason coming over?" Alex asked her.

"Yes, but he has babysitting duty. Chloe doesn't need much. She's only five months and will play happily with her toys on the floor. She's not quite crawling yet, so we're probably safe for this Christmas. Next year, she'll be getting into everything."

"Who is Chloe?" Courtney handed Ashley the knife.

Ashley took it and started slicing the tape holding the box together. "She's Jason's niece. His sister lives with him and his parents. She had a rough time with postpartum depression, but she's better now. She's finishing up her G.E.D. and is going to surprise her parents with her diploma on Christmas Day."

"Terrific," Courtney said, helping pull the box open.

Soon there were two big pieces of tree they'd pulled out of the box. Alex and Paul took over because they were taller, and easily plugged the two pieces together. Once they stuck the trunk into its holder, everyone started fluffing the branches.

As they started to decorate, Jason showed up with Chloe. They all took a break to coo over her. Then Jason laid her on her blanket in the middle of the living room with her toys, and they started decorating the tree.

Alex turned on the Christmas music, keeping the volume lower than earlier in the day when he and Courtney had belted out the songs on their drive to Bismarck. He smiled at the memory.

"You look happy," Paul said quietly beside him.

"I am. I feel like I'm finally home. It took a while."

Paul bumped Alex's shoulder with his own. "Sometimes things take time."

"Good things," he agreed.

They didn't say any more. The women were more vocal as they hung ornaments, and Alex enjoyed listening to them talk. Since he'd been away, he felt like this was a way to catch up on some of the community happenings and people.

They hung the last ornaments and took all the empty boxes out to the garage. They stood around admiring the tree and the garland and lights hanging on the door frames. Alex set a few gold and red candles at various places around the room, and there was a nativity scene set up on a table in the corner.

Then they all collapsed on the chairs and couch and sighed as one.

"That was fun," Courtney said. "Thank you all for the help. This was a great idea."

"I believe it was your idea," Ashley teased her.

"Right. I will take credit," Courtney agreed.

Alex punched Paul lightly on the arm as he headed into the kitchen. "I got a prize when I married her."

"Don't you forget it," Courtney called across the room.

Ashley joined him in the kitchen. "What can I help you with?"

"You can see what everyone wants to drink. We have water, soda, or apple cider. Or I can make hot cocoa. I'm feeling hot from all that work, so it's not likely anybody will be interested."

"Sure. I'll ask."

While Ashley started divvying up drinks, Alex got the cookies and a plate of fancy cheeses together. Then he pulled out paper plates and napkins and lined them all up on the island. "Snacks are served. Help yourself."

Ashley didn't even wait to sit down before starting to munch on one of the cookies. "Yum. Ginger cookies. My favorite. No one makes these anymore, but I could smell ginger when I walked in here today. I was hoping I was right."

"Courtney made those just for you. She remembered you liked them," Alex told her.

"I love them, and they're fresh. Amazing, Courtney."

"Thank you," Courtney said.

Alex thought she looked almost shy as she took the compliment. He decided he better get on the ball and praise her more often. Underneath her tough exterior, she had a soft heart. He should know, after what she'd gone through to stick with him.

When their company left, Courtney and Alex settled back on the couch together. It became their favorite place to cuddle.

"You did a great job hostessing today," he told her.

"So did you." She turned sideways to face him. "You seemed happier today."

"Well, we had a great time going to pick out a tree, didn't we?" Alex hoped she'd agree. He knew he'd had fun, and she appeared too also.

"I did. You have a horrible voice." She poked his stomach.

"I know. I usually don't sing very loud. I try to let others drown me out. Except today. I was having too much fun."

"Trying to be louder than me, but not on key." She laughed and tucked her arm in his. "Remember tomorrow when we're at church to sing quietly."

"I will." He wasn't looking forward to seeing her family tomorrow morning. His family accepted him and Courtney since he'd gotten home, but he wasn't expecting the same grace from Courtney's family.

He knew Courtney warned them to behave, but he would still feel the weight of their thinly veiled displeasure. He had tonight to enjoy the evening before facing them, and he put thoughts of them aside.

CHAPTER 14

Courtney's family treated Alex about like he'd expected when he arrived with her at the church. A few ignored him. A few said a muted hello. Her parents politely continued with small talk. Frowns abounded when they thought their parents and Courtney weren't watching them.

Two of her brothers and two sisters joined them. Her other sibling attended his own church. Alex sat at the end of the pew with Courtney between him and her family. She sang along with the songs, and he sang quietly so only she could hear. He caught her glance at him once during a song, and they smiled.

Attending church again was the one bright spot of the morning. He was glad Courtney refused to join her family for lunch after church. She told them that, after Christmas, they would consider visiting them. He didn't know what else she told them, but they accepted her word.

The following weekend, she was going to join her family on a shopping spree for Christmas, and they were going to have an early get-together at her parents' house. He hadn't decided if he would join Courtney yet or not, so they kept the option open.

When Alex and Courtney got home from church, they stopped at Steven and Barbara's house. They entered the living room together. Mary and Sarah sat there talking quietly.

The girls stopped whispering while Barbara talked briefly to Courtney and Alex.

There was a sudden hush in the room as Steven took a deep breath and let it out. They all looked at him. He was no longer breathing. Alex could tell instantly.

So could the family. Mary took one look at her dad and then looked over at Alex. "You killed him. It's all your fault." She rushed at him with her hands out as if to shove him, tears pouring from her eyes.

Alex held his hands in front of him, palms out. "I'm sorry, Mary."

"You're not sorry. You got what you wanted." She sniffled.

"Enough," Barbara said, taking Mary's arm and pulling her away gently. "Girls, we have to talk." She gave him a meaningful look.

He knew what that meant, and Courtney did too. They both said goodbye to Steven by touching him on the shoulder. Then they said goodbye to Barbara and left through the back door.

"She's going to tell them about their father, isn't she?" Courtney asked.

"Maybe." Alex didn't like what this would mean for the family, but Barbara hadn't totally agreed with Steven on this subject. He likely knew, when he died, she would tell the girls the truth.

"Sad," Courtney said.

"Very."

"Is there anything we can do?" Courtney asked.

"Probably not. The neighbors will be stopping by constantly now with food and condolences, and we're not welcome. It would make it harder for Barbara. She knows she can call if she needs us." He wished they could do more, but there was nothing to do.

He knew the vigil and funeral were already planned, and Barbara just had to go through the motions. And grieve. Unfortunately, there was no help for grief, except time.

CHAPTER 15

Courtney showed up for work as usual the Monday after Steven's death. There were a lot of customers, and she was glad she'd been assigned to work. They picked up ingredients to make food for the Hanson family and for Christmas. Christmas was the following week on Friday, and there wasn't much time left for those wanting to bake.

She overheard people talking about lighting candles and standing outside Steven and Barbara's house singing hymns. The weather would be frigid that evening. The temperature dipped to the single digits, and snow was forecast for the next day.

She knew from Betty, the vigil would be tomorrow, and she and Alex talked about whether they should attend. Alex thought it would be best to steer clear, considering many of the townspeople believed his actions at the bank made Steven sicker. Most of them reasoned he treated Alex like a son, and Alex betrayed that trust.

Alex refused to tell anyone the truth. Courtney knew she and Alex did the right thing, and they weren't going to the vigil. It would make it easier for Barbara and the girls. She and Alex said their goodbyes yesterday. Steven was in Heaven now and knew how they felt.

While she restocked shelves, she considered Alex's dream to help people. She knew he was meant to follow that path, but she still didn't see the way they could make it work. She needed to pray more about it. She'd been concentrating on praying Alex would be okay in prison and been relieved when he returned safely home.

He changed, but she still loved him. They were returning to the closeness they'd had before he left. They might even be getting closer than before. Despite everything, there seemed to be an additional level of intimacy in their relationship.

That was probably due to Alex's new relationship with God. She sighed, realizing suddenly that meant she had to help Alex make his dream come true. She'd been fighting the idea. Now, she knew why.

She liked to know Alex was safe at home. She didn't want him to go out into the world and be unsafe again. Why hadn't she realized the reason for her reluctance sooner? Because she was still adjusting to everything. Getting out of Chokecherry Valley was of paramount importance to their continued survival. They'd never get out from under the cloud of Alex going to prison.

After helping Betty, she returned home that afternoon. The day continued to be busy, up until her exit from the store. She'd asked if Betty wanted her to work later, but Betty waved her away. She stressed that Courtney should keep supporting her young man. Courtney smiled at the old-fashioned term and at Betty. She couldn't have asked for a better boss.

Betty knew she couldn't wait to leave the store every day since Alex got home. Yes, she wanted to be with Alex, but she also felt the tension when one of the townspeople spent their time in the store scowling at her. Courtney was thankful the people in town stayed kind to Betty.

She got home to find Alex sitting on the couch reading his Bible. She smelled something good cooking in the oven. "What are we eating this evening?"

"Pot roast, baked potatoes, and apple pie for dessert." Alex laid his Bible on the coffee table and got up.

"Yum. I need comfort food after today." She'd removed her outdoor wear and joined him by the coffee table. After a quick kiss, she sat down on the couch, and he sat beside her.

"Was it a difficult day?" Alex asked her.

"Busy. Everyone's getting ready for the holiday. Of course, there were also the shoppers for hams and casseroles and everything else people will take to Barbara." She laid her head on the back of the couch and closed her eyes.

"The Hansons' attorney called and wants us to be at the vigil tomorrow."

She jerked upright and turned to look at his face. "Are you serious?"

"Do I look serious? I wouldn't joke about that."

Although he'd been restless since he'd gotten home, he'd never used a sharp tone with her. She understood his view though. She felt the same reluctance about going to the vigil he did.

"I'm sorry." She took his hand, leaned back against the couch again and pulled him over to her. "Come cuddle."

He promptly slid next to her, but his frown remained. "I don't like this. Just because Steven wanted us to be there. We loved each other. He was a second father to me, and I believe he felt like I was a son."

"He wants you to know his feelings. He wants you to have the same opportunity as everyone else. The ability to say goodbye."

"But he knows we said goodbye at his house."

"Maybe he told Bob to call you before you were even out of prison," Courtney suggested.

"Bob said he just talked to him a few days ago and stressed I should be at the vigil.

Courtney sighed. "I guess we've been through worse things. That sounds terrible. I didn't mean I don't want to go to the vigil to support Barbara. But Mary and Sarah aren't going to like it. We're a reminder to them now."

"I know, but I guess we're stuck because I also got a call from Barbara asking me to come. It was one of Steven's last wishes." He groaned. "I can't wait to move out of here in the new year."

"I agree," Courtney said. "I guess this is a good time to tell you something good. I was thinking about your dream to become a pastor or do missionary work. I was hesitant to let you do it." She laughed as she sat up and grabbed his hand.

"What about it?" he asked, surprised.

"You're a grown man."

He smiled into her eyes. "Yes, I am."

"But I feared losing you. When you start helping people, you're not mine anymore. You belong to everyone in the community. And you belong to God. You aren't mine anyway." She brushed her hand along his cheek. "But I realized something else."

"What's that?" he asked.

She noticed his smile was gone, and there were tears in his eyes. This meant a lot to him, and she hadn't understood until today. He had come home, only to still feel alone. She thought she was helping by shielding him, but she wasn't helping at all. Thank goodness he had God to see him through.

"I realized you already belong to God. I realized you're meant to do work for Him on Earth. I realized I love you and want you to have what you want in life to be happy. Since you've been chosen by God, and that's what you want to do, then we'll find a way to work it out. I'm sorry I didn't understand the importance sooner."

He pulled her into a big hug. "What did I ever do to deserve you? I can never repay you for all the things you've put up with since marrying me."

She couldn't see his face, as her own face was buried in his soft sweater, but that didn't matter. They would be okay together. "No repayment. We're one in the sight of God. You are a remarkable man, Alex Richmond. God recognized it sooner than I did. Of course, He had the advantage of making you."

CHAPTER 16

Alex didn't want to be at the funeral home for the vigil. Bob Fuller, Steven's attorney, convinced him to attend the service. He would have stayed away if Barbara hadn't also asked him to be there.

He sat in the back row, along with Courtney. Paul and Hannah brought Ashley from Bismarck to be there, and Jason arrived with his family. Everyone in the small community knew Steven, and that included Jason's family. They were seated right in front of Alex's family.

Alex couldn't help but be aware of the hostile looks thrown his way. He'd overheard more than one person asking why he was allowed to stay. He tried to sink into the seat, but there was no hiding his presence.

He saw Steven's brother, Parker, talking to the funeral director, and the funeral director looked Alex's way. They weren't standing far from where Alex sat, and he heard Parker tell the funeral director to have him removed.

The funeral director headed in his direction when Bob intercepted him.

"Alex stays," Bob said. "It was one of Steven's final wishes. I'm sure you don't want to go against that." He put his hand on the brother's shoulder. "Alex doesn't want to stir anyone up. He's going to sit there quietly. I'm guessing he doesn't want to be here either, but I asked him to come, and he did."

Parker grudgingly nodded and sat down without looking in Alex's direction again.

"I don't understand what's going on," Courtney whispered in his ear. "Why would Steven put you through this?"

Alex shrugged. "We were friends. He knew I wanted to be here to say goodbye."

Courtney leaned back in her chair.

On her other side, Paul patted her shoulder. "Hang in there. This is going to get more interesting."

Courtney swiveled to look at him. "More interesting? I want peace."

"Soon. You'll get it soon. You're right. This is all unusual, and I believe a plan was put into action."

Soon the doors at the back of the room were closed, and the pastor stepped up to the podium to begin the service. He started out with a prayer for Steven's soul. After he stepped down, Parker read a Bible passage, and then Mary read a verse from Psalms. The funeral director stepped up to the podium.

"Before we get to the part where everyone shares any memories or prayers for Steven, we have a special request. Steven called me a few days before his death, and I stopped by to visit with him. He wrote a letter when he knew he was dying. He asked his close friend and attorney, Bob Fuller, to read this letter to us now."

"No!" Alex shouted and stood up. "It's not necessary."

Bob was already standing behind the podium. He looked at Alex with sympathy. "It's what he wanted."

To Alex's surprise, Barbara stood up from where she sat in the front row and joined Bob. "It's time."

"It isn't necessary," Alex said to Barbara.

"I appreciate your position, Alex, but it's time," Barbara repeated.

Mary and Sarah went to stand beside their mother and nodded at Alex. He had no choice but to sit down. They weren't going to stop.

Courtney whispered to him, "What's he going to say?"

"Listen," Alex responded, his eyes focused on Bob. He clenched his hands into fists. Steven hadn't needed to do this. Tears stung his eyes. He felt Courtney rubbing his back, trying to comfort him.

Bob adjusted the microphone at the podium and started reading.

Dear Friends and Family.

Thank you for being here for my family. I'm honored you took the time to come. I've appreciated your trust in me and all the times you have been there for my family and me. Serving you as bank president was a dream come true. During my time at the bank, I hope I helped you navigate your financial futures in a wise way. I tried my best.

At this point, if I were standing in front of you as I should be, I'd be clearing my throat. Because what I have to say next is not what you would expect and does not reflect well on me or my character. In fact, I have been a coward not to tell you this information sooner. Before my death. To leave this world and ask my good friend Bob to read this is dishonorable.

I apologize to all of you. And I apologize to my daughters, who were unaware of the true circumstances of everything that happened two years ago. There is no hiding from you now. Or from God's judgment. May He have mercy on my soul.

My wife urged me to tell you at once. I hope, as soon as you know the truth, you won't treat her badly.

Two years ago, money was stolen from the bank. That is common knowledge to this community. What isn't known is I took the money. Alex did not. Alex has been blameless in this entire situation. He tried to put the money back into the bank to save me from prosecution. I was going through my first chemo treatment and was short of money. I figured I'd take the money, pay for treatment, and then, with my next paycheck, return the money.

It didn't work that way. There was an audit, and Alex tried to cover for me so I could spend more time with my family. We did not know the outcome of the cancer treatment at that time, so when the auditor saw Alex tried to put the money back, he assumed Alex had taken it in the first place.

He didn't. I did. I'm begging for your forgiveness now for my family. As I said before, I have been a coward. They don't deserve to suffer for my actions, and my daughters were unaware of what I did. Every time Barbara tried to talk me into confessing, I refused to listen.

This next part will sound like an excuse, but it's just an explanation. There is no excuse for what I did. When I went into remission, I was going to confess. But I didn't. Then the cancer came back, worse than ever, and I knew this was the end.

Alex told me many times he was fine with the way things worked out. He told me prison wasn't that bad. I'm sure it was a lie. Courtney also paid the price by being away from Alex, and by being a pariah in the community. She handled it gracefully and said she agreed with Alex. They both deserve your respect for letting me spend my final years at home with my family, and for upending their lives for that to happen.

Now it's time for the truth to come out. Alex didn't do anything wrong. I did.

I apologize now, when it's too late for me to allow you the chance to tell me face-to-face what you think of me now you know the truth.

My desire is you will treat Alex and Courtney with the respect they deserve for their great sacrifice. I never had two better friends than them.

Thank you, Alex and Courtney, for putting your life on hold. I plan for this letter to be used by my attorney, Bob Fuller, to have your record cleared. Bob holds a further letter with full details for the courts.

I want to clarify two things. Bob never knew the truth. Alex and Courtney were unaware I would ever reveal the truth.

There's really no way to end this letter, except with an additional apology to you all. I hope you remember the good times and forgive me for my greatest failing.

May Christ's Peace envelop you all.

Steve

CHAPTER 17

There was a long hush when Bob finished reading the letter. He moved back from the podium and sat down again in the front row of chairs.

Barbara stepped up to the microphone. "I'm sorry."

As tears fell down Barbara's cheeks, her daughters led her back to their chairs. Sarah and Mary looked shocked at the news that had been unleashed on the mourners.

Alex tried to control his own tears. He felt Paul's warm hand on his shoulder. When he felt more under control, he stood up. He didn't look at anyone, but he could feel their eyes on him as he walked down the aisle toward the front of the chapel.

Courtney suddenly jumped up to walk beside him. Always with him. He took her hand, which was as sweaty as his.

He stopped and stood in front of the microphone, Courtney beside him. He started talking directly to Barbara. "Your husband was a fine man. I loved him like a father. When my siblings and I were growing up, we had little support. The whole town knows how my parents liked to travel without their children. Steven and you were and *are* my family." He looked at Mary and Sarah and smiled. "And Mary and Sarah are two extra sisters for me."

He looked out at the congregation. "You may be feeling cheated and let down by Steven right now. I've never felt that way. He made a mistake at a time when he was sick and desperate. Who among us hasn't made a mistake in our lives?

"Some of our mistakes have been small, and some have been big. But even the small mistakes have ripples. Ripples we may never understand on Earth. I know when you all have time to process this news, you will remember the good things about him and forgive him for his mistake. I pray you will treat Barbara and her family with respect."

445

He looked at Courtney. "We did what we could to give Steven time with his family. He had so little of it left. We were happy to help ease some of his misery." He smiled at Courtney, and she smiled back.

He stepped away from the podium, touched Barbara on her shoulder as he walked by her, and walked back down the aisle and out of the building.

His family quickly joined him outside. Paul gave him and Courtney their coats and hugged each of them. Hannah took her turn with hugs, and Ashley followed her example.

"Let's talk when we get back to the house," Paul suggested.

They had all come together, squeezing into one car. They walked to the car in silence and drove back to Alex and Courtney's house.

When they'd all gotten their winter outerwear put away, they trooped into the living room and dropped into their respective places on the couch and chairs. Alex looked around at his family.

Ashley was curled up on one end of the couch beside Courtney, who sat beside him. Hannah and Paul each took seats on the stuffed chairs across from them. The only one missing was Jason, who attended the vigil with his family and stayed with them.

"Well," Paul said. "That was quite a shock." But he didn't sound surprised at all.

"I'll say." Ashley nudged Courtney. "Why didn't you two tell us?"

Alex shrugged. What could he say? He and his siblings drifted apart by that time. Paul was drinking. Ashley moved to go to college. He and Courtney felt it best not to put the burden of keeping the secret on anyone else.

"Does Courtney's family know?" Paul asked.

"No. The only people who knew were me, Courtney, Steven, and Barbara. Their daughters didn't know until last night. Barbara told them yesterday because she had a feeling it was going to come out somehow. Maybe Steven warned her. I didn't know he was going to have his confession read at the vigil."

"It will change your life, you know," Ashley said.

She sounded so adult to Alex, who still thought of her as younger. She only had one week of school left to earn her four-year degree although the graduation ceremony happened in the spring.

"I know. But the change will be gradual. There will always be people who won't believe what Steven wrote. And people who will be mad at them because we did keep this secret. But I don't care. If Courtney and I are good, I'm good." He put his arm around her shoulders and leaned back on the couch. He took a big breath and let it out.

"It does feel good to not have a big secret weighing on me anymore. Especially with all of you. You're my family, and I know we haven't been as close as some families. However, I did miss you while I was in prison. I made the promise to myself, when I got out, I'd develop a relationship with you all if you were interested." He smiled.

"Am I jumping to conclusions that's what you want too?" He looked from Ashley to Paul and Hannah.

Paul got up and clapped him on the shoulder. "Even without the truth, I was ready to accept you." He turned to look at Courtney. "You too. You're my sister."

Ashley and Hannah each got up and took their turns hugging him and Courtney.

"I know we've hardly even spoken yet," Hannah said. "But I'm claiming sister status with you all right now." She hugged Alex too.

Ashley headed to the kitchen. "This calls for refreshments."

Courtney jumped up and joined her, and Hannah followed. Alex and Paul moved to stools at the island, watching the women search through the cupboards and fridge.

Courtney said to Ashley, "You were seriously a pain in the neck. Coming into my kitchen, like you did my house a month ago."

Ashley smiled at her. "That's what sisters do."

Alex could tell the two of them had made peace and were trying to lighten the mood.

They were soon all eating cheese and crackers, washing them down with soda and water. They talked a bit about Christmas, and all of them agreed to come back and celebrate Christmas with Courtney and Alex at their house. The good mood gradually turned somber.

"Are you going to the funeral tomorrow?" Paul asked Courtney and Alex.

Alex replied, "I hadn't intended to go. I didn't want to go tonight either, but Barbara and Bob convinced us to go. Now I know why. Barbara would be fine either way. I'm not sure what's best. If we go, there will be a lot of staring, which I'm used to, but that detracts from the reason we're all there. But if we're there, we can support Barbara. I don't know what the best thing to do is."

"Go," Courtney and Ashley said in unison, then looked at each other and laughed.

"We'll go to honor Steven," Courtney said.

Ashley nodded. "It's about him. It's like you said at the vigil. He was a mentor to you. You deserve to say goodbye, like everyone else. I don't think anyone will say anything to you or to Barbara about the embezzlement. They may look, but that's all."

Paul nodded. "I agree. If you want to go, I'll go with you."

"Me too," Ashley said.

"I guess we're all going."

The gathering broke up, and Hannah and Paul took Ashley back to Bismarck.

CHAPTER 18

After locking the front door behind their guests, Courtney and Alex wandered back to their favorite spot on the couch to cuddle.

"Well," Courtney said.

"Yeah," Alex agreed, "this changes a lot of things."

"Does it?" Courtney asked.

He looked at her in surprise. "Of course. Now we can stay here in Chokecherry Valley. Once everyone is used to the idea I didn't embezzle any money, they'll start treating you normally again."

She shook her head. "I don't want that to stay here. Besides, if you're going to help the neighborhood wherever we settle, we both need to get good jobs. That way we can pay for your college courses."

"I can probably find a job around here now." Alex wasn't sure what he'd do. People might be willing to hire him, but what kind of jobs were available in a small town like Chokecherry Valley and the surrounding area? He'd have to at least travel some miles to get a decent job. People around here didn't have much to pay an employee.

"Do you want to stay? I mean really, Alex. Do you want to stay here in this house, or would you rather move? We have a chance to make a fresh start anyplace if you want." Courtney's voice was reflective.

He couldn't tell if she wanted to move or stay. "What do you want? You're half of this team. I can take a lot of online classes. If you want to stay here in Chokecherry Valley, then we can stay. We'll figure out the money later. It's been an emotional day, and it's late."

She sat there quietly snuggled up to him for a while. Finally, she said, "You're right. It's late. I don't know what I want right now. It's been a crazy day. Let's sleep on this and consider things for a few days."

"Good idea," he said. "We agreed we weren't doing anything before Christmas anyway." He lifted her chin and looked into her eyes. He felt close to her tonight. It was time. "Do you want to stay with me all night?"

Her eyes lit up her whole face, and a wonderful smile curved her soft mouth. "I'd like that. I've been waiting for you to feel comfortable at home."

"I'm home with you. It's going to be okay." He believed it now. The unbearable secret they'd been carrying for two years was finally off their shoulders. The relief surprised him. He thought he had come to terms with living with the lie the rest of his life. He'd learned lies were toxic.

CHAPTER 19

The funeral was sad, but there were no outbursts from anyone. A few people shook Alex's and Courtney's hands and apologized. Some still avoided their gaze. Probably embarrassed. They'd come to terms with the new status quo eventually.

The flurry of the week before Christmas continued at the store when Courtney was at work. Alex saw a new light in her eyes when she got home and knew she was feeling the same relief he was that the truth of the embezzlement was known.

Steven's attorney called and was trying to get Alex's case reversed, but Alex didn't care. Yes, it might help with his reputation, but he didn't feel it would make any huge difference in his life.

His biggest relief was Courtney's family knew the truth. They surrounded her with love while he was in prison, but he knew she had to deal with their wrong assumptions about him. She'd been hurt but was willing to hide the truth. He was glad she didn't have to worry about their judgment any longer.

Christmas day drew nearer, and he and Courtney hadn't discussed whether they would move or not. He gave it a lot of thought and leaned toward moving. He briefly considered he'd be helpful to Barbara by staying, but she informed him her sister lived in Virginia, and she was moving there as soon as the girls graduated from college.

Could he sell their family home? His parents had lived here, and his grandparents in their time. Would he be the one to sell it? When he bought it from his siblings, he assumed he'd live the rest of his life in the town. Things changed. God changed him. His path in life would never be without unknowns. He'd learned that lesson.

Although he felt led to help others, he was uncertain of his abilities. He kept reminding himself he would have God to

451

lead him through it all. And God gave him Courtney to help him. He couldn't doubt that after what she'd been through and still stuck with him.

His greatest joy was that she had started asking him questions about God. It showed him she was serious about deepening her own faith.

He decided he'd done enough sitting around for the day and took a walk to see Barbara. A few other women were there when he arrived, and they greeted him cordially.

Barbara's sister from Virginia was staying with her. Barbara's daughters were also with her now until the New Year because school was over for the semester.

After checking if she needed anything, he left, reassured she had the help she needed. He would leave it up to her as to when she wanted to talk to him again.

He did his usual cooking after baking more things on the list Courtney wanted to serve for Christmas. Then he went online and started researching the process to become a pastor. The information he found showed it would be a lengthy process.

Courtney was right. They were going to have to earn some money first. He would contact the church liaison to begin the process of acceptance into a program, but classes would have to wait. In the meantime, he could help in whatever community they decided to live in.

In the middle of eating that evening, Courtney put down her fork and announced she'd made a decision. They were sitting in their favorite spot in the bay window at the table in the kitchen.

"We should move. Your family is in Bismarck. My family is spread around the state, but my parents are in Bismarck too. I don't want to work at the grocery store any longer. Betty won't need me when the holidays are over anyway."

Alex gazed at her across the table. "That's a good idea. I second everything you've said."

The relief on her face was obvious. She jumped up and kissed him, and then sat down again on the bench with a blush on her cheeks. Her eyes glowed brightly. "Good. Because there's something else I've never told you."

He looked at his vibrant wife, who suddenly appeared more alive than he'd ever seen her, except on their wedding day.

"I've always wanted to start a retreat center. A place for people to go to reset when life has dealt them a blow. A sanctuary for people who have lost loved ones, or are making a big decision, or," she paused. "Well, anything where a person needs a break for about a week."

She held up her hand to stop him before he could speak. "I know. It'll take money."

He got up and joined her on the bench in front of the bay window. "We'll find the money somewhere. It's an absolutely wonderful idea. Let's do it. I'll be helping you, which is helping other people. It's exactly what we both want to do. Becoming a pastor is a long process anyway, and you'll have my help for a long time before we need to make any other decisions."

They were ready for a new life.

CHAPTER 20

Alex and Courtney joined her parents at their church in Bismarck for Christmas Mass. The evening service was beautiful with the church decorated in bright red and green. The nativity scene at the altar had been repainted this year, and everything gleamed with newness.

At least Alex felt that way. It was like he'd been living in a bleak desert and had finally come out into the light of a green oasis. He knew he and Courtney had a long road ahead of them, but in his heart, he was already settled.

Courtney's family greeted him enthusiastically, and all of them individually pulled him aside to apologize. Her parents had come out to Chokecherry Valley a few days ago to express their regret over their behavior and talked to them about the whole situation.

He'd been happy to tell them there were no hard feelings. He did what he had to do by taking the blame for Steven and hadn't expected anyone to accept that with equanimity.

He loved the new glow on Courtney's face as she finally felt accepted by her family again. Since they made the decision to move and follow their dreams, she had been happy and lighthearted.

This Christmas felt like the best Christmas he'd ever had. He felt closer to his own siblings than ever before. He felt purpose in his future with Courtney as they worked together to build a retreat center. Courtney's acceptance of his dreams and God's call were miracles.

After church, they returned home and started the meal. They worked well together in the kitchen. Alex set out candy and cookies on the coffee table and the other decorated table they'd set up in the living room for Christmas.

Hannah and Paul arrived first. Ashley and Jason soon followed. Jason said he could stay until after the meal, and then he was going to join his family with Ashley. They all gave Ashley a hard time about leaving them.

She blushed and laughed at them. Alex could tell Jason made her happy.

After that, the day was one laugh after another. They talked over each other often.

After they'd eaten the big meal of turkey and all the fixings and desserts they could handle, Paul held up his hand to get everyone's attention. "Hey, guys," he yelled.

They were finally quiet.

"Hannah and I have something to say." Paul and Hannah were seated on the couch together, where Alex and Courtney usually cuddled at night. Paul took Hannah's hand, and she held it out to show everyone the bright ring on her finger. "We've finally chosen a date."

Courtney and Ashley screamed and jumped up to hug Hannah. "Congratulations!"

Alex and Jason chimed in their congratulations, and Alex hugged the happy couple too. Jason settled for smiling at them both.

"When's the wedding?" Ashley asked.

The happy couple looked at each other. "Next year in May. We're keeping the wedding small. Friends and immediate family."

"That's wonderful," Alex said. "As long as we're sharing news, Courtney and I have news to share too."

"We're selling the house and moving. We're looking around western North Dakota for a larger place." Courtney explained their plans, and there were more congratulations and offers of help.

Courtney's eyes glowed happily. "I'd love any help we can get."

There was more hugging, and then Jason and Ashley had to leave. Hannah planned to stop at her sister's house also. They left shortly after Jason and Ashley.

Courtney looked at Alex when they were gone. "That went well."

"Definitely. No one even questioned us selling this house."

"Were you worried about it?" Courtney asked.

Alex considered it. "I didn't think so, but the relief when no one brought it up was a comfort, so I guess I was."

They soon found themselves settled on their favorite seat on the couch.

"Merry Christmas." Alex brought a small box out of his pocket and handed it to her.

She took it from him in surprise. "We weren't giving each other gifts this year. We agreed being together was gift enough."

"We did, but I couldn't resist." He smiled as she fumbled with the wrapping paper.

When she opened it, she found a small, exquisite gold angel on a chain. She looked up at him with awe and a huge smile. "It's gorgeous."

"So are you. She reminds me of you. My angel." He kissed her.

~~~

**Check Out The New Series Featuring Courtney and Alex
Crocus Hill Inn Mystery Series
Picture of Book 1 – The Last Owners**

Missing persons and half a million dollars in jewelry...
~~~

When Courtney purchases a quaint house in the countryside, her dreams of transforming it into a cozy, inviting inn appear within reach. But beneath the charming exterior lurks a tangle of dark secrets. The previous owners vanished without a trace—eight years ago.

Driven by curiosity and a sense of justice, Courtney and her husband Alex team up with Gary, the son of the missing couple, to unravel the mystery. The clock is ticking. The promise of treasure draws fortune hunters to dig up the tranquil backyard.

When a fresh murder shatters the peace, Courtney realizes that the truth might be buried even deeper than she feared. As the stakes rise and the body count grows, Courtney must decide how much she's willing to risk to bring the truth to light—and whether some dreams are worth dying for.

A traditional, twisty, mysterious whodunit set in southwestern North Dakota...

https://www.jeanrezab.com

COPYRIGHT

ABOUT THE AUTHOR

Jean Rezab writes from her home in North Dakota. Having grown up on a farm, she enjoys all things country, especially wildflowers, wheat fields, and winding lanes.

She likes to entertain her readers with everything she writes. Since reading has always been a means of escape, she enlivens stories with complex relationships, sweeping her readers into other worlds. She writes intriguing mysteries and women's fiction with messages of love and forgiveness.

www.ingramcontent.com/pod-product-compliance
Lightning Source LLC
Chambersburg PA
CBHW031153310726
48969CB00001B/73